THIRST FOR REVENGE TRILOGY

Book 3

I0692972

Lawrence the Ghost

By

John L. Kinsler

Thirst for Revenge: Book 3: Lawrence the Ghost © *2013* All rights reserved by John L. Kinsler

No part of this book may be reproduced or transmitted in any form or by any means, graphic, electronic, or mechanical, including photocopying, recording, taping, or by any informational storage retrieval system without prior permission in writing from the publisher.

W & B Publishers

For information:
W & B Publishers
Post Office Box 193
Colfax, NC 27235
www.a-argusbooks.com

ISBN: 978-0-6159468-8-7
ISBN: 0-6159468-8-7

Book Cover designed by Dubya

Printed in the United States of America

"The beast alone was reacting... The beginning and end of all his thoughts was hatred; that hatred which, if not checked in its growth by some providential event, becomes a hatred of society, then hatred of creation, revealing itself by a vague, incessant desire to injure some living being, no matter who. Jean Valjean "is a very dangerous man."

... Les Miserables 1863, Victor Hugo

A THIRST FOR REVENGE: TRILOGY

BOOK ONE: LAWRENCE THE FATHER
- CHAPTER ONE: Prelude To The Son, Peter's Gunfight
- CHAPTER TWO: Llewellyn Lawrence's Friend
- CHAPTER THREE: Father's Fall
- CHAPTER FOUR: Father's Fate
- CHAPTER FIVE: Father's Duty
- CHAPTER SIX: Father's Hell
- CHAPTER SEVEN: The Lost Father

BOOK TWO: LAWRENCE THE SON
- CHAPTER EIGHT: Killing The Dog
- CHAPTER NINE: The Dog Killer
- CHAPTER TEN: They Killed The Ice Cream Man
- CHAPTER ELEVEN: The Fight
- CHAPTER TWELVE: Feeding A Bear
- CHAPTER THIRTEEN: The Cat Eater
- CHAPTER FOURTEEN: The Beast
- CHAPTER FIFTEEN: The Falls
- CHAPTER SIXTEEN: Beast To Beast
- CHAPTER SEVENTEEN: A Beauty
- CHAPTER EIGHTEEN: Beauty's Beast
- CHAPTER NINETEEN: Beast of the Mother
- CHAPTER TWENTY: Breast of the Mother
- CHAPTER TWENTY ONE: Feast of the Beast
- CHAPTER TWENTY TWO: Who Are the Beasts?

BOOK THREE: LAWRENCE THE GHOST
- CHAPTER TWENTY THREE: Haunting
- CHAPTER TWENTY FOUR: The Followers
- CHAPTER TWENTY FIVE: The Ashes

Dedication

Dedicated to All of My Children: my book, read or not, my DNA will be history.

JLK

CHAPTER TWENTY THREE

Haunting

"Lawrence?"

Lawrence knew it would happen but hoped it might not happen. He put down the phone knowing he had to go back.

"Mr. Lawrence?"

He did not answer.

Lizzy had left his name in her personal papers. He was listed as a tutor for the Niagara City High School when she was notified that Henry was being assigned to the halfway house. The hospital had tracked him down through the school. Even though he had resigned, he had no qualms letting Nuevello or Fannon know where he now lived.

"Hey, Mr. L? You gonna to respond or something?"

The phone sat there in front of him, the voice filling the silence.

Alexis Katherine Winters knew better than call Lawrence by his initial. He hated people calling other people Mr. this initial or Mr. that initial, even people whose last name was so foreign a translator would have trouble with it, which is why she did it. Still it was his name and unlike other people he was not ashamed of being a Lawrence, proud to be a Lawrence.

"Kat, you know better than call me Mr. L. You want to be reporting on events at the Virginia City Library from now on? Give me a couple minutes. Bet you haven't even finished you mocha from Starbuck's since you are late, you know?"

"Oops! When you got a minute or an hour, call me."

He was not serious with Kat because he knew she was a great reporter and when he was zoned out, calling him by a letter got his attention quickly. While everybody that knew her called her Alley Kat, Lawrence just settled for Kat. She was a very thin and tall blond with short, irregularly cut hair much like a page boy, like a mother would do to save money. In her case Lawrence knew that her boyfriend, whom she stood a good three inches taller than, probably did the hair job. She was also a quick speaker who kept at you during a conversation until you heard and understood her. This was not impolite. It was a trait that served her well as a reporter for the V City Server which was the name Dr. Judge Sauers had given to the old Virginia Gazette after he purchased a half interest in it. Kat talked with people softly and slowly. Even though it was just Kat's way, it was the best way a good reporter could interview. If you ignored her, she kept at you until you did pay attention or she told you to fuck off. That aggravated the Judge but pleased Lawrence. Kat was a recent graduate from VCCC, Virginia City Community College, who refused to follow the money trail necessary to get a four year college degree. Lawrence had offered to have the paper pay for her bachelor's degree and let her keep her job at the same pay while she earned her degree. She thanked him and told him that no offense to his degree in English, but she did not want to waste four years of her life in the unreal world of academia.

Lawrence was mentally out of touch when he received the phone call telling him Lizzy was dead. DeGraff Hospital in North Tonawanda, New York had called Lawrence after they were told to go fuck themselves by Uley Hawkins. Uley refused to acknowledge any relationship with Lizzy and hung up on them after cursing them. The nurse on the phone had told Lawrence that there was no one else they could turn to concerning her funeral and burial arrangements. Lawrence asked them how she died and the nurse refused to respond, to which Lawrence responded by telling them he would not help them unless he knew how she died. The nurse put him on hold for nearly ten minutes until a doctor picked up the receiver. He told Lawrence that she had been found dead in her trailer with severe degrading rigor mortis. Lawrence pushed for more until the Doctor said it seemed, but he would not verify it, that she had somehow broken her neck during a struggle since her face was excessively bruised. Lawrence thanked the doctor and told him that he should cremate her body and send him the ashes. He would pay all the expenses including the shipping. When asked if the police were investigating her death, the doctor hesitated.

Lawrence knew he had to go back.

He leaned backward in his desk's swivel chair, laced his fingers together, and gripped the back of his head. He would deal with Western New York after the ashes arrive.

"Okay, Kat, come on in."

Lawrence was the only person he knew who could make Kat Winters smile. She came through the glass door of his office and closed it which meant this conversation was between the two of them only. She had with her the ubiquitous lined note pad and mechanical pencil.

Kat spoke, "You know that woman whose been charged with criminal child neglect in the death of her six month old child?"

"Yeah, but you're not on that story. What's up?"

"Just let me fill you in from my notes. It'll catch you up. A neighbor tried to wake her that morning but got no response. The neighbor knew she was at home since the neighbor gets up way before sunrise to get her family off to school and to work. She sees the woman leave with her child every day. She has trouble getting the baby into the car seat. It's one of those complicated ones with all kinds of belts and stuff."

Those were not Kat's words because she was reading directly from her notes.

"You've talked with the woman?"

"No, these notes I are from Clark. I'll return them to him when he gets here. We share notes all the time. I went through his when I got here. Anyhow," Kat's vocal volume was only a breath from a whisper and forced Lawrence to sit up, tight against his desk, "the woman is in jail because," she flipped over her notes, "the neighbor called the police. Not seeing the neighbor that morning, she knocked on her door, got no response and found the door unlocked. Afraid that there had been a robbery or something, she went into the apartment and found the baby hanging off the side of the crib, dead. The baby had squeezed through the slats and got caught."

"And the police charged the mother with criminal child neglect because the woman was drunk as a skunk, right?"

Kat smiled and went on, "yes, they found a fifth of scotch, cheap scotch at that, next to her bed. Putting two and two together, they figured she was too drunk to hear her baby crying."

"This is what bothers me about Clark's report. If the baby got its head caught, how could the baby cry, let alone scream?"

"Forensics, Lawrence. Police forensics did an autopsy on the baby and found the baby's throat completely swollen and chafed. It's damage matched the throat of a human who had screamed themselves to death."

"So, the baby screamed, the mother was drunk and passed out, and you've got a whopper to throw at me, right?"

She smiled, "pick up your receiver."

"Excuse me? Why do you want me to make a phone call?"

"Lawrence, just do like I ask and pick up your phone and dial my home phone number."

Lawrence dialed the number from memory, let it ring and spoke, "I'm getting your message. What now?"

Kat told him to dial in her password number which she gave him written on a piece of scrap paper. He hit the play messages number when the phone voice asked for a menu selection.

"This had better be good or I'm going to start calling you … Okay here's the first message."

"Hit the number button until you get to the message for the date and time I wrote on the scrap paper."

Lawrence listened but was confused, "are you sure it's for this date and time? I can't hear anything because of that damn noise in the …"

"Is the message over? Did it ask if you wanted to hear it again?"

"Yeah, but why would I want to hear it again."

"Click on your speaker phone and hit the asterisk for a replay."

They both listened to the noise but when Lawrence tried to lower the noise, Kat told him to turn it up.

"Why in the world would I want to do that?"

"Listen, okay? Tell me if you hear anything at all."

Lawrence got next to the speaker phone and just as Kat was about to ask if he heard the voice Lawrence said, "there's a woman's voice. Can't make out what she's saying. Here, let me try it again but I'll listen through the receiver."

He clicked off the speaker phone and put the receiver to his left ear, "yes, it's a woman. Sounds like a young woman trying to talk with you. She keeps bitching about the jet noise outside her window. Don't blame her since it is eleven o'clock at night."

"That's a girlfriend of mine. She can't leave a message that I can decipher because the jet planes from Oceana are cruising right over her house. She called me the next day without jet noise in the background. I'm kind of lazy about deleting my phone messages. I just forget they're there. Did you notice the date and time?"

"Yes I did. Let me see your notes a second."

Kat had a clipping of the newspaper article which Clark had written and handed it to Lawrence.

"Okay, your undecipherable message is the same day and same time as when the woman's baby strangled trying to get out of the crib," Lawrence was beginning to see where Kat was going.

"My friend lives on Realty Lane which is ironic since she sells real estate. The woman whose baby died also lives on Shipp's Lane."

Lawrence recognized what Kat had uncovered. The question of cause was circumstantial and coincidental. "Where have you gone with this?"

"Called the hospital, Sentara General on First Colonial. You need to thank them for being helpful with this."

"How's that?"

"That cover story you wrote a few weeks ago on their emergency room made them look very good. Few hospitals can best their quickness at handling ER. The hospital verified that the baby's death was in the same time frame as when that jet noise was going over my friend's house."

"And over the home where the baby died. And according to the autopsy, the baby's throat ..."

Kat picked it up, "was scarred and swollen from screaming and crying."

Lawrence was afraid to hang up his phone. "Listen Kat, you've got to get out of here right now and secure your phone. Bring it here and I'll have the message copied. We might even be able to get the background noise cleaned up some. It's a shame your friend didn't stay on the line longer."

"So where do we go from here Lawrence? Police?"

"No way. We settle ourselves down and think."

"Don't trust V City's Police Department?"

"I don't trust any government body. I especially don't trust the Feds. This has got to go through them, not just the locals. You know the argument this brings up?"

"Yep, the jet noise. Maybe it killed the baby."

Lawrence got up from his seat and moved to the chair next to Kat. He took her left hand in his, "Kat, you have done one great job here. But you're young."

Kat thought Lawrence was going to pull her off of the story. "You're not going to ..."

"Shush. Nobody can do this story better than you. You're going to do it. I'm going to set up some leads for you, most of which you probably have already been turning over in your mind. You have got to do this slowly and covertly. No matter how close you are to anybody, don't let it out until you've sewn the story up tight. You understand?"

Kat's face had reddened slightly. She looked scared but was wide eyed in anticipation.

"What's to be your first step?"

***

Lawrence had been reluctant to move to Virginia City for a few reasons. Being a North Easterner, he was not sure he could endure living in the south. He liked having four distinct seasons and even though he complained about the harsh winters, especially for Western New York, to not have snow and wintry fires seemed a farce. He could survive the weather but he did not know if he could survive the newspaper business, especially the newspaper that Judge Sauers had bought into. Judge had been one of Lawrence's professors in college and Lawrence had enjoyed his class. Judge gave him one of the better learning experiences at the university. Dr. Sauers did not lecture. You worked and you shared work with your classmates. Judge taught journalism and the class was very simply a make shift newspaper. The classroom was a newspaper office. Judge was editor-in-chief and the students were the reporters. He made everyone take a desk at the paper. Each student wrote a front page story, a human interest column, interviewed one or more the college's athletes or coaches, and went as far as doing help wanted ads for the pseudo newspaper.

No, Lawrence had no problem with Judge. The problem was with the Virginia City paper. It was basically an advertising brochure delivered to "free, take one" boxes at every other corner in Virginia City. Copies were on the counter of every hotel. The free newspaper survived not by readers buying the paper but through the advertising paid by the tourist industry. Each winter the newspaper nearly collapsed since the tourists to Virginia City Beach were few and far between. Lawrence did not even like the newspaper's name, The Virginia Light House, since there was no light house within 25 miles of the resort.

With his Nuevello nest egg in an off shore bank, Lawrence had the financial maneuverability to bargain with Judge Sauers about the job. He did not have to do much negotiating. Dr. Sauers laid out the position up front and Lawrence's only one qualm was the name. Lawrence would be the Editor-in-Chief of the newspaper. Sauers was the Managing Editor. Lawrence ran the news and Judge ran the advertising, period. Sauers admitted that the name, The Virginia Light House, was pathetic and promised Lawrence that if the paper grew in readership, as the owner he would change the name to whatever Lawrence chose.

Lawrence's tactics were simple and Sauers saw readership revenue increase. There was a strong possibility that the "Lighthouse" could become a real newspaper. Lawrence went out to every school in the Virginia City area with his camera and took hundreds of photographs. He went through the stacks of photographs, began writing the stories that went with each one and published them in the weekly paper. Mothers, fathers, grandparents gobbled the newspaper up as soon as it hit the street corner machines and hotel counters. Even if the Virginia Light House was not free, it still would have been gone within hours every week. This success precipitated into Lawrence and Judge's first battle. The hotels, restaurants, boardwalk vendors, amusement ride venues, and every other advertiser were all over Judge Sauers since there were few ads to read. There were no newspapers left for tourists since the community grabbed them.

No sooner had Judge started challenging Lawrence's local photojournalism campaign than Judge saw the smile on Lawrence's face and knew the reason for it. How stupid could he and the advertisers be? It was so simple that they had not thought of it; print more newspapers since more people were reading the newspaper. Lawrence would always remember Judge smacking his own head like some dummy that just woke up to reality. The problem of finding the money to print more newspapers was Sauers' problem, not Lawrence's. Lawrence tossed in the promise that Judge had made to him, renaming the "Virginia Light House." Sauers give Lawrence his due.

The paper was now the "V City Server" and it cost the public fifty cents. The advertisers and the tourist venues got bundles of free issues to pass out to their customers just like they used to get with the "Virginia Light House." Judge got the advertisers to start running more ads but with coupons. The advertisers got discounts for their advertising for every hundred coupons they returned to the newspaper. The newspaper had actually become a competitor with the larger Norfolk and Richmond papers.

Lawrence's next step was to hire reporters. Being the Editor-in-Chief as well as the only reporter, he needed to do this so the newspaper could cover not only local community happenings but also news events. Judge was reluctant again. True, the revenue had increased but having to pay reporters would get the paper back into the red again. Lawrence found the solution by going to Virginia City's Community College English department and proposed that they offer a journalism class where the students would be interns working for the V City Server. Having Dr. Judge Sauers with him, who was a retired college professor in journalism, sold the deal. The paper would get college student intern reporters each semester.

***

"His name is David Johnstone," said Kat, "Commander David Johnstone, Lawrence."

"Whose name is David Johnstone?"

"He's the pilot that flew over my friend's apartment when she tried to call me."

"Which means he's the same pilot that flew over the woman's apartment? The mother who's been charged with criminal child neglect? How did you get his name?"

"Are you sure you want to know?"

"Oh come on. What did you have to do to get it?"

"I called the Oceana Air Base and asked for the base commander. The operator wanted to know why. So I told her that we ... that would be the V City Server ... were going to do a story on the base's history and I'd like to start with the base commander. She passed me along to the base commander's secretary who wanted to switch me off to the base publicist. I was ready for that and explained that I wanted to do an interview with the base commander as the lead in to a series on the base. I told her that it would be good to have the commander's own words in print along with his picture. She put me on hold."

"And when did I approve doing a story on the Oceana air base's history?"

"Just now, because I told the commander yesterday that the story and his picture would run in two or three weeks."

"You are kidding? Right? You already interviewed him?"

"That's what I said. I interviewed him yesterday on base in his big boring office."

Lawrence could have never imagined having to fire an employee but Kat was up against the wall right now. Yet he knew her well enough to know that she leaned toward melodrama.

"This better be good."

"I had a bunch of questions prepared. All were favorable to the base and the jets. I had researched the good admiral well enough to know he's a real blow hard, at least according to the bartender at the air base drinking spot. He got a bunch of praise dumped on his head for his days flying over Nam and napalming innocent children. No, don't start yelling at me. I didn't say anything at all about the napalm, just his sterling record. You know that son of a bitch had to dump a plane into the ocean right after takeoff from a carrier? Shame they rescued him."

Lawrence just shook his head, shrugged his shoulders, and held his hands up in surrender.

"Anyhow if you ever want to know the history of the Ocean Air Base, I've got it. And if you want a nice 8 X 10 of the admiral, I've got that too."

"Story? Have you got a story somewhere in here?"

"He took me to lunch on the base. God the food was awful. He downed a couple gin and tonics but he surprised me. He did not make a pass at me. I had him very relaxed, telling his war stories. I told him how great his stories were and how amazing it was that he survived. When his cheeks got a little too red from the gin, I nailed him. I told him that a few weeks ago my best friend and I were out on her patio doing some late night drinking when one of his planes roared over our heads."

"Would this be the same day and time as your answering machine recorded that loud noise blasting away?"

"Yes, and the same date and time when that baby was crying."

"How did you get it out of him?"

"I told him that my friend said the plane was an F-14 Tomcat but I told her it wasn't. I said it was a F/A-18 Hornet. Seeing as we were a little bit loaded and had no concept of what we were saying, we made a hundred dollar bet on which jet it was, not even realizing we'd never be able to find out which one it was."

"So you hit on the Admiral to find out which plane?"

"No, he was one step ahead of me. He drained his gin and tonic, walked me back to his office, and made a phone call. It's amazing how you males just have to show off to us poor little girls. In less than five minutes in walks Commander David Johnstone."

"Come one, Kat. That's bullshit. You're just jerking me along here."

"Nope. The Colonel was piloting a Hornet on that exact day, at that exact time. His flight path went right over my friend's ..."

"Apartment, the apartment of the woman whose baby was crying! You've ..."

"Let me finish, sir. I said to Commander David Johnstone that we could almost see him in the cockpit. He said we should have waved since he was only a couple hundred feet from us."

"Those jets are not suppose to be lower than 825 feet over populated areas!"

"So where do we go from here, Lawrence?"

"Damned if I know. David Johnstone, huh?"

"Yep, he invited me out for a drink. Gave me his phone number and said to call him when I'm available."

Lawrence sat back with his fingers laced together. Kat was a very eager reporter. She would go far but not with the V City Server. This story could put her into the big times. It would have to be her decision whether to pursue the Colonel any farther.

"Are you comfortable with meeting him again? Especially off base and for a few drinks?"

"I don't know, Lawrence. You get with these military studs and all of a sudden the testosterone levels start rising along with his ..."

"I get the point. Think on it."

"Do we need more than what I got?"

"Unfortunately, yes. It's your word against theirs right now. Very simply, they could say that they messed up the dates and times on Colonel Johnstone's flight. Or that those were not the times you gave them."

Lawrence lifted his hands, fingers still laced together, and stretched his arms so his palms rested on the back of his head. He reclined the swivel chair backward and rocked it slowly back and forth.

"I think I need to be with you. Do you have a problem with that?"

Kat smiled. "You are an angel, Lawrence. There is no way I'd like to go one on one with David Johnstone."

CHAPTER TWENTY FOUR

The Followers

Kat asked, "Lawrence, did you see the news yesterday?"

"You mean the Waco, Texas incident?"

"The media are going crazy about it. The Waco Tribune-Herald did a study on this guy David Koresh. He's some kind of guru, a Branch Davidian that believes Jesus lives just outside of Waco at a place called Mt. Carmel. Wasn't Clint Eastwood the mayor of some town named Mt. Carmel?"

"In California, Kat. I didn't pay much attention to it yesterday. What's the big deal about a bunch of religious zealots setting up home in Texas?"

"Guns and explosives according to the Treasury Department's Bureau of Alcohol, Tobacco and Firearms. UPS delivered hand grenade casings to Mt. Carmel."

"Hand grenades? You got to be kidding?"

"Not only that, when the ATF went through some shipping records, they found that 90 pounds of powered aluminum had been used to make destructive devices, like hand grenade powder, when mixed with gun powder was also delivered there. And get this, Koresh whose real name is Vernon Howell, spent over 40 grand on 104 AR-15 rifles, rifles that are a close match to the M-16s used by the American military. Only difference is that AR-15s are semi-automatic instead of automatic like M-16s. Which makes no difference anyhow since even semi-automatic weapons are illegal."

"So that gave the ATF just cause to attack Koresh and his followers?"

"No, in fact the ATF's search warrant was bogus. They got a search warrant based on their assumption that the Branch Davidians were retooling the semi-automatic weapons into automatic M-16 type rifles. The ATF never gave any evidence to prove that the Davidians were planning to do that.

The stupidest thing about it is that if you go anywhere around Waco, most people own a shotgun and a hacksaw."

"Meaning they're making illegal sawed-off shot guns."

"Koresh is a bold son of a bitch. He actually told a Special Agent who called him that he and the ATF were welcomed to come out and see his guns."

"Kat, before we can get into this, I need to know more about these Branch Davidians and Koresh …"

"Here, I'm already ahead of you. Clark helped to."

Kat handed Lawrence about twenty sheets of papers with scribbled notes all over them. "Tell me, the short version. The gun sales' angle on this has got me curious. I might just know a man who can give us a better slant on the rifling changes. I'll call him after you bring me up on the clan that's out there in Waco."

Kat went through her research with Lawrence. Koresh's followers were an off shoot of the Seventh-Day Adventist Church which was formed sometime between midnight and noon on October 23, 1844 by William Miller. Adventists believed in the coming of Christ. One in particular, Hiram Edson, saw in a corn field "heaven open to my view, and I saw distinctly and clearly telling me a great event had taken place. Jesus would not tarry in His labor. The End - - or the Judgment of the living was shortly at hand." Two years later nineteen year old Sister Ellen had a vision of God showing her the Ark with two angels guarding each end. Jesus lifted the cover and showed her the stones on which were written the ten commandments. This was God's truth and it was beyond the understanding of mere mortals. Only the select, who personally connected with God, Jesus, and this source of wisdom could understand and explain the scriptures as written in God's bible. The Adventists spread to Waco Texas where Victor Houteff, a Maytag washer salesman, established a community devoted to King David. Believing he was the resurrected Elijah, a direct descendent of John the Baptist, Houteff named his followers at Mt. Carmel the Davidian Seventh Day Adventists. They believed Jesus would return and confront the heathens. After defeating them Christ would move them to Jerusalem.

Kat smiled and spoke up. "By the way Lawrence, good old Victor Houteff happened to marry a seventeen-year-old member of the flock when he was fifty-two. See, there's hope for you old folk."

"I don't know, Kat. Just keeping up with you youngins down here in da South be very hard, my, my. How does Koresh get into this?"

"Now he's a story to pity or loathe. Koresh or Vernon, whatever, had one tough childhood. His father abandoned him which was probably for the better since his father basically screwed little girls. Mama on the other hand, was an alcoholic who lived with an alcoholic who was brutal. She shipped Koresh off to his grandmother when he was four. When he was eight he was gang raped. In school he was dyslexic, illiterate, and placed in special education classes. Ironically he was able to memorize the entire New Testament by the time he was eight years old."

Lawrence knew about special education classes and students; Koresh obviously had not belonged in special education. He was probably just dumped there.

"When he was nineteen he knocked up a 15 year old girl and joined the Seventh-Day Adventist Church. In 1981 he moved to Waco and became a Branch Davidian. He also started sleeping with the prophetess and leader of the sect who was then 78 years old."

"Come on, you're making that up. He knocks up 15 year olds and does 78 year old women?"

"Lois Roden. She claimed that God had chosen Koresh to father a child with her. The child would be the Chosen One. Roden's son, George, wasn't too thrilled with Koresh and chased him out of Mt. Carmel. Koresh migrated to Israel where he had a vision. Returning to Mt. Carmel after Lois Roden died, Koresh said that he was the Lamb of God and God told him to go forth and have many wives. Where once monogamy had been the law of the Seventh Day Adventists, polygamy was now its leader's path."

"Which meant he could screw anybody he wanted?"

"Which he did. Any and all. By the way, he and his good old-step brother or should I say his step-son, George? Whatever. They had a contest between them to raise the dead. Obvious neither could do that but Koresh was able to drive George so crazy that George wound up killing a man, Wayman Dale Adair, who claimed to be the Messiah. He did it with an axe blow to Adair's head. With George being sent to prison, David Koresh now ran Mt. Carmel. The name Koresh is a poor translation of the name Cyrus who was the King of Persia."

"So right now the reincarnated son of God is trapped in a compound in Waco Texas?"

"That's about it. It's a good place for him to be trapped. He's probably screwing every little girl in the compound. The government's problem is that the Feds, ATF and the FBI, can't get him for statutory rape. He has not only convinced the girls that he's a prophet sent to fuck them, but their parents have signed an agreement to let their daughters become his wives. It's Texas, does that surprise you?"

"Why are you laughing Kat?"

"It's like really stupid. Why in the world does the United States government have to get into this? The Davidians are just a bunch of crazy people, and they ought to just leave them alone. Koresh actually told a reporter that the intelligence of his gonads bids him to do his work."

"Before a standing army can rule, the people must be disarmed," quoted Lawrence.

"What's that mean?"

"Noah Webster made it clear in 1777 that's how the country would have to run. It's America's way of controlling its citizens by cracking down on an armed citizenry. I know a man who's been harping on that message, putting it in people's ears for a few years. He's a gun dealer, and more. He's a yellow dog dealer. Before you ask, it's a dealer that does the paper work in his name so your name's not on any papers when he sells you a weapon."

"That's kind of dumb, isn't it? I mean, what if you go off and kill somebody? The gun's in the dealer's, the yellow dog's name?"

"No, he just claims the weapon was stolen. Hand me the phone. I'll call him."

Lawrence had a list of phone numbers that he kept on a laminated index card in his wallet. On it was Tim McVeigh's name and Lockport phone number. Lawrence waited through five rounds of ringing before the answering machine picked up. He left his name and his newspaper office number along with his personal home phone number.

***

"Mr. Lawrence, I'm sorry it took so long to get back to you but I've been down in Texas. What can I do for you, sir?"

"Were you in Waco?"

"Yes sir. I'm here right now in a motel room."

"First Tim, let me make sure I don't take advantage of you. I'm a newspaper editor down in Virginia City at the V City Server now. If you don't want me to use your name for any reason, tell me. I won't."

"No, that's okay. What do you want to know?"

The Mt. Carmel site had been laid to siege for over four weeks without any movement from both sides, so to grill McVeigh would be a waste at this time.

"Lawrence, it's a typical American show. Hell, there are women carrying crosses walking back and forth in front of the fucking ATF snipers. Vendors have set up tables and are peddling everything from hot dogs to T-shirts. I've been cleaning up with my bumper stickers, the ones that say "Fear The Government That Fears Your Gun" and "When Guns Are Outlawed, I Will Become An Outlaw." They've sold out. But, hardly anybody's bought "Politicians Love Gun Control.""

Lawrence smiled, "you mind if I put you on speaker phone? I've got a very gifted reporter with me and she needs to take notes on what you've been through down there."

"No, I'm okay with her listening, Mr. Lawrence."

"Lawrence Tim, no mister, please. Have you been near the compound?"

"Can't get near it. I drove up this real rural road thinking I'd go around the blockades, and bam, out popped six federal agents. They surrounded my car and there were eight more off to the side of the road. I told them this is a public road and I'm visiting friends in the compound."

"So of course they said we're sorry Mr. McVeigh and let you go up to the compound?"

"I know you're smiling, Mr. Lawrence. They told me that if I'm not the press, to turn around. Which I did. This was one little road, almost a dirt road. They had an Army tent erected on it and a military truck for transport of personnel. All of them were armed. I mean armed to the teeth. It was like being back in the desert, you know?"

"So you didn't really see anything?"

"No, but I'm staying for a couple more days. I think this siege might go on for quite a while."

"What do you personally think about the situation?"

"Fucking government wants to disarm its people. You know that hierarchy because you told me about there being only three levels in society? You know the royalty, the warriors, and the workers?"

"Yeah, I remember. This situation sounds like that?"

"You don't think so?"

"Actually Tim I'm glad you brought it up. It sure does seem the rulers are sending the warriors to quell the workers. What do you think'll happen?"

"Should be over soon. Can't imagine the Davidians cooped up like that. Got to be scary in there, you'd think."

"Well it's been pretty long now, what three weeks this Sunday?"

"Yeah, but on the inside the wait is a killer. Government guys are getting high just like they did at Ruby Ridge. I think it'll happen again, Mr. Lawrence. Say how's your ..."

Lawrence knew what McVeigh was going to ask so he cut off the speaker phone and picked up the receiver. Kat gave him a desultory grimace as if he had deprived her of an important conversation.

"I'm okay, Tim. This stuff drives you crazy, doesn't it?"

"Damn right, Mr. Lawrence. It makes me want to blow the fucking Feds to kingdom come. Hey, Mr. Lawrence got any new books for me to read?"

Lawrence paused, realizing that he did indeed have a new book for McVeigh to read but whether to tell him about it, since it would probably rile him up even more, was uncertain. Still Lawrence had no right to control or decide another man's thoughts.

"Yes, but it might be hard to find. Try some of those old book shops up in Toronto because I doubt it's in many book stores in the United States. It's titled A People's History of the United States, written by Howard Zinn. He used to be a professor at Boston University and a leader in the civil rights and antiwar movements. It'll get the hairs up on the back of your neck. Especially when he covers our noble country and its great leaders. But what do you expect; he's a native New Yorker, if you count Brooklyn."

"Sounds good. You want me to call you if I hear anything about Waco?"

"Do that Tim. Bye."

Kat was on Lawrence as soon as he put down his phone, "siege and government agents trying to storm the Alamo. Can I use what he told you?"

"Tim's a strange young man. He's not really very social. The Army and Desert Storm ripped his morals apart. Go ahead, write what you think, but be ready for me to bounce it around a bit."

***

"Judge, Judge, calm down. It'll only cost us a couple hundred dollars. We'll get the bond money back after the trial."

"Yeah, if she shows up for the trial. For God's sake, Lawrence, the woman's probably wanted by INS for deportation. I'm surprised there's even a bail set."

"Listen closely Judge. Let me go over it again, step by step. Here, take this note pad, jot some notes. Okay?"

"I heard it the first time, why ..."

"Because you blew a gasket and missed what I have on the Navy. The woman was passed out but technically not intoxicated. Her blood alcohol was below the drinking and driving limit. She was asleep, that's all."

"Again, you're telling me that this Commander Johnstone's jet plane flew over her house and the noise didn't wake her? I can't buy that, Peter."

"When's the last time those jets woke you out of that afternoon old man's nap you take?"

Dr. Sauers shook his head, smiling. He knew, like everybody else living near a flight path, that you get used to the jet noise as far as sleep is concerned.

"That's what really locks it. We're all so used to the jet noise that it blots out any other noise including a crying baby. Judge, the pilot was even below the 825 foot level which the airbase claims they keep to. You heard the noise from the tape I made. Want me to put it on again, turn up the volume to the 110 decibels these jets can reach and see if you can hear me crying?"

"I don't understand this ten thousand dollar bail the judge set. Why so high?"

Lawrence did not understand it either. He got the impression that there was more going on than criminal child neglect charges against the woman. He watched Dr. Judge Sauers walk to his desk, open the top right drawer, and pull out a checkbook.

"How much?"

"A thousand."

"Lawrence, you said a couple hundred for Christ's sake!"

He did not want a response. He signed the check, ripped it from the pad of V City Server checks, and handed the check to Lawrence. Going back to his desk, Sauers pulled out a file, took a sheet of paper out of it, wrote on the sheet, and handed it to Lawrence.

"It's an agreement of exclusivity. Do not ... let me repeat this, Peter, do not put up one penny if she refuses to sign this agreement and make sure you have a witness, an official employee at the city jail like the desk clerk, sign it. Any problem with that?"

Lawrence took the check made out to him, since the court would only take cash. He would go down to the Virginia City jail.

"Peter, this is good. I hate being such a pest about it, but I'm always cautious. You've got this story close to being tied up and in our hands. As big as this story could be, still every step's gonna make me edgy."

"Judge, I know how you feel. What bothers me is what we discussed. This case, the mother's arrest, is too plebian for the bail. Jailing a mourning mother with so little to go on sounds like somebody doesn't like little old Cuban ladies. Maybe there's some kind of racism going on. Who knows? I'll let you know how it went when I get her released."

"Lawrence, do not put up the bail until you have talked with her. You understand?"

Lawrence was glad for the close friendship and sage educated advice of Dr. Sauers, but he was especially grateful for the monitoring. He had intended to go post bail and then talk with Louisa Santiago after she was released. Dr. Sauers caught him possibly making a big mistake.

***

If Lawrence expected a little middle aged Cuban lady to be shown into the prisoners' visitation room, those expectations fell apart when he saw Louisa Santiago. She was nearly as tall as the prison guard who escorted her into the open cubicle where Lawrence had been waiting ten minutes. She was not a scared and pitiful alien being horrendously dragged into jail. She stood on the other side of an unbreakable plate glass partition that separated her and Lawrence. Her hands were akimbo and she scrutinized Lawrence up and down. She had dark red, extremely bushy hair that looked like it had been combed by a lawn mower. Every few seconds Louisa would toss her head, shaking the hair from in front of her eyes. There was a steak of grey that ran over the top of her brow. That the city jail had prisoner clothes for women that tall or blouses that covered her more than abundant breasts would be difficult to believe. It was obvious as she bent down to look Lawrence eyeball to eyeball, that Louisa wore no bra. This was unusual since suicide by hanging was quite possible with such an undergarment. Louisa had thick eyebrows which served well to reduce the sexuality of her aqua blue eyes. Her facial lines were severe and her nose arched from her face like a shard of glass. Her mouth was wide enough to keep up with her tongue, which never ceased to spew out words. Her mouth was extremely seductive in its thinness and moisture.

"Sit down now or I'll take you back to your cell. Understand?"

Louisa flailed her hands, palms up in front of her body but sat at the guard's command.

"So who the fuck are you?"

Lawrence just smiled, "I'm the editor for the V City Server."

"So?"

"I'd like to talk to you about the death of your child and ..."

"Maggot! You're a fucking maggot. You want a story about me killing my baby? Mother fucker, you ain't the first."

Lawrence knew that other newspapers had run stories about Louisa's case but none had talked to her."No, I want to get you out of here. I don't believe you ..."

"Get me out of here? You're shiting me. How you gonna to get me out?"

"The question is, am I going to get you out of here? I need to talk with you first."

"Probably want some pictures of my poor dead baby? You're just like the others."

"If I am, then why are you not sitting in your cell? In fact maybe you can explain something to me?"

"What?"

"Why did they set your bail so high? Is there somebody that has it in for you?"

Louisa sat back into her chair, crossed her right leg over the left, and rested her hands on her thigh, messaging the muscles gently. "My bail's high? I don't know nothing about bails."

"At the worst, what happened to your child was an accident. There was no intent or no violence committed by you. I checked and you have no prior record for anything except for pandering."

"Pandering? What the fuck's that mean?"

"It means you were selling yourself for sexual relationships."

"Hey, those charges were dropped! How come you know about them. They were supposed to be exorcised ... or is it exercised from my record?"

"Removed is an easier word. They were removed from your record despite the police undercover evidence that pretty much nailed you. The newspaper keeps records on computer of every charge registered at the police station. We don't delete them since you never know what might come up in the future. You're a good example."

Louisa Santiago was furious as she stood up cussing. The guard came up behind her, told her to sit down or she was going back to her cell. As she tossed her hair from her irate eyes, Lawrence was startled by the energy of her outburst and the sexuality of her body. The eyes were satanic and mesmerizing. He was stunned. She turned on the guard but stopped short and gave him a smile to stimulate his perverted male ego.

Lawrence got back to his questions concerning her prior recorded interrogations, "Louisa, who's this guy, the seed?"

"Czeed, you fool. Everybody knows Czeed. He runs this fucking town. Kenny Czeed ..." she stopped quickly. Louisa was not a smart woman and her aggressive physical drive not only got her into sexual relationships but also into trouble. Always too late, she recognized when she had gone too far and was in danger. She shut up, wrapped her arms around her bosom, and stared at Lawrence.

Lawrence knew who the seed was. Only the man's name was pronounced more correctly by making the "s' into a "z" which followed a silent "C." Kenneth Czeed was the Virginia

City Town Manager, second in rank only to the mayor. Actually since Czeed's office was not an elected position. Czeed had more power and more control than the elected mayor and the Virginia City Council. Lawrence knew he could not push her anymore here and now. It was too risky. Lawrence had to get her out of jail.

"Louisa, why didn't you try to post bail? Or why didn't you get a friend to get you out? Do you have a lawyer yet?"

"No."

She was being petulant now. Lawrence knew this was good. Yes and no answers are a reporter's forte. "How about this Czeed guy?"

Silence, "Come on, Louisa. If he helped you before, why not now? I'm sure that if you ..."

"No he wouldn't. He said if he ever heard from me again, he'd report me to INS."

"You're not a citizen? Are you saying immigration wants you? How the hell did you get here? Where did you come from?"

"Cuba. My momma was a Cuban but my father was a Dago off an American oiler. He brought her here after I was born but before they could get married, he was killed in a car accident. His family exiled us so we moved to South Carolina."

Lawrence could see she was beginning to calm down. "The law says you were drunk and your baby died because you were too drunk to hear her cry. What do you remember about that night?"

She was reticent but was no longer aggressive as before. He guessed it had to do with her admitting to being an alien. According to Louisa's timeline, Lawrence could not see her being sent back to Cuba. It had been twenty-five or thirty years since she was brought to the United States. Czeed was snowing her for whatever reason about her deportation, more likely the reason being that if Czeed's amorous affairs with Louisa got out, his city manager position would be lost, not to mention losing the money he makes, the trophy wife, and his four children who now attend private schools.

"Do you remember the jet plane that went over that night?"

Louisa's eyebrows squinted, "who remembers those stupid airplanes?"

"They're loud, Louisa. So loud you can't even hear the television or the telephone ringing."

"Mr. Lawrence, have you been here very long?"

"A few years, why?"

"Those planes don't mean anything anymore. You kind of don't hear them after they've blown your hearing apart night after night. I guess I'm immune to them. Except when those fuckers interrupt General Hospital. That really pisses me off."

Lawrence pulled out the exclusivity contract and held it up to the glass for the guard to see. The man nodded his head and picked up a telephone receiver. Lawrence could hear a phone behind him ring almost immediately. The door behind him opened and another guard came in and asked for the exclusivity contract. He read it over, had no questions, and left. Somebody, somewhere else in the building, must have had to approve sending it on for it took more than ten minutes before the contract got to Louisa.

"Read it over slowly, and if you have a question as you do read it, stop and ask me."

Louisa took her time. She had no questions. She started to sign the bottom but Lawrence told her to stop. He picked up the telephone receiver, waited two rings before the guard picked up and asked him if he would watch Louisa sign the contract and then initial it as a witness. The guard started to question if he should be doing this until Lawrence told him it would earn him a hundred dollars in cash, right now. The guard signed it, Louisa signed it, and the guard called in another guard to take the signed agreement to Lawrence.

"Louisa, it's going to probably take a few hours but I won't leave until you're free. Be patient!"

Lawrence had not allowed for Virginia City's bureaucracy and its low level, poorly motivated employees. It was dark by the time they walked out of Virginia City's jail facility.

***

"You posted bail for a whore?" Kat Winters would be Katherine for the night and she was dressed as a Katherine should be. She was going to be wined and dined by a jet pilot commander of the Ocean Airbase at the exclusive Officer's Club. Lawrence had also been invited, although the pilot had been reluctant. Katherine told Commander Johnstone that she needed Lawrence to explain the story frame work for the proposed special V City Server edition that would extol the Oceana Airbase's extreme value to the Virginia City economy. She had arrived earlier than Lawrence.

"We'll talk later Kat. I think you'll find Louisa a match for your snobbish condescension, my dear Miss Winters."

Lawrence noticed no commander and raised his hand for a waiter. The maitre d ' told them that Commander David Johnstone had left the table a half hour ago to spend a few minutes with some of his Navy buddies.

"How long have you been here?"

"Forty-five minutes, maybe an hour. I think he wants to hit on me but is afraid I might be jail bait. But he's talking, bragging about all of his risky and dangerous roaring flights up into the wild blue yonder."

"So he wants to take a flight into the wild blue yonder with Kat Winters, does he?"

"That's pretty good Lawrence. And before you correct me, I know wild blue yonder is Air Force. I think he's over there weighing his anchor next to the other testosterone oozing jet men. By the way, I hope he's not flying tonight since he's put away many a glass of Chevis."

"Drinks that much? Let me think on that for a while," said Lawrence as a waiter came and asked if he wanted a drink.

"Just a beer, whatever you got on tap."

Lawrence knew when to have all of his smarts.

"Take a look at this," said Kat pulling an 8 X 10 photograph out of a manila envelope that showed Commander David Johnstone posing next to a Tomcat. Ludicrous and self-aggrandizing, it had the commander's signature at the bottom wishing Katherine good luck.

"Ah, you must be Peter Lawrence, editor-in-chief of the V City Server," said Commander Johnstone as he returned to his reserved table for three and stretched out his hand to Lawrence.

"Yes, sir."

Lawrence had gone through in his mind what he knew, what he needed to know, and how he could learn from Commander David Johnstone. It had kept him up last night since Lawrence had to fight his own prejudices and preconceived notions about not only Commander Johnstone's being a military man, but the whole bravado that surrounds the world of being a soldier, whether an Army foot soldier, a Marine gunner, an Air Force ace, or a Navy Tomcat flyer. Within that perspective Lawrence had to keep his initial dislike of the military to himself and bring no personal interpretations of how these men chose to live.

"Here, let me get you a drink ..."

"It's on its way, Commander."

"Katherine, need another diet Pepsi?"

Lawrence just looked at her, recording in his mind that she was very smart, smart enough to not get high in the situation about to unfold.

"Yeah, that'd be good."

"Here comes the waiter now. Looks like he's headed here with Pete's drink. Listen Katherine, while he's here let me ask him if they got any dinner specials back in the kitchen that cater to diabetics."

Lawrence dared not look at her as it would draw too much attention to them. He waited until Johnstone turned away to talk to the waiter.

Lawrence mouthed the question "diabetic?"

Kat just smiled as Lawrence shook his head back and forth shaking of his head.

Commander Johnstone had went through what he knew of the airbase's history which Lawrence recognized as a litany drummed into the heads of all personnel stationed at the base.

Both he and Kat knew nearly every item the Commander recited since they had prepared for this encounter. There would not be a good cop/bad cop scenario. Lawrence knew that as soon as Johnstone recognized such a tactic, they would lose him.

"So I assume we're going to have the Air Show soon?" Kat asked already knowing the date.

"October as usual. Are you going," replied Commander Johnstone?

"I've been going since I was a little kid. Lawrence, you ever been to the Air Show?" Kat asked knowing that he had never attended and probably never would.

"Is John Mohr going to be there? I've seen him flying that old biplane on television. What kind of plane is that, Commander?"

"I believe it's a Stearman. You know his grandfather Fred knew Charles Lindbergh? Mr. Lawrence, how come you'll go see an old barnstormer perform but not our jets? Blue Angels are going to be there."

"Noise gets to me, Commander. I've got an inner ear problem that sends me into vertigo if it gets infected."

Kat picked up on the conversation. "Can't be that loud, Lawrence? I mean my parents took me to every air show at the base year after year. It was neat climbing through the planes and riding the kiddy rides. Jets would make me jump and clasp my hands over my ears but you shouldn't be such a baby about it."

"I'm not the only baby about it, Katherine. Why do you think Cecil Field in Jacksonville, Florida kicked the Navy out?"

Johnstone finished his sixth or seventh scotch, signaled the waiter, and he asked Lawrence and Kat if they wanted another. He sent the waiter off for another saying, "make sure you put this on my chit, okay? The dinner too."

Lawrence noticed that Commander Johnstone's eyes were clouding a bit. "Mr. Lawrence, they didn't kick us out. We packed up and left. Not enough room down there. Hell, we sent 180 F-14 Tomcats and F/A-18 Hornets up here where we'd have some room. You know how many people that brought to this 'nowhereville? Over 11,000 people and that didn't include the military families. Place was a barren cow pasture before the Navy got here."

Kat responded, "I've done some research for our feature on Oceana. You guys opened in 1952, during the Korean War but the land you took over had been settled back in the 1880s."

"Oh come on!" Johnstone was sipping his fresh scotch faster than the ice cubes could melt, "they were just a bunch of hayseeds, farmer folks. If it weren't for Oceana you guys would still be raising cows and growing corn. Look what Oceana did to the economy of Virginia City?"

"Sure did help the economy. The noise and danger potential of the jets forced the closing of the high school and an elementary school," said Lawrence. "Do you know that your Hornet ..."

"Tomcat, I fly a Tomcat!"

Lawrence was getting to him and kept it low keyed to not cause the man to erupt. "Okay David. We're just talking friendly here. Don't take it so personal, okay?"

Kat reached over and put her hand on the Commander's arm which gained her a smile. Lawrence knew he had to be careful, not push the edge and lose the catch, "... your tomcat is one very bad ass jet? Might be the best fighting machine in history?"

Lawrence had no idea if that was true. For all he knew John Mohr and his biplane could shoot down a Tomcat.

"Fuckin' A!"

It was too loud and Kat shot a look at Lawrence before speaking. "Mr. Lawrence, do you know how much money Virginia City would lose if the Navy packed up and left here? Over a billion dollars a year. Not only military losses but their families have homes here or live in apartments and pay rent here. The squadrons increase jobs and obviously produce revenue for the businesses here. I bet some of those jet plane pilots might even read your esoteric and boring editorials."

Lawrence smiled at her. "Boring? Esoteric?"

"Yeah, what's esoteric mean?" Asked Johnstone.

"Information requiring knowledge used by a small group of intelligent people," said Lawrence.

"Ignore him David," said Kat gaining the edge that was set up by Lawrence's esoteric definition of esoteric. "It means he's a snob."

Lawrence just laughed, "You're both probably correct. I see Virginia City without Oceana Airbase as a bunch of farmers whom when daunted by sounds louder than a rock concert or a pile driver, just sit back and say 'sons bitches fly a 100 feet above us, we've gotta stop talking and start sipping our beer until we's gets our hearin' back!'"

All three of them laughed and Lawrence stood up. "Having mentioned beer, I've got to use the bathroom. What is it you Navy heroes call the outhouse? The head?"

Commander Johnstone had recovered from the anger that had been building and laughed at Lawrence's self deprecating comments about intellectuals. "That's right, sir. We call it the head. You want to know why it's called that?"

Lawrence smiled, "hope she's not wearing lipstick?"

Kay just groaned, ignoring her two macho masculine dinner compatriots and their now comradely conversations. She had gained a whole new perspective for her editor by seeing him in action.

Lawrence visited the head. As he was leaving, he found the Maître De for the Oceana Airbase Officers Club. "Can I speak to you for a second?"

"Yes, sir. What can I do for you. Have you enjoyed your meal?"

Lawrence had hated his meal. If the officers ate like this, the enlisted men must suffer, "yes, very good. I noticed that Commander Johnstone is writing off our meals on a chit."

"Yes sir, that is his privilege," responded the Maître De.

Lawrence could not help but detect a slight grimace in the man's demeanor with the response that Johnstone pays on credit. "I'm the editor-in-chief of the V City Server and we're here, that young lady sitting at the table with Commander Johnstone and I, as part of our job."

Lawrence reached into his back pocket and pulled out his wallet. Opening it, he took out two one hundred dollar bills, "don't put our bill on his credit. It's part of our expense account at the newspaper. This should cover it, plus a tip for the waiter."

Before the man could reply, Lawrence took out another hundred dollar bill and handed it to the Maître De, "this is for you. Commander's kind of a proud man, so whatever you do, don't let him know I picked up the check."

"That's very kind of you, Sir. Commander Johnstone would greatly appreciate it if he knew."

There was some overtone in the man's voice that stopped Lawrence, "you know, I was here with him a few weeks ago and I believe he picked up the bill. Do you have his unpaid chits somewhere?"

The Maître De smiled and spoke, "yes, sir. Would you like to pay those also?"

Lawrence gave the man the date that Louisa Santiago's baby died and asked if Johnstone had a chit for that day. Lawrence would pay it, but he would need a receipt so he could get reimbursed by the newspaper. The man left and came back with Commander Johnstone's signed chit for that day. Without looking at it, Lawrence asked how much and paid it in full adding a tip to the Maître De. He returned to the table.

"Commander, it is getting late and I've got to be going. Great dinner, Commander. When you go up again?"

Lawrence had not sat down so Johnstone rose to shake his hand. "Tomorrow. I've got a morning training flight with a cadet and the day after I'm doing a night flight out over the Atlantic. Thanks for stopping by Mr. Lawrence."

"Hey, I heard you already met Katherine's girlfriend?"

"How's that, sir?"

"I did her a flyover in your Hornet, oops, I mean Tomcat. When was that, Katherine?"

Johnstone responded before she could with the date and time.

"You've got to be stringing these young ladies along. Come on, your couldn't really see them through their windows. You can't fly that low without crashing into something," Lawrence had made it a challenge.

"Sure can, Sir. One of our pilots got nailed buzzing his ex-wife's apartment at 600 feet whenever his kids told them that Uncle Joey was spending the night and she couldn't come to the phone right now. She did not have any brothers."

Lawrence just shook his head and snickered, "Katherine, can I give you a lift?"

"No, I'm fine. See you tomorrow Mr. L," she said grinning.

***

"So Katherine, did you get home without Benny and his Jets hitting on you?"

It was the next morning and Kat had just walked into his office.

"Lawrence, he was so swacked his joy stick wouldn't work."

"Wait, you got into a position with the Commander that …"

"No, we didn't go anywhere to fuck if that's what you're thinking. It wasn't because he didn't want to …"

"How about you?"

"He's an icky old man to me. My grandfather's his age for Christ's sake. I was worried a bit when we left, shortly after you. He was just waiting for you to go so he could weigh his anchor, as you politely put it. Fortunately his anchor had too much booze running through it to weigh anything."

Lawrence chuckled; thought more about what she said, and nearly went into a paroxysm of laughter. "What? Excuse me, but I need to catch my breath. What happened?"

"He escorted me to my car and tried to be romantic with me. You know, that come on bullshit of smooth-talking, getting closer, saying what great eyes I have, and … Now don't choke this time, but the asshole ran his knuckles over my face like it was going to get me all hot!"

"His knuckles? Does that ever work?"

"Not on me? Want to know what will?"

Lawrence looked her in the eyes, "Kat, I had never seen you dressed up like you were last night. Am I attracted to you? Yes. Would I make love with you? I don't know. You're of age but it's not mine. People working together and sleeping together can be dangerous for both. Us included. Let's just have some fun with it for now, both of us wondering what the other sees and would do. Okay? So how did you get him off you in the parking lot?"

"Just as he started rubbing his hips against my thigh, I said that the newspaper didn't have any information about his family but that the Admiral had told me he was married and had a couple adorable kids. Anchors away, my friend! Tears came to his eyes."

"Sounds like it's a good thing he flies a Tomcat cause he sure couldn't get anything else up, up, and away."

"So continuing Lawrence. You got him admitting he flew over the apartment for ... what's her name?"

"Louisa, Louisa Santiago. Yes, he's nailed. He's nailed more than you think."

"How's that?"

Lawrence had the chit from the Maître De on his desk. He pushed it over to Kat, "take a look at this."

"Our boy sure likes to down his scotch. So?"

"Look at the date on the chit and the time."

"Holy shit, it's the same day that the child died and what, only a couple hours before the time of death according to the autopsy?"

"That's our problem. All I wanted was enough evidence to clear Louisa Santiago. Just his admission to a high noise fly over under 800 feet at the same time of the child's death would be enough. It shows reasonable doubt that she could not have heard her child screaming so loud that it ruptured the blood vessels in the baby's throat. Reasonable doubt, period. She's free."

"But?"

"You tell me."

"Johnstone's buzzing below the flight zone meant he was responsible for the child's death. What's that called?"

"Involuntary manslaughter."

"Holy shit! And he was intoxicated as well. What would his level had been with those amounts of drinks ... wait a minute. Maybe we're jumping to conclusions. Maybe he was hosting somebody at the officer's club and hadn't been drinking himself. I mean a lot of people drink scotch, especially Chevis Regale."

"Look at the chit. Looks like a check civilians get at a bar. See the boxes at the top? See the one that says guests? That means number of guests. There's a one there. He wasn't even downing them with his buddies. He was drinking alone."

Lawrence got up from his desk as Kat, who had been standing, eased her way over to the chair in front of the desk. She sat down slowly. After closing his office door, Lawrence went back to his seat.

"This has just erupted into something way more than we signed up for. It's much more than just saving an innocent woman from prosecution."

"Jesus, Lawrence, what we got will put him in jail ..."

"The brig, he's military. He will also be dishonorably discharged after serving his time in the brig. The question is, do we take him down?"

"No, you're missing the big picture Lawrence. We're only looking at one pilot, one pilot that we weren't even trying to find. All we wanted to do was get Santiago freed. Now we not only have a man who has committed manslaughter, but is he the only one?"

Lawrence knew what Kat meant. He had not worked it out in his mind yet, "we at least know the Navy will react. Hell, maybe that's only a possibility?"

"Only a possibility? Are you crazy? The Navy will be breath analyzing every pilot before they take off. They'd have to after we print this story. Which also means ... when are you going to write this?"

"Not my story, Kat."

"Then who's ... No, Mr. Lawrence, this is too big for me. I just got out of ..."

"You write it, period. I'll deal with getting Louisa off."

***

Lawrence had packed up and moved to Virginia City Beach lock, stock, and barrel. To accommodate all of his belongings, he rented what had been an in-law floor added to the top of a garage. The in-law had been long gone, had actually died in the rental which turned off other potential renters. "Death lingers o'er the spot" was a line from some poem which Lawrence could not remember except that death does not haunt the living, only takes the living. Lawrence never feared death and was not going to fear the ghost of the old lady who lived on the top of a garage.

His apartment was only blocks from Virginia City's beach, boardwalk, tourist bars, and restaurants. It was far enough from these venues to maintain privacy but still accessible to the bay to the west which give Lawrence a place to canoe. When he had the time and energy, he could actually leave his back door, and haul the 18 foot Grumman canoe out of the garage and launch it into Back Bay. If needed, he could canoe out into the bay, go north into the Chesapeake Bay or south down the river systems of Munden Point Bay and into North Carolina's bays on the west side of the Outer Banks. Across the road from his domicile was the Atlantic Ocean.

Lawrence's home was also only a few blocks from the newspaper plant. This was also a great benefit to Lawrence since he really did not like cars or driving. Both took his mind away from whatever was running through it. His daily walks to work let him contemplate in forty five minutes what his plans would be once he, the editor-in-chief, got to the V City Server's office. All of the United States Eastern Shore Coast from South Delaware's Dewey Beach, to Virginia's Eastern Shore, Virginia City Beach, and on and on through North and South Carolina unsettled Lawrence. Home had been Western New York and the mountainous forests with refuges from humanity and resources of fish and game. Now he lived on a gigantic plateau of marshes, bogs, sedges, and tree breaks few and far between. It made him restless. A restless Peter Lawrence was a challenged Peter Lawrence. He needed a lair, not one from which to stalk and kill, but a hide-away to put the human world out of his mind, or at least out of contact and beyond humanity's reach. This he accomplished.

During his first two months in Virginia's coastal area, he spent weekends driving north and south, east and west, over single lane farm roads and deserted farm roads, usually getting lost which was what he wanted most. The upper Back Bay area just below Chesapeake Bay was over populated and out of the question. Lawrence bicycled to the Back Bay National Wild Life Refuge and found exactly what he needed, almost. It was owned by the United States Fish and Wildlife Service under the Department of Interior. He could not own nor build his Eden there but if needed, he could not only get lost in the refuge but he could disappear into North Carolina very easily, even by bicycle along the flat, hard packed sand beach that ran south.

One Sunday after stopping at a local produce stand and buying some excellent peaches to eat on the spot, Lawrence crossed Gum Bridge Road in Pungo, just off an extension of Princess Anne Road. He decided to see if there really was a Gum Bridge, which there was not. Instead he got deep into the farm and marsh land abutting Shipp's Bay. He made a right turn on Charity Creek Road only to find no Charity Creek, but instead Muddy Creek Road. Choosing to head toward the bay, he made a left hand turn, followed the road north, and found himself deep into farm land. He also found the true end of Gum Bridge Road's after going about two miles. It ended in a dirt road along a plowed farm. With nothing to lose and needing to stop somewhere to wash the peach juice off his sticky hands, he made a right turn on a twisting dirt road that that ended at a farm house about a half a mile from Muddy Creek Road.

He was lost in Pungo but maybe he had found a link. Just south of Gum Bridge's dirt, Muddy Creek Road passed over a small creek flowing eastward, probably ending up in Back Bay. He parked his bike, walked to the stream, and rinsed off his hands. He followed the creek, through a copse of pine trees that lined both sides of the steam. The vegetation was extremely dense considering that it was a pine biome. After a quarter of a mile or so, it opened up into a plain of dense marsh and a large cove. Lawrence cursed himself for not putting his canoe up on the roof of his car, knowing he would not try to venture through the soggy marsh, rife with sand pockets that would sink his legs knee deep. Looking at tracks in the damp soil, he saw that it was probably home to cotton mouth snakes. He would return later.

Three weeks later he did. Before returning he had researched, with the help of the real estate agent that found him his garage home, the area around Landing Cove which was the name of the body of water he had found. As far as the realtor knew, there were no deeds on the entire area. It was written off as unsettled marsh on the federally owned Back Bay Wildlife Reserve. She did note that over twenty years ago the city had issued a plot deed to some duck hunters from New Jersey granting permission to build a cabin off a small stream that emptied into the tributary that flowed from Landing Cove into Sand Bay. The plot deed was still valid and the duck hunters had the unique bureaucratic enigma of owning a parcel of land prior to the U.S Government declaring ownership. They could no longer access the property however since the farm bordering Landing Cove had changed ownership and the new farmer labeled his property with No Trespassing signs and threatened the New Jersey duck hunters with bullets when they tried to visit their hunting plot. The duck hunters put the small area on the real estate market but obviously nobody had any interest in owning hunting blinds in the middle of a United States Wildlife Reserve with No Trespassing Signs.

Lawrence needed to see the property so he put the Grumman canoe up and headed the ten plus miles down General Booth, over to Princess Anne and into Pungo. The plot map that the realtor got from the city deed's department showed the duck hunter's shack to be over a mile away. Lawrence had noted of this before his trip and opted to hit the cove as the tide was falling. The area was barren, with random pine trees and marshes along with one or two other small creeks terminating in Landing Cove. He headed directly east toward a peninsula north of the only outlet for Landing Cove. It was a dense pine forest. Lawrence guessed that very few people ventured through this wilderness especially since it had been labeled a protective wet land only a few years ago.

Gliding through the inlet with the tide's current, he paddled north to find the creek leading to the shack. It did not take long. There was a large sand island due to erosion in the center of the stream. He had to portage the Grumman for about twenty yards around a 20^0 bend in the stream. This was good since it prevented any visitors canoeing or kayaking up the stream. Less than fifty feet to the east he found the duck blind, which turned out to be more like a hunter's cabin. It was obvious that the duck hunters from New Jersey had spent muscle, time, and a bit of money building the cabin. The siding was substantial and the windows were covered with drop boards to keep intruders away. There were two windows to each side of the front door and one window facing east at the back of the cabin. The hunters had been cheap when it came to the hinges, though. Very few people put value into the prevention of corrosion of simple hardware like hinges. This is especially sinful when living in a salt water environment. The front door was sturdy and padlocked but like the windows, the hinges were cheap and it took little effort for Lawrence to use a stone to crush them. The door swung open, staying upright only by the padlocked clasp. Inside it was dark. The cabin had not been lived in for many years by a human. No matter what an owner does to seal a wildlife area abode, living creatures penetrate. He rolled the stone into the dark cabin and heard the rustling of critters heading for hiding places. He recognized the sound of slithering snakes and took the chance they had gone into hiding. Walking into the cabin, his first thoughts were to get the windows open. Since they were only latched from the inside, this was no problem and soon he could see the interior of the cabin. He was very pleased. It was clean and organized, almost too neat to be a hunting cabin. There was an old fashioned crank pump affixed to the kitchen sink which needed a new leather seal. There would be fresh water or close to fresh water available once fixed. There were three bunks. The hunters did not have a generator, Lawrence would have to install. They had used kerosene lamps for light. He also discovered that they were dentists from the dental magazines lying on the table in the middle of the hut. Two different dentists' names were listed on the mailing address stickers and he assumed the third duck hunter was also part of the same fraternity.

Once back home, Lawrence bypassed his realtor and, using the information from the mailing labels, personally contacted one of the dentists. The man was ecstatic to finally get a potential buyer, so ecstatic that he got his partners' signatures on the paper work within two hours, and sent it FedEx to Lawrence. The good doctor and his buddies were so ripe to sell the cabin and the land lease that Lawrence got both titles for only a thousand dollars. They did not even question who Lawrence was and accepted the purchaser's name as John Clayton. Lawrence, or it should be said John Clayton, now owned the inaccessible plot of land and hunter's hut. He had his hide away, surrounded by signs telling people to keep off or be arrested. He could not ask for anything better.

Lawrence took his time rebuilding his sanctum sanctorum. He wanted to ensure that it stayed his holy place, his Eden, or his DumDum as John Clayton would have called it. His access via the creek that ran under Muddy Creek Road was not an option since it was too visible and there was no place to hide his car when he left it to canoe to Landing Cove. Ironically it was Muddy Creek, the Muddy Creek which was two miles north of Gum Bridge Road that gave Lawrence his egress to Landing Cove. A boat launch inlet ran right out from Muddy Creek into Shipps Bay. Lawrence paid the storekeeper who ran the boat launch a yearly fee and was able to park his car there and canoe out into the bay. Mr. John Clayton, as he was known by the boat launch owners, paid yearly in cash, so no questions were asked.

At first Lawrence made a concerted effort to rid the cabin and its environs of cottonmouth snakes. He had not realized their value until he revisited the cabin and found it overrun with rats. He left the snakes alone. The other visitors did not bother him. It was not uncommon for Lawrence to find a squirrel sitting on his table when he awoke in the morning. Twice he was able to take a deer down within yards of Dum-Dum and dress it for the venison. The flow of nutria, foxes, a couple of feral pigs every once in a while, combined with the abundance of snakes, meant he had no human visitors. Lawrence never missed the human contact but felt lost when he visited the cabin and found none of nature's life within it.

Lawrence was here in DumDum, the place to filter out, arrange, modify, and plan his assaults on life. Nothing could interfere with him at Landing Cove. His vow when facing a challenge was to not leave until his decisions were made and plans were set and he was here now to make a decision. There had been two that kept him here for more than two weeks.

***

Lizzy Hawkins had been beaten to death in March of 1993. Lawrence would avenge that he would not accept that Lizzy was worthless and needed to be exterminated. It took only one call to know her killer. Dr. Nuevello's secretary answered the phone but no sooner had she put him on hold then Nuevello was on the line.

"Lawrence, why the call?"

"Nuevello, I need information and it has nothing to do with our relationship. We're cast in stone by the collateral we both hold."

There was a change in Nuevello's tone that made Lawrence's inquiry easier, "okay, what do you need to know?"

"I got a call from De Graff Hospital that Lizzy Hawkins had been beaten to death. My guess is Uley?"

"You know I can't tell you anything."

"You mean you won't tell me anything. She was beaten to death. That doesn't sound like ..."

"Lawrence, what I don't know can't hurt me. Ever hear that expression? Trite isn't it? Almost childish. Unfortunately it works. I'm going to hang up. Hope I've been helpful."

Lawrence called Dr. Judge Sauers and told him that he was going to be away from the paper for about a week, giving no reason. Sauers had gotten used to Lawrence abruptly taking a few days off and accepted that Lawrence needed personal time. Since Lawrence's time outs had ended up with tremendous improvements in the V City Server, Sauers just told Lawrence that he would take over the daily management while Lawrence was gone.

As Lawrence packed he noticed that he was low on ammunition for his Colts and the Remington. He did not want to wait until the next day to buy more so he packed both weapons and headed out for the twelve hour journey up north in hopes of buying ammo from Tim McVeigh when he got to Western New York. At least the traffic would be light since it was late on a Monday night.

Lawrence took a room at the Grand Island Holiday Inn and called McVeigh reaching his answering machine, "Tim, Peter Lawrence. I'm staying at the Grand Island Holiday Inn and need to buy some ... some supplies. Can you give me a call or maybe stop over?"

Rejuvenated after a long shower, Lawrence picked up his ringing phone and heard McVeigh's voice, "You don't know, do you? Waco's blowing up. The Feds are attacking right now. It's on the fucking news. There's armored tanks ramming the walls of the compound. Hell, the whole building's in flame ... "

"Hold on a second, Tim. Let me put on my TV." Lawrence quickly grabbed the remote and hit the channel button until CNN came on. "Wow! When did this start?"

"Mr. Lawrence? Look, I'm in Michigan on a friend's phone, Terry Nichols. All I know is that I was outside his farmhouse changing the oil in my car and I heard screaming from inside the farmhouse where I'm staying. The wooden complex where Koresh and his worshippers were housed was on the TV. It was totally engulfed in flames. How fucking cold blooded can you be to set a building on fire with women and kids in it?"

Lawrence watched the television in disbelief.

"Mr. Lawrence? You still there? Hello!"

"Yeah, Tim. I can't believe it either. What justifies what these ATF soldiers are doing?"

"I know of nothing but a search warrant. There's one called a "no-knock" search warrant."

"That lets them attack civilians with a massive assault?"

"No, it doesn't. They never got one. All they got is a normal search warrant from back in February. Says they have to announce their search and define their duty."

"How does either one justify bombing with incendiary?"

"It don't. Look, you got on CNN?"

"Yes."

"That's automatic fire at the doors of the compound. Listen, we're heading down there. Let me give you a name. Here"

McVeigh read off the name of a gun dealer in Lockport and continued, "this is it, Mr. Lawrence. This is fucking it! Somebody's got to take these assholes down. I mean really down. Make them pay in double or triple, blow the sons of bitches to hell where they belong."

"Tim, you better slow down. Cool off a bit."

"Sorry, sir. I'm passed it now. Ruby Ridge and now Waco. It's sort of like you said. The three levels, royalty, warriors, and workers. Gotta go. My man in Lockport will take care of you."

Lawrence watched enough of Waco to chill his blood and then turned off the TV. He could not chance having another gun dealer knowing his name or face. He checked over his available bullets and felt that he had more than enough for Uley Hawkins. The truth was that Lawrence knew he did not need more ammunition. He just used it as a reason to talk with Tim McVeigh. To Lawrence McVeigh was the picture of a tragedy waiting to end in horror. Lawrence mused on this for a few minutes. A tragedy waiting to happen, almost Shakespearian. McVeigh was almost there. Hell, Lawrence was almost there but had one more task in Western New York.

Uley no longer worked for Niagara City Schools. Whether he had been fired or just let go, Lawrence had no idea and did not care. It cost Lawrence a hundred dollars to buy off a former coworker of Uley's. Uley was a UPS driver working out of Rochester New York. Lawrence hated driving in Rochester better known as the can of worms roadway. Only having visited Rochester a couple times when he lived in Western New York, it was enough times to get him lost trying find destinations that seemed to have been washed off the face of the earth. The same happened as he spent two days visiting UPS delivery facilities. Eventually he found Uley but he was out on a delivery, which worked well for Lawrence.

Watching the brown vehicles come and go, Lawrence was able to identify Uley and his truck. He followed him. The UPS truck made a delivery to an Eastman Kodak plant near Lake Ontario, then kept along the lake road heading east toward Syracuse. Lawrence kept his distance and bided his time. Uley stopped at a McDonald's and picked up take-out, drove back along the lake, and stopped at the pull-off. It was a place where people could take in the beach and swim but not in Upstate New York in April and not during the week.

Lawrence had one of his Colts in a snap-on belt holster at his back. He was wearing his hooded Buffalo Bills sweat shirt. He parked about a hundred yards from Uley's truck and walked slowly down the parking lot, giving Uley time enough to enjoy his last meal, Chicken McNuggets with fries. Lawrence stayed behind the UPS truck so his only chance of being seen by Uley would be in the rear or side view mirror.

Vengeance dominated his thoughts. His mother, Evelyn, had always applied her Catholic heritage by using religious adages, one being "vengeance is mine sayth the Lord." He had no conflict with Evelyn once he learned he could not change her devout and pious mind. His concept veered well off from Biblical terms. Man was not created in God's image. God was created in man's image. Through all of his religious upbringing and indoctrination Peter Lawrence saw the obvious. The Bible was written by a man, or many men. The image called God is always described as human. Vengeance was a human trait, rarely seen by any other species. Vengeance is mine I say. I am God's image. Uley was another Frick. Lawrence would kill him without guilt.

He smiled. It was dichotomous and he was proud to coin it. What does it mean? I am made in God's image or I created God in my image?

Uley opened the driver's side door and exited, carrying a white MacDonald's bag while sipping his super-sized drink loudly. He headed to a trash can chained to a pole light three car spaces from the UPS truck. At least Uley was depositing his trash ecologically and not throwing it out on the tarmac.

It was obvious that Uley had added something extra into his MacDonald's drink. He was reeling side-to-side as he threw the food bag at the trash can, missing it completely.

Lawrence made the man jump, almost out of his pants which were unbuckled with the fly open. Lawrence did not want to know what Uley had been doing in the truck with his pants down. Nothing like whacking off while eating a cheeseburger.

"You missed Uley! Now you'll never get into heaven."

It was getting late, almost dark. The wind, like no other wind, blew in their faces as it came off of Lake Ontario. Sharp bites of sleet bit at their faces, turning their cheeks red. Uley did not hesitate and went into his front pocket struggling to pull out a collapsed hunting knife. He could not get the blade to swing out. His finger nails were bitten off to the quick leaving him no way to lift the blade at the notch.

Lawrence had his Colt drawn, "you're going to die, Uley."

He shot the man in the gut and Uley went to his knees. Within seconds he was vomiting.

"Why am I doing this Uley?"

"Cause we beat your ass in the garage?"

Lawrence shook his head slowly, "how much pain did you cause to Henry?"

Uley screamed as another bullet ruptured more stomach tissue and ripped through more nerves. Uley grasped his stomach and Lawrence heard the sounds of Uley defecating. Each sphincter spasm brought more pain and Lawrence could smell the offal. Still he would not kill Uley although he knew he could not risk putting it off much longer. The road here had been barren but that did not mean a motorist would not show up at any given time. Still, who was going to visit the dismal, cold, sleet freezing rain of the lake shore at dusk on a night like this?

"He ratted you out Uley?"

"Who?"

"Nuevello," said Lawrence, letting Uley go through another five minute sphincter contraction of pain before he put a bullet into Uley's head.

Lawrence drove back to Virginia that same night, a ride of many miles, many hours, and many thoughts. God was not one of them. He had now been responsible for the deaths of three people. Frick did himself in. Lawrence had killed Fitzgerald Ledger and now Uley Hawkins. It was true that Lawrence felt less and less guilt with each killing. It was not getting easier though. He was now morally estranged as a human. These three dead men were no better than rodents. A rat has no sin for its life. It behaves as it needs to survive. No so Frick, Ledger, and Hawkins.

Lawrence made it to Syracuse without any police sighting. He was still in the midst of an early spring snow storm. Heading south on Route 81, he let go of the fear of being caught and begin to go over in his head an editorial on the Waco Massacre. While McVeigh had given off a wide stream of anti-government challengers, Lawrence could only note them for source verification. The radio only sporadically mentioned Waco and then mostly in terms of right wing, religious radicals living using children for incestuous sexual acts. Just like Tim McVeigh, Lawrence knew that the media was being used for government propaganda. There were contacts he would have to make and news reports he would have to read before he could write the editorial.

"No. There wasn't," his thoughts erupting within the silence of the car's interior. Not even in his most patriotic mode could he believe the government had cause to burn to death women and children. Questions had to be asked many, too late though for the lives of twenty dead children.

***

His trip to Western New York resulted in his first challenge issued to the readers of the V City Server via the editorial page. His first editorial piece was on Waco. It was the first challenge to the people. He called the first editorial "ten questions to ask Janet Reno." Subsequent editorials would be shaped in the same mold, always keeping the style. They would rile many and rally others. Dr. Judge Sauers had to either let it run or dissolve his partnership with Lawrence. It did not appear for two weeks, the first week having been spent at Landing Cove writing it after first researching through the news media and contacting leads that Tim McVeigh had provided. McVeigh admitted without hesitation that any information he had was second-hand and prejudiced. For all his angers and faults, Tim McVeigh would not prevaricate.

He sat in his cabin alone and enjoyed his well-filleted flounder. He ate only pieces of the croaker he caught, avoiding the small bones. He put together his "ten questions to ask Janet Reno." Each question was gleaned from a separate source but Lawrence double checked each story to insure its validity.

***

"For Christ's sake, Peter! What did you … No, I can see what you put on our front page. The question is why?" Judge Sauer was more upset than Lawrence could have imagined. He was an extremely religious man. Lawrence had never even heard Judge say damn. Now he took the name of the Lord in vain.

Once back from killing Uley Hawkins, Lawrence had researched, written and printed his editorial column on the Waco Massacre. Today he ran it without Judge Sauer's knowledge, only two weeks after the attack on the Branch Davidian's compound. Running the paper without Judge Sauer's approval was an agreement Lawrence had forced on him if he wanted Lawrence as his editor-in-chief. There would be no censoring of the editor-in-chief except by termination after the fact. Today was after the fact. Lawrence's first set of ten questions to ask …might also be Lawrence's last ten questions.

"Read them Judge."

"No, read them aloud. Read them here in front of the staff. They're as stunned as you but they can't fire me."

"Want me to take a vote on firing you? We're all going to lose our jobs and dumping you might be the only way to …"

"Judge, slow down! You're going to have a heart attack."

"I sure as hell hope I don't. I won't have any money to pay my medical bills. You know why I'm here this early in the morning?"

"I'm betting," said Lawrence, "that a couple of ad runners have bailed?" Lawrence exuded cool and calm.

"A couple? Try five this morning. I stopped answering my phone!"

"Judge, read the column aloud so we can all hear you. You're good at that. That is why I liked your class in college. Read it to us."

So Judge read aloud, "Dear Reader, I am the editor-in-chief of V City Server and this will be the first time you have read a column by me. I chose early on to let our reporters do what they do best at."

Kat interrupted, "Lawrence, shame on you. A dangling participle? What did you do that for?"

The newsroom's atmosphere lightened considerably with laughter.

Judge continued, "The recent events in Waco Texas have startled and scared me into putting what I have seen personally before your eyes. We at V City Server have followed the Waco Texas confrontation day by day providing you, our readers, with news copy from national news networks. Having read through paper after paper, magazine after magazine, and watched network news day by day, I find myself bewildered by the plethora of events, most of which contradict each other. Who really knows the facts? In a society like ours, the United States, one turns to its leaders. That responsibility fell on the shoulders of the Attorney General, Janet Reno. Once the confrontation started on February 28th, it fell into her lap quickly. The agencies were hers, ATF (Alcohol, Tobacco, Firearms) and of course the FBI which we all know. Now we have four federal agents dead and 82 Branch Davidian Followers dead.

What happened, Janet?

Can you answer these ten questions?

1. What law did they break? I do not know. Your search warrants are not only ambiguous but invalid since there was no intent listed on them. The AFT tried to force a search without reason.

2. Did you really need U.S. Army tanks, plus two Apache war helicopters and a Blackhawk to take out the 96 Branch Davidians? You had 75 ATF agents, 25 FBI agents, a couple hundred Green Berets, and fighter jets all at full alert to face off against mostly women and children.

3. Who was the idiot that claimed the ATF had the right to make a bust since the Davidians were making and selling methamphetamines? There was absolutely no evidence they were involved in making, doing, or selling drugs.

4. Did you really have the CIA fly a spy plane over the complex?

5. Is it true that one of your ATF agents shot an innocent dog hanging around the scene because the dog's barking annoyed him? Did you get a writ from the SPCA and Waco's Animal Protective Services before you blew away the dreaded cur?

6. Why did an ATF agent arrest a senior citizen couple who just happened to be in the wrong place at the wrong time on a weapons charge? The man had no idea how to fire the AK-47 that the ATF claimed he owned and the woman could not even lift it.

7. Can you wire us a picture of your tank commander who mooned the Davidians and every bystander within fifty feet? I understand how frustrating it had to be for him since he stated that you were a chicken and you should just order him to kill them all.

8. Was it necessary to shoot the man who was only there to paint the graying water tower in the head? Maybe your agents did not like the color he was using.

9. Why did one of your agents put three bullets in the head of an unarmed man and leave his body where it fell to rot for four days? You might include with this question why bodies were left in the morgue to decompose before an autopsy could be conducted. It seems that is a sure way to destroy evidence.

10. On your orders, ferret rounds of CS gas and methylene chloride were launched into the compound by the Bradley tanks. The FBI knew what would happen in such a confined space. The vapors flooded the compound and ignited into flames. Without verbally calling into the shell of the building to see if there were survivors, your bulldozers rushed the building and plowed down the walls, not only covering evidence of this heinous crime, but crushing six mothers and their children who had survived the holocaust of flame you threw on them. In order to answer this last question you need to look at the picture at the bottom of this page. It shows the charred remains of a woman's skeleton wrapped around the charred remains of a baby she was clutching. Take a good look at it.

Question ten is appropriate for your obvious actions. Do you like your Branch Davidian mothers and children well done or pink on the inside?

Except for Lawrence, everybody was crying. They had seen the original photo on Lawrence's desk. Everybody, including Dr. Sauers, had to sit down.

Sauers spoke, "Peter, I'm sorry, very sorry. I only skimmed your column and selfishly thought only of the calls. Reading it aloud made it too real. I know you Peter. I know you well enough to know you can back up every word."

Dr. Judge Sauers knew Lawrence and Lawrence did not respond.

"You have made a great statement here but I fear you'll have to pay for it."

"How's that Judge?"

"You think the Feds will let it go?"

"No, but this is only the spark. Reno will want to go after me and maybe the V City Server but Billy Bob Clinton won't let her. You know why?"

"Go ahead, Peter."

"Just yesterday Clinton and Reno, plus the FBI, stated that there's evidence the Branch Davidians set fire to themselves as if it was some kind of religious sacrifice to their God."

"You're kidding? With all the video and photographs and the on-site reporters watching, Clinton believes they self-emulated? Can he really be that dumb?"

He really could be. Lawrence found that out the following Monday. He was going over the next week's layout and assignments when he glanced up from his desk and looked out the glass windowed walls. He saw two grey suits come into the newspaper office. They did not stop to ask for him at the desk counter, coming straight to the swinging half door that separates the customer area from the newsroom. Kat stood up and asked if she could help them but was ignored. Lawrence put his hands behind his head and guessed Uley Hawkins had caught up with him. Trying to flee was useless since he recognized the bulges under their suit jackets as weapons that would probably be draw now since they opened his office door and walked in. They did not do that much, to Lawrence's surprise.

"You Peter Lawrence?"

"That's me. What can I do for you?"

"We're from the FBI," said the tallest one. Both were young, mid-twenties, and both had close-cropped military haircuts. They could easily be brothers even though the one doing the talking appeared to be better built physically. There was no evidence that either one had ever been in a fight but it could also mean that they had been and were never hit. The tall one flashed his badge so quickly that Lawrence was not able to catch his name.

"You are to come with us. Now."

Lawrence kept his hands behind his head, fingers interlaced, and rocked in his desk chair.

"You have a warrant?"

"Listen Buddy. We're FBI and the reason we're here does not necessitate a warrant. Get up now and follow my associate out the door. I'll be behind you, so watch it."

"Let me see your ID, now."

As Lawrence hoped, the FBI agent reached with his right hand into his inner suit jacket pocket and pulled out his ID which meant the revolver that Lawrence had seen earlier could not be pulled out. The agent flipped open ostentatiously the coveted FBI photo badge and held it for Lawrence.

"Wow, there really is an Efrem Zimbalist, Jr. in the FBI," said Lawrence. Having made the agent flinch, Lawrence took advantage of the agent's loss of control for a split second and grabbed the man's right wrist with his left hand. He forearmed the agent at his left eyebrow. The agent went down fast and Lawrence kicked the other agent in the knee so hard that he heard the crack. The man went down, grabbing his knee. When he went for his weapon reacting a bit too slowly, the heel of Lawrence's right shoe broke his nose. He was down and out. Lawrence grabbed the agent's revolver and clicked off the safety. The weapon was familiar to him.

"Kat! Kat, you out there?"

Kat slowly peeked around the doorway and Lawrence could see that the entire newspaper staff were up from their desks looking in his office.

"Hey folks, I'm in control here. Got a couple of bad little boys here. Kat, call the city police and ... No, call the sheriff's office. I get along better with them. They'll spread what happened here faster than the townie cops. Go!"

The first agent was groggy. He tried to sit up as Lawrence spoke, "now let's try again. What are you after?"

The man made no comment as expected.

"You see those people out there? I've got witnesses. I've got assault and battery charges against you plus assault with a deadly weapon."

Lawrence held it in his palm, "you got the same make revolver?"

There was still no answer.

"Listen, dick head, you're in a newspaper office. The sheriff is coming to arrest you. Now I know the big boys up in DC will get you off but I won't. I'm going to have a photographer in here in about ..."

A flash went off before he could finish. "Well you have been photographed. I got a feeling you're going to be leaving the FBI very soon. In fact when tomorrow's edition of the V City Server comes out, I'll bet the DC boys won't be able to can your sorry ass fast enough. You can save your ass right now. Here's the sheriff himself."

Captain DeTangua walked into Lawrence's office, surveyed the situation, and closed the door. Then he went to the shades on the glass walls and pulled them down, "Mr. Lawrence have these guys been harassing you?"

Lawrence and DeTangua knew each other from gym workouts they both did at the same center. Neither could find a partner to box at the center. It was a rarity in Virginia City, where exercise usually meant riding stationary bikes or running on treadmill machines, or worse dancing exercises with the blond and annoying instructor. Lawrence and DeTangua had talked, found they had a common interest, and quit their memberships at the health club. They joined a ratty boxing gym in Portsmouth.

"They're deciding now," Lawrence looked over to the second agent, his nose bloody and head still wobbling, "or rather this one's decided now about pressing charges."

"Pressing charges on who?"

"Themselves, cause if I don't get some answers, I want you to arrest then for ..."

The senior agent rose and stood, his face on the left side now visibly swollen, "okay, let's deal. I tell you why we're here. You don't bring charges and you keep your mouth shut. Deal?"

Lawrence just nodded his head and smiled.

"We got nothing on you. Reno's pissed about the article in your paper. She knows she's got nothing on you because everything you wrote is pretty much true. So she got us, the

FBI, to come down here and screw with you a bit, extract a little revenge. You know, scare you so you'll leave it alone?"

"Tell Jan, I call her Jan since we're so close. Tell her you did scare me. Were you involved in the Waco massacre?"

The man made no comment and Lawrence continued, "bad wasn't it. You might not speak to me but I can read the answer in your eyes. If I were you, I'd go back and tell the FBI director, that's William Sessions, right?"

"Not for long. Sessions won't play ball with Clinton and Reno. He didn't want me being here. Said so but he had no choice."

"It's good to know there's some of you people out there who aren't Gestapo. Tell him I get any other visitors, he'll read about it, and not just in this paper. Captain, you got something to say?"

"Why don't you just shoot them?

***

Lawrence smiled as he finished eating and extinguished the stove's fire since it was getting dark. Going back over his first front page editorial almost two years ago and the dramatic change it made in the V City Server and now alone now in his sanctum sanctorum, Lawrence could weigh the backlash likely to occur when the paper attacked Oceana Airbase, Commander Johnstone, and thanks to Clark Kent's research, Virginia City's tolerance of the domination of the Navy in its backyard. The paper had hired a lawyer to get the charges against Louisa Santiago dropped. Lawrence still did not know why it had been so difficult. There was no evidence that supported the charges against her. Sober or not, Louisa could have never heard her baby crying when an intoxicated Commander David Johnstone flew a few hundred feet over her apartment. Yet somebody, somebody with influence wanted her to be charged.

He walked out of the cabin and scanned the high marsh weeds and twisted pine trees that encircled his lair. Never, in almost three years, had anyone invaded his property. Still, he faithfully patrolled his hide-away. Satisfied there were no interlopers, he traveled the circuitous route that he had created to the east. The path to Shipp's Bay ended on a crest that dropped sharply down to the water which was about ten feet below. The ground was hard- packed sand and earthy mud. At first sight there appeared no path but behind the oversized sign posted by the U.S. Fish and Wildlife Service which warned visitors to stay away or be prosecuted to the full extent of the law, he came to the gully. He had built a façade cover over the eroded gully which, when pushed to the side gave him easy access to the bay. Once on the narrow beach that bordered the shore, Lawrence looked around in the darkening night. He had to eliminate any potential observation of his presence. Too dark now to be seen, Lawrence stripped down and walked slowly into the very cold water. Back Bay was in the south and earlier in the year the area had experienced a heat wave. However Lawrence knew the end of March would keep the water ice cold. He paid no mind to the cold as he waded slowly deeper in water, remaining alert to what my lay lurking in the bay waters. As the water reached his chest, he swam, using a breast stroke, until a hundred yards off shore, then flipped on to his back, sculling in place with his hands. It was cogitating time.

The paper was ready, the type set, and all Lawrence had to do was give the word. It was not a staff decision although Lawrence had met with every employee from the top echelon on down to the men on the delivery truck. It was a four hour meeting, without Dr. Sauers presence. Judge had been given a preview of the articles, making no comment. What he did say was that after the Waco Massacre, Lawrence's attack on Janet Reno and his run in with the two FBI agents; that he, personally, would never allow politics to run his paper. Lawrence did not know whether Judge's comment referred to the freedom of the press or the fact that the V City Server had made a major change as a newspaper due to Lawrence's "ten questions." The first few advertisers that had pulled their ads from the paper had later begged Dr. Sauers for their spaces back once they saw the newspaper's circulation double. This was thanks to the national newspaper media picking up on Lawrence's editorial. All the major papers were running it. The television news media also picked up the story, calling the V City Server that "little newspaper in the south with its gutsy editor." Lawrence refused to appear on any of their shows, but he did return calls making sure to mention that he had been harassed and physically attacked by the FBI. It was at that point that Judge vowed to never step in the newspaper office again except to place ads.

Lawrence, now floating in the bay, would make the final decision. His staff was scared. The paper's articles would attack the Naval Airbase, a group of tyrants who did not care how close pilots buzzed over the houses of the hicks living in Virginia City. Kat's bio piece on Louisa Santiago and her dead baby labeled Commander Johnstone as a drunken killer. Accompanying the article were photographs of her little baby and Louisa behind bars. Clark Kent's article could earn him a Pulitzer. He had visited every hospital within twenty-five miles of Oceana Airbase, gone through records, and found that the number of children admitted into the hospitals in noise zones was four times greater than any other zone. The reasons for these excessive medical admissions, occurring during times when airbase fighter planes were on maneuvers, ran the gambit from children having damaged ear drums, children and adults with tinnitus - - symptomatic ringing, hissing, or buzzing in the ears, children with mononucleosis due to lack of sleep, children and spouses suffering physical abuse from parents or partners, injuries from automobile accidents, patients entering alcohol and drug abuse programs, prenatal miscarriages, and suicides.

His story of a teenage girl who almost died one morning during a jet low level flyover was guaranteed to cause shock waves throughout the community. The girl suffered from Long QT Syndrome which causes an abnormality of the heart's electrical system, meaning a rush of adrenaline or a sharp rise in blood pressure. She was near death because she had to be awakened gradually each morning. Any sudden noise while she slept could cause a heart attack. Jets were flying over her home at decibels exceeding 100. Ironically, if she were at a job with noise over 90 decibels, OSHA would demand the wearing of hearing protection.

Kent interviewed a number of patients during nights of excessive flyovers and jet noise. Since the hospital would not give out patients names, Clark waited outside the hospitals until the Tomcats and Hornets soared over the area. When people began showing up in the emergency room, or when ambulances arrived, he entered the emergency room feigning pain in his lower abdomen. Anybody who has ever been in a hospital emergency room on a busy night knows what it is like. Sick and injured people sit on uncomfortable steel and plastic chairs waiting for their turn to be seen. They wait for hours, sitting with nothing to do but talk to a fellow suffer and talk they do. Kent wrote it all down, symptoms, injuries, aches and pains.

As Lawrence continued to float in the bay, he smiled remembering when he asked Clark what happened when he was finally him into the examination room. Clark said that he would pass some gas, say "oh my, that's better", and leave. Clark had the entire staff laughing over that.

In total darkness Lawrence turned over and swam back to shore. He sat naked on the narrow strip of sand, not to dry off but to decide if he really wanted to take on the United States Navy. It was a shame that Tim McVeigh wasn't here to see this happen, thought Lawrence. It might be a learning experience that McVeigh could use in his battle with the United States government. It sure would do more than McVeigh's idle threats to take out the ATF and FBI.

On such a clear night, Lawrence would have liked to have seen some sign in the sky, giving him direction. All he saw was Orion's belt. Without dressing, he returned to the camouflaged barrier that covered the gully, and walked back to his cabin. It was an easy and undisturbed walk. His excellent night vision, was perfected over many years of hunting with his grandfather, meant he needed no lights to show him the way. Once inside, he took the pad of paper on which he had written 13 questions for the admiral, crossed out four of them and added one more. The questions were ready and so was Lawrence. All he needed was strong brandy and a long sleep before returning to Virginia City.

When Lawrence pulled his car into the driveway in front of his home, he found his space taken. This was not unusual especially during tourist season, since he lived within walking distance of the beach. The yellow Mercury Grand Marquis, which Lawrence guessed was a 1976 or 1977 model, was occupied by a man who appeared to be asleep. No need to call the police or a tow truck. Lawrence parked on the street and walked up to the intruder's car.

Knocking on the window he yelled to the man, "hey, you're in my driveway. How's about ..."

Tim McVeigh rubbed his eyes, ran his hands over his military haircut and gazed at Lawrence, "oh, Mr. Lawrence. You weren't home when I pulled in last night so I figured you wouldn't mind if I just slept out here. Okay?"

"Let me know and you can stay here anytime. I'll give you a key. Come on up. I live on top of the garage. The steps are on the side."

Once inside Lawrence put on the coffee maker machine and asked McVeigh if he wanted a bagel egg sandwich. McVeigh nodded. Lawrence got two sausage patties out of the freezer, placed them in an iron skillet to cook at medium heat. He put two bagel halves in the toaster, got two eggs and two slices of Velveeta cheese from the refrigerator. By that time the coffee had finished burping its way to being brewed. Once the sausages were brown, Lawrence added some butter to the pan to fry the eggs.

"I noticed your car Tim. You made it all the way from Buffalo in that?"

"No, I came down from Michigan. Only cost me $300 but I did have to shore up a seal leak in the transmission. Burns damn oil almost faster than I can fill it."

Lawrence put the bagel sandwiches on the kitchen table and sat down.

"Thanks for putting me on to Zinn's book. The man's really good. I was amazed at how we teach our children about our so-called founding fathers and how humble and fair-minded they were. That one quote from Walt Whitman, the Walt Whitman who wrote 'Leaves of Grass.'?"

"Yeah, I know the one you mean. Whitman who seemed to be such a quiet and peaceful man, telling the Mexicans that we aren't looking for a fight but if you get in our way we'll wipe you out?"

"Crush you is what he wrote. Same meaning, though. I stopped here to show you something," said McVeigh, taking a large bite out of the sandwich. "Is there a place 'round here where you could like set off some fireworks without anybody calling the cops?"

Lawrence needed to get to the newspaper office soon. The type had been set, and the printers were warm and ready waiting for his editorial piece, "is it going to take long?"

"No, just a couple minutes."

"Finish your sandwich and you can follow me in your car. You're looking a little dragged out. Want to take a shower before we go?"

He did and when he finished Lawrence took a quick shower and dressed so he could go straight to the newspaper after McVeigh finished showing Lawrence his fireworks display.

"Nice T-shirt, Tim. You better be careful because you're in da south now, boy!"

McVeigh's T-shirt had a picture of Abraham Lincoln on it with the famous Latin quote 'Sic Semper Tyrannis' which means Lincoln basically got what he deserved from John Wilkes Booth. On the back was a tree bleeding the blood of patriots and tyrants.

Lawrence led McVeigh into a marsh area adjacent to First Landing State Park and they parked at a small, sandy beach. No one was in sight. McVeigh popped open the Mercury's trunk and pulled out a Gatorade jug filled with beads that looked like BBs.

"These are ammonium nitrate prills."

"You mean pills, Tim?"

"No sir. Prills are beads. Some you can use to purify water," said McVeigh. He took out a bottle labeled liquid nitromethane, a piece of what looked like sausage, and a blasting cap like Lawrence had seen worker's on road gangs use when laying railroad tracks.

"Back off when I say now. Back to those trees. You'll have time. I set the fuse for ten seconds. Go!"

From the trees Lawrence saw the Gatorade jug explode much like a hand grenade. He hoped there were not any runners or bikers going through the south entrance to First Landing State Park at this hour of the morning.

"There's the answer Mr. Lawrence. Right out of The Turner Diaries,"

"Answer to what Tim?"

"Ruby Ridge, Waco, what the United States Army did in Iraq at Desert Storm to innocent people. What they tried to recruit me for."

"Tim, it's going to take a lot of Gatorade jars to take down the AFT and the FBI and the United States Army. You're being ridiculous."

"Piece by piece, Mr. Lawrence. How about a ten ton truck filled with ..."

Lawrence had to stop him before lost total control, "Tim, you're tired. I've got a newspaper whose presses won't run until I set them off. I can't help you right now. Wait and read the paper tomorrow. In fact, go back to my apartment. There's a spare key in a magnetic key box underneath my electric meter. Get it, go upstairs, and crash out on the sofa."

McVeigh's eyes were wide, gaping, irritated, "I don't have time. Today's April 14th and I can't wait."

Lawrence had no idea what McVeigh's rush was. All Lawrence could do was watch McVeigh drive out of the park, smoke filling the air, and acid dripping out of the exhaust pipe. The jug was not the bomb. The man looking for a ten ton truck was the bomb.

CHAPTER TWENTY FIVE

The Ashes

"Mr. Lawrence, Katherine has told me too much about you," said Melanie Winters as she opened the door to her condo.

"That's kind of scary. Nice place, top floor of Ruby Inlet Condominiums. Most people call me Lawrence."

"I'm not like most people, Peter. You don't mind if I call you Peter?"

Lawrence just smiled as Melanie Winters closed the door behind him. The living room was directly opposite the entrance with its south wall nothing but large windows. To the right was a fireplace with a gas fire blazing even though it was the middle of April.

Lawrence walked over to the windows to take in the view of south Virginia City as the sun was setting. "What a great view. I can see the Naval Base and what appears to be the Back Bay. It would make a great photograph right now with the sun dipping below Pungo. Hey, maybe you can answer me a question? Why's it called Ruby Inlet? Some guy named Ruby settle here?"

"Peter, it's a legend probably concocted by the town council a hundred years ago. Supposedly a famous pirate … I don't know his name, Blue Beard, Red Beard, Black Beard who knows … dumped a treasure chest of rubies into the tide here before he was captured by our ancestors."

"Ah, Kat long time no see," Lawrence smiled as Katherine Winters came into the living room.

"Yeah, an hour ago Lawrence," said Kat as she sat down in front of the fire. "Want a cocktail or something?"

"You got Southern Comfort and soda?"

Kat got up and went to the kitchen where her mother was now preparing dinner. Lawrence had been invited many times to the Winters' home for dinner but had begged off, leery of getting too close to an employee. This was sort of ridiculous as he and Kat had been working very close on the Oceana Air Base story for many weeks now. She finally got him to accept her mother's dinner invitation. While Kat was making his drink, Melanie Winters came out of the kitchen with what appeared to be a vodka gimlet, "so Peter how come you haven't tried to seduce my daughter?"

Lawrence had been well prepped by Kat. Her mother enjoyed making people nervous, trying hard to prod them out of their shells. "Isn't she a little young for me? I'd be robbing the cradle, wouldn't I?"

"What are you Peter? Twenty nine or thirty?"

"I'll be twenty-eight in October."

"Kat's only eight years younger than you. How's about we flip the age gap around a hundred and eighty degrees? Would you be uncomfortable going to bed with me?"

"That's a little bit different, wouldn't you say? No, I wouldn't have any problem going to bed with you."

"Why you'd be as much jail bait to me as she is to you. I'm thirty seven. Are you too young for me?"

Lawrence just shrugged, "I don't think Mr. Winters would much approve of it?"

"There is no Mr. Winters. Never has been. Kat has my last name. Her father knocked me up when he was stationed at Oceana before being sent to Viet Nam. Before he shipped out, he was kind enough to explain to me that he was already married and had a son. Somewhere out there Kat has a half-brother she's never met. She has chosen to not seek him out."

Kat returned with a cocktail glass holding soda water with a slight yellow tinge. "Down south we call it SoCo, not Southern Comfort, Lawrence. Yes, I chose not to meet my half-brother."

"And your father? Not even curious?"

"My father was shot down in Viet Nam and died in a prisoner of war camp. He never told his family about me and I don't really give a fuck."

"So what happens if you accidently run into your step brother?"

"If his name is Gilbert Logan Junior, I'll probably punch him in the eye."

The name jolted a memory in Lawrence, that he could not place.

Melanie went into the kitchen, followed by Kat while Lawrence enjoyed the SoCo and the sunset from the condo windows. He was not sure but felt he could see the Back Bay area of his sanctum sanctorum, DumDum. Called to eat, he took one more gulp of SoCo and headed for the dining area.

"Meat loaf? You've go it to be kidding me. I haven't had good meat loaf for years. Hell, moi mere hates it and never cooks hamburger."

Melanie looked questioningly at Lawrence and spoke. "Your what?"

"My mother is French, mostly Canadian French. All the years of being raised in a family who spoke French more often than not, rubbed off on me."

"So you guys blew away the good old Admiral and the City Council today?"

Lawrence responded. "Mostly Kat's article did. Her piece on Louisa Santiago had people calling the office wanting to send her money. I mean sending Santiago money, of course. Clark Kent's ripping history of the base and its medical effects on the people living anywhere near a flight path, kept the phones humming with readers wanting to close Oceana down. At least half of the calls were from people who experienced similar problems with the jet noise."

"According to Kat your Ten Questions To Ask City Council and the Admiral got more than a phone call. One of our dear town leaders paid you a visit?"

***

There was a calm after the initial storm which in effect cleared the air, just like a healthy spring rain does. Readers wanted answers to V City Server's Ten Questions.

Question #1: Admiral, do you really believe that Virginia City is just a bunch of farmers?

Question #2: Admiral, what is the favorite cocktail for jet pilots before they fly over our city on maneuvers?

Question #3: Admiral, have you talked to the people at the ABC stores about increased alcohol sales? Your advice to people who get upset about jets flying under a hundred feet above their heads, suffering from ruptured ear drums is they should just drink booze and wait for their hearing to return. The Alcoholic Beverage Commission might give you a finder's fee for increased sales.

Question #4: Admiral, can you tell me where I can buy a better sound meter? The one I used for your flight paths for one week all read over 110 decibels. According to a letter from you to the Washington Post, your jets only average 60 decibels.

Question #5: City Council members, your survey missed a few items. Can you explain why your survey asked citizens about day time flights? Might it not have been a good idea to ask about night flights?

Question #6: City Council members, did your survey forget the 30,000 citizens that live in the take-off zone? Not one citizen in the take-off zone that we called ever saw a survey taker. Maybe the survey taker was having a before take-off drink or two with the Admiral's pilots?

Question #7: City Council members, did your polled citizens really say they were more interested in having the roads improved than ending jet noise? Probably that was because they want to get out of town faster and find a quiet area.

Question #8: City Council members, how many children have suffered medical problems due to jet noise? No! No! You cannot look at our article on that research. You could use your survey that cost $30,000, except the survey did not ask about the medical effects.

Question #9: City Council members, did you really authorize Town Manager Kenneth Czeed to turn down $2 million from a housing developer who wanted to build condos in the areas that the city condemned?

Question #10: City Council members, did you know that the LLC that you granted building permits to was going to build condominiums and apartments in the jet flight and noise zones and your own Town Manager, Kenneth Czeed, is its Limited Liability Partner? It might have been a good idea for the town attorney to review state property law before letting Kenny erect those domiciles. Of the renters and lessees in those housing units that we interviewed, not one knew that they were buying property in a noise and accident potential zone. That they should be notified is required by Virginia State Law. I wonder if the state agency, which also has to approve all LLCs, knows this. After contacting the National Securities and Exchange Commission, we found that one of the investors in the jet flight zone development is our beloved Admiral who just happens to play golf every Tuesday morning with Kenny Czeed. I will bet that no jets fly over the base golf course when the Admiral is putting.

The reaction to V City Server's issue on Oceana Air Base was extensive. Calls after calls came in asking how to solve the problem. Lawrence referred the callers to the CAJN, Committee Against Jet Noise Coalition, the leader of which had called Lawrence very early that morning, telling Lawrence that this was just what the coalition needed to combat the city's continual ignoring of the problem. Lawrence was asked to speak at the next City Council meeting. He responded with "I would have to think about that."

Lawrence did not have to wait long for the reaction of the city leaders. Kenneth Czeed was in the newspaper's office before noon. Lawrence not only saw him enter the office but heard him yelling and posturing himself to the receptionist who kept people from entering the news room. He ignored her and barged through the swinging gate, looking through each of the glass enclosed offices, until finding Lawrence's.

Lawrence had never met Czeed. However he had researched him thoroughly. He was raised by a wealthy family that controlled a large land area in Norfolk and Virginia City. His father was an investment banker and Kenneth attended private schools. He had left the University of Virginia, not because he was a failure as his records demonstrated, but according to the family, they did not want their son mixing with the those kinds of people. Czeed's grandfather still liked to brag about owning slaves. Czeed got a degree with honors at some little innocuous Mid-West college and a MBA from another innocuous college in Florida. He walked into his father's real estate company, quickly learned how to manage limited partnerships and made a great deal of money. His investors lost money even though they thought they were making money by paying less taxes to the Federal and State IRS. Czeed was a big man, a good two or three inches taller than Lawrence. While a bit overweight, Lawrence could see that Czeed took part in some type of exercise regimen, other than just playing golf with the Admiral. He was also a bully and loud mouth who threatened most people simply by his vocal power and large physical presence.

"You the editor of this rag shit hole?"

"No, but if you've got to go that bad, there's a men's room down the hall only we don't use rags. But there's plenty of soft tissue paper. Good-bye."

"You know who I am?"

"Isn't that a Neil Diamond song? No, it's "I Am I Said." Sorry you got me on that one. Again, good-bye."

Lawrence stayed seated, his fingers interlaced, a big grin on his face.

"I'm going to see this place closed down. I 'm the Town Manager here and you're in big fuckin' trouble, boy."

"Boy? Jesus, I hope you don't call my black sports editor that. He'll kick your ass real good. Now stop trying to push me around and sit down, Mr. Czeed."

"So you do know who I am?"

Lawrence ignored Czeed's comments, left his seat, went to his office door, and called Kat into his office, "Mr. Czeed, this is Katherine Winters my public journalist. She's going to sit with us while you explain to me why you're here."

"Your Mom's the principal of one of our schools, isn't she?"\

"Yes, sir."

Lawrence lowered an eyebrow at Kat for her subjugation to Czeed's self-image. "Kat, all you have to do is listen and take notes. Okay?"

She shook her head but fear showed in her eyes.

"I want a retraction and an apology to me, City Council, and the Admiral of the Oceana Air Base. You are to apologize for your slander, defamation of character, and libel against the leaders and people of Virginia City. I want it out tomorrow or I'll ..."

Lawrence liked interrupting people filled with their own sense of self -worth, "whoa, slander? That means telling lies, doesn't it? What lies did we write?"

"Well, how about my using my influence to buy condemned property?"

"But you did use your influence to buy condemned property and ..."

Czeed leaned over Lawrence's desk his palms flat on the desk top, "Listen, you ..."

"Sorry but touching my desk is out. The sweat coming off your hands leaves stains. Get them off and sit back in your chair." He saw Kat's eyes widen.

Czeed's back was up and getting higher. "You bastard. You heard what I said. I want a ..."

"Mr. Czeed! Kenny, my boy. Let me make it simple. I don't think that kind of language is appropriate in front of a lovely young lady like Katherine. Please apologize."

"I'm sorry, miss. I'll keep it under ..."

Lawrence had a big smile on his face when he spoke. "Good, now get the fuck out of my office!"

***

"Katherine, he didn't really tell Czeed to go fuck himself?"

"Yes he did, mother. You should have been there. Scared the hell out of me. I thought they'd get into a fist fight, right there on the spot. Czeed jumped up angry as a city dump dog. Lawrence didn't move, just stared at him and smiled. Well, not really a smile, more like a funny looking sneer. Czeed said he'd be back but not alone. Lawrence did not a say a word and Czeed was gone."

"And did he come back?"

"Not yet mother. This was just this morning. I think he's going to try and find loop holes in our articles."

"Kat, he won't find a one. Even Judge went over them. Didn't like what they said, but it had nothing to do with what was written. Judge didn't like reading about his city and his country, especially the part about the U.S. Navy's, but like the stories told, it was pretty incriminating."

Katherine cleared the dining room table, directing Lawrence to the living room to keep her mother busy and away from the kitchen and from bugging her. Lawrence followed Melanie Winters into the room and sat on one end of the sofa with Melanie at the other.

"Another SoCo and soda?"

"Not right now. The meatloaf was great. I've got a question for you that if it bothers you, just tell me to leave it be. You're a school principal, right?"

She smiled and nodded at Lawrence who was looking about her condominium.

"Principals get good pay but this is sort of hard to fathom, this condo on Ruby Inlet, especially one at the top. How can you afford it?"

"Pornographic videos."

Lawrence gasped, laughter escaping deep from within, "okay, like I said if it bothers ..."

"I'm not lying. Pornographic videos paid for it."

"Okay, if you say so. One other question. Why did you get a gas fireplace. Firewood is so much better and much more romantic."

"I answered your question Peter. You still haven't answered mine. I'm nearly nine years older than you. Would you have sex with me?"

Lawrence knew the answer when he met Melanie Winters for the first time. She physically reminded him of Eileen, which frightened him at first. As she talked with him and revealed her lack of respect for male dominance, she became more and more attractive to him. "Yes, I would."

"You think I'm kidding about pornography paying for this condominium, don't you?"

She was smiling, a smile that hinted at sexual teasing, "did you ever hear of the Masked MILF?"

To admit he knew the Masked MILF, would divulge that he watched pornographic movies. She knew she had Lawrence in an embarrassing position. When he gave it up and admitted that he did indeed know the infamous Masked MILF, she continued.

"I guess it was about four years ago. I got involved with one of the Naval Officers over at the Navy Base off of Dam Neck Road. The irony was that his wife was also a principal, a high school principal. Hard ass, definite hard ass. That this Navy warrior could put up with a bitch like Rhea Ashley made you afraid that we were being protected by milk-toast military men like him. She was dirt ugly, had fat calves and thighs and totally bleached blonde hair. She wore black horned-rim glasses which actually was a benefit to her since it hid most of her sorry face."

"Rhea went to the superintendent of schools, the one that ruled the district back then, a Dr. Benne. He was a little twerp with an inflated ego that didn't get along with anybody unless they kissed his ass. Rhea told him that I was the Masked MILF in pornographic videos. She even gave him a copy of the VHS she owned. She told him that her husband lead her to the discovery. Some of his sailors had picked me up in local bars. Benne went berserk, had security walk into my office and take me out."

"Wow, how in the world did you get your job back as principal?"

"Easy Peter. I sued the hell out of the school district. Benne acted without any investigation, totally accepting Rhea's word."

"That doesn't surprise me. I'm guessing Kat told you that I used to teach. I know the power hunger of school administrators and how they react spontaneously without thinking. They love to throw that power around."

"He looked at the videos and saw that this porn star looked a lot like me. She looked so much like me that the idiot terminated me. You should have been there, at the trial. One judge, it was that simple. He watched the video. Actually everybody in the court watched it. It was a scream seeing people glance away from the TV monitor. They were afraid somebody would catch them eyeing all of the sex going on. But there's one feature of all the Masked MILF videos that won it for me and that Benne ignored. She never takes off her mask. The judge ruled in my favor, including the five hundred thousand dollars in damages I asked for. Plus they had to reinstate me. After paying the lawyer and the IRS, I bought this condo and resumed my career in education."

"What happened to your accuser?"

"Rhea got transferred. Administrators rarely get fired unless they take their mask off. Dr. Benne went to a local college as Dean of something ... Assholes I guess. So look around you, Peter. It was a bad time but I won and ..."

Kat interrupted her mother, "Mother, I'm going out, then back to my apartment. I'll stop over maybe Friday." She leaned over and kissed her mother on the cheek.

"See you, tomorrow, Lawrence. Bye."

They wasted little time and the warmth from the gas fire felt exhilarating against their naked bodies. She was good. Melanie could dominate, bringing Lawrence near the edge or she could submit, having Lawrence bring her to the edge. It lasted for over an hour, and then ebbed into drinks before the fire, their naked bodies feeling the afterglow of shared orgasms.

"Damn you're good. Never have gone off that long or that intense," why he whispered was without reason for they were alone.

"You're the first man I've known who knew how to bring me off with his tongue and lips. Pretty good, Peter. Yes, you do have a pretty good peter, Peter."

They both laughed. "Now you know why as a kid I made people call me Lawrence."

She took his glass away and started at him again.

"I'm not sure we're going to make another one this soon Melanie."

She smiled, kissed his nipples, licked his penis, and went into her bedroom. Just as he thought maybe he should join her, she returned. Only he was not sure it was really Melanie.

"Let's see if my Mask can help this mother that you'd like to fuck, get you off."

In their whole time never once did Lawrence ask the question, nor did Melanie ever respond to the other obvious question. Who was that masked woman?

***

It was a little after 10:00 AM on April 19th, when Lawrence saw Czeed enter the news room followed by Chief of Police Jack Jekyll. It did not take Czeed long to counter-attack Lawrence. As Jekyll was holding up his ID badge, Lawrence pulled out of the right hand top drawer of his desk a copy of his weapons license, and reached behind him to draw his pistol from the holster on his belt. He placed the Colt M1911A1 in the drawer, keeping the drawer slightly ajar. Lawrence did not rise as Czeed and Jekyll came to his glass door. Instead Lawrence smiling at them, knowing they expected him to get up and open the door for them, he called Kat's phone extension.

"Kat, get your steno pad. Let these two men into my office, and take a seat away from them. No matter what they tell you, do not do anything they say."

Jekyll saw Kat approach the door and say something to Czeed. Both men backed off as she opened the door, raised her left hand, palm up, leading them through the door. She followed as Lawrence had asked and sat herself quickly in the heavy leather seat and opened her note pad, ready with a pen.

Czeed spoke first, "What's she doing in here?"

Lawrence spoke. "I invited her in here but I don't remember you being invited."

"Listen you son of a ..."

"Ken, stay out of it," said Jekyll. "I'll handle this. The girl makes no difference. Sir, you are Peter Lawrence? Is that correct?"

"Yep"

"You are to come with me to the police station."

"You have some identification on you?"

"You know I'm Chief of Police in Virginia City. Let's go, sir."

"You are required by Virginia State law to present identification. Do it, Jack."

Jekyll had no facial expressions. Dour would best describe his image. He held up his police badge and a police ID with his photograph on it. Lawrence was pushing Jekyll. They had met a few times before when Lawrence was working on articles dealing with crime in Virginia City. Jekyll stood about three inches taller than Lawrence and was very narrow from top to bottom. His hair was very black from an obvious bad dye job that did not erase the grey streaks at his temples. Lawrence knew the man as a no alibi man, meaning whatever you told him was useless until your case went to court.

"Cut the bullshit, Lawrence. You know Police Chief Jekyll. Do as he says."

Jekyll held up his right hand in Czeed's face. "You brought me here to do a job, now keep your mouth closed and let me do my job."

"Mr. Lawrence, please get out of your seat and come with me, sir."

"Jack, do you have an arrest warrant for me?"

"No, I'm only taking you to police headquarters to answer some questions."

"Jack, do you know what just cause is? I don't have to go with any police tough guy unless you advise me of why you are sequestering me to your lair."

"Lair? What do you mean by that?"

"You really are a dumb fuck, aren't you?" Lawrence watched Jekyll's face turn red. The man was starting to boil. "Why don't you have a seat and we'll have your little interrogation right here with Miss Winters taking notes for me. You afraid of something?"

"I want you up and out of that chair, now!"

Lawrence leaned backwards in his desk chair and laced his fingers together, never letting the smirk leave his face. After rocking back and forth in the desk chair three times, he unlaced his fingers and put both palms down flat on his desk, a foot apart from each.

"There's a copy of a weapons license in front of you, right there on my desk. I suggest you read it, now!"

Lawrence noticed that Jekyll's .38 service revolver was latched with a leather thong. Lawrence could not get beaten. Jekyll picked up the weapons license and spoke.

"So? I can get this revoked with one telephone call."

Lawrence had no fear of facing off against Jekyll. "I hate cops Jekyll, especially cops like you. You think you're tough guys, can push people around with your badge. Yeah, I've heard the stories about you. What'd you got there in that holster, a Smith and Wesson? Good weapon if you carry a reloader. I am not moving from this office. You have not provided just cause to detain me in your custody. What we have is a stand-off."

"You get up now before I pull my weapon and do arrest you, sir!"

"Jack, you want to be Wyatt Earp? Well, here's your chance. I've got a Colt M1911A1 automatic in my upper right hand drawer. Go for your gun, cowboy. Just like the movies. I might even take out Czeed here. That would be purely accidental, of course. But it's you I want Jack. When I take you down, there's going to be only one witness and it won't be Kenny boy."

No one moved. Jekyll was roiling, his ears turning red. Never could Jekyll have imagined that any person would stand up to him. That he should be faced off in a duel with the editor-in-chief of a newspaper was unfathomable. He could feel Lawrence's confidence, smell the sweat of the predator, and run know without a doubt Lawrence would have no qualms killing him in this show down.

It was a little after 10:00 AM and reporter Kent was knocking repeatedly on the glass of Lawrence's office door. Jekyll turned at the sound but Lawrence's eyes never left Jekyll. Jekyll was a dead man now. He turned back quickly but stopped, did not unlatch his pistol. Lawrence was leaning back in his chair with his hands laced together behind his head. Jekyll backed off what might have been an opportunity.

"Bang, you were dead," said Lawrence as he waved Kent into the office.

"Lawrence, this is bad. Somebody or some radical group just blew up the FBI offices in Oklahoma City. It's on the TV out here. Turn yours on. CNN's got it. They're hauling bodies out right now."

"That's all, Jekyll. You and Czeed get out of here. Now!"

After Jekyll and Czeed turned tail, Lawrence went into the newsroom to watch. There was a live feed showing what was left of the Murrah Building. You could see empty office spaces on the north side, like huge honeycomb cells with pipes and debris still falling out. CNN was struggling to find the story. The estimate at this point was that fifty or sixty people had been blown up. Fire trucks were arriving with long booms that extended into the blazing fire of the building, as firemen worked tearing apart the debris in hopes of finding any survivors. Helicopters were dodging other helicopters as they circled what remained of the building. Most astounding were the photographs of the Murrah Building before the explosion. This had to have been the work of high level assault terrorists. Hundreds of police cars encircled the building, the smoke still pouring out of the tons of fallen concrete. A reporter came on with a story of a woman who survived the blast only because she was under the bodies of six people who died as the walls of the sixth floor fell on top of them.

Two more bombs were found in place ready to blow up the rest of the building. They appeared more explosive than the first but were never ignited. Video tape pieces saved from the building video surveillance cameras showed a white van driving past the building's entrance just minutes before the blast. Video links showed people running from the Murrah Building as the bomb disposal squads were moving in to defuse the bombs. The bombs, according to the authorities, were very sophisticated. President Clinton spoke with the police and FBI terrorist teams were sent in since these bombs had to have been created by professional munitions experts.

"Clark, I want you to go down there. Book the first plane out. I'm not after the details. We're going to get them off the news releases and TV news. You need a people article. You know what I mean, right?"

"Done it before, Lawrence. I'll make the call to the airport right now."

Kat called to him, "witnesses say they saw a Ryder Truck in front of the building just before the blast."

Lawrence got to the TV just in time to see a Ryder Truck caught on the surveillance camera. "They got the bombers on tape. Look at that. There were two of them sitting in the parked truck in front of the building. Damn, try to park on some street in Norfolk and you'd be towed before you could turn the ignition off."

"Look, here's the first one getting out of ..."

Lawrence stopped. The tape was very blurry but there was something familiar about the driver. You could not see his face but there was a unique slouch in his posture.

"Look at this replay of the explosion. Look at all that black smoke," said Kat.

Only Kent left the newsroom that day. Lawrence stayed glued to the television well into the night.

Two days after the bombing, a report came in that a prisoner was being held in the Noble County Jail. On the day of the bombing, a report that a man had been arrested for carrying weapons in his yellow Mercury Grand Marquis came in around noon. Stunned, Lawrence watched the video from the dash cam of the state trooper. The trooper had stopped the car because the rear license plate was missing. He knew for certain now that McVeigh was involved in the bombing. Lawrence recognized the car instantly. He recalled the bomb test in First Landing Park he had witnessed only months ago. Even without an ID, Lawrence knew the driver was Timothy McVeigh. It became obviously McVeigh had been trying to recruit Lawrence when he stopped over in Virginia City and met with him. McVeigh had been stopped for not having a license plate. What a pathetic, stupid error to make. Only fifty miles or so from the Kansas border, an hour or less to safety, and a dumb error got him.

"Lawrence, what's got into you?" It was Kat. "My mother says you've not even responded to her phone messages?"

"I'll call her tonight. Promise. This Oklahoma bombing catastrophe is puzzling me. Do I write an editorial or not? Kat, I've got something to tell you that might be impossible for you to believe. This bomber that they arrested? His name is Timothy McVeigh and he is an acquaintance of mine."

"You know McVeigh? You're lucky the Feds aren't all over you."

"I don't know him that well. I'm a hunter and I bought some guns from him. He's a Western New Yorker like I used to be. I know he came back from Desert Storm very disillusioned about the U. S. Army and the country. I just never thought of him as blowing up all those people."

"You do remember that we have a petition to put to the Town Council next Tuesday? That's only six days away, Lawrence. Why don't you let the big boys handle your friend?"

"Kat, he's not really my friend," Lawrence felt a pull in his chest because McVeigh was his friend but Lawrence had to be careful. "Our paths just crossed every once in a while. And we've got the petitions all in, all 50,000 of them!"

"Why didn't you tell me? That's great."

The petition was an outgrowth of CAJN, the Committee Against Jet Noise. The newspaper spread that the V City Server did on Oceana's jet noise had lit a flame under many of the citizens of Virginia City. The CAJN people discussed solutions with Lawrence and together they came up with a referendum to revoke the lease that Virginia City had with the U.S. Navy. CAJN had presented their referendum to the Town Council. The Town Council had given little thought to the referendum since they believed that the minimum signatures required to produce a successful referendum could not be met by knocking on doors, handing out street flyers, or telephoning recruits. The Town Council, along with its Town Manager Ken Czeed, believed it to be impossible for a campaign to collect 50,000 signatures; the number needed a referendum to be held. What the City Council, Ken Czeed, the Navy, and Judge Sauers did not know was that Lawrence had agreed to support the referendum by doing free ads in the V City Server. Despite Dr. Sauers' expostulations after seeing the full page advertisements were actually written by Lawrence and members of the staff, it was too late to put a stop to the campaign so he and Mrs. Sauer took a month's vacation in Toronto.

"Kat, I trust you deeply but since all of us were pushing to get the referendum passed, I wanted to tell everyone together before the town council meeting. Let's go tell them."

***

Lawrence knew when he was defeated. He looked down the long aisle of the auditorium. It was an end to two years of trying to overcome the U.S. Navy and Virginia City's government. No, to be more specific, it was a battle to best and oust Kenneth Czeed and his city council cronies. They could return Virginia City property to the citizens. Lawrence and CJAN had all their enemies by the throat because signers of the petition were enough to end the Navy's leasing of the air base. The people had voted them out. There were indeed enough signatures to force a referendum forcing the Navy out. It was a two year legal battle against Virginia City's lawyers who tried to void the petition by challenging and verifying each and every signer was challenged and verified by city council staffers and the city's legal representatives. As expected many, petitioners were voided for minor errors in signing the petition. Still there remained the requisite signatures to force the referendum. It was challenged and delayed, restarted and stopped as more legal challenges arose from city council. The final referendum, written and rewritten, made it to the voters.

It was a done deal, but not for the supporters in favor of ousting the air base. The referendum failed to gain enough support to revoke the government's lease. Lawrence was stunned. Even with more than enough petition signers for the referendum to pass, it failed, narrowly. Lawrence had no idea why. Kat wrote a front page challenge to the people of Virginia City asking why people voted down what they had petitioned to support. Expecting scores of letters to the editor, there were none. The local television news stations stopped people in the streets, questioning how they voted, only to be ignored.

It took little effort to find the reason. All that Lawrence had to do was read his own newspaper, specifically the real estate section. Property in the noise zone was being bought hand over fist at prices low enough to scare home owners, but high enough to force them to sell. Two thirds of the purchases were by Limited Partnership consortiums. A quick investigation, led to general managers using pseudonyms and registering in foreign countries. The V City Server challenged the Limited Partnership legal status, seeking a list of the officers, especially the general managers. The newspaper's attorneys advised them to not waste the money. Since suing foreign governing bodies for the illegal purchase of property by Limited Liability Partnerships would take at least five years before any action would be forthcoming. Nothing could be done in the United States against these consortiums. Lawrence knew better than to pressure Dr. Sauers into international legal action; it would bankrupt Judge and the newspaper.

Lawrence was not yet ready to concede to Czeed and his cronies. He still had a connection through his foreign bank that had been set up by Judi Dougherty. Rather than involving

Judi's syndicate connections that might cross wires with the Limited Liability Partnerships Lawrence was tracking down and tangentially involve his mother, he instead took two days off and left the country. Ostensibly using his off shore bank to recommend real estate investments for his personal portfolio, Lawrence plowed through investments with his advisor for two days. He struck gold twice. Pressuring his investment manager to reveal the specifics before investing large sums of money into a GP, a General Partner's pocket, the investment manager folded to Lawrence's demands and named names. The first one was the base commander at Oceana. The second LP general manager was Kenneth Czeed.

***

It was to be a simple City Council meeting. The agenda was short. The air base referendum was history. The base would stay. The mayor and the other nine city council members were hoping for a quick and non-aggressive public meeting. There was little on the agenda that could upset the citizens who were attending.

Lawrence came walking down the center aisle, a strictly forbidden action. Nobody could just walk into the meetings and speak at the city's microphone.

"Excuse me sir!" Iris Joseph, City Clerk, was always ready to catch the abusers, those who dared violate the proceedings. She was already rising from behind her bench seat to stop Lawrence as he approached the podium. She was an old gal whose white coiffure that little children and turned off what was left of their husband's sexual hormones.

"You will stop where you are and return to your seat!" said Iris chastising him as she approached the podium.

Lawrence smiled and waved to the old bitch as he grabbed the microphone, "let's see. Yes, I think everybody can hear me."

He saw Kenneth Czeed talking with one of the city council's representatives. Both were now standing behind their seats. Czeed gently patted the man on the shoulder, moved him away, and yelled "DeTangua! Arrest that man, now! Do it!"

Captain DeTangua was standing by the American flag, waiting to salute it during the pledge of allegiance that always opened city council meetings.

Lawrence continued, "before there's an attempt to have me handcuffed and taken away, I would like Captain DeTangua and City Manager Kenneth Czeed to notice the uniformed gentleman walking down the aisle to my left ..."

"Sir! I am not going to tell you again! I determine who speaks to ..."

"Iris, you old bitch. Shut up and sir down. You're going to enjoy this! This man is a United States Marshall and he is armed with an automatic pistol. He has with him seven subpoenas to be issued to the following six Virginia City's council members."

Lawrence read off each name, smiling as he finished the list, "plus our City Manager, Kenneth Czeed. These subpoenas were written yesterday by a Federal judge in the United States Court House, 600 Granby Street, Norfolk Virginia. The U.S. Marshall has delivered these subpoenas to the designated persons and they are to appear in court on the date noted on the subpoena. These individuals are to appear in court to explain their complicity involving real estate transactions in Virginia City, Virginia and their knowledge of said investment frauds. Their testimony will include but not be limited to the following: artificially inflating the value of a home to obtain a larger loan; inflating the value of a home so the buyer can receive cash back at closing's, submitting false documents to secure financing, including phony paycheck stubs and fake W-2's; taking out multiple mortgages on a property that collectively far exceed the value of the property; selling a home without disclosing to the buyer that it has a tenant, and finally selling the same home to several different buyers."

"Ah! Then there is City Manager Czeed. Kenny, you don't have a court date. You are being charged with fraud. The U.S. Marshal has a warrant for your arrest charging you with the following: manipulating lenders ability to obtain loans by conspiring with appraisers, straw buyers, or other insiders; property loan applications completed with falsified information; securing loans for people who couldn't otherwise qualify to borrow and purchase homes which they could not afford; and selling real estate to people with elevated risks of defaulting and then fore closuring on those properties after which you purchased the same properties at drastically lower costs."

Lawrence watched as the U. S. Marshall walked over to arrest Czeed and was greeted by Virginia City's Chief of Police. Lawrence was too far away to hear the exchange between the two law officers but he knew what was being said. He saw the U.S. Marshall hand over the arrest warrant for Czeed to Jack Jekyll and, leaving him to arrest Czeed. Czeed would not go to jail. Instead Jekyll would go to police headquarters, register the arrest warrant with the bailiff and leave Czeed free on his own recognizance.

Still standing at the podium and waiting for Iris to chastise him again, Lawrence turned to face the crowd seated him. As he expected, most were leaving, thinking all the commotion had ended.

"All of you people sit down. You think I've caught the bad guys and it's over? Sit people and learn who the truly bad guys are."

Strange looks washed over the faces of the people. They had already seen a beaten and scarred City Council being charged for crimes, the crimes Lawrence had cited. The audience could see the accused council gathering their notes and pencils, readying for their exit as ignominious as possible. What was left?

"The true guilt here lies not in the criminals accused. You, the people of Virginia City, are the real criminals. You allowed your names to be removed from the petition that could have stopped the destruction of lives in our community. For a mere pittance of money that was gorged out by a money machine that made millions of dollars in profits, what did you accept from them? I know the answer. Less than a thousand dollars. You gave your city to the vermin sitting before you and the money whore Kenny Creed. Because you ceded your name on the petition, people lost their homes, went bankrupt or just plain died in homes they could not heat, along with family they could no longer feed. You fed those victims to the money rodents. And all for a few bucks that was spent in a flash."

"You people are vile and inhuman. Each of you and your children breathe out the broth of selfishness. Because of you others had to walk away from their lives, scarred and defeated. What a debacle! You sons-of-bitches! You've fucked your neighbor good!"

A man had started towards Lawrence, anger glowing in his eyes, his face bright red. Lawrence did not care. His battle had been lost, not by the money czars and sycophants, but by their victims. As long as they were not a victim, they did not care. The man stopped and turned away ashamed. He knew he had $827 after taxes in his bank account that would pay for a trip to Disney World with his kids. Yes, Lawrence was more than right.

"Fuck you," the man said, never really understanding that he and the rest of the paid-off citizens had been financially raped and pillaged by Czeed and his investors.

When Lawrence got to his car, he found Melanie Winters leaning against the right front fender, a smile on her face. "You did it! You beat them and ..."

"No, all I did was pin them against the wall. It'll make them find another way to get to me."

"What are you talking about Peter? Czeed is going to jail right now. Christ that's one down and one less to deal with, right?"

"You didn't see the U. S. Marshall give him the warrant, did you?"

"No, everybody was standing by them. I assumed that the marshal cuffed him and took him away before people started leaving. I could see the empty council seat where Czeed had been. By the time I could see, he was gone."

"Gone with Jack Jekyll. The marshal gave Jekyll the arrest warrant since it was Virginia City's territory. Jekyll will take Czeed to the bondsman who will let him go on his own recognizance with no bail. He'll be out of there in an hour."

Melanie was stunned. "All those charges against him and he goes free?"

"Yep, and he probably won't even go to court. Nothing was won today."

"What is the matter with you? It went off just like you planned. You nailed them all."

Lawrence was trying to control himself. His breath was deep and through his nostrils, trying to help his body maintain a calmer demeanor. He knew his face was getting red, so he took another breath through his mouth, rid his face of the redness. He felt an oxygen surge in his sinuses.

"Nailed? I nailed them all? Yeah, that's a good way to see it. I had the nails and tried to drive them deep. They were weak and only dented the surface. They are all falling out."

"What the hell are you talking about?"

Lawrence started to respond, but held his hands up, palms facing Melanie Winters, "hold a second. I think Captain DeTangua is coming over to talk with me."

DeTangua was Virginia City's sheriff and his main duties were investigating minor crimes, setting up liaisons with Virginia City schools to control drug and alcohol violations by students, and acting as a Constitutional Officer for City Council meetings. Melanie Winters knew DeTangua quite well since he frequently visited her school. He was a regular visitor to her teachers' class rooms, talking to students about the law and the consequences of violating those laws.

"Hello, Mrs. Winters. How's school going?"

"Fine Sheriff."

"You mind if I have a little talk with Mr. Lawrence?"

"No, go ahead. I'll get in the car and ..."

Lawrence cut her off, "is there a problem with Miss Winters listening in?"

"No, no problem at all. In fact, knowing how well Miss Winters guides her students, she might be of benefit here. You know Czeed is not going to jail?"

Lawrence looked at Melanie, putting his hands out, palms up, "we just discussed that. I saw what happened with the marshal."

"Jekyll's with him now down at the court house getting him released on his ..."

Melanie could not resist finishing his comment, "own recognizance."

DeTangua had a winning smile. It showed his embarrassment at not knowing the answer before Melanie. Along with that was a faint red blush that covered his face. He was very deceptive, making people think they knew the answer to a question before he did. This was rarely the case, but he used his countenance to calm and assuage people, usually evoking more information from them.

"Yes Ma'am. You knew it would be that way all along, didn't you? How about you, Mr. Lawrence?"

"What did you need to tell me Sheriff?"

"You better stay clean Mr. Lawrence."

"Are you threatening me?" Lawrence regretted the question even before he finished it.

DeTangua's back stiffened along with the hairs on his neck. He had interactions with V City Server many times in the past. Lawrence had always been courteous and professional with him. In a few cases that Captain DeTangua needed help getting information out or tracking down information related to crime in Virginia City, Lawrence and the reporters had always been willing to help DeTangua apprehend the perpetrators. Now here was Lawrence challenging him.

"Mr. Lawrence, I'm just warning you. If I'm out of line ..."

Lawrence would not let him finish, "look DeTangua, I didn't mean it. You're a good man, a great peace officer. I appreciate the warning."

They shook hands and DeTangua went out to his sheriff's car and drove off. Lawrence opened the door for Melanie and then got into the driver's seat of his car.

"Is all of this just talk? What about those council members that got warrants? They ..."

"You got it wrong. None of the city council members got a warrant. They got subpoenas. They have been charged with nothing."

"But they approved all those deals and property assessments. Aren't they liable?"

"My place or yours?"

"Have you forgotten my fireplace and the fold out sofa bed in front of it?

"Ah, yes! And you have the best cognac on the entire east coast!"

"Only because, unlike you, I'm willing to pay more than five dollars for a bottle."

***

Melanie could live with Lawrence being a difficult man to decipher. There was no doubt in her mind that he was not at all pleased with what happened at the city council meeting. Yet, he did not allow those feelings to affect their love making.

"You are really upset about what happened, aren't you?"

Lawrence took a post coital slow sip, of his cognac and shrugged.

"Was I bad at what we just did? Sorry."

"You are an asshole but I still ... " She was not ready to tell Lawrence that she loved him.

"I'm your asshole?"

Melanie smiled and pulled the sofa spread off the back and wrapped herself into a cocoon. Lawrence remained naked, enjoying the intense heat from the fireplace. He finished the last of his drink.

"There is nothing more this world can give me than the unadulterated pleasure of your legs wrapped around my back, forcing my body deeper into yours as my life explodes into your womb."

"What bullshit!"

Lawrence stared at her, unsure if she believed he was being honest or sarcastic. "When you have an orgasm, I watch your eyes. They close."

He had startled her. "You watch my eyes?"

"Yes, they're the path to your passion. I watch it in your eyes. When it's not there I feel bad that I was not able to get you off. Is there any better physical pleasure that you can think of?"

She was not sure what was going on between the two of them. She had never had intercourse with a man that cared so much about her pleasure. She often watched him as the physical ecstasy encompassed his entire being, so much so that that she was afraid for him.

"Melanie, what happened tonight was irrelevant to my life and yours. I make love to you and that has meaning to my life. And yes, I am bothered about the city council meeting. It was a waste. I didn't realize just how much until it was over. We had them, Czeed and the council dead in their tracks. They are guilty. But the people sitting there, listening to the charges, knowing these people were criminals, knowing they had committed crimes against them and their neighbors for profit, meant nothing to them. They could not even see that the lousy, fucking eight hundred or nine hundred dollars bequeathed to them by the perpetrators of fraud and scams were like throwing an old chewed-up bone to a dog living in a cage. They just don't fucking care."

"What did you expect?"

"Melanie, it was their family and neighbors, who were robbed of their own homes. Those people didn't give a damn and worse, set-up the city to keep doing the same thing, over and over again."

"No, Peter. It can't happen again. They were caught with their hand in the cookie jar. Maybe nobody actually goes to jail, but the same thing won't happened again. You've exposed their crimes. You've exposed the bad guys."

"Right now while we're talking, Czeed is plotting another scheme. We both know that. How else can he support the millionaire life-style. No, that's wrong. Czeed really doesn't care about his millionaire status. It's the thrill of taking life from others. Stop, I know what you're going to say. Yes, he did not physically harm anybody. But he sucked the life out of them, none the less leaving them without home and hearth. And you know what? What really sticks into my crawl? Not one person at that meeting cared. They didn't get scammed so far as they are concerned, Czeed can go on being a conniving son of a bitch. And the same city council members that are facing a federal inquiry, those same people will get re-elected."

"So what can Peter Lawrence do about it?"

"Are you making fun of me?"

"Absolutely not. Who I care about is you. Through all of this you see no victory. You see only that part of your life was wasted. Why is that?"

Melanie had just helped him more than he could have ever imagined. Lawrence was a loner, had been as a child, a teenager, a young adult, and today. She stood up, the sofa blanket revealing her naked body. Reaching for his empty glass, she ran her hand over his face slowly and gently, and then walked into the kitchen to refill his glass with cognac. Lawrence was still naked, mesmerized by the fire. She handed him the glass, kneeled in front of him and with her cold hand, brought his penis back to life. They had now made love to each other so often, that each knew when the stimulation was to fuck or excite their love for the future. This was the latter.

"You've asked a serious question. What I can do. You deserve a serious answer. Life is more than us sitting here, loving each other. What life is scares me because we are just a small part of it. What is the meaning of life? What always comes to me is what Jack London wrote about living. '*There is one task in life and that is to perpetuate it.*'"

Melanie stirred. "And that's what London says life is? Making babies? What meaning is there to us, then?"

Lawrence knew Melanie was upset. They had been honest with each other from the beginning, and despite the anger and disagreements were the better for it.

"You might not want to know the one law of life."

"I'm a big girl. I've read Jack London, read him to sixth graders in fact when I was a teacher. Tell me. What is the law of life?"

"You must die."

CHAPTER TWENTY SIX

Beast With Dead Eyes

"Why am I here Tim?"

Lawrence saw a version of McVeigh he had never seen before. He had expected McVeigh to be beaten, destroyed, and maybe even regretful as he faced his last day alive. He was not. His avoided eye contact and though not cold, his eyes were perpetually looking down, pensive as thoughts were flashing through his brain and he was having trouble capturing how he wanted to respond. McVeigh's speech was soft and slow.

"I was allowed to choose four witnesses."

"And you chose me because ...?"

Again there was slowness to the response, as he searched through his thoughts for an answer. Lawrence wondered if McVeigh might be drugged.

"You saw Waco and Ruby Ridge as I saw them."

"Not exactly, but close. Still, why me?"

"I got the book you sent me when I was in Super Max, People's History of the United States by Zinn. Thought it was some sort of school book. Went right through the prison censors," said McVeigh.

"I don't think many prison guards or administrators know Zinn was a civil rights leader and antiwar during Vietnam," replied Lawrence.

Since Lawrence could not get McVeigh off Zinn and into why Lawrence was here in Terre Haute, Indiana waiting for McVeigh to be put to death, he opted to let him go with what stirred his anger.

"Each page made me wonder why the real history of this country is never taught in school. We're like you told me years ago, an ant colony, the royalty, the soldiers, and the drones. Every war we fought made the the rich richer by throwing bodies onto the battlefield. Iraq was a perfect example of that. Kill the people, run over their government, create your own leaders and you'll make the arms dealers, tank builders, and every arms supplier to the war richer. What cost? A few dead soldiers."

"Tim, you know that you killed more people in Oklahoma City than American soldiers who were killed during the Iraq war?"

"You're kidding?"

"Only 148 Americans were killed. Tim, why am I here?"

Again McVeigh's eyes glossed over and he kept his head down. It was not submission, like that of a recalcitrant child.

Lawrence had no idea what was running through McVeigh's mind. There was not a lot of time left for Timothy McVeigh's and Lawrence was getting edgy that McVeigh was wasting his finale minutes and seconds of breathing for little or no reason.

"You know they're recording what we say, what we talk about?"

"No doubt whatsoever. Sounds to me like they're just wasting their time and more importantly ours," said Lawrence trying to get McVeigh's head on straight.

"There's going to be a book about me by writers from the Buffalo News. I won't read it," said McVey grimacing when he realized why he would not be reading it. "I don't know what'll come out, how much the government will censor about my life. Zinn's life shows how powerful the royalty and soldiers are. Maybe in my book they'll be able to spell out just how vicious and violent government agents really are."

"Tim, but you've done a very vicious and violent crime."

Again McVey's eyes turned blank and he stared at the floor behind the Plexiglas barrier between Lawrence and himself. Some sadist had installed a large clock in the visitor confines, the large second hand sweeping away each second of McVeigh's life.

"Prison has been rough but it did have one great moment for me. When they sent me back to Reno, the guards had to be changed since the regular force were Oklahomans and they feared one of them might try to kill me. They brought in Texans to guard me. Like that was a safer force. I didn't have much to do with other prisoners. Some respected me and some were afraid of me. Ironically some actually asked me for an autograph. But the best was one day when I was working out in the exercise cage. I could see another prisoner through a tiny window in his jail cell. He held up a piece of paper with a big letter G written on it."

"That's it? A piece of paper with a letter on it?"

"No, he dropped it and held up another with a large capital O. One by one he dropped a letter and replaced it. Together they spelled GOODBOMB!"

Lawrence smiled.

"That was rare. My regret though is the pain I feel for my relatives, especially my sister. She knew I was planning a major operation. At a Christmas party she told friends that something big was going to happen. She knew it would be against the Feds. FBI agents immediately went after her, tailed her where ever she went. They followed her into restaurants intentionally showing their holstered handguns. She would leave stores and find agents searching her pickup truck. The FBI looked at her as a suspect, a conspirator. Eventually they invaded her house and took her into custody."

"They had warrants?"

"Yeah, of course, but at that point in time almost any judge would have granted them one if they needed it. Hell, they had already wire tapped my father's house. When the agents were holding my father for questioning, they were watching the news about the bombing, right in front of him. When my picture appeared on the screen they made the comment that you'd have to be a scumbag to give birth to a piece of garbage like that."

"The worst of the agents were two assholes, Yrac and Etroc that harassed my sister, causing her to suffer a mental collapse, almost insanity. They claimed that she was hiding evidence from the investigation. During the search they found letters I had sent her. It was my mistake that got her in real deep shit. I had her package and ship a large quantity of bullets to me. She didn't know it was a federal crime to do that. They changed their tactics a hundred and eighty degrees. Etroc had tried playing the mature fatherly type with her, treating her friendly. As if her helping them would be good for me during the trial. He was always well-dressed with a smile on his face when you pleased him and a frown when he felt you were not cooperating. Like she's that fucking dumb. Yrac is the bad ass. He is short but very muscular with a penetrating gaze. His skin is light brown with just an Asian tint of yellow. His hair is butch-clipped, nearly bald, and black. He could easily pass as a sumo wrestler. He jumped down her throat for hours upon hours. For two weeks he questioned her for close to fifteen hours straight. The threats and aggressiveness were not just Yrac's. The FBI has a psychological profile unit that Attorney General Janet Reno - - as in the same Janet Reno who sent tanks into Waco - pressured to break her. After hours of being threatened by Yrac, Etroc would replace him. He was a little less friendly and tried to brain wash her. They threatened her, telling her that if she didn't help she could be prosecuted."

"Reno's boys stooped as low as you could go. They gave Yrac photographs of dead babies from the Oklahoma bombing and told her I was going to fry and that she might end up sitting right next to me. They even made an FBI poster listing every charge and penalty she faced for aiding and abetting her my crime. Dead babies, can you imagine how sick these people are? Etroc pleaded with her, telling her that they had to believe she was directly involved unless she showed them she wasn't."

"What they did served only one purpose. It got her so mad that she turned on them, dared them to arrest her. As soon as Etroc started with his gratuitous plea of 'now dear, maybe you need a moment to see how we're only trying to help you', she laid into him and Yrac. So angry by now she fiercely defended me. They used her verbal onslaught against her, telling her it was obvious she was involved in the bombing, an out and out lie. She told them she had little sympathy for the victims. She walked out on them and hired a top-notch Buffalo lawyer. He was able to limit their interrogations about my letters and political beliefs, but she could not be prosecuted by the Feds or the State of Oklahoma."

"Your sister is quite a fighter Tim."

"Better than I would have believed. Well after the bombings, she was in a bar and a patron recognized her. He got into her face and called me a baby killer. She punched his lights out."

A guard came into Lawrence's booth and told him that he had five minutes left.

The time had gone by fast, faster for McVeigh than Lawrence. "I'm still not sure why I'm here Tim"

"My family was beaten down and threatened for a crime in which they had no part in. My family really doesn't understand what I did. I think you do. I've been reading your paper over these many months. I've talked with you off and on. What happened in Virginia City is just more of Zinn. Somehow it has to stop."

Lawrence was even more confused. "Yes, but we lost. Actually I lost. Nobody else seems to care."

"That's what's wrong. The Aggies keep winning and Huggies keep being poor and helpless."

Lawrence laughed. "You remember my view of life. Aggies and Huggies? Yep, that's about it. You own the land, you own the people who work the land for you. Yes, that's how life is."

"No, you're wrong. It doesn't have to be that way. Huggies, hunters and gatherers, maybe ..."

The guard returned, "you'll have to leave now."

McVeigh spoke, " ... maybe Jim Hawkins could help you?"

Lawrence smiled at McVeigh as he got up from his seat. McVeigh just sat there, knowing his time was out as Lawrence turned to leave. Lawrence stopped and turned around.

"Sir, you'll have to leave now," the guard was now reaching for Lawrence's arm but Lawrence put his hand on top of the guard's and released the man's grip. Lawrence ignored the man.

"Tim, one thing I forgot to ask."

McVeigh looked up, the same gaze that permeated their entire meeting, was searching for something in his mind, something he wanted to say.

The guard addressed Lawrence, "Sir, now!"

"You're unarmed. Touch me again and I'll hurt you!"

The guard left to get help, giving Lawrence the time to ask his question, "why no license plate? I don't want to hear about somebody being able to identifying your car. You would have been ignored by the trooper. He would have had no reason to pull you over. Hell, a missing license plate will always get you pulled over. You put yourself in a bad situation. "

McVeigh smiled, "everybody likes to think I was going north to Michigan. Nobody would stop a car going to Michigan."

Two guards grabbed Lawrence without a struggle. On the other side of the Plexiglas another guard escorted McVeigh to the 9-by-14 foot cell with its tan walls, bed, sink and toilet. The ever present guard kept watch over him from the outside.

***

McVeigh walked the 500 yards to the death house cell, a red bricked cell without windows. It would be the first time in years he was able to see the sky and the moon, and it would also be his last time. He had spent two hours with his lawyers, mostly writing to relatives and saying a couple of goodbyes over the phone. He was strong, strong enough that, unlike the usual inmates facing death, he neither asked for nor needed help climbing up on the medical gurney.

Lawrence was one of four witnesses. The execution room looked like a hospital room to him. McVeigh was stretched out on the table in the center, a white sheet covering him. The sheet covered the tubes that would send chemicals into his body and kill him. They also hid the straps keeping him fastened to the table. Over 200 spectators in Oklahoma City were watching via closed-circuit television. They were the surviving bombing victims and relatives of non-survivors. He could not see them and he did not care.

McVeigh could see his four chosen witnesses by rotating his head and looking into the room. Although chairs were available for the witnesses, no one, including Lawrence sat. They were separated from the window to the execution room by a steel bar two feet from the floor. It was 7:00 a.m. Monday, June 11, 2001. Two witnesses were able to reach the window and they pressed their hands against the glass. A woman, whom Lawrence did not know, tried to reach the glass but could not. McVeigh's eyes roamed over to the media representatives in a separate room. While the closed circuit audience in Oklahoma could see McVeigh, he could not see them or the victims and relatives who came to the prison to watch. They were behind a one-way mirror.

A U.S. Marshall lifted a red phone to check for any last minute reprieves. These could only be made by the President or the Supreme Court. McVeigh did not bother to look at the Marshall. He had accepted his fate.

"Warden, you may proceed with the execution."

McVeigh had not given any thought to a reprieve. He ignored his death knoll by staring at the witnesses. They were alone in their room, no guard and no possessions other than a writing pad and pen. Lawrence printed eight large letters on his writing pad and held it up to the viewing window. McVeigh smiled as he was read GOODBOMB.

The first chemical, sodium thiopental, ran into McVeigh's right leg at 7:10 a.m. Being an extremely strong sedative, McVeigh's eyes were closing as he looked directly into the camera that was sending his death over the airways to Oklahoma City. McVeigh fell into unconsciousness but for some strange reason his eyes stayed open. Within a minute after the first injection, pancuronium bromide was started into his veins. This drug shut down his lungs and after two final gasps, McVeigh stopped breathing. His eyes were still open. At 7:13 a.m. the coup de grace, potassium chloride, sealed his fate as it ran through his blood vessels and stopped his heart. McVeigh's lips turned light blue, his skin yellowed. His eyes remained wide open. It was 7:14 a.m. when Timothy McVeigh was pronounced dead. All that remained of Timothy McVeigh was a handwritten statement saying "I am the master of my fate: I am the captain of my soul."

**

As Lawrence walked behind the other three witnesses to McVeigh's death, he felt the June heat enter the air conditioned hallway from an open door behind him. He glanced back and saw the two prison guards that had been escorting them sneak outside. Lawrence turned and caught the closing door to the recreational area of the prison. It was grey outside and even though still early in the morning, it was hot. He could hear singing outside of the prison. By far the loudest and largest group, were the anti-death penalty adherents.

The two guards had stopped at a blind, windowless corner and were in the process of lighting up cigarettes.

"Sir, sir you gotta turn around and go back into the building. Don't let that door close it'll ... Ah fuck! It's shut and there ain't no way back in. We're going have to escort you out here! Shit!"

"Why don't you just finish your smokes? Nobody knows you snuck out to grab a smoke. You came after me and you have no idea how I got out here."

The guard looked at his companion, smiled, and drew in a big whiff of tobacco smoke. "Work's for me but you's ass is grass when the warden gets you. Wanna a smoke?"

It sounded good, Lawrence could almost taste that nicotine lift a cigarette gave him. It had been almost twenty years since he stumped out his last cigarette.

"Nah, I gave up. Besides I only smoked Parliament. They still sell those?"

"Damned if I know. They were those crazy smokes, weren't they," said the guard, inhaling slowly through his mouth, exhaling through his nostrils. "They had some kind of tube for the mouth, didn't they?"

"Recessed filter, supposed to cut down the nicotine that you inhaled. Nobody smoked for less nicotine. We smoked them because you could run the tip of your tongue around the recesses like you're ..."

"Eatin' pussy! Fuckin' I remember that. Ain't no pussy I ever ate had a hole that small," said the second guard. All three laughed.

Lawrence let the two guards finish their cigarettes without bothering them. He looked back at the execution building and could still see in his mind Timothy McVeigh's opened eyes. Contrary to legend, a dead person's eyes open when rigor mortis sets in; which was why dead bodies would have weights put on the eye lids. Lawrence also knew that ancient myths had their own legends, the most notable one that coins being were placed on the dead man's eyes to pay the ferryman carrying the dead body across the River of Forgetfulness. If you didn't pay the ferryman, the dead man would rise from death and roam the earth blindly, seeking his living enemies.

"Let's go, Boss. We're takin' you in. Big Boss goin' nail yo ass!"

The guards opened the doors opposite the execution building. These doors had outside key locks. No sooner did they enter the hall, then a loud announcement roared throughout the prison.

"Mr. Peter Lawrence, you are to be taken immediately to the warden's office. Any prison employee knowing where Mr. Lawrence is should call the warden's office and escort him there now!"

Both guards led Lawrence back to where he should have been in the first place. In front of the solid grey, steel-reinforced warden's office, a closed circuit camera picked up the two guards and Lawrence waiting.

A voice came over the speaker above the door. "Guards, do a thorough search of this man's body and signal when you have ascertained he's unarmed."

Lawrence put his hands up against the wall as one of the guards shook him down. The guard signaled the camera and Lawrence could hear metal on metal scraping as the door unlocked. The guards led him in. Lawrence was surprised that they had not handcuffed him. Another guard was waiting on the other side of the steel door.

"It wasn't your guards' fault. I just needed some fresh air so ..."

"You're talking to the wrong person, sir. I'm just here to escort you to the warden's office. You two can leave. I will deal with you when I am finished here with Mr. Lawrence. Go."

The warden's guard was white, probably a good four inches taller than Lawrence. As expected his attire was tight and sharp, flawless. He carried on his Sam Browne belt a holstered Smith and Wesson semi-automatic pistol which Lawrence guessed carried 15 rounds .357SIG in a magazine. As expected he also had a belt holstered TASER X26 pistol which transmits NMI impulses through wires into remote targets at distances up to 35 feet. Surprisingly, the guard had a mustache, usually not allowed in the military-styled personnel of a Federal prison.

The warden could have been the twin of the associate warden, escorting Lawrence into the office. Both were tall with narrow faces and receding hairlines. Their mouths hung in a sanguine mope suggesting that they did not appreciate anybody bothering them or interfering with their job. They said what they needed to say. Not once did they smile or show some sense of understanding for what anybody else had to say. The military could not have been more military.

"Mr. Lawrence, I am prepared to have you arrested and confined right here, right now. You are guilty of two crimes. You attempted to disrupt a Federal Prison execution and you disobeyed the regulations to which you agreed."

Lawrence did not hear the warden, distracted by Yrac and Etroc sitting to the left of the warden, directly beneath the American flag.

"Agent Yrac, McVeigh didn't do you justice. I'm surprised you're not roaming Terre Haute looking for Hooters girls. Although you probably think Indiana is the Home of Hooters. It's Hoosiers by the way Agent, not hooters."

"You know Lawrence Agent Yrac?"

"No warden. I've never met the man. I don't know why he's making those comments."

"And good old Agent Etroc, are you having trouble staying awake?"

Etroc spoke, "Mr. Lawrence, Mr. Lawrence. Why are you involved in this? Why are you even here? We'd just like to understand why you were involved with McVeigh."

Lawrence spoke to the warden. "First, before your boy TAZs me, let's cut out the threats here. How did I attempt to disrupt a Federal prison execution?"

"That message you signaled to him - - good something?"

"As a representative of the press and as an American citizen, I have the right to say, either out loud or in writing, anything I wish to say. Second, what regulation did I violate?"

"We specifically told you; in fact we had it put in writing which you signed off on, that you would limit yourself only to where I or my staff allowed you to migrate. You exited into an unprotected and dangerous area of my prison without permission. That alone will get you arrested."

"Go ahead. Try it. You know you're talking through your ass."

Lawrence could sense that the warden wanted to tell his associate warden to shackle Lawrence, arrest him, and lock him up. But the warden knew it would fall apart and he would become the laughing stock of the Federal Penitentiary System.

"Mr. Lawrence, these two gentlemen are here, assigned by the Federal Bureau of Investigation. Obviously you know the both of them."

"No, only by reputation and seeing their photos in newspapers. Go on."

"I'll let them explain. Mr. Etroc?"

"The FBI has information that Timothy McVeigh was involved with more than just Terry Nichols. We know for a fact that McVeigh on at least two occasions discussed with you ..."

"In other words, you tapped my telephone?"

Yrac spoke. "We had a legal subpoena for the wiretaps."

"That'd be wiretaps, as in more than one?"

Etroc continued. "Yes, it would. And I'm sure you realize your conflict in Virginia with the United States Navy Air Base allowed us to get Federal wiretap warrants."

"Agent Etroc, do you have a drinking problem?"

Yrac raged, "that's none of your business ..."

"So he does? I've been warned about your aggressiveness agent Yrac. McVeigh hit you right on the head. Chubby little Asian boy that the other kids picked on. What do chubby little boys do? They pick on the girls."

"That's enough Lawrence!"

"No warden, you haven't seen enough. You got your own little world, a world you control one hundred percent. How about it, Yrac? Can you go at me, head-to-head?"

Etroc saw the frown on his cohort's face. He ignored it, thinking he was breaking Lawrence down. "Lawrence we got you talking with McVeigh about Ruby Ridge and Waco ..."

"Were you or your buddy at either place? One incidence was enough to justify McVeigh's anger. One of your snipers assassinated a mother and her baby! Did you see it? Then the son-of-a-bitch goes bar hopping, bragging about blowing apart a mother's brains while she's holding her baby, her baby that is now dead because of your Federal agent. And you call McVeigh a murderer? What the fuck is the FBI?"

No one spoke. Lawrence knew he had wasted his breath. He sits in the lair of the beasts. Those that sat with him were the death merchants of humanity, people who would kill babies, drop atomic bombs on civilians. Lawrence looked about him, four men who do not run a country but kill for a country that runs them.

Yrac changed tactics, leaving in the dust each atrocity Lawrence pinned on them. "Did you ever buy a weapon from Timothy McVeigh?"

There were three answers here - - none of which Lawrence liked. If he said no, he could be caught in a lie and arrested. If he affirmed that he did indeed purchase guns from McVeigh, the FBI could go after him on a weapons charge. McVey might not have had a license or his records might have revealed the .45s and holsters - - which probably were illegal.

Lawrence played the odds. If they already had McVey's records of gun sales, Lawrence would be in jail by now.

"No, next question."

Etroc took over, "we've laid it out Mr. Lawrence. Yes, we wire tapped your phones but it had nothing to do with you. The FBI does not believe, at this point in time, that you were in anyway involved with Timothy McVeigh's bombing of the Murrah Building. But you need to help us understand some of the conversations McVeigh had with you. It is very obvious from the tapes that McVeigh did not engage you to help with the bombing. What we have been trying to do today, and Agent Yrac and I are guilty of being accusatory with you ... we have information spoken between you and McVeigh that we cannot disregard."

"Such as?"

"Jim Hawkins? What the hell does Jim Hawkins mean?"

Lawrence smiled, interlacing his fingers and wringing them between each other while looking directly into the eyes of both agents. He had longed plan on Jim Hawkins and now the moment was here. With fingers still wrestling fingers, Lawrence leaned back in his chair, and abruptly stood, making the associate warden reflex and put his hand on the TAZR. Lawrence limped slowly around his chair.

"Didn't mean to scare you but I've got a bad knee. I've to stretch every once in a while," slowly pacing and massaging both knees with his fingers. "Hurt it running high hurdles in college."

"Tim and I talked books back when I was an English teacher. One book that hit home with Tim was Stevenson's Treasure Island. When he returned from the Gulf War, he found that the government he believed in so much was actually betraying him and the people of America. He said it reminded him of Jim Hawkins having so much faith in Long John Silver, then having it washed away by the pirate leader's treachery. So Tim looked at the United States like that."

"You know what scares me the most though? Watching a person have his life taken away. The execution of Timothy McVeigh was horrible, synthetically staged so well that the victim went through the whole death scene like a good soldier dying for his country. Fuck, it was good old American melodrama, the dead man playing his role line-by-line."

Lawrence walked over to Yrac's chair. "McVeigh killed the right people, the basic people, the drones of America, the workers."

He put both hands on the arms of Yrac's chair, "Agent Etroc, you do your job. You make it as easy as you can. You go home, ignoring the atrocities of life during your eight or so hours on the job. You are a good little soldier, a warrior, getting old and still fighting the bottle."

"Can't eyeball me, can you Yrac?" Lawrence eased down so he was face-to-face with Yrac. The warden put his hand up in front of his associate warden, preventing him from interfering.

"You totally destroyed a family that was not responsible in any way for what McVeigh did. You fucking attacked them, just short of physical torture. His sister, his sister became your prey. You followed her into restaurants, called her a suspect in the bombing. You wired her house, then you grilled her eight or nine hours a day You told her she was going to fry. Fry? She would get the electric chair? That's brutal. I bet you even had a hand in trying to frame her by putting explosives on her clothing."

Lawrence backed away from Yrac, " ... and you showed her a series of photos of babies mutilated and killed by her brother's bomb. Was that a Janet Reno decision? What, no comment?"

"You still got the poster? The poster listing all of the crimes she had committed and all the penalties she would suffer for her brother's crime? You stuck it right in her face, didn't you?"

Lawrence turned his back on Yrac, "dead babies! Pictures of dead babies!"

"Listen to me you slit-eyed Asian pig," said Lawrence. From his peripheral vision he saw the movement of the warden and his second-in-command. Turning back to Yrac, Lawrence said, "I'm going to make you number 169."

Lawrence saw Yrac's eyes widen and knew that Yrac would react instinctively, in a pure rage. He came straight at Lawrence, no plan and obviously no knowledge of hand-to-hand combat. Lawrence had intended to enrage the bull. Lawrence could have gone down when the man came at him, both hands open at chest level. Yrac's eyes were bloodshot, and his mouth was full of snarling teeth. Instead of engaging Yrac man-to-man, he dropped backward, putting the weight on his right leg and forcing Yrac to turn to his right and lose his balance. Lawrence caught him with two quick jabs just below the left eye followed by a blow to his nose with a right cross. Lawrence turned quickly knowing the associate warden would either pull his pistol or TAZR.

"Put that fucking TAZR away for God's sake," said the Warden now standing, his face white. "Mr. Lawrence might have goaded the man into a fight but these two FBI agents should know better than attack him for verbal insults. Sit down, everybody sit down! Mr. Lawrence, please sit. You have my word that I will report this agent to the FBI for conduct unbecoming an agent of the Federal Government."

Lawrence did not sit. "Unless you want to take me into custody and are ready to charge me with a crime, I'm out of here. Warden, I've got no beef with you. You did your job. Neither of us like killing people. McVeigh died as mercifully as possible."

Lawrence walked over to Etroc who was helping his cohort up off the floor. "I know and you know, we're not finished. There's going to be only one ending between you, the Asian pig, and me. Maybe next time. You better get some ice on his face or he'll have even fatter jaws than he does now."

Lawrence was personally escorted out of the prison and to the parking lot by the associate warden. As Lawrence opened his car door the man spoke, "don't know how to figure it, Mr. Lawrence. Can't see how you justify what McVeigh did. I mean he killed children, innocent women and kids. You really think what he did was right?"

"I knew Tim, but not know well. His belief in this country was one hundred and ten percent loyalty. Then he went to Iraq. It got to him. He did horrible things, killings like those at Waco and Ruby Ridge. That's what bothered him so much. It's funny .. No, that's really not true. Killing is not funny."

It was hot outside now. The mid-June morning was passing by in in Middle America. Lawrence rolled down the driver's side car window to let the car air out. Leaning against the car he decided to leave the door open as well and he continued talking, "this country trains soldiers to shoot to kill, to build bombs, and then to use those bombs to kill people they are told to kill. Then it turns those same warriors on the United States' own citizens. It doesn't add up. You're an officer of the law. How would you like it if the government took away your ability to defend yourself?"

The associate warden just shrugged. Lawrence reached out and shook the man's hand. "Is there a book store around here? I'm staying at the Best Western off of Route 70."

"There's a Books-A-Million just south of there. Honey Creek Square Shopping Center's has a store and there's a Walden Books near the entrance of 41."

Lawrence got into his car, closed the door, and aimed his left hand, thumb up, and finger completing the pistol shape, "thanks."

***

After returning to his motel room, he showered and ate breakfast in the motel's restaurant. His omelet and minced potatoes tasted like Styrofoam. Lawrence drove to the Honey Square Shopping Center and found at Waldenbooks what he was seeking, a book of road maps for North America. A major gap existed in McVeigh's trek that Lawrence could not understand. McVeigh appeared to have made a stupid and irrational decision with his escape from the Oklahoma City bombing. McVey had plotted, planned, created a weapon of mass destruction, and mechanically ignited it, killing 168 people yet he allowed himself to commit an error that any moron could avoid, driving without a license plate. McVeigh had been adamant about not having his license plate showing. Neither his lawyers nor his biographers could make sense of it. His stories about a plan to clear out his storage shed in Kansas and go camping at Geary Lake for a day or two then visit Arizona before starting another attack, this time hunting down and picking off federal agents one-by-one, was ridiculous. Lawrence knew it was totally fabricated. There simply was no logic for not having a license plate.

What happened between him and the police officer in Perry, just miles short of Kansas, was difficult to understand. Did McVey truly think a hick cop from a boondock hick town could not nail him? It seemed that McVeigh had played along with the patrol man and nearly made it but Lawrence noticed an anomaly in McVeigh's escape route. McVeigh was not heading anywhere near Arizona, or any other place west. McVey was stopped on Route 35, heading north. It made no sense. There was no way that a police officer or anyone could have known that Timothy McVeigh had blown up the Murrah Building in Oklahoma. No agency had any records on McVeigh to put them on his trail. McVeigh was a total unknown. He knew that. It gave him a great edge in his escape. Tim McVeigh could have driven to Washington D.C. and toured the FBI building and still not been arrested.

The logical place for Tim McVey to go was back to Western New York, Buffalo or maybe Michigan where his cohorts were. He could take Route 44 out of Oklahoma City, through Tulsa, across Missouri, and follow Route 70 to Columbus Ohio or pick up Route 69 to Lansing Michigan. With the radio on, McVey would have heard reports of citizen sightings of any possible bomber fleeing Oklahoma City, in which case, he could have changed to a less open route. The odds of success on random escape routes were tremendously higher than riding without a license plate through Kansas.

Lawrence took a yellow highlighter out of his attaché case and marked off the two routes to Lansing and Buffalo. Then he took a red highlighter and started up Route 35 through Kansas, into Iowa and stopped. At Kansas City

McVey could follow Route 35, going east but he would be in heavily populated areas and there would be police troopers patrolling the roads. If he took Route 29 at Kansas City, he would be going through South Dakota and North Dakota. There would be less chance of being pulled over even if he was speeding.

He could wind up in Canada and that made no sense. Lawrence highlighted that route in red and stopped at Winnipeg. McVeigh would never have gotten through customs without a license plate. Looking at the map with the yellow route to Western New York and at the red route through the Dakotas and into Canada, Lawrence saw why McVeigh got caught. The plan was actually very smart. There was no route that guaranteed success. He had to increase his chances to survive, and he almost did. If he had a license on his car from the get-go, there was bound to have been someone seeing the fleeing car and noting the license plate numbers. In fact there were people who had reported a description of McVeigh's car. None could give the police a license plate number. Because the descriptions were so scant and varied the police had written them off. Traveling all the way to New York would surely have gotten his unlicensed car pulled over. Traveling through the largely rural farm and ranch area of Route 29 would be a very minimum risk. The patrol officer that picked up McVeigh had no idea at the time that he had captured the Oklahoma City Bomber.

"Tim, you almost had it made," Lawrence said to himself, sitting at the desk in his motel room.

Once off Route 35 his chances were excellent. When pulled over, he had hoped to just get a ticket and be written off by the cop. Outside of Perry, Oklahoma, it almost worked. McVey had one more chance at that point in time but backed out of it. He could have easily shot and killed the patrolman. While his chances of escape would have decreased, there would have been a chance of escape nonetheless. McVey had read the officer as a yahoo. He did not know that the trooper was a nineteen-year veteran who had made a name for himself by catching traffic violators.

Had McVeigh reached the Canadian border, Lawrence knew that McVeigh would have somewhere back down route 29, put on his original license plates. The chances that the Canadian border patrols had been warned of a vehicle matching Lawrence's plates would have been minimal. His chances of going through customs were excellent. Having no license plates would have had him caught and handcuffed before he could bat an eye. Where would McVey go once in Canada?

McVeigh might have given Lawrence the answer, "ask Jim Hawkins." To do that meant going to McVeigh's grandfather's apple orchard and opening the apple barrel. That meant a drive from Terre Haute Indiana to North Tonawanda, New York, nearly eleven hours. He had to call Kat to tell her to keep running the newspaper without him for at least three or four more days. Lawrence got up from the desk and went to the phone. As he passed by the window overlooking the parking lot, he stopped.

"You got to be fucking kidding me," said Lawrence.

Sitting in a nondescript gray Ford LTD sedan, four rows behind Lawrence's car in the motel's parking lot, was Etroc, at the driver's wheel, and Yrac in the passenger seat, still holding an ice pack to his face.

Kat answered the phone, "hello, news desk. How can I help you?"

"Kat, this is Lawrence."

"Wow, how did the execution go? I saw news broadcasts on television. There were more people wanting him pardoned than wanting him executed. Is that how it really was?"

"Yeah, listen Kat. I've unearthed more information. I had a very good interview with him. I'm going to fax it to you as soon as I can."

"Why don't you just wait until you're here?"

"I'm not coming to Virginia City. I've got a very strange lead that I need to play out. Could be nothing, but I really don't think that's the case. I've got to keep it to myself. Can't tell you anything about it yet."

"You don't trust me?"

"It's not you. I want you to be absolutely quiet for ten seconds. No noise at all," said Lawrence as he flipped the switch next to the window to turn on the air conditioner.

After counting silently to ten, Lawrence continued, "did you hear a humming sound?"

"Yeah! Shit, is somebody tapping your motel room phone?"

"I don't know but I can't take the chance. I shouldn't be more than one or two days."

"Before you hang up, Mom's doing okay. They didn't release her because of her temperature. She should be out ..."

"What are you talking about?"

"She went in for the abortion. Oh my God, you didn't know? Oh My God, I thought you knew."

Lawrence was stunned. He had no words that would speak of his pain and certainly none to voice his anger. He hung up.

"How, how can I lose another child? Eileen, Eileen, how I miss you," Peter Lawrence was in tears. All the pain of that night in Allegheny Park came back. His mind would never lose his last minutes with her.

CHAPTER TWENTY SEVEN

Son of the Beast

If the scenery was beautiful, Lawrence not only did not notice, but could have cared less. He was sure that Indianapolis, Columbus, Akron, Cleveland, and Erie were great places to visit, but Lawrence saw nothing of them. It was not because Routes 70 and 90 had no views nor was it because Susan Yoder had been pregnant without his knowledge and that she had his child murdered. Neither was it due to his anticipation of what the apple barrel would tell him. It was the cat and mouse game being played with the two FBI agents that captivated his thoughts.

Lawrence knew Yrac and Etroc had probably determined his destination since they had been tailing him from the start. The end of the trail was obviously Buffalo, New York, although, to be specific it technically would be Niagara Falls. What they had no way of knowing was where in Niagara Falls Lawrence was headed. They did know that McVeigh had passed along information to Lawrence, information that the FBI wanted. Lawrence had to get rid of them before he arrived at McVeigh's apple orchard.

Not expecting any conflicts, Lawrence had driven to Terre Haute just to interview McVeigh as he requested and to witness McVeigh's execution, also requested. He had not expected any conflicts or complications because of it. Yet here he was headed to Western New York with two FBI agents on his tail. He had not brought any weapons with him, and this bothered him.

The sun had finished setting as he drove Route 90 north, past the exit to Erie, Pennsylvania. Lawrence could see the signs for Route 86. Had it been another day in another lifetime, Lawrence would have his canoe atop the car roof heading east on Route 86 through Jamestown and into Allegany State Park. The memories of Eileen O'Hara Ledger would never leave him. He made a vowed that when he finished dealing with McVeigh's final words to him, he would come back, put his canoe in the water, and return to camp where her spirit had left the real world.

The long ride from Terre Haute ate away at his conscience. One more death had pierced his life, the death of his first child. Did he care for Susan Yoder as much as he had for Eileen? Until talking to Kat, the answer most definitely would have been yes. Now there was doubt, no trust. Lawrence tried to imagine all the reasons that would have kept her from telling him about the pregnancy. He could not come up with a single one. He needed to leave Susan Yoder behind until his trip to the apple orchard ended.

Entering New York State just south of Ripley, Lawrence could see far off the lights on Lake Erie. There was still another hour and a half of driving before reaching Buffalo. When trucks heading south on the opposite side of the divided highway came at him with their bright lights on, the illumination in the rear view mirrors let Lawrence to know that Yrac and Etroc were still tailing him. He was sure they spelled each other during the last nine plus. Exiting at a rest stop to gas up, Lawrence had seen them stop before the exit off Route 90 to switch seats.Lawrence had to lose them before he got to the apple barrel on McVeigh's grandfather's orchard. He needed to make a decision soon. If he went directly to the Grand Island Holiday Inn where he had a reservation and then tried to escape the FBI agents tomorrow or the next day, they would have the advantage since they would have him pinned down and could call for additional help from the FBI and local police. Lawrence needed to find McVeigh's stash before dawn. It was late and this gave Lawrence an edge. He lived here and knew the area better than the agents.

Lawrence smiled.

The route to Grand Island was best taken by catching 290 east and north going past Greater Buffalo International Airport and around Tonawanda. Lawrence went west instead, taking Route 190 through the west side of Buffalo. Lawrence had no intention of staying on 190. He slowed well below the speed limit, so much so that cars were backing up behind him. The LTD was not behind him. They usually kept at least two or three cars behind Lawrence, obviously ignorant enough to think he had no idea they were tailing him. At the Peace Bridge and Canada, Lawrence pulled out into the passing lane but still maintained a slow speed. Cars were honking, forced to pass him on the right. At the Peace Bridge exit sign, Lawrence merged quickly into the right lane in front of a pickup truck, barely escaping getting rammed. He could see the LTD trying to get over. Unfortunately for Lawrence they made it but Lawrence was not through trying to lose them.

He crossed Peace Bridge and got to the customs booths. Even though it was late at night, there was still a backup of cars since only one booth was open. This was the edge Lawrence needed. Although he could not see the FBI car, he knew there were at least three cars between them.

The border patrol officer at the booth checked Lawrence's credentials, asked him his destination, a business trip to Toronto, and let him through. From the Peace Bridge to Toronto, meant the QEW all the way. Had it been daylight, the border patrol officer might have noticed Lawrence turning off at Route 124, Central Avenue and heading south, instead of north. At route 1 Lakeshore Road, Lawrence made a left and headed north along the Niagara River via Niagara Boulevard. The LTD and its occupants would never have the chance to catch up to him. Lawrence stayed on Niagara Boulevard all the way to Niagara Falls, Canada.

He needed to get to Lockport and Upper Mountain Road. He could cross back to the United States at the Rainbow Bridge or go all the way to the Lewiston-Queenstown Bridge. Crossing at the latter into the United States would take him directly to Route 104 which turns into Upper Mountain Road. He guessed that Yrac and Etroc would realize by now that Lawrence had shaken their tail. They would also know Lawrence would have to cross back over the border. The border patrol officers would be United States ones, not Canadians.

All it would take to catch Lawrence was a quick call to them to report Lawrence's car and license plate. The question was would they stop Lawrence until the agents got to him? Probably not. Having Lawrence detained would ruin their chances of tracking him to his final destination.

Lawrence crossed over at the Rainbow Bridge, enjoying the night lights of the Falls while remembering his showdown with Zig Ledger at Three Sister's Islands. The border patrol officer on booth duty confirmed the accuracy of Lawrence's hunch concerning the FBI agents. He took Lawrence's driver's license and car registration into the booth. Lawrence could see him on the phone. The man returned without Lawrence's credentials.

"Where are you headed Mr. Lawrence?"

"Grand Island. I have a reservation at the Holiday Inn and I'm damn tired. Can we get this interrogation over officer?"

The patrol officer did not answer but went back into the booth and picked up the phone. He did not take long.

"Here's your license and registration. You can get to ..."

"Thank you. I know where I'm going," said Lawrence. He pulled out onto Prospect Street heading south to the Robert Moses Parkway. He saw the border patrol officer standing outside the customs booth watching as the car headed toward Grand Island. Lawrence would not allow himself to look as he passed by where he tutored Henry Hawkins. Memories of Henry, Lizzy, and Ulysses still gave him nightmares. When Lawrence got to the on ramp for Route 190, instead of off ramping onto the Grand Island Bridge, he stayed on the Robert Moses, caught Buffalo Avenue and headed north to Upper Mountain Road and the apple barrel.

***

The little black coffee maker sputtered and spewed, a continual orgasm of explosions, finally easing off, and then dying. Lawrence picked up the insulated cardboard cup and poured coffee into it. It was a bright shiny day outside the window at the Grand Island Holiday Inn, overlooking the Tonawanda River with its opening to the Erie Canal nearly dead center between North Tonawanda and Tonawanda. Jack London had walked here and been arrested here. Death had been here.

He finished his six ounces of harsh but intoxicating caffeine and picked up the phone, connecting to the front desk, "Yes, you can help me. Is there a couple of gentlemen going by the names Yrac and Etroc staying here?"

Lawrence knew had seen their Ford LTD in the parking lot.

"Good, could you connect me to their room? Thanks."

Lawrence poured another six ounces into the cardboard cup, "Etroc, right?"

There was silence on the other end. Lawrence waited until Etroc responded. "Yeah, what?"

"I've had enough. Let's talk. I'll be in the hotel restaurant. See you in a couple minutes," Lawrence said, putting the receiver back in its cradle.

The Holiday Inn had a breakfast buffet. Lawrence made up a plate of scrambled eggs, two rashers of bacon, and some diced red potatoes with onions and green pepper. After taking a large tomato juice, he found a table in front of the huge picture window facing the same direction as his room. His back was to the dining area entrance. He was a bit stunned when Etroc came up behind him and pulled out a chair.

"Yrac will be here in a couple minutes. Mind If I get something to eat?"

"No, go ahead. Us citizens are paying for it, right?"

By the time Yrac showed up, his compatriot was sitting down with a full plate.

Lawrence saw that Yrac's face was still swollen. "Told you to ice it, Yrac. Ice won't do any good now. Let it be. Tomorrow try wet heat."

"Go fuck yourself, asshole."

Lawrence smiled, "let's get down to it. I'm playing with a bad hand, maybe a pair a deuces if I'm lucky. After all this time, after all these confrontations, it's just not worth it."

As the pacifier Etroc saw his opening. "Mr. Lawrence, how you choose to see Timothy McVeigh is your right. He might be an avenger, a hero to you. To us, to this country, he is a murderer, was a murderer."

"Yeah, that says it pretty well. I've heard his life story directly from him. What he went through and what his country asked of him was too difficult for Tim to handle. And he couldn't. That's my predicament too. Part of me sees a country killing its own people, like at Waco and Ruby Ridge."

"Obviously, Yrac and I can't comment on that. It's part of our ..."

"Duty? I'm not questioning what your life is and what you think you owe the U. S. of A. What you're willing to accept because you're a soldier horrifies me."

Yrac took the ice pack off his face and looked Lawrence directly in the eye. "Soldiers? We're not fucking soldiers."

"Cool it Yrac. Mr. Lawrence doesn't mean soldier in the military sense."

Lawrence had to explain. "It's a social classification, like ants and bees. There's the royalty, the owners of this country, the queens and kings. To keep the colony, the United States, running and in order to satisfy the greed of the rulers, there has to be soldiers, police, and enforcers. To feed the colony, the country must have drones, workers. They are so many workers that eliminating a few or many of us has little or no effect on the colony."

Etroc spoke. "That's all very esoteric. Esoteric is the right word?"

"Yeah, it'll do. What McVeigh saw was the misuse of violence by the soldiers at war in Iraq. When he returned to the land of the free, he saw the same misuse here."

Both agents had nothing to say.

Lawrence knew it was a waste of time and energy trying to explain the power structure in the United States.

"So you still haven't figured out what Jim Hawkins means, have you? Did you ever read Stevenson's book, Treasure Island?"

Yrac said, "it's a kid's book. I saw the movie."

Lawrence shook his head. Jerking them around, he asked, "Disney's or MGM's? Bobby Driscoll was a bit whiney in

Disney's but I'd give Robert Newton an edge over Wallace Beery as Long John Silver. Anyhow, where was Jim Hawkins when he found out that Long John Silver was a pirate and was going to kill off the crew and steal the booty?"

"Shit," said Etroc, "in the apple barrel! McVey's message wasn't about learning that Silver and his mates were the bad guys. McVey's message was to you. So where's McVeigh's apple barrel?"

"I've been there with him. Probably I put the idea in his head. He was showing me some firearms at his grandfather's orchard. He used the farm as a firing range. There was an apple barrel sitting right where we were firing weapons. My guess, from what he said to me before he was executed, is that he hid information there, in the apple barrel. There's only one way to find out."

"You mean there's a real apple barrel? Not some wild guess that winds up being bullshit?"

"That's my guess. Only way to find out is to go there."

Lawrence finished his coffee while the FBI agents ate their breakfast. Neither agent was going to let Lawrence out of their sight. As Etroc rose, Yrac quickly swallowed down his grapefruit juice, and wiping off his mouth said, "okay, let's see what you got, Lawrence."

Outside the agents walked Lawrence toward their car. "I'll take mine."

"No way. You ain't dodging us again," said Yrac. "Where's your car?"

"Over in the River Oaks Golf Course parking lot."

"Why'd you park there?"

"To screw you up. Figured you'd think I took off on you. How'd you know I'd be here at the Holiday Inn?"

Etroc responded, "Aah, Mr. Lawrence, let's just chalk it up to FBI magic."

"As in wiretap magic?" Lawrence did not wait for a response and started toward the golf course.

Yrac spoke, "hey, asshole, where you goin'? You ride with us."

"I won't do that. But if one of you wants to ride with me, let's go."

Yrac was reday to erupt but Etroc stopped him. "I'll ride with him. You follow."

Lawrence unlocked his car but Etroc told him to stop and open the trunk. Lawrence popped it open and Etroc did a thorough search of it. He shut the trunk and got into the passenger seat.

Lawrence headed west down Whitehaven Road, "looking for anything in particular?"

"We don't take chances. I probably should have shook you down too."

Lawrence had anticipated this. He had already deflated his spare tire, popped one rim edge with the tire iron, secreted his two Colt M1911A1's inside the spare tire, and then reinflated it. The only problem would be if he got a flat tire and had to put on the spare. At Grand Island Boulevard he made a right and headed to the north bridge. Catching I 190 he passed through Niagara Falls, making a right turn just before the Reservoir State Park. He headed east on Saunders Settlement road. When he reached the community college at Route 429, he made a left and headed north. He tried to not think of Eileen Ledger as the car went under the bridge at Upper Mountain Road passing the Schimschack Restaurant.

"You boys ought to come up here and have dinner at Schimschack's" said Lawrence. "Best prime rib on the East Coast."

"I'm afraid my good buddy Yrac only likes pork. Something to do with his being a Samoan. We close?"

"Yep, just ahead. We make a right on Lower Mountain Road. McVeigh's grandfather's orchard is on the north side, his home is on the south."

They reached the apple orchard and Lawrence pulled up in front of the grandfather's house on the south side of the road. Yrac was right behind them, pulling up on Lawrence's right. The three of them exited the cars and Lawrence walked up to the front door.

"Better let them know we're here," said Lawrence.

Lawrence tried the doorbell button twice. He could hear it ringing inside the house. He knocked on the door. Again, there was no response. He gave up and turned back to Etroc and Yrac to join them.

"I didn't think the grandfather would be here so soon after the execution. Probably staying with relatives or friends. Tough to be alone after your grandson is executed."

Both agents raised their heads and stared at Lawrence. Yrac was going to say something but Etroc stopped him and spoke, "actually it's better for us. The old man might get defensive and force us to get a search warrant. Where's this apple barrel Lawrence?"

Lawrence turned around, facing north and the apple trees across the road. "See that loading dock over there to the right?"

Lawrence pointed the dock out, "nothing much there. It's early in the season. They load up baskets of apples for market delivery from that dock. Trucks back into the docks. The workers pick through the baskets, yanking out the ones that are too damaged for shipment. Some of the trucks pick up the ones less damaged and are sent to the processing center for sauces and juicing. If the apples are rotted, they get dumped into the barrel on the other side of the dock. Eventually that barrel gets dumped in a compost pit."

Lawrence started walking across the road to the loading dock, turned to make sure Etroc was with him, and saw that Yrac was also following. "One of you ought to stay here in case somebody shows up. A neighbor might call the cops on us."

Etroc turned to Yrac. "That's smart. Yrac, there's a barn and a garage behind the house. I saw them when we were pulling in. Take a look. There might be somebody back there."

Yrac stared at Lawrence. The hate was still there and needed and wanted a chance to take on Lawrence again. He turned and went around the back of house. Lawrence was already at the loading dock when Etroc crossed over Lower

Mountain Road. He noticed Lawrence had his hands up, walking around all sides of the dock, shaking his head.

"Got a problem Lawrence?"

"Yeah, there's no barrel."

"You're shitting me? Right?"

Etroc could see the frustration on Lawrence's face. He started roaming around the loading dock looking for a barrel. There wasn't one.

"Listen, Lawrence. You're fucking with us. There is no apple barrel ..."

"The pit, that's the place. The compost pit. It's over there, to the right. See that mound? It's the dirt piled up from digging the compost pit. Come on. I'll bet it's there." Lawrence went east about fifty yards before Etroc could catch up with him. Lawrence was still shaking his head and waving his hands.

"Lawrence, you've fucked with us one too many times now," said Etroc drawing his service pistol. "Put your hands behind your head. I'm arresting you for providing false information to a government agent in the line of duty. Good, now turn around so I can cuff you."

Lawrence faced the orchard, knowing there was no barrel out there.

"Okay, right hand behind your back," said Etroc as he held his weapon to Lawrence's head. His left hand snapped the handcuff onto Lawrence's right hand.

"Now the left. When Yrac finds out how you led us on this wild goose chase, I'm not going to stop him from kicking your ass. You're in real deep. Taking federal enforcement agents from Indiana to fucking Buffalo on some trumped up story is going to put you in federal prison for a couple years."

He finished cuffing Lawrence and told him to turn around and slowly walk back to the house. As they crossed Lower Mountain Road, both noticed the absence of Yrac. Etroc kept hold of the hand cuff chain with his left hand while keeping the pistol barrel at Lawrence's right ear. He pulled Lawrence to the right and pushed him toward the back of the house. They got halfway around when Yrac came out from behind the house, nearly running into the now handcuffed Lawrence.

"Yrac, this son-of-a-bitch has fucked us over big time. There is no ..."

Yrac walked up to Lawrence and put his face inches from Lawrence's. He smiled as he hammered Lawrence in the stomach with his fist. Lawrence doubled over and before Yrac could take another blow, Etroc grabbed the Samoan's arm and pulled him back. Lawrence fell to his knees.

"In the back. There's a barn and a garage and an apple barrel. Smells to high heaven, though."

"You assholes, take the cuffs off. I told you there was a barrel." Lawrence had shaken off the blow to the stomach but he barely made it to a standing position.

"No Lawrence, we'll wait and see if this is Jim Hawkins' barrel. Move."

The agents followed a smiling Lawrence around the house and to the barn. It was much easier to find in daylight.

"So what's in it Yrac?"

"Apples"

Lawrence started laughing, ignoring Etroc's stares.

"Wow Yrac! I'll bet you remember that from elementary school. Your teacher told you to look at the red fruit, Yrac. It is the first letter in the alphabet. So "a" stands for apple!"

Yrac ignored Lawrence.

"I don't know what else. I just saw these rotten apples. Smells bad. Well not real bad. Fact is the smell kind of gets to you in a way."

Etroc spoke, "they've fermented. You're smelling apple cider. Take another look."

"Fuck you, Etroc. You stick your head down in that. Ought to be right up your alley. Get yourself on one of your booze trips whiffing rotting apples."

An angry Etroc turned to Lawrence, "turn around."

After taking the handcuffs off, he told Lawrence to have a look. Lawrence went to the barrel and kicked it over. It was only about a third full, maybe one bushel of rotten apples falling out. Lawrence up righted the barrel and walked away.

Etroc had put his pistol back into the holster and walked over to the barrel.

"Nothing Lawrence! We've got nothing. A bunch of apple ooze and rotting odors."

"So what do you want from me! Let's cut the arrest bullshit. I didn't tell you assholes to follow me to Western New York. I was coming up here, plain and simple. You've got nothing on me. McVeigh screwed me over. You followed me and got screwed"

The sun was bright enough to now see into the barrel. Lawrence knew he had them. He walked over to the apple barrel and looked into it. "Wait."

Lawrence walked into to the barn and returned with a rake. He turned the rake upside down and put the handle into the barrel, using it to knock on the bottom of it.

"You hear that?"

"Hear what, asshole," said Yrac.

"Shut up and listen," said Etroc.

Lawrence knocked on the bottom again, once more getting a hollow sound, "Bottom is on the ground, right? If it's on the ground, there shouldn't be a hollow sound. Let me try something else."

Lawrence put the rake handle all the way to the bottom of the barrel. He grasped the rake at the lip of the barrel. This gave him the depth of the barrel. Lawrence held the rake outside of the barrel. The rake did not touch the ground.

"Shit," said Etroc, "there's a false bottom."

Yrac did not grasp what Etroc was saying, "how the fuck you know that?"

"His hand, Yrac. Look at his fist. Same place outside as it was inside. But look at the rake handle. It doesn't go the depth of the barrel ... Unless, the bottom's built up from the sides."

"I don't get it."

Etroc did not waste time trying to explain. Instead he went to the barrel, told Lawrence to pull the rake out, and kicked over the barrel.

"Damn, the bottom goes the full length as the sides. It means ..."

Lawrence broke in, "the boards I'm hitting are a false bottom. Look at how far the inside of the barrel is. There's got to be a space under the false bottom of nearly a foot."

Etroc walked into the barn, roamed around for a few minutes and walked out with a hammer, ready to bust out the bottom.

"You might want to think twice about busting out the bottom," said Lawrence.

"Why," replied Etroc.

"You don't have a search warrant for one. Remember, Tim McVeigh was an expert in explosives."

"Fucking right, Lawrence. What can we do?"

Lawrence said. "Let me look in the garage a second. Be right back."

Lawrence turned, and as he walked away he could not help but smile. They were falling hook, line, and sinker for Lawrence's plan. He knew what he needed and found the screw driver that he had used last night. He picked it up and waited a few minutes until Yrac yelled for him to get on with it.

Returning he held up the screw driver and spoke, "my guess is that McVeigh made sure he could open and close this space with ease. Probably thought of it back when we had talked about Treasure Island and Jim Hawkins. Wouldn't have booby-trapped it, though."

"Why not?" said Yrac.

Etroc responded, "think, Yrac. It's his grandfather's orchard, his grandfather's apple barrel. All it would take is somebody to accidently damage it while loading or unloading and bam, it would explode. Plus he might also set it off himself."

Lawrence spoke, "which means there's a way into it. One of you want to try?"

"No fucking way, Lawrence!"

"How about you, Etroc? Got some balls?"

"Just try it. Blows up, we'll send your pieces to Virginia City."

Lawrence turned the barrel upside down where he could see the screw head slots. It was much easier than last night. McVeigh had covered the screw heads with brown clay. Lawrence let them be, but for the benefit of the FBI agents he made motions as if he were brushing off areas of the bottom.

"Hey, look what we got here! Two flathead screws embedded into the wood."

Removing the screws, Lawrence pried open the bottom with the screwdriver and exposed the insides. "There you go!"

Yrac pushed Lawrence back and looked into the hidden storage space, "Etroc, we got 'em! Look. All kinds of paper work. Hey, there are even some maps."

Etroc brushed past Lawrence, eager to survey Timothy McVeigh's stash. Lawrence watched them slowly pull out the materials that Lawrence had left in the secret barrel bottom last night. None of what he left there was useful to him. The FBI would now have lists of McVeigh's guns and firearms sales, long lists. McVeigh was good at selling arms and better at keeping records. Every name and sale had been done within the boundaries of the law. Etroc and Yrac would have a couple thousand potential terrorist names to go through, but not until Lawrence no longer needed surveillance. The secret storage area had contained materials that were now secured in a leather satchel in the safe at the Grand Island Holiday Inn where Lawrence had deposited them the night before.

"We got you, Lawrence. Right here. McVeigh sold you two Colt M1911A1's. Guess we got to take you in after all. This is going to be a great pleasure for me Lawrence," said Yrac.

Etroc spoke, "shut the fuck up, Yrac. We don't have him."

"What you mean? They're illegal in ..."

"Look! See this receipt book? It's a license register. Lawrence lives in Virginia. McVeigh sent in the required licensing receipt."

"He's not in fucking Virginia now!"

"He's also not carrying now. I searched him before we left. You searched his room ..."

Lawrence had anticipated the searching of his room which was why he had placed the leather satchel in the hotel's safe.

"How about his car?"

"I told you. I searched him and the car. Forget about it. Lawrence is small potatoes. It's going to take the bureau a month to track down all of these names."

Lawrence spoke up, "how long you guys going to be here?"

Etroc spoke, "probably a day or two. This might not be all we find. Why?"

"I've got to get back to Virginia City."

Lawrence knew that they could hold him as a material witness, could even sequester him for the entire length of the investigation.

Etroc got up from the porch where he had been going through the stash of papers hidden in the barrel. He went up to Lawrence. "While I don't really want to do this, you've played fair. I don't like you, Lawrence. I think there's more to you than we know. Yet there's not enough to keep you in custody. Watch yourself. Next time we'll come down on you like ..."

"Gang busters? Try it. Someday, somebody's going to stop government thugs like you. I hope I'm one of them," said Lawrence. "I'll enjoy the taste of revenge." He turned and went back to his car.

***

The New York State Thruway was still the most boring road in the world thought Lawrence as he exited at Syracuse and headed south on Route 81. He was home in fifteen minutes. Evelyn Southern was watching Wheel of Fortunc when Lawrence walked into his mother's house.

"I am home, Mon Mere. You want to wait for Pat Sajak to do the final spin before you kiss me and welcome me home?"

"Yes, mon fils. Sit down here, next to me on the sofa."

"So where's ...?"

She cut him off.

Sajak had spun the five thousand dollar slot, adding another thousand to make the puzzle worth six thousand dollars for each letter. Evelyn solved the puzzle before any of the contestants got farther than three letters on the board. "He's in jail. I want the young red-headed women to guess an 'r'. She'll get three of them for eighteen thousand dollars."

The woman guessed an 'l'. "You stupid bitch. You don't deserve to win."

With that she clicked the remote, turning off the television.

"Yes, Mr. Dougherty took the rat for his mob boss. The fool."

"Took the what?"

"Rat, Petra. Took the rat so as his boss did not go to jail." She leaned over and grabbed Lawrence by both cheeks, pulling him to her for a full kiss on his lips. Lawrence had hated her thus showing affection when he was a child. It embarrassed him when kids asked if he stuck his tongue down her throat It still bothered him.

"Rap, mama. He took the rap."

"Rat, rap, whatever. He's still in jail while I sit here like a lonely widow with no a man to excite my female body with kisses and caresses."

Lawrence knew Evelyn spoke this way to tease him. "Damn, I needed to talk with him. How long is he going to be in jail?"

"Two more weeks. The judge gave him a month."

"He got sent to jail for a month? What was the crime?"

"Gambling. The police busted the back of Giordano's restaurant and caught them running a roulette wheel."

"So? Everybody knows there's a table there every Friday. Caesar Constanzo runs them all over the city. He's been doing it in front of the police ever since Atlantic City went legal. How come now?"

"The priests got him. They were losing money at bingo so they went to the judge who happens to be up for reelection. Told him the good father, the bishop, would tell his lambs to vote for the Mick candidate instead of the Dago who lets the mob's gambling go on during their bingo game night. Judi had to jump in and claim it was his doing."

"I can't wait two weeks, Ma Mere. I need to talk with Judi tomorrow."

"So go down to the precinct jail and visit him."

"That's ridiculous. Cops'll hear everything we say. I don't need that."

"Take him for a walk."

Lawrence started laughing, "take a prisoner for a walk. I'm going to be able to get the police to let him take a stroll around the city with me."

"Yes, we do it every other night. Mon fils, the chief of police is Irish and was at our wedding. Judi's "associates" contribute thousands of dollars to the Police Benevolent Society every year. My husband is a proud and well-known man in this city. He just has to pay off Constanzo's debt to the fucking Catholic bingo players."

"So I just walk on down to the police station tomorrow and they let him out?"

"He'll have an ankle bracelet on his leg. Ooh, how I hate that damn bracelet. It bangs against my shin when we're ..."

"Stop, I don't need to know."

"Petra, you seem to have some problem back down in Virginia Park?"

"Virginia City, Ma Mere. Why do you ask me this?'

"You have been getting phone calls from there. I took messages. Let me get them," said Evelyn. She paused, perusing the categories for Jeopardy! Lawrence could make a good guess about whom called.

"Two women, one sounded maybe as old as me. The other a child? And yes, an older man, a doctor somebody. Here are the messages, Petra."

The man was Judge Sauers wanting to know when Lawrence would be back running the newspaper. The two women were mother and daughter, Susan and Kat Yoder. Kat was after the same answer he would give Judge Sauers tomorrow.

"She's not as old as you. She's just got a deep voice. I need to know what you think about this problem I have with her, Mon Mere."

"You've never asked me for advice about your women. I know how much you were destroyed by the woman in Western New York."

"Eileen, Eileen Ledger. Yes, it almost totaled me. No, it's ..."

Lawrence could not convey how deeply he felt about Susan Yoder's abortion. "She killed your grandchild."

Lawrence regretted the words as soon as they left his mouth.

"Mon Dieu! What are you saying?" Tears formed as she cried.

Lawrence had been wrong to word it as such but this was his mother. His mother had gone through transgressions and battles far worse than this. He was surprised at her frantic reaction.

He put his arm around her as she held her hands against the flow of tears coming from her eyes. She nestled her head on his shoulder.

"I'm sorry I shouldn't have said it that way. I don't even know all that happened. All that I know comes from a phone call from her daughter Kat, the younger woman that called here. I talked to Kat about running the paper while I was gone. This was after McVeigh's execution. Kat let slip that her mother ... Her mother and I had been having a very close sexual relationship. Kat told me she was still in the hospital after the abortion."

"Petra, you didn't know she was having an abortion?"

"Mon Mere, I didn't know she was pregnant."

"Mon Dieu, how sad, sad for both of you. Have you called her?"

"No. I can't. I'm too involved in this McVeigh execution. I don't have time to ..."

"Petra, you shame me. This woman ..."

"Susan. I don't feel sorry for her. Not yet any way. I am not going to confront her hundreds of miles away over a telephone line. It is too difficult and way too painful to do that."

Evelyn raised her dampened face and gently kissed Lawrence on his cheek. "You are a good man. I know she's in pain because I know for her to have called here she must love you deeply. You are right. It cannot be fair for her or you to face this ... I don't know what to call it. I want you to listen to me. Do you love me, Mon Fils?"

"Yes, but of course Mon Mere. Why?"

"Do you trust in me, see me as a person who loves you and loves helping people?"

"Your point?"

"I gather that if you need to see Judi then you have much on your mind. You will probably be many days, maybe weeks resolving this McVeigh problem. Am I right?"

"Of course. My guess is a week or two."

"I will call her, Mon Fils."

Lawrence started to protest but Evelyn pulled his face to hers and shut his mouth with a kiss.

"She will know you have love for her and will be with her as soon as you can. She will know I am your mother and what I tell her is a reflection of you, my son."

***

Lawrence just shook his head as he and Judi walked up North Washington Ave.

"I can't believe it. They let you just walk out, with me no tail."

"But Peter, I've got my cute little ankle bracelet. There's no escape."

Lawrence had grown to love Judiah Dougherty, not as a father but as a close friend. He was the kind of friend you fight for, even kill for.

"So I gather from my mother you can even bop her with the ankle bracelet on?"

"Peter, you don't need to talk like that. Doesn't it embarrass you talking about your mother?" Judi put his arm around Lawrence's shoulders and laughed.

"So what's so important you got me signed me out for my daily exercise?"

"You know about the Timothy McVeigh execution, right?"

"Yes, there are many who felt he got a raw deal. Should have been life. That fucking looney-tune Manson sure deserves it more than him."

"McVeigh and I had some dealings a few years ago. He basically went off on the Ruby Ridge and Waco massacres. You know about them?"

"Yeah, a bit. Don't know the details but from what I heard the Feds killed off some innocent people."

"Children included, Judi. One fucking sniper shot a woman and the baby she was carrying. Blew the kid's head off."

"So you're involved with ... or maybe it's better to think you were involved with ..."

"Neither. I felt exactly like he did about the killings but did nothing. McVeigh requested that I be a witness to his execution."

"Oh, that's bad shit Peter. You actually saw him get wasted?"

"It was nothing Judi. You ever have to put down a pet?"

"Yeah, my dad had an old setter, Irish and as red as an orange peel. Took her behind the garage, over on Emmet Street. Had himself a little .22. Put it to her ear and ..."

Lawrence could not believe it. Tears were coming to Judi's eyes, this from a man that Lawrence was sure offed a couple of people in his time. There was something different about a pet, though.

Lawrence let Judi's malapropism go by. An Irish setter cannot be as red as an orange.

"McVey just laid there. Men put needles into his legs and he fell asleep, asleep forever. Scary, might even be more scary than hanging or electrocution."

"You talked with him before they did him?"

"Yeah, which is why I'm here. How much range they give you with that ankle bracelet? Come on, they let you hump my mom. How about we stop up the street at Brixx Grille and Tavern for a quick one? It's just around the building between here and Dix"

"I don't know, Petra. They catch me, they'll slap a couple more weeks on me. Maybe send me to the state pen to finish it out."

"Your call," said Lawrence as they continued up South Washington Avenue. "I can't tell you everything, but McVeigh lead me to a stash confronting all of his plans for the bombing. It included an escape route."

As they neared the turn south to the Brixx Tavern, Judi stopped and held Lawrence's arm. He looked up and down South Washington, pulled Lawrence through the parking lot and checked out South Dix Court to see if they were being followed.

"Just one cool one, Peter. They'll never smell it on me."

Judi scanned the tavern for blue suits or anybody that might recognize him. He led Lawrence to a booth in the back near the restrooms. Judi sat facing away from the men's room to avoid being seen, then raised two fingers and out loud yelled, "bartender two cold ones right here, if you please."

Lawrence never failed to be astounded by Judi Dougherty.

"Judi, the problem McVeigh had was that he got caught. He got caught by some redneck farm boy. That ended it for him. Everybody thought he was headed back to Michigan where Terry Nichols lived, but he wasn't."

"How do you know that? He tell you?"

"No, I figured it out by following his route. Why did he not have a license plate on his vehicle?"

"So he wouldn't get IDed at the scene," said Judi as he downed the beer mug and ordering two more before the waiter got five feet from their booth.

"It wouldn't be the license that was easily identified. It would be the car leaving the explosion. I don't know how many times I tried to get a license plate number of some asshole to report him to the police. Never got one. It's almost impossible."

"Don't make much difference Petey," said Dougherty. "What would the police do if you did get his number?"

"I'm guessing McVeigh was headed to Winnipeg Canada, going straight up Route 81. If his plate number was caught by someone, he could never get past the border. They'd be waiting. He gambled that it was safer to have no plate than to have someone get the plate number by pure chance. He probably had plates and would have put them on when he got near the border."

Judi raised his hand for a third beer but Lawrence stopped him, "no more, Judi. They'll jail me for letting you get drunk during your exercise period. Still doesn't make much sense, does it?"

"Peter, I think you're obsessed with this. He could've been going anywhere. There's no way that you can show me that he was headed ..."

Lawrence pulled out a AAA road map. "This was in his satchel."

"The satchel he lead you to?"

"This map and a bunch of contacts, people he sold arms to and bought from. There were ammunitions dealers all over the country and Canada. I finally had a chance to go through his satchel last night at my mother's." Lawrence failed to mention that he had also found five 3.5 inch computer discs. "He was not headed for Winnipeg. He was headed to Thunder Bay."

"Petey, what do I have to do with any of this?"

"That's what struck me about McVey's leading me to his cache. Same thing. Why did McVeigh lead me to his hidden papers? They had nothing to do with me. But I was wrong. My name's on the map. Look just above the Indian name. See it? Says meet with Grayrock and Lawrence."

Lawrence looked at his watch. Time was running out for Judi's exercise period so he had to get to why he needed Judi's help, "Judi, I've got to get there."

Lawrence quelled Dougherty's obvious rejoinder. "Even if I'm not the Lawrence in these notes, I need to know what McVeigh had planned. I need contacts in and around Thunder

Bay and I need help to get my personal weapons across the border. Obviously his plans included connected people. It wouldn't be much of an escape plan to get stopped in the middle of a large Canadian city. I don't have connections and that's what I need from you."

"Peter, you're obsessed, that's for sure. But you're right. If someone else tracks this down, you could wind up as an accomplice in the Oklahoma bombings. Fuckin' government don't give a shit how little evidence there is. They'd just arrest you because your name was on that map."

Judi grabbed Lawrence's wrist and looked at his watch, "damn, not enough time for another brew. Let's go, before they come after me."

When they got back to the police station, Judi stopped Lawrence at the front door, "more I think about it, more you better watch your ass. That map you got? McVeigh's fingerprints are all over it. You'd be dead meat if somebody turns that over to the Feds. Makes you look like an accessory. Get rid of it. Burn it. You already know what's on it. It'll do you no good, only fuck you over. I got more weeks in here. Can't help you ..."

Lawrence shrugged and Judi grabbed Lawrence's shoulders and looked him in the eye, "no, I couldn't do much myself even if I was out. You'll get a call. You might not like the conditions but I'll try to get them as less demanding as I can."

He pulled Lawrence into a hug, patted his back with heavy, knurled hands three times, and said, "tell Evelyn I miss her real bad. I'm starting to look at some of these other scum bags in here. Might give'm a try. Don't tell her that! I'm just jerking you around."

***

"Okay mother, where did you shack up with Judi? I mean how could you have got him all the way here and back in that short a period of time? That would be one quick fuck."

Evelyn Southern smiled at her son, "who said we came here?"

"So you took him to some hotel room for a quickie?"

"You know, it is a real shame that prisoners have to sleep on those metal bed springs and skinny mattresses. I don't know how they can even go to sleep."

"I don't believe you! They let you go into his cell and do the deed?"

"Best orgasm I ever had. Was like fucking John Dillinger."

Lawrence quickly ended the conversation before she compared Judi to John Dillinger's famously body part.

"Mon Fils there was a call for you. You are to meet with Caesar Constanzo tonight at 11:33 PM. Here are the directions."

***

"Mr. Lawrence, I am glad to finally meet you. I have known your mother for her many years with Judi. Lovely woman. I regret not meeting her in my younger days," said Caesar Constanzo as he greeted Lawrence at his front door.

Lawrence was always amazed at the number of men sexually attracted to his mother. "Judi has spoken very well about you Mr. Constanzo. Or should I call you Dom?"

"It must be my spitting image of Marlon Brando," Constanzo responded, wrapping his two hands around Lawrence's right hand. "No, Caesar is fine. It made me a king in my dear mother's eyes, now long gone but forever remembered. Please come with me to my library. This way."

The house did not impress Lawrence. He had thought Constanzo would live on an immense estate with high walls surrounded by acres of forests and patrol dogs. Constanzo lived in a row house in the Little Italy part of the city. The maple paneled library shelved with books from floor to ceiling was quite impressive.

"I feared your mother might have followed you with a gun to shoot me. For some reason she is blaming me for poor Judi's arrest and incarceration."

While never having met Caesar Constanzo face-to-face, Lawrence was well aware of Constanzo's get down to business and cut the bull shit method of dealing.

"I can't help you Peter. You do not mind if I use your first name?"

"Lawrence, most call me Lawrence. They think it's my first name."

"Fine Lawrence. You are dealing with the Mafia. I am the Consigliore for this family but I am Consigliore for a very small town which is more Irish than Italian."

"I'm aware of that."

"Good, then you probably know that our venues are very small compared to say New York or Jersey or even Chicago. You also know what quid pro quo means?"

"I have no problem paying you in kind."

"Yes Lawrence I know you are a hard man and I know you are a made man."

Lawrence was stunned by Constanzo's knowledge of his killings, but held his tongue.

"Yes, we find more about people than the police. We also recognize a need for men like you, men who could help our family. Unfortunately, Canada is not one of our markets. Especially the Thunder Bay area. You know how many Italian speaking citizens live there? None! How many Italian restaurants do you think are there?"

"It's not that small a city. My guess would be a population of a couple hundred thousand?"

"Just short of a hundred and ten thousand. It only has four Italian restaurants. No, Lawrence we have nothing in Thunder Bay to help you and no way you could help us. Place is heavy in frogs, though."

"Frogs? Excuse me, Mr. Constanzo but what's frog's ..."

"French, Lawrence. I'm sure you know Canada is heavy with the French. It is probably why the Italian population is rare in Thunder Bay."

"Are you pulling my leg? Are the French and Italians still at each other's throats?"

"Yes, Italians, the syndicate. It is our cause célèbre. It is our raison d'être and will always be. You do know the French are responsible for the syndicate being called the Mafia?"

Lawrence did not know that and Constanzo continued, "Morte Alla Francia Italia Anela. Translated as 'Death to the French.'"

Lawrence could recognize that Constanzo, the elder consigliore of a Mafia family, loved telling stories and legends like many aged leaders. He was on a tear. Lawrence had enough respect for Constanzo and knew enough to show him the respect a capo deserved, "how did that come about?"

"Lawrence, you are a wise man. Judi says you are a newspaper editor. It is a story you should run in your paper. It is a love story. Many years ago, hundreds, back to the thirteenth century in Palermo, in Sicilia, in Italy, a beautiful young lady and her lover went to the Church of the Holy Ghost to be married at its altar. They could not find the padre so the young man let his betrothed wait in front of the church while he searched for the good father. Her heart was beating, throbbing with happiness when Druet, a drunken Sergeant of the French garrison, came up behind her, grabbed her, ripped open her bodice and buried his face in her pure white bosom. She screamed and tore herself from him. In seeking to escape, her dainty feet slipped on the church steps and she fell. Her beautiful head smashed into the church cornice. She lay in a pool of blood where her lover found her dead, the blood from her brow oozing over her long tresses .."

"Tresses? Right?" Lawrence's smirk drew a smile from Caesar Constanzo.

"Let me finish, my friend. Her lover caught Druet, knocked him to the earth and drove his steel stiletto deep into the blackguard's heart."

"And this is how the name Mafia came into existence?"

"Morte alia Francia! Death to the French! A crowd drew around the dead child and her lover. Silence filled the church steps until someone yelled Morte Alla Francia Italia Anela, death to the French is Italy's cry! For three days the citizen's roamed the streets, slaughtering the hated French. Knowing the French would retaliate, the citizens of Palermo formed a secret society using the initials of their call to arms "MAFIA!"

"This is how the mafia became ..."

Lawrence responded, "the hidden enemy of the dastardly French bastards."

"Yes, my friend. The mafia went out and attacked the rich and mighty, fighting for the poor and downtrodden."

Lawrence had a deep respect for Constanzo and he also liked living but he could not resist some light hearted banter at the expense of the old, Italian capo, "I think you made all of this up. It sounds like you're describing the movie Zorro."

Constanzo stared into Lawrence's eyes, not missing the easy smile Lawrence wore. "Yes, my role was played by Anthony Hopkins."

As Constanzo turned to his liquor cabinet and poured out a scotch for Lawrence, both men began laughing. Lawrence had not been asked if he liked scotch but was glad to have it.

"Here's an envelope for you. You will find tickets in it for an airplane flight, first to Minneapolis and then on to Thunder Bay. There is also a hotel reservation. None of these can be traced to you or me. They are open reservations so be careful with them. Since you have not made plans for your return, there is a voucher for return flights."

"I asked Judi about getting weapons across ..."

"Unless you need to have your own firearms, there is no reason to take guns with you. On the outside of the envelope, turn it over, call that number when you deplane in Thunder Bay. A man will deliver a car to you and he'll bring with him a variety of small arms weapons. If you like, he will also chauffeur you while you're in Canada. Knowing a little about you, my guess is you would prefer being on your own?"

"That's right. But wait a second. After all you went through how can I pay off this ..."

"You don't. I am not doing this for you or for Judi or even your lovely mother. I am doing this for Timothy McVeigh."

Lawrence was stunned, "What's McVeigh got to do with you or your family?"

"How many did he kill? One hundred and sixty eight? Yes, one hundred and sixty eight, most Federal employees. Were some FBI?"

"Yes, I'm not sure how many."

"We fight the same enemy, Lawrence. Our family is just that, family. You could look at all the syndicates as tribes. We are the basis of life on this planet, Lawrence. The owners of property and rulers of slaves, we are not. We share our family's existence through work and pride. That is not what this country is now. I don't even know how to configure what we have become in this country but it is the rulers and the slaves. People don't need air to breathe or food to eat in the United States. They feast on ownership and lucre."

"The United States is ruled by money merchants, is the best I can come up with Caesar," said Lawrence. "The world was hunter and gatherers. The people on the earth lived as tribes and life was sharing to survive. Now life is owners and their slaves. Agriculture, owning and ruling the land. It came right out of the Mideast. The blood tie that kept people together has become property, ownership. I don't know much about your organization but I do know you take care of your own."

Constanzo spoke, "I have only one small recommendation for you when you make your trip. I have talked with my people in New York and they do have ties in Canada. None in Thunder Bay, though. Mostly they use their sources for smuggling drugs into the states by way of the St. Lawrence and at times across the Great Lakes. But they did say they have used in the past sources in the Winnipeg and Thunder Bay area for arms smuggling across the lakes. That might be where you should start since McVeigh I believe was also an arms salesman in the states, right?"

"Yeah, that he was. Probably I'll go after information through as many gun and hunting shops as I can find. Thanks. They could maybe link me to McVeigh's plans," said Lawrence. He intentionally did not mention Greyrock's name.

"There's one other item that should interest you. The Western New York syndicate put a hit out on you soon after you left Buffalo."

"Shit, I've been up there a couple times since then. Their shooter must really suck."

"No, Judi paid a visit to some dago named Dr. Nuevello? He was very apologetic to Judi and the hit has been rescinded."

***

Evelyn drove Lawrence to Philadelphia International Airport to catch his 9:55 am flight to Minneapolis. He would arrive around noon with two hours to catch his connection to Thunder Bay at 2:10 pm. Unless there were flight delays, Lawrence should be in Thunder Bay somewhere around 5:00 pm. As to be expected, Evelyn brought up Lawrence's relationship with Susan Yoder.

"You do not understand women Peter! This woman is in her late fifties. You are thirty four. If she has a baby with you, she'll be almost seventy when the child graduates from high school. Sacre bleu, Mon Fils! You expect too much from her and ..."

Lawrence hated the times when he and his mother parted in the midst of disagreement, "Mother, and I say mother because I am an American. It is none of your business."

He had already yanked his suitcase out of the back seat and leaned into the driver side window, kissing her left cheek quickly before the power window rolled caught his head. He waved and went into the United Airlines terminal. When he opened the ticket envelopes, he noticed the cost to the Constanzo syndicate for his trip. The $1,500 that he saw was only for airfare one way. Lawrence did not want to think about the total cost of this trip he was making. As usual the plane sat on the runway for nearly a half hour before takeoff, making Lawrence and the other passengers that had to connections to make in Minneapolis look at their watches frequently. They had a good pilot and once airborne he notched up the throttle and was able to land almost on time.

The Delta flight to Thunder Bay took off at 3:30 pm, over an hour delay but it did not matter to Lawrence since it was the last leg on his journey.

Lawrence brought with him McVeigh's leather satchel from the apple barrel. He had gone through it twice now and most of the information dealt with arms dealer contacts. One set of papers answered one question about Timothy McVeigh's mysterious life. Like many veterans of Desert Storm, McVeigh was exhausted by three months of continual stress while waiting for an enemy gunner to put a bullet in his head or blow up his Bradley. That kind of pressure takes time to dissipate. As soon as he returned to Fort Bragg, he was pressured to return to the Gulf War. With gung ho veterans all around him screaming they were ready to go back, McVeigh signed up to tryout as a Special Forces soldier but he failed all the tests and resigned from the military. His duty to his country had run out.

Immediately McVey was contacted by a private military company known as Bloodcreek, who operated a paramilitary training facility in North Carolina. Kirk King, the owner and president of Bloodcreek, was a wealthy land owner and part of his land holdings included a river. The creek water flowed from cypress trees whose tannin sap would seasonally turn the stream blood red. King himself was an ex-Navy Seal and used his wealth to support the Republican Party. This gained King many no-bid contracts. King's organization had an extensive program of examining discharged military personnel for potential recruits in their organization.

Bloodcreek wanted Timothy McVeigh. King's analysis of McVeigh was based on McVeigh's record of kills and his weapons expertise shown during the Iraq war. Bloodcreek had been there as a contractor and seen McVeigh in action. McVeigh would fit well in their training programs: hand-to-hand combat, precision arms marksmanship, and operations using armored personnel carriers.

The fifteen page missive Bloodcreek sent McVeigh was in front of Lawrence. McVeigh was a hot candidate in spite of failing at the special forces tests. McVeigh had thought deeply enough about Kirk King's offer to do research on Bloodcreek. His notes demonstrated just how distraught he was about government, especially the United States Government's military industrial attack on the freedom of the citizens. Lawrence read through McVeigh's annotations on the letter King had sent to McVeigh. King provided personal monetary support to specific candidates during elections. He spent millions of dollars digging up incriminating actions by the opposing candidates. Those same elected officials ensured that millions dollars in contract money was sent King's way. Bloodcreek would never have to put in a bid for contracts. One of King's subsidiary companies was paid $21 million dollars to guard the chief of a coalition authority, without any bid. Another branch of Bloodcreek shipped cases of automatic firearms to Iraq, no permits and no tariffs.

McVeigh's notes included hired killers provided by Bloodcreek. Bloodcreek security staff in Iraq shot nearly 200 Iraq citizens, not only shooting first but being in violation of the company's own alcohol and drug policy for weapons use. It was a deadly game that Bloodcreek paramilitaries called the fastest gun. McVeigh had found information indicating that Kirk King himself had been accused of murder, perhaps while trying to be the fastest gun. His military arms specialists were accused of using prostitutes, including child prostitutes. McVeigh's last notes were, "great, just what I want to be. A mercenary who shoots people money for no reason other than, fucks little kids, crashes cars with bombs into schools, and says here is America, a force , a culture, where everybody is a gun for hire."

One small notation puzzled Lawrence. Bloodcreek had just obtained a contract of several millions of dollars from the CIA to locate and assassinate the top officials of Al Qaeda. Kirk King had written to McVeigh that this would be a good assignment for him with his experience in the Mid-east and his extensive abilities with arms.

This information astounded Lawrence. Bloodcreek's headquarters were very near Virginia City. He had had no idea they even existed, let alone were a paramilitary, billion dollar industry. They were another provider of soldiers to the royalty.

He replaced McVeigh's documents in the leather satchel and looked out the plane's window. Land was finally visible after hours of flying over Lake Superior.

As the plane neared Thunder Bay, a very large island identified by the pilot as Isla Royale National Park, came into view which the pilot. It was less than forty miles from Thunder Bay and belonged to the state of Michigan. The pilot mentioned that Isle Royale is world famous for its long-term studies of the wolf (Canis lupus) and moose (Alces alces) as a predator/prey ecosystem.

The plane banked sharply to Lawrence's left readying for the landing. The pilot pointed out the Sleeping Giant Provincial Park which got its name from the view as seen from Thunder Bay. The cliffs, valleys, and mesa cuestas are the framework of what looks like a Sleeping Giant. The native Ojibway legend identifies the giant land mass as Nana bijou, who was turned to stone when the secret location of a rich silver mine, now known as Silver Islet, was disclosed to white men.

From the air Thunder Bay Airport is tiny and as the plane descended, it did not get much bigger. It had only one runway that could land the Delta jet. Lawrence was not the only one smiling when the brakes were applied and the plane brought to a stop before winding up in the river just south of the airport.

Thunder Bay's airport terminal is smaller than most K-Marts. The walk to, thru, and out of the airport took minutes. Parked in front of the airport exit was a black Jeep Cherokee with the words Nardo Harbor Funeral Service printed in grey across the side. A tall, extremely thin, curly black-haired teenager with an obvious Italian family inherited nose, stood leaning against the passenger side door holding a sign with "Lawrence" written in red marker.

"I'm Lawrence. Am I dead?"

The boy smiled. "Not yet. Give us a chance though", and shook Lawrence's hand. He handed Lawrence the car keys.

"You want me to drive?"

"Family called, said get you a car. My Papa guessed you would want to avoid the Mounties. Drive our Cherokee and nobody bothers you. My name is Tony, Little Tony Nardo. Actually my name is Antonio Nardo the fourth, but Antonio three and I are the only ones still alive Everybody calls us Big Tony and Little Tony even though my Papa's only five-three. You ever make mention of his being short ... Well, you'd be floating up from the bottom of Lake Superior in about September. Go ahead, you drive. I'll direct you."

Little Tony took Lawrence's suitcase and tossed it on the rear seat, sat down in the passenger seat, and gave Lawrence directions. "Catch the expressway, Route 61. You want to go north. You'll make a turn in about five or six kilometers."

"Miles, Tony. I'm from the States remember."

"Yeah, sorry bout that. Gonna be more like nine, ten miles. You're looking to pick up Harbour Expressway, Route 11 goin' east."

"Where you have me being put up?"

"Family said you wanted something not fancy, so you're at the Voyager, about a block from our business."

Little Tony Nardo reached behind him for a box as Lawrence hit 100 kilometers per hour. "You need a gun, right?"

"Yep, makes it easier getting through customs. What do you have?"

"How about a Ruger SR9c 9 mm stainless steel, small and only weighs 23 ounces?"

"That's good. I've shot Ruger's before. Very reliable and handle well. Sighting is great. Only problem I see with it is that it has a low scare factor. Idiots you point it at think it's a toy. That's their problem though. Holster?"

"Didn't know how you'd carry, so here," said Little Tony, pulling out a shoulder holster, a belt holster, and an ankle holster.

"Here's Route 11, where to?"

"Two miles, or so the expressway becomes Main Street. It's a dead end. You go left. It'll be Fort William Road for about two or three miles then it becomes Water Street. Water becomes Cumberland which'll put us at Nardo's Harbor Funeral Home in about fifteen or twenty minutes."

"Lot of boat docks down here. Pretty big railroad yards, too."

"Most of what you see is sitting there rusting. Things ain't the same as years ago. That's what Papa told me. He was here when he was a kid."

Lawrence was not seeing anything in Canada that he had not seen time and again in most urban locales in the States, especially the older cities that never regained industrial development. Thunder Bay's waterfront had been a shipping mecca during Canada's grain, forestry, pulp and paper years. Lawrence went by grain towers and silos left over from those years. Railroads ran agriculture, lumbering, and manufacturing right into Thunder Bay from Western Canada, shipping across the Great Lakes up the St. Lawrence Seaway to North America's East Coast. There was no other way short of trucking to the Pacific Coast which had one major problem; no highways. That is no highways until the Trans-Canada Highway was finished.

"Wow, look at this! You guys actual have a Dairy Queen," said Lawrence as he passed Clarke Street and the DQ. "Jesus, there are more used car lots, auto repair shops, and rusted vehicles abandoned on side streets here than there is in Buffalo!"

As Lawrence expected, Nardo Harbor Funeral Home was in the center of the Italian district of Thunder Bay with a view of the harbor, as its title suggested. The harbor could only be seen by walking or driving down Powley Street for a little less than a half mile. Within yards of Nardo's was the Voyager Motel where Tony's father had booked a room for Lawrence. Considering it was the middle of the summer, Lawrence would have expected at least one other guest at the Voyager. There were none. The development on the Northwest side of Thunder Bay was single family, frame houses with neat lawns. The proximity to Lake Superior verified the few boats backed into driveways awaiting the weekends and vacations. Little Tony told Lawrence this was considered the Bay Algoma area. It was almost one hundred percent Finnish and Italian families. They negotiated a peace in the 60's. Little Tony made it clear to Lawrence that while Tony Senior insisted there was a negotiated peace, the Finns living in this neighborhood understood they did as Tony Nardo told them. If not, he would graciously provide them with a free service, courtesy of his Harbor View facility.

"My father has directed me to invite you to dinner at our home tonight," said Little Tony as Lawrence, dropped left him off at the funeral home. "You need be here around six or six-thirty. No, you cannot bypass my father's invitation."

Nardo's Funeral Home was an old two story school building modified to include mortuary facilities and fitted with steel doors on the lower levels, including the garages. Lawrence guessed this was to prevent raids by the authorities. Little Tony told him that no matter what was going down, never call the Royal Canadian Mounted Police. Little Tony warned Lawrence to ignore anybody roaming around the motel especially at unusual hours.

Lawrence was tired. It had been a long trip from Philadelphia to The Voyager Motel on the edge of Lake Superior. He needed a shower and really wanted to sleep even though it was only a little after 6:00 PM. He had to accept dinner with the Nardo's so he showered, got into the bed, and figured that Little Tony would call him from the motel lobby to wake him. Just before nodding off, he remembered Little Tony's package and checked out the Ruger SR9c 9 mm stainless steel pistol. Being new Lawrence noticed its chambering was a bit tight so he pumped it a few times without cartridges, then added three cartridges and chambered the rounds. It was still a bit stiff. The ankle holster was probably useless but one never knows. The shoulder holster leather was also rigid, he would have to pick up some leather softener to loosen it. Most likely he would keep the pistol in the belt holster, the grip facing forward and off his left hip. This meant he would have to wear a coat to keep it hidden. He started going through his list of gun dealers but once he put his head back on the pillow, he was out.

***

It was Friday June 15th, less than a week since Timothy McVeigh had been given his lethal dose of drugs. Lawrence was very close to giving up. Did he really care whether his name was in McVeigh's secret papers? He did, which was why he laid back in his motel bed after spending the day trying to track down Charlie Greyrock. He began planning his itinerary for tomorrow.

The day had started out well, a bit cool at 14^0 C, which in his world was about 58^0 F. The perpetual lake effect kept it windy. Lawrence had two choices to start his morning. He had a list of arms dealers from Tony Nardo and the phone directory, mostly hunting establishments. The list totaled over twenty locations, nearly impossible to do in one day. His advantage was that he was seeking Charlie Greyrock a Native American, although he was probably a native Canadian. He searched through the phone book for First Nation connections and found over a hundred. Which connection would have a data base with names? His first choice was The Association of Native Child & Family Services of Ontario on Anemki Drive, a good ten or so miles south of the motel. It gave Lawrence a chance to grab some breakfast and coffee on the way. He drove almost the identical route as from the airport but made a turn on James Street south, going over a meandering river that connected to City Road. At Mission Road he made a left; Anemki was just two blocks south.

Child and Family Services was in a three story, modern building in suite 106. Lawrence's approach was simple. He was an editor for a newspaper in Virginia City, Virginia, USA who was doing a feature on Native Americans living in the Virginia City area who may have relatives living outside the States. He explained that when interviewing tribes and their families back in Virginia, he had met a family who had a long lost relative that had emigrated north during the recession. The clincher to this fabricated story was that the family had made a fortune from selling their land to the U. S. Navy for an airbase. This meant that the itinerant relative had a fortune just waiting for him in Virginia.

The Native Child and Family services representative fell for the story. It bothered Lawrence that he was lying through his teeth to her since she was very helpful to him. She explained to Lawrence that the information she had was privileged so she could not let him examine the files, but if he had the time to wait she would go through them looking for Grayrock. He did wait, for three hours. She did not find anybody with the name Grayrock since her service department was probably too limited. A Child and Family service had contact mostly with native Canadians of the child-bearing age. She did however give Lawrence three other organizations that might be made helpful.

At the First Nations Organization facility he was referred to Lakehead University. By now it was nearly two in the afternoon and he was ready to give up. Instead he decided to take one more stab at tribal contacts through the University. Tomorrow would be Saturday and public service organizations would be closed. If he drew a blank, he would have to try the hunting and arms sales stores over the weekend. He headed to Lakehead University on Oliver Road.

Lawrence was in an area of Thunder Bay unlike the urban semi-slum city. Here Thunder Bay was a modern city with forests and well paved streets he had seen so far. He drove by the Thunder Bay Country Golf Club, long, green and picturesque. Lawrence guessed golf was played maybe four months out of the year this far north. Regardless of the limited use, it painted a better picture of Thunder Bay than the Bay area and Algoma.

The woman at his last stop had been quite accurate about Lakehead's dedication to Aboriginal Cultural & Support Services. Lawrence quickly discovered the professionalism at the front service desk of the Lakehead administrative building. The receptionist was prepared for Lawrence's arrival and greeted him warmly. While she was not a native Canadian, she knew the college and explained to Lawrence how the university was set up to provide a culturally supportive environment to all Aboriginal students whether they are Status, Non-Status, Inuit, or Métis. The university is there to assist all Aboriginal students academically as well as to those only interested in learning more about Aboriginal culture.

A young undergraduate student approached the front desk and was introduced to Lawrence. She escorted him to the top floor of the building and to the office of Aboriginal Studies where he was introduced to the Aboriginal Student Liaison/Advisor Student. She shook his hand, asked him to take a seat next to a huge picture window while she called up a graduate student to assist him. The view from Lakehead University was breathtaking. Lawrence could actually see the fabled giant on the Sibley Peninsula lying on its back across Thunder Bay.

The undergrad was a young native girl from Winnipeg who was studying to become a social services director when she returned home. She escorted Lawrence to another room where she logged on to a computer. As she searched for Charlie Grayrock, she read out so many details about native Canadians and their needs that Lawrence was lost. He wondered whether her propensity for data and statistics would be of any help to the families without income or a reservation on which to live. In the states he had seen many inspired college graduates taking on the underprivileged, believing the bar graphs and PCs could be of help. She found nothing. The Lakehead University aboriginal culture resources were the most inclusive in Canada. Charlie Grayrock did not exist.

Lawrence was ready to thank her and leave but a thought running through his mind made him hesitate. He asked her if she had access to information that covered all of North America. Smiling she returned to the keyboard and hit pay dirt. While she could not find Charlie Grayrock specifically, she did come up with a tribal name having a Grayrock in it. Charlie was not Canadian, he was a Comanche. There are no Comanches in Canada. Lawrence pushed her to search further but she told him once again the Comanche populations in Canada are nonexistent.

Lawrence was ready to concede defeat and return to Virginia. On his way back to The Voyager Motel he bought a bottle of Chevis Regal. Sip by sip he told himself to give up. The more he drank the more he kept thinking, go home there are no Comanches in Canada. When his sober self-woke, his Scotch induced cognitive errors came to light. He still had that list of arms dealers.

"I'm sure if I had asked that dear graduate student for Mafia names, there would be none in Canada," thinking out loud in the shower while the alcohol tainted thin layer of sweat formed from a restless sleep washed away.

***

Saturday's weather was not much different from Friday's except the wind had picked up. It was still early for a Saturday, but he could drive around to some of the addresses for gun shops and maybe get a handle on the chances of any of them knowing the Comanche. He headed south down Cumberland Street. The rail yards and their carriers dominated the east side providing no view of the lake. Lawrence went past the address he was given and made a U-turn at John Street. Driving slowly down the street he could find no stores at John Street and Water. All he saw were tractor trailers lined up, most with their tail bumpers backed up to buildings. He stopped at one that had "shooting range" painted the side walls. It was open. From the look of the counter it must have once been an auto repair shop. There were old labels on the shelves for batteries, ignition coils, and other automobile parts. The shelves were empty but a sign above the door leading to the rear of the store read "6-port, 20-yard range that has been approved for .22 caliber rifles and all calibers of handguns." It was written in English and French.

The man behind the counter spoke to Lawrence, "need some shootin' practice, buddy?"

"No, I'm looking for a gun store called "Armoury Specialties, LTD?"

"Yer here, bub. What ya need?"

Lawrence knew by the accent that the man was an American, maybe from Chicago, "some 9's for a Ruger."

"Ya licensed to carry a Ruger?"

"Nope. It's back home in New Orleans. Ammo's cheaper up here I've been told. You can do a shipment for me?"

"Against the law. No can do."

"Sorry to bother you," said Lawrence and turned to leave.

"Hey, 'for ya go, how'd you get our name?"

"Indian I met in New York gave it to me. I'm up here on business and remembered him telling me about you guys."

Lawrence decided to take a chance. Either he would get thrown out of the auto store turned armory or get the information he had been chasing down. "Charlie led me to you. I guess he was bullshitting me. You know Charlie?"

"Fucking Redskin. Damn my Daddy told me never trust an injun'. Yeah, I know good old Charlie."

Despite his comments, the man's face showed no anger. The man chuckled a bit and spoke, "Charlie nail you for something?"

"I don't know if I was chiseled but he sold me an AK47, totally automatic. Illegal but he got it for me."

"It's what Charlie does for us. See those trailers out there? They get empty, Charlie comes along and fills 'em up."

"So the trailers are Armoury Specialties LTD?"

"Sure are. We get word of a raid and they're gone. Even if we're busted, we don't have title to them. Say how's about I sneak your 9's order through? How much a box of Remingtons go for in the states?"

Lawrence had to make a legitimate estimate. He had never bought ammunition for a 9 mm, only ammo for his Remington and a shot gun, "box is around $40 American but you can get 10 boxes at $37.50 a pop."

"Shit, they'se stealin' from ya. How's $35 each?"

"I'll give it some thought. I'll stop here on my way back," said Lawrence walking toward the door. "Say, how do you ever get in contact with Charlie? I tried to get a hold of him when I came up here Thursday but can't find his name anywhere."

"Nobody can. Injun don't give nobody his place of business. He just knows when to stop by, that's all. Guess he's got a good mind for knowing his customers. Sorry," said the man turning to go into the back room. At least Lawrence now knew there is an Indian named Charlie and that sometimes Charlie appears in Thunder Bay.

"Hey, you know you might just get lucky. He's a drinker but then all them damn Redskins like to put down the hooch.

That's why we kicked their asses and took all their land. If Charlie's in town, he usually hangs around The Wharf It Down bar. It's across from the loading docks and railroad yards. Might just catch 'em there tonight. Never know. We're open here 'til twelve, so if you want the 9's stop by. Might go to $34.50 by tonight. See ya."

Lawrence got in Nardo's Cherokee and drove back up Water Street to check if The Wharf It Down actually existed. It did, but from its shabby looks it might not survive falling apart much longer.

***

Lawrence and Little Tony sat in the Cherokee across from The Wharf It Down bar, waiting for some patrons to appear. It was still early for a Saturday night. Lawrence would have preferred checking out the bar and looking for Charlie by himself, but as soon as he mentioned the bar to Big Tony Nardo, he had no choice but to take Little Tony along. There was a reason. The Nardo's owned the bar and the bar was not just a bar.

"You got a gaming facility in that building?"

"Hard to believe, ain't it? See that big galoot coming out to have a smoke? That's Otto. Pop gave him ownership couple years ago."

"Ownership with a piece of the profits, right?"

"Getting to know us, hey Mr. Lawrence?"

"Lawrence is just fine. I'm old enough without some goomba Italian kid putting me down. Why'd people, especially tourists, come here to this dump?"

"Tourists don't. Who does come are natives, Indians. Especially Natives living on the dole. Government catches them putting down bets and they'll lose their government checks. The Wharf ain't no open gambling joint. Even if the Mounties raided it, they wouldn't find a loonie on any table, or even a fucking piastre."

"A what?"

"Frog dollars, called piastres. Loonies what limey's call a buck, a dollar, cause the fucking bird's on it."

"But there would be cards on the tables?"

"Sure, no problem Mister Redcoat. Having a good little game of war."

"War? War like in the child's game where you play one card at a time and the highest picks up the losing cards?"

"Got it again, and I thought you were a gorby."

"I'm guessing that's an American tourist?"

"Yeah, but you ain't. Mounties don't got the time to screw with a little pisspot operation like this. Bay police just ignore it most the time. A few officers will take a shot at us couple times a month."

Two old and beat up Renaults pulled up in the parking lot on the south side of The Wharf.

"Frogs, fuck! Frogs are always starting it up. Get popping drugs with the booze and they's ready to storm the … What the fuck was that French place?"

"Bastille, prison in Paris. What's their problem?"

"Hate everybody, especially Nish. Nish are Natives, Indians, First Nations people. Only worse hatred Frogs have is for us Dagos. They used to call us Mangia-Cakes because Canadians have the habit of eating sweet dessert, cake, after a meal but Italians normally eat fruit after a meal, not sweets."

A huge black Ford F-150 truck pulled up across the road from The Wharf, parallel to the train tracks. It was about a hundred yards in front of their Cherokee. It was dark, making it difficult to see the man getting out. All they recognized was that he was tall, taller than Lawrence.

Little Tony reached under the driver's seat and pulled out a bottle of whiskey but Lawrence declined a slug. They waited until the bar had taken in a few more customers and it was completely dark outside. Lawrence adjusted his ankle holster with the pistol grip bottom aimed forward on the inside of his right leg, took three practice strap unlatches and quick draws. He did not chamber any 9's in the Ruger which would have given him valuable micro seconds for a quick draw and fire. He was not anticipating the kind of confrontation where he would need to fire his weapon that fast.

"Let's go, Tony. Introduce me to Otto like I'm some gorby. That right?" Lawrence continued after Little Tony's nod. "I'm here on a visit, that's all."

The back doors to the gambling room had not opened yet making the bar nearly full. Immediately Otto came from behind the bar to shake Little Tony's hand, "hey, how's it goin' Ton? Dad fitting you in?"

"Nah, I'm just a tour guide for these Yankees comin' over to see how good we's got it. This here's Mr. Lawrence. He's in from Philadelphia."

Otto shook Lawrence's hand and asked what they wanted to drink. Tony ordered a beer and Lawrence did the same. Both sat at the bar and scanned the wall-to-wall mirror behind it. Lawrence saw the huge driver of the Ford F-150 sitting by himself at a booth near the door. Instinct told him who the man was. If Charlie was an Indian gun runner and an ammo dealer operating a large network in Thunder Bay, the man in the booth was Charlie, the only Native in the bar. Lawrence got a fast look. He wanted to make sure the man did not catch him eyeballing him. The bar noise was getting loud as the French men started in on Otto to get the games going. Otto told them to keep their shirts on. They cursed at Otto which meant nothing to Otto since he only spoke English and German.

Thanks to his French teacher mother, Lawrence understood nearly every word the Frenchies spoke. The Frenchies were denigrating all of the Canadian Natives in the bar, but were especially harsh on the Indian. Lawrence guessed they had made a bad choice in thinking the big native in the booth could not speak their language.

Charlie had had enough from the French boozers in the bar. They were now speaking English and making fun of his chewing on a peyote button while he was waiting for another beer. He struggled getting his extra large body out from the booth. He walked up to the Frenchmen. "You harp Frogs go into your church and talk about Jesus. Us Comanches chew cactus buttons and actually talk to Jesus."

Lawrence smiled. This huge, crag-faced man was a Comanche. There was little doubt he was Charlie Grayrock. Charlie Grayrock was wearing a gray herringbone dress **suit** with a flat pink shirt, no tie, but a lanyard knotted with multicolored feathers. Lawrence guessed the suit cost two or three hundred dollars. He was off by four hundred and fifty dollars. Charlie's face was rock solid. It was not too dark to discern his eye color. Lawrence knew it was rare for natives to have Grayrock's blue eyes. They were narrow, almost like slits and very penetrating. His hooked nose was indigenous to many Native North Americans, his very deep. The suit had to have been specially tailored since the suit's arms were taut.

Anticipating a fight, Otto stepped in between the Frenchmen and Grayrock. Charlie did not move but the Frenchmen were obviously glad to move. Charlie watched the men go to an empty booth at the other end of the bar, their tails between their legs.

Grayrock spoke to Otto, "set those fucking frog's up with drinks on me Otto. Guess they didn't know who I am. Give'em each a mimosa, cause that's what those French fags like to drink. Put it on my tab."

Grayrock started back to his booth but turned and approached Tony and Lawrence, "Tony Nardo, right?"

"Yeah, how'd ya know?"

"Your father's the only man within a thousand miles who has a Roman nose near as big as mine," he answered, extending his hand to Tony and then to Lawrence.

"Name's Charlie," he said to Lawrence as he shook his hand.

Otto opened the doors to the kitchen, leading to a double door made of steel at the rear. Once open all those who wished to play war entered, leaving no one in the bar. The bar was now closed and Otto extinguished the exterior lights. Saturday night was for playing.

War is a card game, a child's game. Everybody lays down a card and the highest card wins all the other cards. This made it a favorite of the Native Canadians. They did not have the gaming ability or the money necessary to play the high stakes games at Casino Thunder Bay on Cumberland and Pearl Streets.

The back room here had five round tables with five seats at each. Each table was one money level of the card game. The table with a placard showing the number one was just that - - one dollar. Each player started with one deck of cards. Two cards were randomly removed by the dealer, so the value of each hand at one dollar per card, was a fifty dollar ante for each player. A full table would have a pot of two hundred and fifty dollars. Busting the other four players would win the pot. There was a time limit of one hour per game if nobody had won before then. The game started by each player anteing up, the house dealer gathered in the pot. The house took ten percent, leaving two hundred dollars if there was a sole winner. If nobody ran the other players out of cards, each player having cards left got a dollar for each one.

Table one always filled quickly with Native Canadians. Table two, with a two-dollar might get one or two Natives if they had won at table one. Rarely did a Native risk table five, the highest betting ante at two hundred and fifty dollars. The total pot now was one thousand two hundred and fifty dollars. A clean win at table five, was one thousand one hundred and twenty-five dollars. This was big time and for most it was only a one-time shot since it meant dropping a couple hundred bills. Lawrence and Little Tony sat at the five dollar table with the Frenchmen. Charlie started to sit at the four dollar table but with only one other high roller, they might as well flip a coin as play cards. Instead, he joined Lawrence, Tony, and the three Frenchmen to fill out table five.

"Guess most Yanks, Dagos, and Frogs can't roll'em high," said Grayrock.

The first game lasted the full hour. Nobody got wiped out losing all their cards. Little Tony was in the poorest shape, having only one King to take any tricks. By the end of hour two, Tony was gone. Lawrence had an ace and two kings with a shot at winning the table until one of the Frenchman matched his ace. Lawrence went down in a face-off, showing a three to the Frenchman's ten. In the final hour of play, Charlie wasted everybody except one of the Frenchmen who had four cards remaining.

The Frenchman started up, "you're a fucking cheater! There is no way you could have won so easily."

Charlie counted out his cards and told the dealer, "looks to me I've got a thousand and thirty coming."

Otto had already figured out Charlie's earnings and passed them to him.

Charlie tossed his cards in the middle of the table. "Now listen to me Frog! Just how in the world could I have cheated? I'd like to know, so I'll have an even better chance the next time."

"I don't know! I just know you cheated!"

Lawrence reached toward his ankle when the Frenchman stood up, knocking over his chair. He did not have to be ready to pull out the Ruger because Otto was already standing behind the Frenchman with a baseball bat. The Frenchman's friends grabbed him and in French told him to back off and get out of here. Lawrence sat back into his chair and watched the three men walk out of The Wharf.

Charlie spoke to Lawrence, "What did you say your name was?"

"Lawrence, Peter Lawrence."

"Come on, Petey. Let me buy you a drink. Little Tony, you get'm free or I'd buy you one too," said Charlie as they walked back into the bar area. Otto was closing up the gambling room, putting the iron bars across the doors and padlocking them.

Lawrence ordered a brandy that was watered down. "Charlie, I've been looking for you."

Lawrence saw Charlie lean to his left and with his right hand, reach behind him.

"No Charlie, I'm not a cop or Mountie. What you got back there anyhow?"

"Smith and Wesson Bodyguard 38. What's in your ankle holster?"

Lawrence smiled, "Ruger 9'er. Let's go outside where it's a little quieter."

Little Tony was about to complain to Lawrence. Lawrence's words sounded like he thought The Wharf was wired but Little Tony decided to let it be.

"Come with us, Tony. You need to hear this. Your father knows but probably hasn't said anything to you."

The three of them walked out the bar, crossed Cumberland Street, and slid around the hordes of rusted railroad boxcars, cars that had little chance of delivering anything over the rusted tracks. Lawrence passed three of the railroad tracks before he stopped.

"I'm a newspaper editor from Virginia City, Virginia. About a week ago I was a witness at a federal execution in Indiana. You know who Timothy McVeigh is?"

Charlie had his Smith & Wesson out and fired before Lawrence could even blink. "I got the other two covered. Turn around Lawrence. Our French friends decided to follow us."

Lawrence turned and saw two men less than five yards from them, their hands up. It was too dark to identify them. Lawrence put his right foot up on the brake hose hanging between two CNN box cars and drew his Ruger. Lying in front of the two trapped men was the third man, dead. Lawrence kept the Ruger aimed at the chests of the two living ones and walked to the body.

"Yep, you got the bastard. It's the man that went after you at The Wharf. Damn, that little cap pistol of yours got a big wallop and is extremely accurate. You shot him right between his eyes," said Lawrence, laughing. "Tony, come here. You gotta to see this."

Tony Nardo had out a .22 caliber target pistol that he had pulled from his back when Charlie had drawn, shot, and killed the Frenchman. He was ready to fire well before Lawrence had drawn his ankle pistol. Nardo started laughing. "Shit the poor fucker's crossed eyed. What a fucking way to go."

Lawrence and Charlie could not keep from joining in on the laughter, even in front of the dead man's compatriots.

Tony spoke up. "What about these shits? Rough'em and let'em go?"

Lawrence had never killed in cold blood. "What do you say chief?"

"Cops be here in about twenty minutes. No way we can get rid of this body. Cops'll trace down these two and we'll be IDed. Bad men, these are bad men. Problem is cops find three bodies they'll be over at The Wharf getting testimonies. We're in deep shit."

Little Tony shot both Frenchmen at center body mass killing them instantly. "Let me get the Cherokee. Be right back."

Charlie turned to Lawrence as Little Tony hustled across the street, "that boy leaving us?"

"No, Little Tony's smarter than the both of us."

"How's that?"

"Jeep Cherokee belongs to Nardo's mortuary and has body bags in it."

"Holy spirits of a dead eagle! Boy's a warrior and a chief. Now don't tell me. My guess is that there's going to be cuisses de grenouille in Little Italy tonight. You know what that means, Kemo Sabe?"

Lawrence's mother used to bring them to her French classes, disgusting everybody, "Mais oui, Mon Ami! Frog legs that taste like chicken."

Tony backed up the Cherokee, turned off the headlights, unlocked the rear hatch, and went to the rear of the vehicle. "We're fucking lucky. Got three body bags in here. Give me a hand. I'll show you how to bend the body. Got to be quick or the muscles'll cramp up making it fucking difficult."

They loaded the dead men into the back of the Cherokee, shut the hatch and were ready to leave when Grayrock spoke up.

"Yeah, I knew Timmy. Was a good man. How'd he take the execution?"

"No tears, no regrets. But I need to talk with you. Both for your sake and mine."

"Figured that Lawrence. Tomorrow morning you come down there," said Charlie pointing south. "The docks below here are nearly abandoned. I want you to come down to this wharf," he had out a business card and was drawing a rough street map on the back. "Don't let anyone ever get this card. You do, Kemo Sabe, and I'll hunt you down and kill you very slowly over a fire!"

"I didn't know you Comanches were cannibals? Gonna to roast me well-done?"

"Yeah, right after I cut off your dick and dice it into a salad. Go all the way to the end of the wharf. There's a big granary right on the lake shore. Blue colored building on top. Walk the steps to the top, slowly. I'm not a friendly neighbor. About 8:00 tomorrow morning"

***

It seemed to Lawrence that anywhere you wanted to go in Thunder Bay meant traveling up or down Water Street. He grabbed a large coffee at a Burger King and drank it slowly for two reasons. One, it was only a little after seven and he did not want to pop in on Charlie Grayrock too early. Secondly he did not need a lap of hot coffee. Water Street became Fort Williams Road the declining industries of Thunder Bay laid out along either side. The area was filled with scads of silos and granaries in addition to tracks upon tracks of railroads, some rusted and abandoned, others crammed with granary cars. He made a right on Central Avenue and headed northeast until the road sharply turned due east. After crossing the bridge went up and over the rail tracks, the road ended at Maureen Street. In little more than a hundred yards, Lawrence was in front of the abandoned grain and wheat buildings on the lake side of the road. Five storage silos, each connected by a conveyor trestle emptied into an operations building. Lawrence pulled the Nardo's Cherokee, minus the dead bodies up to an abandoned office building painted aqua. The over grown grass and weeds proved the granary had not been in use for a long time. Grayrock's diagram showed an arrow that led Lawrence to an opened two-door garage. Rats ran for shelter as Lawrence noisily trod through weeds and wooden frames lining the passageway between the two buildings. Behind the abandoned garage, a trestle-framed stairwell led to the uppermost building of the four tube-shaped grain processing buildings. After climbing the six stories up to the conveyer shed, he went around to the back and continued up two more levels. Instead of being the scaffolding like the first set of stairs, these were riveted to the granary elevators with only a pipe railing for safety. Some stairs swayed back and forth as Lawrence climbed to the top landing, the landing sagging and making creaking noises as he stepped on it. There was an opened door. Lawrence could smell fresh brewed coffee as he entered.

"Hey, Kemo Sabe, you got up here without falling to your death. You know us Indians ain't got no fear of heights. That's how we got jobs doing those skyscrapers in New York City."

Lawrence reached out and shook Charlie's hand. "I always thought that was bull shit."

"Well my friend, you are right. We're damn near as afraid of heights as any white man. Only reason we'd go up there was it was the only job we could get. Coffee?"

"I thought Thunder Bay was this great seaport feeding the world?"

"Yeah, it was fifty years ago. Once the Trans-Canada Highway got completed, Great Lakes shipping to the East fell apart. Didn't disappear, just declined. Thunder Bay still does a good amount of business, but unless you got political pull like Keefer Terminal odds are you'll wind up like this granary."

"Good coffee, you grind it yourself?"

"Sumatran, straight from Africa to here. Yep, I only drink what I grind."

While the outside of the elevator roof building looked like it was part of the Great Depression, years of rust destroying all hope of survival, the inside was immaculate with paneled walls, wall-to-wall carpeting, department store furniture, and a fairly well-equipped kitchen. The east windows facing Lake Superior had been broken by ransackers and local thugs over the decades. They had been replaced with bullet proof glass and were obviously washed frequently.

"What a great view Charlie. According to Thunder Bay's Chamber of Commerce, I should be seeing ships all over the lake."

"Sometimes you actually can see one or two. Hard to believe, isn't it? Ever see the Sleeping Giant?"

"Yeah, when I was at Lakehead College trying to track you down. Like your view better."

"Didn't have much luck over at Lakehead did you?"

"You're quite a specter aren't you? How'd you get this place? By the way, where's your truck?"

"Getting an oil change and tune-up. Business I'm in lets me meet quite a few losers. Man who owns this terminal went belly up when his hiring defied the First Nations Council here. It was during a time when pressure was on the Canadian government to rectify how they've treated us Natives. Son of a bitch owner here did a bankruptcy and nobody got a dollar. He kept the title, still has it. Put me down as the security agent for the plant. Pleased everybody, including First Tribe."

"You stay here all the time?"

"Nah, but nobody bothers this place. I might be here once every couple of months. Vandals know better than mess with me. Once I killed off a few, they left it alone. Nothing here for them anyway except a place to smoke up and sell drugs. They can do that damn near anywhere they want in Canada. They love the laws here."

"What I don't understand is why couldn't I track you down through First Nations or Lakehead University?

"Didn't use my real name. Used my grandfather's name, Isa Tai. You'd looked that name up there'd be a lot of property listed."

"Isa Tai? That's a Comanche name? Sounds like a Jew with an Asiatic parent?"

"Comanche medicine man. He and Quanah Parker led the Comanche into the Great Battle of Adobe Walls. Of course they got their asses kicked but my granddad wound up making a fortune by selling dumb white fucks protection for their cattle grazing on Indian land. He was a great story teller."

"Must have been if he led the Comanche into the slaughter and then turned around and sold his services to the enemy."

"Comanches are tough. Try to chase down a Comanche and you've got no chance of catching him. Comanche'll ride a horse into the ground, cut out his guts, wrap his intestines around his neck, and take off on another horse while eating the guts as he goes."

Charlie pulled out his Smith & Wesson .38 and aimed it at Lawrence's center body mass, "got that Ruger with you? Of course you do. Reach down with your left hand and .."

"Wearing a belt holster."

"Same difference, Kemo Sabe. Left hand, two fingers to unsnap and lift out. Lay it facing you on the table."

Lawrence smiled and did as he was told.

"Got a problem with you, Lawrence. Yes, I am the Charlie that knew Timmy McVeigh and yes, my name's probably in McVeigh's records. Did you bring them?"

"In the Jeep. Want me to go get them?"

Charlie Grayrock smiled, "why didn't you shoot those Frenchies last night?"

"Killing doesn't bother me. Dying does. I saw McVeigh go under. Wasn't like a hanging or the chair, but it bothered me. I don't jump at killing."

"Couldn't be because you're from the FBI?"

"Charlie, how many agents did you see surrounding this hideout when you got up before dawn this morning?"

"None. How'd you know I got up before the sun?

"How old are you? Sixties?"

"I get what you're saying. I wouldn't be seventy-two and still breathing if I didn't cover my ass, eye ball my domain here. I got a couple questions for you Petey before we go any further."

"Do them."

Charlie put his .38 Smith & Wesson back in his holster, but he did not let Lawrence pick up his Ruger. He sat diagonal to Lawrence who was facing the large windows with the a view of Lake Superior.

Charlie put his left elbow on the dining room table, his hand angled toward Lawrence, fingers spread. "Give me your left hand, elbow on the table."

"Are we going to arm wrestle?" Lawrence was smiling but grasped Charlie's left hand firmly. "I always wanted to Indian wrestle with an Indian."

"Comanche, asshole. No wrestling, besides that ain't how you Indian wrestle. Whether you want to believe me or not, my great grandfather, Isa-Tai, was a bona fide medicine man. He could talk to the dead and read minds. I'm not that good but I know when a man's lying. Do it."

It was easy to read Grayrock's face. His eyes were narrow slits that bored through Lawrence, knowing a lie. Lawrence laced his fingers and flattened his palm against Charlie's fingers. Both men gripped hands and started sweating.

"Back about six years ago, McVeigh contacted me because he needed help. Timmy was a smart kid. Wouldn't tell me what was going on, only that he would need to get out of the states and disappear. I guessed the Feds and maybe some State cops were catching him selling illegal weapons. Happens all the time to us gun runners. We just ease off for a year or two move to a new market, and they forget."

"As you know I deal arms, explosives, and weapons from other countries. For some reason I can't figure, German lugers are always hot. Got to be right from Germany, not those cheap shit American mock-ups. How do I get them into Canada and the US? I pilot them in. Outside that window you're looking through there's a Cessna 182 fitted with amphibious floats. Just got that one last year. I had a similar plane bought back in 95. But because I needed a little more range and the old one was running down, I upgraded to that one."

"Told McVeigh I could get him lost real quick, nobody'd be able to track him down. I didn't really have some isolated hide-out for him. Asked him what's going on and he said I didn't need to know and it was in my best interest to not know. He was damn right about that!"

"But I did tell him that I had a client up north in Ontario that could hide a jackass in a Senate committee. I'd ask him about putting Timmy away. Which I did. McVeigh went for it. Deal was simple and McVeigh put up half my fee but ...."

Grayrock hesitated in saying the contact's name, "man up north didn't want a penny to take in McVeigh. I guessed he wouldn't. Sssh, hold on. I'm almost there."

"I was all gassed up and waiting for McVeigh to pull into this granary. We'd lose his car off one of the abandoned deep water terminals and be on our way. I sat here for two days. He never showed. Didn't know why until they caught him and I saw his face all over the television. For nearly two years, I sweated out him dropping my name to the Feds for nearly two years. I was right about McVeigh. He never got me caught up in it. I could have been in jail right now, it's why I'm playing it close with you. No statute of limitations on a terrorist attack."

"You don't know how close you were Charlie. Two FBI agents were all over me trying to get the satchel I have in the car. It's how I found you. If the Feds had it, they'd nail you too."

"I got some questions that might be pretty heavy for you Petey." Charlie still held the grip with Lawrence. "You got two uncles?"

"Yeah, so?"

"One of them used to be a boxer, did some prize fighting? What's his name?"

"Ralph."

"Got one that fought in Nam? Good with a knife?"

Lawrence started to get up from his seat, "What do they have to do with ..."

"Whoa, hold them horses Kemo Sabe. What's his name?"

"George."

"Is your father's first name Llewellyn?"

Lawrence's fist tightened, forcing him to put his other hand over the grasping hands.

"That Lawrence written on McVeigh's map? Lawrence you told me about? Not you. It's your father."

Lawrence unlaced his fingers from Charlie's hand. He leaned back, on the dinette chair. His eyes glared at Grayrock, narrowed slits of vision. His father was alive and in Canada. All these years and his father, Llewellyn Lawrence was only a day's trip from his son but he never made contact.

"In fact I talked with him last night. He's got a smart phone he bought in France under an assumed name. He also waited for McVeigh that Wednesday morning but he didn't care if the authorities knew it. They're after him anyhow. He calmed me down. Told me that if they catch me and take me into custody, he'd contact them, tell them all I did was give McVeigh his name. Never came to that, though."

" Whoa, you're almost breaking the bones in my hand, Lawrence."

"Charlie, what's next here? I'm at the end. I'm not the Lawrence that McVeigh labeled on his escape route. I don't know this man, my father. I need to know him. How did you two get together?"

"Nam. In case you don't know, your father turned on his country. He got captured by ..."

"Charlie, I know most of it. You, I don't. How did you come together?"

"Lot of time for that, Lawrence. Lot of time if you up to meeting him."

"How? He's wanted all over the world. How could I ever get to him without jeopardizing his life?"

"Come here Lawrence," motioning Lawrence to the window with a view of Lake Superior. "Look down there. See the Cessna right below us?"

Lawrence stood in front of the huge window and nodded.

"Where your father is makes it damn impossible for anyone to catch him. Even if they could tail you and me in the Cessna, even the plane can't take us all the way to where your father is. Besides nobody really gives a buffalo's ass about my little old airplane, let alone figuring out I'm taking you to a fugitive from the Vietnam War. There is no tie-in between me and Lew."

"Family used to call him Lew."

"He knows you're here. I told him you might want to meet him. You got a problem with it?"

"What did he have to say about meeting me?"

"Scared, scared about as much as you are. Told me to make sure your mother doesn't know."

"Why did he say that?" Lawrence was getting a little irritated.

"Cool down. Lew's got handles on just about every ... I got to watch what I say. The man knows your mom is under deep surveillance especially now that the Feds are on your tail. He wants you to come. He was stunned that you tracked me down through you being close to McVeigh. Wants to know you. Are we going or not?"

"Now?"

"I need the rest of today to do some deals in Thunder Bay, then we go. You alright to go? Got something better going on in your life?"

Did he? Lawrence had basically quit the Virginia City Server after talking to Judge Sauers. But there was also Susan Yoder. A part of him missed her, especially when she straddled his loins, forcing him to grab her hips as she pumped him to his explosive, near oblivion orgasm. But there was hatred as well knowing she aborted his child. It weighed heavily on him. He felt jealous imagining that she was probably fucking another man now. She needed sex even more than Lawrence.

"What time you want me here?"

***

Little Tony Nardo left Lawrence off at the dilapidated shed in front of the towering grain elevators. "You gonna to trust riding in that Injun's plane? Shit, he lives in a junk pile. Just look at this mess. Boy, you got some balls."

"Two of them. Hope the smell from those body bags goes away. Tony, you're a good man. Need anything and I can give you, you got it. Tell your Papa many thanks. I'll tell Constanzo about your family's service to me." Lawrence took Little Tony's hand to shake but both men wound up in a tight hug. Little Tony would be the future Don of Thunder Bay.

Grayrock had been watching from the scaffolding on top of the storage silos. He waved to Lawrence who returned the salutation as he headed to the stairs leading to Charlie's domicile. Charlie, carrying a large backpack descended the stairs while Lawrence waited.

"Already Kemo Sabe? Follow me around the silo to the bay."

On the other side of the granary the Cessna 182 with amphibious floats was belayed to a floating dock five feet below the pier and extending into Lake Superior. Lawrence followed Charlie to the dock. There was a long stretch to the plane, reached by the plane's wet and slippery floats. Charlie opened the pilot's door and secured it the left wing strut. He called to Lawrence to grab his backpack and hand it to him. After stowing the pack, Lawrence handed him his travel case and the McVeigh satchel. Charlie stowed them below the two rear passenger seats and stepping on to the float, hefted himself up on the floating dock.

"Okay Boss, you go in first."

There was not a lot of head room for Lawrence and even less seat space for Lawrence's long legs as he negotiated across the pilot's seat to the right side of the plane. Charlie followed Lawrence without any hassle, plopped into the pilot's seat, pulled the door closed and locked it. He told Lawrence to double check the passenger door to make sure it was also locked.

"Don't want you to fall out unless you're some dumbass U.S. Army Major."

Charlie started up the 230 horsepower Continental O-470-R flat six piston engine that drove a two blade constant speed propeller. He had to let it run for a few minutes to get the lubricants flowing.

The noise level was deafening and Charlie had to speak loudly. "Noise'll drop down once she's oiled. It'll still be bad so you got to yell a bit. Got some good weather. Visibility's about 15 miles and wind speed's 9 miles per hour. Gotta watch ourselves though since the wind's gonna to be a bit gusty. Maybe 20 or 22 miles per hour. You get air sick?"

"Never have but I've not ridden in a small plane for long time. How long and where are we going?"

"Wunnumin Lake First Nation is the first stop. Be about two, two and half hours maybe three if the weather changes. Wunnumin Lake's a good 350 or so miles north, due north in fact."

Lawrence could see the pilot's gauges leveling off.

Charlie slowly reduced the throttle. "She's warm and ready."

The airplane crept slowly forward, pontoons against water friction, as Charlie negotiated a 90^0 right turn and headed north. The water speed picked up gradually. The huge floats splashed water as the plane rose a bit and then dropped. Charlie turned on the wipers. Before Lawrence even noticed it, there was no more splash as they headed up. Charlie banked a bit to the right causing Lawrence's shoulder to push into the passenger side door. Looking out the window, he got a tremendous view of a few tankers and cargo boats leaving a wake behind them as they headed toward the Port of Thunder Bay or east to Sault Ste. Marie, Lake Erie, and the St. Lawrence Sea Way.

Charlie spoke, "See that island down there?"

"Looks like a big mesa in the old west. Flat as an iron but those sides are cliffs all around. Looks like it's impossible to get to the top except by helicopter."

Charlie continued, "Instead of big mesa, think meat pot pie with a crust."

"Yeah, sort of looks like that. What's its name, Pie Island?"

"Sure is. French used to own it and called it Le Pate or meat pie with a crust. Discovered silver on it and there was a big fight many years ago about who owned, the French or Canadians. Now there's a big fight about whether it belongs to First Nation or Canada."

"When are you going to tell me how you met up with my father? Were the two of you in the same company in Vietnam?"

"Nope, never met Arens until he broke me out of prison."

"Arens? How did he come up with that name?"

"You know he saved a Vietnamese family from the U.S. Army, don't you?"

"My Uncle George was there with him until my father deserted. I know about places like Mai Lai and the other tragedies."

"You better think twice about calling your father a deserter or traitor in front of me, Petey. I don't want to have to kill you."

Lawrence could hear the tone. He was acting like a border line jerk.

"Charlie, you're a good man, a brave man. From what I've seen, you're a good friend to those who help you. What you're saying about my father is he was one of those during Nam. Don't judge me because I'm ignorant of what really happened. I don't fucking know. My uncle George and my mother's sisters told me a lot about Llewellyn Lawrence before he left for Nam. What they don't know is Llewellyn after he became a renegade. You were there after he turned on America."

"Petey, I never apologize. It makes you look weak. What I know is you're in an unbelievable situation. I respect that. You're a lot like your father."

"Arens, you mean?"

Charlie laughed. "The Vietnamese couldn't pronounce Lawrence correctly. They called him Awrence, leaving the 'L' off. Eventually they shortened it to just Arens. Didn't seem to bother Lew much."

"You don't know why do you?"

"Why he didn't care if they called him Arens? Guess it made him feel closer to the people. Hell, he lived with them for over twenty years."

"There's that too. You'd know better than me. I know from Ma Mere that his favorite movie was Lawrence of Arabia. You ever see it?"

Charlie was laughing. There was something exciting in how Charlie laughed. It was a deep laugh, coming up from his gut and making his face red. It was not loud but came across like the rat-a-tat-tat of a machine gun.

"Fucking 'A', sounds like that son of a bitch. Yeah, I've seen that movie. The Arabs called Peter O'Toole Arens. Good handle on how one person cannot change the world."

The plane shook and Charlie opened the throttle a bit, taking the Cessna higher. "Months after your father, Arens, went over to the Viet Cong, I was flying a copter over ..."

"You flew helicopters during Vietnam? How in world did an Indian ... Damn Charlie, I'm sorry. You know it's a habit, a bad habit."

"Don't sweat it, Petey. I'm not ashamed to be an Indian. You want to know how I got to flying a Huey Cobra gunship? Hell, we got a good three hours to go. Might as well lay it all on you.

"I lived on a reservation in Oklahoma, Lawton Oklahoma to be exact. We were treated just like slaves, no more like prisoners. Eventually, after a lot of pressure from all of the reservation chiefs, the U.S. Bureau of Indian Affairs stepped in and started educating us more, instead of just housing and feeding us. Didn't even have schools for us back in the 1880's. Twenty-two children were entered into the United States Indian Industrial School for grades one through five. School was in Lawrence, Kansas. Holy shit, another Lawrence! I've been guided all my life by fucking Lawrence's!"

Lawrence laughed as Charlie continued with his story.

"And a fine job they did. You know what they taught Injuns back then? Take a guess."

"I'd guess basic ABC's, some math, probably history?"

"Fucking wrong, Petey. Boys were taught wagon making, blacksmithing, shoe making, tailoring white men's clothes, and how to paint a white man's barn. The teaching took place at some local farmer's barn and the school would get a supplement check from the farmer."

"Nah, don't believe you, Redman. Go ahead. Anything useful?"

"Yep, farming but again it was for ..."

"The white man's farm. How about the girls? Cooking and sewing?"

"You are one smart asshole, Petey. Left out homemaking. After ten years of Tribal complaints, the school went to a full time high school. Even got them to learning typewriting. Actually had five typewriters."

"And I'll bet the practice work was issued by companies in the area?"

"You got the picture. Maybe I'm a little too bitter about it. For one thing, when I was there I was five or six years older than most of the other Comanches on the reservation. I had a wife and two kids. I had been working at a garbage disposal company in Lawton. I couldn't hardly feed my family. My wife was a dishwasher for the Army officer's club and still we nearly starved. It's why I went to the school. Indian agent gave me all these promises about the great job I'd get. Got my degree in '63, industrial technology degree. Not one fucking job was available. The agent that promised me a great job was gone. Reservation was going to pot. Government stopped much of the money coming in, demanding we support ourselves, except there were no jobs."

"After a little more than a year, the best I came up with was being a storeroom janitor at a fucking K Mart. Paid shit, I even worked the night shift. I slept while my family went from house to house in Lawton trying to find a job any job, just to provide food. One of the K Mart lowlifes came in one night carrying a draft notice. Boy was scared shitless. He was ready to blow off his toes to keep out. I saw an opportunity. I saw a way my family could have income if I served the government. I ignored the fact that the government had destroyed my ancestors and turned our reservation into a slum. Even so I enlisted."

"By pure chance, during advanced infantry training, a Master Sergeant was looking for copter school candidates. All you needed was a technical degree. I had my wife send me a copy of my degree and took it to the sergeant. Guess what Petey?"

"He didn't even look at it."

"You hit it right on the head. I could have told him I flew jets for Pan Am and he'd a still signed me up. I thought I was to be an infantry soldier with a chopper company, but they put me right in pilot school. The idiots told me to forget everything about flying planes because they were going to teach us from ground zero how to fly a Huey Cobra and kill gooks at the same time. Six months and a big raise in pay. Boom, I was sent to Nam. And that's what I did, flew choppers with guns out the bay door mowing down slope heads."

"Would have been good for a year I had to reup for three years. That hurt, but they were generous with leaves and I got home every three months. Sometimes if we killed enough Vietnamese, they'd give us an on-the-spot bonus of two weeks leave."

"My family was on base back home, being taken care of by the United States Army. Even though I missed them for two years, I knew they had a decent home, plenty to eat, and were safe. Safe until a drunk Second Luie from Georgia broke into the house and raped my wife and killed my kids. Army tried him, convicted him, and hung him. They offered me a reassignment home for the remainder of my duty. I didn't take it. I wanted to kill, kill anybody, anywhere. But I was able to control it. Nobody read anything into or even cared that my Huey was doing more kills than any of the other three choppers."

"Then it got ugly. The Company Commander began his strafing raids of villages. It was about that time when we were hearing from the States that Americans didn't support our effort, wanted the war over. They were marching in the streets and on college campuses. It pissed off everybody in our company. It got worse when Mai Lai made the news."

"I saw the pictures and knew I was doing the same thing Calley and Medina were doing. I went to the Company CO and told him I had enough, wanted a transfer. Problem was the CO had been running bets with other CO's about which company could get the most kills. I was winning him a lot of money and prestige. He climbed all over me and I almost ... "

Charlie's face was getting red. Lawrence could see sweat around his collar, "He was a mean son of a bitch and a vain asshole. I did a 180, said I see his ways, and I'd be okay. It was just getting tiring to me that was all."

"He was Mister Nice Guy after I told him that. Gave me a week's leave in Saigon, along with a bunch of Vietnamese dollars. I took them, took the vacation on one condition. I needed some positive reinforcement on these flights, some help finding villages to destroy. Asked him to come along on a sortie to see what I mean. He'd help us get more gooks."

"He bounced around on that, equivocated but said he'd go on the next raid."

Lawrence was enthralled by Charlie 's story, "equivocated? Cheesy little technical school taught you multi syllable words?"

Charlie turned the helm clockwise, lifting the port wing to a 70° angle, easing slowly against the fuselage and making Lawrence lean on the starboard door. "White boy want to fly like an eagle?"

Lawrence was pretty sure Charlie was messing with him but not so sure to keep the hairs on the back of his neck from standing up.

"That turn had nothing to do with you, Petey. Just keeping the flight plan intact."

"So what happened?"

"The CO went up with us. When I say us, besides me, there was a copilot and two gunners. It was daylight when we took off and within a half hour we were over a Vietnam village. CO said he didn't know there was a VC infiltrated village so close. I told him it's real easy to figure out if the village has VC."

"He smiled, acknowledging my ability. I hovered over the center of the village. There were Vietnamese running all around, trying to find shelter. They knew what a chopper meant to the village. The CO just stared, not saying a word. He was sweating like a pig with his bullet-proof flak jacket covering his chest. I told him he should get on the gun and take some shots. He was getting very edgy and said we should do our job and get back to base."

"I told him he was a fucking coward. His eyes went wide as he stared into my goggles. Ordered me to head back to base right then. Told him shoot them like you want us to shoot them. He was still standing at the door port, hands on the mounted gun. He ordered my co-pilot to take over flight controls. I pulled out my service .45 and shot the co-pilot through the left ear hole of his helmet. The two gunners were next, both through the bridge of their nose. A center mass would probably have done the job but who knows? They had on flak jackets. Now it was just me and the CO. I landed in the middle of the village and forced the CO out."

"The villagers were watching from their huts. I could see their heads poking out. I yelled, asking if there was anybody who spoke English. One old man lifted his hand to me. I called him over."

"I told him to translate to the villagers what was being said. I looked around the huts and told them I am one of those who was trained to kill you and your families. I was evil and did not deserve to be alive. This man with me has ordered killings of many villagers and is proud to have killed citizens of your country. I threw my service pistol into the sand and the CO went after it. Before he got there, three Vietnamese men grabbed him, forced him to the ground on his knees, yanked his head back and slit his throat. I awaited my death."

"They didn't kill you?"

"Petey my boy, you really are one smart asshole."

Lawrence put his hands up, covering his face in embarrassment and said "duh!"

"They never said a thing?"

"Nothing. Their message was clear. I was still the enemy but not their enemy anymore. And they were right. I got back into the Huey and flew back to base."

"What the hell happened when you got back? What lie did you tell them?"

"None. I told the truth. I thought they would jail me, try me, and hang me. Instead they put me in the brig and assigned me an officer from the Army JAG Corps. I'm alive because they gave me a Native American. He had just got out of law school back in the States. Fucking ass-kissing Cherokee, but he got me off with manslaughter due to battle fatigue. I got ten years in the stockade."

"Where were you incarcerated?"

"That's where the Army got its vengeance. I was cuffed and hooded. I found out later that they flew me south of Saigon to an abandoned prison built by the French. I got there in the middle of the night, still hooded I was stripped naked and forced almost to my knees. I had to waddle like a duck through a small entrance and into a cell. Then the door was slammed shut. I had no idea where I was and what my life would become. It was total darkness even with my hood finally off, but I managed to find a steel cot to sleep on. There was no mattress but it made no difference. I was so scared that sleep never came."

"At daybreak I got my first view of the prison. I was cuffed and taken out of my cell to the infirmary where a medic examined me and gave me some shots. A guard then took me to the warden's office, outside the cellblocks on top of a huge wall. Warden told me that nobody cares what happens here. I would be executed on the spot for any violation of prison rules. The guard took me away and showed me around the prison. Place was a dead ringer for the Bastille. Big, thirty-foot walls of granite with five cellblocks radiating from the central room where the guards had a clear view down every cell block making it nearly impossible to escape. Each cell was ten feet long and six feet wide with an exit only four feet high, the door made of cast iron. There was a slot at knee level where food was passed into the cell."

"My cell had a skylight about three feet long and six inches wide letting in minimal light. The outside wall opposite the cell door had an opening to a cage where a prisoner could exercise and get some fresh air. The cage was made of rusting steel bars, six feet by four feet with a height of about five feet. To do any exercise I had to stoop so I wouldn't hit my head on the steel bars. I was allowed to use the exercise cage only thirty minutes once a day. No two prisoners adjacent to each other were allowed to use the cage at the same time."

"There was a cement toilet to the right of the cell door. A spigot was directly above the toilet which provided water for flushing excrement down the sewer located under each cell. The same spigot was used for washing and drinking. The smell of shirt permeated the cell."

"Charlie, how'd you ever survive that? I mean mentally."

"At first I thought I'd have been better off executed instead of sentenced to this jail. I cried day and night. Guards would come by and laugh at me. It made it worse. Ten years is a fucking long time. Suicide is what they wanted and there was plenty of ways to do it. They fed me, giving me a fork and spoon, no knife. It made no difference since any fool could use a fork to kill himself. If that wasn't enough, the mattress could be ripped apart and the canvas cover made into strips to hang you."

"But you obviously didn't. So how did you get through it?"

Charlie began chanting ...

"He'e'yo'! Heyo'hänä' Häe'yo! Heyo'hänä' Häe'yo!
The sun's beams are running out—He'e'yo'!"

"That's how, Lawrence. Listen ..."

"Yani'tsini'hawa'na! Yani'tsini'hawa'na! We shall live again, We shall live again.The sun's beams are running out—He'e'yo'! The sun's rays are running out—Ahi'ni'yo'! The sun's rays are running out—Ahi'ni'yo'!"

"Do you know what I'm chanting?

"Sounds like some kind of prayer?"

"It's the Comanche Ghost Dance. Usually it's associated with the Lakota but as White America destroyed more and more of the Native's habitats, many tribes picked it up. It gives us strength and protection from the white man. We even have ghost shirts which repel bullets."

"Sounds like your ancestor, Isa-Tai?"

"Yes it does, doesn't it? Comanches picked it from the Sioux. It was responsible for the great massacre at Wounded Knee. You ever hear about that?"

"Yeah, there was a very good book about it that I read a while back. But go ahead, tell your story."

Charlie banked the Cessna to the right to pick up a small tail wind. "The U.S. government was trying to break up the tribes in South Dakota. Reason? Homesteaders were bitching because the Injuns got better land than the white people migrating west. Government came in to run off the lazy-ass Injuns by cutting their food supplies in half. Native families that once lived off buffalo now had no buffalo, and the reservation food was scarce.

"The Sioux fell turned to tradition. All they could hope for was that our ancestors' ghosts would rise up and give them back their lands. The Ghost Dance went out loud and clear and scared the Be 'Jesus out of the Indian agents. Thousands of troops came riding into the reservation. They arrested Sitting Bull for letting his people sing the Ghost Dance."

"It's a shame they can't arrest those thugs that sing rap songs.".

"I'm with you there, Petey. The Sioux put up their teepees and went into their chants, trying to overcome their hardships. Got the troops scared of a rebellion. Troops went into the village to collect weapons but one of the Sioux wouldn't give his up. He kept chanting the Ghost Dance, over and over ignoring the troopers. It wasn't because he was defying their orders. He was deaf. They opened fire and the tribe went for their weapons, not having much of a chance to use them. U.S. Army started shooting any Indian in sight. They were shooting a Hotchkiss gun, a rapid-fire artillery piece. Still some of the Sioux were able to fire back, killing 25 soldiers. When the dust settled and the bodies were counted, 153 Sioux were dead, nearly everyone being woman or a child. Twenty U.S. Army soldiers were given Medals of Honor for slaughtering women and children."

"I think I know where you're going, Charlie. The Ghost Dance, chants and songs, you've lived with them. It's your history, only not written down on paper."

"In prison I started singing the chants, changing them to fit my situation. I even wrote a bunch myself. If I hadn't, I'd have knitted a mattress rope and dangled myself off the steel bars in my exercise cage."

"So when did Lawrence of Hanoi come riding in on his camel with Bedouin warriors fighting off the ..."

Charlie's voice turned angry, "Don't make fun of your father. He didn't save me from the U.S. Army. Didn't happen that way. Hold on a second while I descend a little to get my position. We're getting close to Wunnumin Lake. I've got to make a delivery there."

Lawrence looked out the window and could see nothing but green woods and hundreds of lakes. How Charlie could find his way through all of this was beyond Lawrence's imagination. The plane dropped slowly as Charlie kept his focus on piloting. A huge island was in front of and below the plane. Lawrence could see dirt roads running through an isthmus to a town. Charlie dove closer and circled to the west, then north, and finally nosing down south, landing on the lake. Since there was little or no wind, the landing was smooth. With the props still running, pulling the Cessna through the water, Charlie slowly eased to shore. The town, no larger than three quarters of a mile across, named Wunnumin Lake First Nation.

"How do we get to where you want to go, Charlie?"

"Walk," which is what they did. "Got to drop off some medical supplies to the Wunnumin Lake Nursing Station and then stop by the police station. But first let me go in this building, Solomon's Gas Bar. He can fill up the tanks while we're busy."

"There's actually somebody in that building?"

"Hey, it's an old grey shed without windows. See the tanks? That's all he does."

"Look at the sign in the resource team office. Sign reads they have a 24 hour crisis line. It doesn't look like they got the call for their own crisis. This place is falling apart, rainspouts hanging down and windows covered with plastic sheets."

"Take a look to your right, Kemo Sabe"

"Damn! An actual teepee! But a modern one with a UTV parked in front of it."

The nursing station was a one level, A-roofed building with two big antennae running up the front door. Lawrence followed Charlie into the nursing station. It was not elaborate but it was clean, well-furnished, and more than adequate for its patients. As Charlie talked with the receptionist, Lawrence walked through the halls and what he saw changed his negative view. People were being taken care of here. The examination room was well-equipped as was the patient care room with its modern equipment. The rooms for extended stay patients were homey and as good as the best nursing homes anywhere. The patient care room had modern equipment and was well organized. There was a family atmosphere about the facility that was enhanced by hand- drawn signs and funny stickers. It was obvious that the patients were cared for by good and well trained personnel. There was no room that he visited that did not have some personal note stuck on a wall or cabinet. Most offices had computers but they were many upgrades behind.

Charlie found Lawrence sipping a cup of coffee in the staff room. He was talking with a nurse.

"We're gonna to be a little off schedule. The chief nurse that I brought supplies for is down at the Wunnumin Lake Police Station trying to get her brother released."

"What did he do? This place looks like a trailer park in the states but the people seem to be pretty upright."

"Don't know. Want to go down and see what's going on?"

"Sure, I always like mixing with cops."

The Wunnumin Lake Police Station was about as large as a two-car garage. It was painted white, with the ubiquitous Wunnumin Lake baby blue roof. A late model white and blue pickup truck with Wunnumin Lake Police painted on the sides was parked in front of the door. Charlie and Lawrence walked in without knocking. Charlie saw the chief nurse and went over to her. She was standing in front of a desk of a police officer. Lawrence noticed the officer was a Native but he had no idea which tribe.

"Charlie, you've landed! Got my package?"

"Yep, two kilos of smack and all the marijuana the town can smoke in a day."

The police officer stood up, shook his head back and forth, and smiling broadly reached out his hand to Charlie. "I thought the Mounties had nailed you by now."

They bear-hugged each other and Charlie introduced the policeman to Lawrence.

"So what's going on here?"

The nurse spoke up. "My brother, again."

"Drunk?"

"No, the rehab finally got him past it. That's the problem."

The officer added, "If I had him on a drunk and disorderly, I'd fine him and kick him out of the cell."

Lawrence looked around the insides of the tiny building and shrugged.

"There's an old out-house in the back. Only cell we ever need. You ever heard of a brick shit house? I've got one."

They laughed.

The officer continued, "he took a shot at some Plate Extract Inc. surveyors that came down from Nemeigusabinsabins Lake to get some supplies. They got a lawyer. He admits he did it. Don't need to go into all the anti-mining gesticulations he spouted off."

Grayrock laughed, " gesticulations? You doin' good for some dumb Injun. You mean he was ranting and raving?"

"Yep, but not drunk. Gotta to hold him for the Mounties."

Charlie just shook his head in bewilderment and turned to the nurse, "package okay?"

"Yeah, you got what my patient needs. Thanks Charlie."

"Listen Dear, walk with me down to my plane, will you?"

Charlie was a big man, tall and strong. He put his arm around her shoulder and the three of them walked to the Cessna. "Can your brother survive them miners in your territory for a year or so?"

"You know he can. We were raised out Nanowin Rivers. Pure living off the land. That's where he belongs. You can get him out of jail?"

"Not me. Friend of mine'll take care of it. Tell your brother to relax for a week or so."

"Charlie, if I weren't so young I'd give you a spin," she said, kissing him on each cheek and his forehead.

She walked back to the police station and Charlie and Lawrence continued to the Cessna. Charlie stopped on the way to pay his fuel bill and asked Lawrence if he wanted a slushie."

"A slushie out her in the wilderness of Canada? You're going to buy me a slushie?"

"Yep. See that brown shed over there? Salomon Mamakwa's - slushies, chips, pop, and condoms. Come on, my treat."

To Lawrence's surprise, his slushie was like none he ever had. Slush ice, but not melted. He dished it out and ate by the spoonful as they returned to the lake.

"Looks like somebody's blocking my plane."

The Cessna was moored to the end of a dock where the fuel had been loaded into its tanks. Tied up next to Charlie's plane was a larger aircraft with pontoons. Plate Extract Inc., Inc. was printed on its side. Charlie and Lawrence looked around for the pilot.

"Hey, you guys up there on the hill. This your plane? Got to move it," yelled Lawrence.

The two men turned and gave Lawrence and Charlie the finger.

"Okay, when you decide to get down here, you better bring a pump with you. Plane's going to be sitting on the bottom of the lake!"

The two men saw Lawrence climb over Charlie's Cessna and begin to unmoor the Plate Extract Inc. plane. Both men came running down to the moorage, screaming profanities. Charlie backed off figuring Lawrence knew what he was doing.

"Get off my plane you asshole," said the man in a grey pinstriped suit. He was very tall, reaching a good six-foot eight or nine inches.

The other man, the pilot, was wearing a leather jacket with a fur-trimmed collar. He started toward Lawrence but Charlie stepped in front of him, "nice jacket. Make you feel like a World War One flyboy? Why'd you pull up and block me?"

"Boss said to."

"Come on, you're an aviator. You know better."

The pilot did know better, his acknowledgement was left hanging in the air as his boss faced off with Lawrence.

Lawrence had unleashed the plane's mooring rope and was standing with one foot on the Cessna pontoon, the other on Plate Extract Inc.'s starboard pontoon, "you want to move it or you want me to move it?"

"Are you fucking crazy? Tie that rope back or I'll knock your teeth down your throat."

"Be pretty difficult swimming in that J.C. Penney's suit," said Lawrence as he shoved the Plate Extract Inc. plane away from the dock, jumped from the port pontoon of the Cessna to the starboard, and then up onto the dock.

The man in the suit took off the custom-tailored jacket and laid it on a picnic table used by fishermen. Lawrence walked up the man, who had now taken the posture of a hand-to-hand combatant.

"Shit, I didn't know you were some karate expert! Look, how's about if I jump into the water and go get our plane?" said Lawrence now only a few feet from the man in the suit.

"Do it, Asshole!"

Lawrence did it but it was not a swim. As the man was pushing his arm back into the left sleeve of the pinstriped jacket, Lawrence hit him with a left jab to the man's right cheek and eye, then caught him with an upper cut to the abdomen, and finally brought another left jab to his face, this time catching the right side of the man's mouth, and loosening two teeth. The man went down on his knees, swooned a bit, and then fell over.

The pilot started toward the fight but as soon as he turned his back, Charlie, kicked him behind his left knee, doubling the leg over. Charlie could hear the crack as the man grabbed his bent knee and screamed.

"Lawrence, you ready?"

"Guess so, Comanche. Turn that engine over and let's get flying."

***

The Cessna headed toward Big Trout Lake.

"Petey, you're good with your fists. There's an ice chest in the back. Had Solomon's Gas Bar fill it up and put in a couple beers. Ice'll keep those knuckles from swelling."

"I know better than jab a man in the mouth. I like the damage it does but it rips the hell out of your knuckles. First aid kit back there also?"

"Yep, lift up the seat cushion on the port side."

Lawrence used some beer to rinse off his cut knuckles, wiped them down with an alcohol swab, and after putting some ice in an old towel he found in the back, wrapped it around his right hand.

"If anybody on the ground sees us, we're headed to Big Trout Lake. Give it a few minutes and we'll be heading due east toward Wapikopa Lake. Our trip ends about two miles west of Tabasokwia Lake. There's a big mountain island in the middle. We'll land next to it. The area is all wilderness. Even a Comanche couldn't find us."

"How about Davy Crockett?"

"Not a chance. Anybody stupid enough to fight two thousand Mexicans probably couldn't find an arrowhead on the end of an arrow."

Lawrence's knuckles were responding to the ice, the swelling receding. "Finish your story, Charlie. How'd you get rescued from prison?"

"Give me a beer," said Charlie holding his hand up to cup the bottle. "Didn't really. The Army put me in that prison for ten years. Like I told you, I would've broken, probably killed myself except for the chants. Comanches have many of them. Went through them all. Then I started making my own up. I wrote stories about every tale the shaman had told me. I chanted them, then changed them, making myself the shaman for the prison. I'd sing them and soon other inmates started picking up on it. Prison officials pulled me out of the cell and beat me until I started putting curses on them. It kind of scared them. Warden said as long as I'm chanting and singing and not using them to plot escapes, they would leave me alone.

"In 1975 I was getting near a possible parole, might not have to go all ten. Then the ceiling fell out. Heard a lot of noise coming from the guards, lot of knocking and clanging like people moving. In less than a day, everybody was gone. The entire prison was empty. Not only were there no guards, there were no prisoners. The whole jail had only one occupant, Charlie Grayrock. I was trapped and left to die."

"Jesus, that's beyond brutality. How did you survive?"

"I'm a Comanche. Remember what I told you? We'd ride a horse into the ground, open his guts, cut out his intestines, sling them over our shoulders, and eat them while escaping. I may have been caged but I had water. The whole prison worked on a cistern system for water. Big water tower catching rain on top of the guard tower. Plenty of water but no food. At least no food until I realized I had gotten so used to rats, snakes, and insects climbing all around and on top of me, that I had taken them for granted. Now I caught them and ate them. Used what I couldn't digest to trap other creatures. I might have given up hope but I would not give up on my life. Kept right on chanting and making up new ones. Even started talking to myself. People would say you're crazy talking to yourself, but it's not true. You aren't crazy if you talk to yourself so you pretend you're two people talking to each other. I got pretty good at it."

"It was probably a year, maybe even two or two and a half when Llewellyn Lawrence found me. I was chanting away, singing an opera in which I played three parts. I was loud, loud enough that some North Vietnamese people who were setting up villages heard me. They were moving from the north into the south since the Yanks left. They heard me but nobody would enter the building. They did not understand my language but they knew I was an American. Word got around that there was a spirit of the enemy still inhabiting their country. Somehow it got back to your father who was now helping the Vietnamese regain South Vietnam."

"He didn't believe them, thought they were just hearing things but when they started quoting lines and singing my chants, Lawrence recognized some of the lines, especially the ones from the Comanche Ghost dance. He had the villagers take him to the prison. He listened and heard a human voice, some words spoken in English and some in Comanche. The prison was wide open, overgrown with vines and weeds. Arens went up and down the corridors until he found my cell. He sent people to find some iron bars that could be used to pry open my cell. It didn't take long. The rust had eroded the door hinges, but not quite enough that I could have knocked them loose."

"Arens asked me if I needed help in leaving the cell but I declined. I had spent every day exercising in my tiny space. I was strong and walked that way out of the cell and out of the prison. I asked who he was, but he said we need some safety and comfort first before we told our stories."

"Your father had saved me. After he heard my story and learned that I had been left to die, he blasphemed the United States. He told me about the victory of Vietnam over the insurgent Americans. I learned the Americans were run out of his new country with their tails tucked between their legs. The American government was even pushing helicopters off of their aircraft carriers."

"That's it?" said Lawrence. "That's the whole story?"

"No Lawrence. I can't tell it all to you. Arens and I must tell it to you, together. When I set the Cessna down near Tabasokwia Lake, we'll almost be finished with our journey. Soon you'll discover everything you've been looking for, and even more."

The plane was approaching Winisk River Provincial Park, "Charlie, what are we looking for down there? The whole area's nothing but rivers, lakes, forests, and huge rock formations?"

"You've just flown over a small part of the Canadian Shield. You're right. Not much civilization down there. If you see any people, they'll most likely be Native Canadians, Crees or Ojibwas. The irony is that this province, Ontario, is the most densely populated in all of Canada. But not here. Go from Thunder Bay east and you've got Kitchener, Windsor, Toronto but go north and west and the populations per square mile go from five to point zero."

"I take it the lack of humans is why Arens lives here?"

"You are one smart white man, Lawrence. Place is like a freezer most of the year but it has an unlimited food supply if you know how to take care of yourself."

CHAPTER TWENTY EIGHT

Cave of the Beast

Grayrock banked the Cessna to port to get a better view of the terrain. "There's Winisk River. We're dropping near the tree tops now. Keep your eyes open for a large rock hill. That'll be in Tabasokwia Lake. You'll see it, a high gray rock escarpment. That's our landing spot."

The Cessna was following the Tabasokwia River. "That the rock, Charlie? Just up on your side's an escarpment. Looks like pure basalt."

"Canadian shield was one big mass of rock millions of years ago. Glaciers cut right through it. We're going down."

The Cessna had a relatively wide stretch of water to use as a landing strip. The escarpment was on the left and a dense forest of spruce, birch, and pine to their right on the very edge of the river. The Cessna turned 180^0 and headed to the trees. Charlie slowly guided the plane within fifteen or twenty yards of the shore. There was no wind as Charlie set the Cessna down easily on the river. Lawrence had no idea where they would portage. The escarpment appeared to be a dangerous climb to the top. The forest was nothing but tree next to tree at the water's edge with no perspective of going ashore. Lawrence kept quiet as Charlie searched the shoreline. After a half mile, they came to a fallen tree partially floating in the river. Charlie pulled up next to it and asked Lawrence to reach behind the seats where he would find a couple coils of heavy rope.

The plane's port pontoon was within a few feet of the fallen tree. Charlie opened the door and stepped out on the pontoon and asked Lawrence for one of the rope coils. Taking one end of the rope, Charlie tied it to a fallen birch tree. The other end he tied to a pontoon and then got back into the pilot's seat. He revved up the engine and slowly drifted down river. Lawrence was worried that the cleat on the pontoon would rip out while trying to pull the birch tree. To his surprise, the birch along with four or five other fallen trees pulled away from their original position and floated down river without hardly any strain on the Cessna.

"You see what we've got here Lawrence?"

"Wow, the trees are bundled together like some kind of platform. Wait a second. Where the trees were is an open shore line with a small cove. Can you get the Cessna into it?"

"What do you think?" Charlie went out onto the pontoon and untied it from the cleat, tossing the rope onto one of the fallen trees. Back in the Cessna, Charlie reversed the engines and carefully guided the plane into the small cove.

"You'd have to be one sharp eyed pilot to see the plane now. Let's secure the plane to the trees. Then we'll unload and get traveling again."

"Traveling, how? Every place we flew by was some kind of island. The whole area's a dense forest. We're going to hike with that load you've got in storage?"

"Who said anything about hiking? What are us Red skins famous for?"

"I doubt you've got any horses tied up around here. Are you going to build us a birch tree canoe?"

"Nope. See that pile of trees down shore, the ones not out in the water? Got a fiberglass Pelican DLX fifteen foot canoe in there. No motor, though. You're gonna have to paddle, white man."

Charlie had several packages stored in the Cessna's hold. He lashed them securely in the canoe. Both men's personal packs sat in the canoe's bottom. They paddled upstream. The current was not too fast and left few rocks protruding.

"Lawrence, if we went the other way, we'd be on the Winisk River. You can actually go all the way to the Hudson Bay."

"Charlie, why all of this secrecy? Hiding your plane, keeping a stashed canoe out in the wilds? My father's not a wanted man anymore. Canadians opened their country to draft dodgers and defectors. U S couldn't extradite him. My mother said they don't even care anymore. Why doesn't he just move into Thunder Bay or Toronto, someplace where there's ..."

"You say civilization and I'll shoot you in the back of your head, Kemo Sabe."

Lawrence kept his eyes forward and dug deep into the cold water, "yeah, it was going to come out that way, wasn't it?"

"Arens is going to have to explain it. He'll do it better than me. I just know him from the time he saved me from dying alone in that prison. Since we've been back to America, he's avoided all people unless they're tribal. You're right, he has no reason, outside of his own, to live in the forests of Canada and fraternize only with Native Americans or Canadians. I have never heard him say one bad word about any Aborigine. But anytime some outsider crosses his path, he's nearly insane with rage. I swear he'd just about kill them all if he could get away with it."

"I guess it bothers me that he hasn't contacted my mother or me. Maybe he figures we're the bad guys too."

"Lawrence, the reason for not contacting his family is quite simple. I'm surprised you don't get it. Think what you told me about McVeigh and his family, especially his sister. The fucking government of the United States is just like the Gestapo in Germany. I know it and so does he. If he made himself visible, the FBI or SS would be ragging all over his family, trying to get him to show up in their territory. I think that's what he sees."

"Yeah, I guess I can see that. I know when I go back, the two FBI agents will be after my ass anyway they can."

It was almost dark now, the sun having fallen behind a large brown rock mesa on the left. Charlie steered the canoe within a few feet of the rock scree, boulders broken off the edge of the brown metamorphic rock layers rising nearly thirty feet above the water. After ten minutes of following the river, the escarpment became eroded rock debris, the beginning of a forest belt from hilltop to shoreline. They went another hundred yards into the forest, closed on both sides. Charlie turned the canoe to port, along the rocky stream edge. There was no shore, just huge boulders. The hill now had a slower rise with many spruce, pines, and birches.

"We're going through those boulders? There's no way through them. Look at the shore. There's no beach to pull up the canoe."

"Don't need a beach. We grab the gunnels, leave the canoe, and walk through the boulders. Can't take too long. Gets dark here fast down in this valley. Let's go!"

They wrestled the canoe from boulder to boulder. Twice Lawrence caught his foot in small cracks between the rocks, nearly twisting his ankle. It took less time than Lawrence had thought. They, with the canoe made, it to the tree line without losing any cargo or breaking any bones.

"Damn, he's really got himself hidden out of sight doesn't he?"

"Not really Lawrence. The Crees and the Ojibwa visit him regularly. This is their land and they live in it like you would in a city. You'll see when the sun's up tomorrow. There'll be Natives all over the river with weirs trapping fish."

"Weirs?"

"The Ojibwa go right into these rocks and boulders and build barriers and fences from the tree brush and latticework done by the Ojibwa women. They especially like to catch sturgeons which have nearly disappeared in many of the other rivers and stream. Besides the nourishment of the fish, after they're dried and pounded, they mix them with fish oil which is loaded with even more vitamins. It takes many months for the mixtures to go bad. What you white people have given up is using all of life's offerings. The Ojibwa make glue out of the sturgeon bladders which waterproofs the seals on their canoes."

Llewellyn Lawrence spoke, "the shield used to be the home of many tribes, tribes that hunted caribou, moose, beaver, and bears. How they used a land with an Arctic climate of long, deadly cold winters with only a few weeks of a cool summer is beyond what America calls the modern man."

He walked out of the darkened pine trees. The sun was setting on the east side of the escarpment. Peter Lawrence looked at his father. He had only seen him in photographs that were thirty-five years old. Despite the fading light, he knew the man was Llewellyn Lawrence. His father was thin, medium height, probably five feet nine inches, weighing about a hundred and forty pounds. Llewellyn Lawrence was sinewy, blood vessels forming ridges on liver-spotted skin. His hair was snow white, pure and uncut, a bushy mess ridged at his temples from wearing a hat. He wore wire-rimmed glasses, the right lens nearly clear glass but the left as thick as a coke bottle bottom. Peter figured that his father could see well with his right eye thus making him able to live and survive without wearing glasses. His hands were muscular, covered with liver spots, worn and wrinkled with his fingernails either broken or chewed, leaving no white edge. As he walked through the pine trees and became more visible, Peter noticed a slight hobbling in his left leg as if he had a knee problem.

"You two jamokes gonna to make me lug that canoe in the trees? Let's get with it here!"

Nothing was said, no one questioned. They portaged the canoe over and through the rocks, eventually lashing it to a pine tree. Each of them grabbed a parcel or travel bag and Lew led them through the pine trees into the dark woods. They followed a path, level by level, up the rock escarpment and through the pine trees growing out of the scree walls. It did not take long before they arrived at a cabin built into the side of the escarpment. Lew showed them where a small fire in a stone faced fireplace was turning to ashes and cinders. Lew placed a few small branches on it. He asked if they would like some gooseberry whiskey.

Both answered yes.

"According to what Chief told me and why I wanted you to visit, is you had some contact with Tim McVeigh?"

"Yes, I witnessed his execution."

"That's got to be pretty hard to take. Watching a man die that took out a slew of government agents."

"Actually there wasn't much to it. Just like watching a man on an operating table being anesthetized for an operation," said Peter Lawrence feeling the gooseberry whiskey going to his head. Anger was rising in Peter that he might not be able to control.

"What is it you want from me? Your trip wasn't exactly a little car hop to the beach on Sunday."

Lawrence watched his father empty his plastic glass and fill it back up again as if they were a couple of old friends shooting the breeze after not seeing each other for a long time. Llewellyn Lawrence picked up a red pack of cigarettes, shook the opened end up, and pulled out a Pall Mall.

"What do I want from him?" thought Peter Lawrence.

The anger festered as Peter responded, "I think McVeigh wanted to protect you and Charlie from being chased by the FBI. You mind losing the cigarette?"

"My house, door's over there if you can't handle the smoke. FBI has no jurisdiction up here. I think that's bullshit. How'd they even know about the chief and me anyhow?"

"He left a stack of papers hidden at his grandfather's apple orchard. Those papers contained a map showing his route from Oklahoma City to Thunder Bay and you and Charlie."

"Why the hell did he do that? Kind of stupid of him looks to me."

Charlie sensed the atmosphere changing, one that if the embers were fed would ignite into a full fire, "Arens, you didn't know Timmy like I did. He pulled off the greatest one man attack made on the United States ever. But he was very loyal to his family and cohorts. Peter and he had a few random associations and he got to know Peter pretty well from them. There was more, much more to his legacy hidden in a barrel than a road map to you and me. He documented all the harassment the government did to his family. My guess is that he was hoping Lawrence would avenge some of the FBI's Gestapo attack on his sister and his grandfather."

Charlie picked up the bottle of whiskey and filled his glass, "and I'm sure he wanted somebody to cover your ass and mine should our names come up."

"More bullshit. Listen Peter, Charlie and I know how to take care of ourselves. McVeigh was stupid riding around without a license plate. Was he begging to be caught or just dumber than I thought? He would be alive today if he had made it to Thunder Bay. Charlie was all gassed and ready to go. I had already set into action a place to hide him in Labrador near the Torngat Mountains. Soon as the Chief and McVey landed, I was going to jump into his Cessna. We'd have had him on the East Coast in a few hours. Nobody would have had any idea where he was. Just me and Charlie. He fucked up and he paid for it."

Peter was feeling the whiskey and to make it worse, he was tired. His father inhaled the cigarette smoke deeply into his lungs and exhaled it back out of his nostrils. The whiskey and his father's arrogance were two conditions that, when combined would lead to a confrontation both would later regret.

"You really think you're Arens the Conqueror, don't you? Took on the United States Army, escaped from prison, fought with the Viet Cong, backed down combat troops, and now you're ready to put down a man who fought the same enemy as you did - - the United States."

"You don't know what I went through. You weren't there …"

"No, but Uncle George was. He told me about you in detail, up until you deserted and turned on the US. My aunt in France has stacks of your letters. She copied each and sent them to me. I know all about you and the Quyens. You were a hero. There's no doubt."

Peter Lawrence reached out his hand. "Here, I want to shake the hand of the hero of the Vietnam War."

Llewellyn Lawrence backed off from his son's hand and chugged down the glass of Gooseberry whiskey, placing the empty glass on a table and flicking the Pall Mall butt into the fireplace.

Peter was not through, "What? You won't shake my hand Rambo? How about a hug? After all, I am your son. But wait. You probably got kids running all over Hanoi, France, and

Canada don't you? Don't hug them either. How long have you been close to me? You could have flown out of Thunder Bay and been in Pennsylvania or Virginia in three hours or less. And let's not forget the woman you forgot."

Peter refilled his glass.

Charlie spoke, "Petey, Kemo Sabe, you ever seen how those gooseberries rot on the ground? Rot right into alcohol and the bears eat 'em up. Drunk bear's a dangerous animal, especially to himself Petey."

"Charlie, I know what you're saying," said Peter and emptied his glass into the kitchen sink. "I'm intoxicated Chief, but not just from bear booze."

Peter Lawrence was somewhat intoxicated but still under control, "thirty-four years and the man was as close as a couple hours on an airplane. Did he know about his son? Did Mr. Marlboro man know how close I was when I lived in Niagara Falls, New York?"

Arens spoke, "I knew where you were. How do you think your aunt's got so much information about me? We shared communications. I couldn't take the chance."

"Now, now Daddy. I got that touch, the touch I've been told you have. You know what I mean. It's how you can sense when someone's lying to you? Mon Mere said I have it, got it from you. You're lying."

Arens turned on him but Peter was the better fighter thanks to Uncle Ralph. Peter partially blocked a right jab that caught the side of his head, feinted to his right but twisted on his right heel as he jabbed Arens' rib cage, knocking the breath out of Arens. Peter held fast even though he could have caught Arens with a succession of jabs to his open abdomen. His father was gasping for air from the first blow and the years of cigarettes.

"Fucking Ralph! You got one of George's shivs to cut me up?"

Charlie stood between them. "Listen Old Man, this boy's gonna to beat the shit out of you. He already beat up a suit from Plate Extract Inc.. I've seen him handle those fists. He's gonna put you down and out. Petey, that's enough. What's this Uncle George shiv stuff?"

"He taught me how to use a knife in combat. Got one belted to the inside of my left calf."

Arens had gotten his breath back. "You don't know what the danger is. You think you've seen how bad the United States authorities can be? Worse than you'd ever expect. If I made contact with anybody in the States, they'd be all over them, probably arrest them and throw them in prison. If you think otherwise, think you'll never get caught, one day they'll eat you up."

"They already tried, Arens," said Peter telling him about the two FBI agents back in New York.

As he heard Peter's description of taking down Yrac at the prison and then conning both FBI agents into trying to find McVeigh's satchel after Peter had already absconded with it, he could not help but smile.

"I don't hug but I will shake your hand."

Peter grasped his father's hand tightly and pulled Arens into a tight hold that Arens did not want. Both fought off tears but lost the fight as they returned to their Gooseberry whiskey.

"You guys more hungry or more tired?"

Both Charlie and Lawrence said tired.

"Okay, there's a couple of bed rolls under that book shelf next to the front window. Floor's your bedroom, bed's mine. I need to stow the packages you brought Chief."

Lawrence had no idea what was in the packages that Charlie had brought with them. He only knew they were heavy. Arens called Peter over to the bookcase on the right side of the stone fireplace.

"Grab here on the edge on your side. Do not try to lift the bookcase. The damn thing'll fall over. Just edge it a few inches at a time, first my side then yours. I'll tell you when we're out far enough."

It was slow going and as they inched it along, Lawrence could see that his reading habit had a lot to do with his father's genes. In this one of four bookcases were probably ninety or a hundred books. When the bookcase was out far enough to get behind it, a chilly flow of air came from behind the wall. His father told him to stop. The back of the bookcase was a black hole in the wall. Arens got a flashlight from the kitchen cabinet and waved Peter over to his side of the bookcase. With the flashlight on, Peter could see that there was a deep cave in the wall, hidden by the bookcase.

"Bear cave. I think this rock here was a molten formation millions of years ago. The cave is probably a tunnel where lava flowed through. Goes back quite a distance."

Peter followed the light from the flashlight as they walked along a tunnel probably twenty-five yards deep from the inside of the cabin. It ended in a huge room, where a light fixture was hanging from the ceiling. Arens flipped a switch and the cave lit up.

"How'd you get electricity back here? In fact how do you get electricity period?"

Arens shined the flashlight up to the ceiling, "see those wires? Go back all the way into the cabin. I put a solar panel high up in a birch tree, wound the wire around its trunk and camouflaged it with clay and chips of tree bark. Look over in the corner. Got five storage batteries that hold charges long enough that I never lose power even if there's cloudy weather for a week."

"Got a computer too."

"It's how I run my ..." Arens stopped short but realized now was the time to trust his son. "I help people fight the law, escape capture. You probably guessed that already."

"It's why McVeigh was set to use you. I know about you and Charlie."

"I heard that white man!"

Charlie had followed them into the cave. "How you like this place, Kemo Sabe?"

"Amazing! Here, let me help you with those boxes."

The boxes were very heavy. "Damn heavy, Charlie. My guess is you got rifles in here?"

"That's the business I'm in. I import them and Arens stores and distributes them. What's the destination for these Arens?"

"Trout Lake. Charlie said you knocked a Plate Extract Inc. suit on his ass and shoved off his seaplane in the middle of Wunnumin Lake. The tribes at Trout Lake need these arms. The tribes are worried about Plate Extract Inc. exploring and exploiting their territory. Right now that's all there is, just exploring. Got Plate Extract Inc. agents, chemists, and workers and thugs, guards with weapons, all over the area just south of the lake. Plate Extract Inc. says they're just looking but there's no way of knowing. Guy you dumped sounds like the number two chief. He'll be looking for you."

"What's Plate Extract Inc. trying to do?"

"Mine anything they can get out of our land. Most likely they have open pit mines looking for platinum group elements like ruthenium, rhodium, palladium, osmium, iridium, and platinum. They all have similar physical and chemical properties, and tend to occur together in the same mineral deposits. The metals have outstanding catalytic properties and are highly resistant to wear and tarnish, making platinum, in particular, well suited for fine jewelry. They have a high resistance to chemical attack, excellent high-temperature characteristics, and stable electrical properties. All these properties are being exploited for industrial applications.

How bad are these extractions? Platinum itself is used as a catalyst for the control of automobile and industrial plant emissions but also a catalyst to produce acids, organic chemicals, and pharmaceuticals. PGMs are used in bushings for making glass fibers used in fiber-reinforced plastic and other advanced materials, in electrical contacts, capacitors, conductive and resistive films used in electronic circuits, and in dental alloys used for making crowns and bridges. Even in jewelry. Nearly every one of these need smelting and chemical interactions to be processed. Fly over Big Trout Lake and look for green forests. Aren't many. The mining's turning them light brown, orange, and red. That's what happens to the forest when you're mining and smelting PGMs."

"How do you know all this?" said Peter.

Arens paused. He had to be careful. How he left the Quyens and where he began his life as a renegade made disclosure a danger.

"I left Vietnam many years ago. I had no particular reason for leaving. I loved the people there, especially the Quyens. They survived the war and are now highly respected in their village. Nam was becoming more and more mercantile. It's why I went to France, as you know from your mother's kin. I belonged to many unions around Paris, took part in many of the union strikes. Evelyn would be very surprised at how well I learned French."

Arens saw Peter's eyebrows rise but went on, "I especially worked with groups hoping to stop environmental catastrophes and help the people who were treated unfairly by the industries in France. I got mixed up with the French syndicate but too deep. They would hire me to assist their members when treated unfairly."

"And how did you help people treated badly by industry and the government?"

"I killed people."

Arens maintained eye contact with his son, "it is my esprit, my inner spirit. There are those who must die and I am the executioner. Do you have a problem with that?"

Peter Lawrence was not ready to reveal his own personal confrontations and lethal actions dealing with those who he needed to kill. "No, Arens, go on with Plate Extract Inc.."

"Plate Extract Inc. is not the real company running this exploration. Boliden, a Swedish mining and smelting company specializing in copper, zinc, lead, gold and silver mining and extraction is the real force behind it. They are totally irresponsible and could care less about the people living near their mines and smelters. They fuck the environment. As long as they make a profit and don't get caught. Last year their Aitik copper mine near Gällivare in Northern Sweden spewed chemicals from an open mine pit filled with slurry ponds over a distance of 120 meters. One of their dams failed, ruptured and sent contaminated water into the environment. According to the report, as I remember it, the cause of the dam failure was either bad conditions in the dam or how the foundation was laid. In truth, the failure was really caused by shortcomings in Boliden's own inspection during planning, construction and repairs. The Vassara River was covered with the white slurry from the break over a 8 km area. It had a lethal impact on the soil and the fauna. It would really piss you off if you ever saw the Vassara River before the break. It was really beautiful with mountains rising to the west and forests as green as green can be surrounding the river as it flowed into the Lina River. From Gällivare the slurry in the river flowed through all this forest biome and into the Gulf of Bothnia. Scientists feared that the reproduction of salmon would be disturbed. In order for eggs to reach development, the salmon roe needs high oxygen concentrations in the water and this was impossible due to the slurry. The slurries stayed in place until the following spring. Added to the slurry contamination was the release of copper into the environment. It was four times higher than what Boliden admitted. Out and out lethal."

Peter was astounded. "You mean the same assholes that virtually destroyed a habitat in Sweden, is going to mine the land of the native peoples of Canada? What did you do to stop Boliden in Sweden?"

"I had worked with some ex-French officers from the Direction Générale de la Sécurité Extérieure, or DGSE, and the Sûreté Nationale on some drug busts for a few months a few years after I emigrated from Nam. It seems the French had no problem with my deserting the U.S. Army and turning traitor. They also looked the other way concerning my aggressive behavior with the Paris Unions and my association with the Italians. After being contacted by an unnamed ecology radical organization, a squad composed of myself and four others attacked the facility, trying to shut it down. Nothing seemed to work. Our best shot was sabotage but the company was so big and wealthy, they either fixed or replaced damaged equipment within hours. We tried something else," said Arens.

"What something else?"

"Instead of blowing up smelters and digging machines, we ..."

Llewellyn Lawrence hesitated.

"Well, what else? These people were ruining the world, running poisons out of the ground and into people's bodies. Why didn't you shoot them?"

"We did. Went after the leaders, killed one or two upper management and a handful of site managers. Made no difference. Company had new managers in place within hours. Boliden even brought in the Piketen which is an emergency response division of the Swedish Police Service, similar to SWAT in the United States. They're called in when situations occur that are too dangerous for ordinary police to handle, like hostage situations, arresting armed suspects, arresting barricaded suspects, or guarding against radicals like us. Piketen is very dangerous, highly specialized and trained with one main task and four secondary tasks. Their main field is dangerous situations in dangerous environments, hostage situations, and insurgent attacks like we were doing. Their other tasks are serving high-risk arrest warrants, maintaining riot control and escorting VIP's and other objects of value."

"You backed off from them?"

"Peter, Boliden didn't care if their management people got iced as long as production continued and that's what changed our approach. We started killing off the workers. Boliden backed off the operation, shut it down, and made extensive changes. Not what we wanted. We wanted to shut down their operation permanently."

"Wait a fucking second here? You killed the common people, the workers? That's wrong, absolutely wrong. Jesus Christ, you're a mass murderer."

Charlie had been silent until now, "you better cool your white ass down Kemo Sabe. Listen to what he's telling you. No, better I lay it on you first. The warriors win wars, not Kings or Presidents or even Generals. Laborers build cars, not plant managers or company VPs. How many principals or superintendents taught you anything? None, it was those people, teachers, who sat down with you in the classroom who produced. Quanah Parker took my people, the Comanche, to war and in man versus man beat you Yankees. Until the United States took out the warriors, the Comanche could not be beaten. Tȟatȟáŋka Íyotake or as he's better known to you, Sitting Bull, didn't win the Battle of the Little Bighorn by killing Custer. He won by killing the troops."

"What do you think was the decisive factor that ensured victory for the North Vietnamese? Killing the soldiers, not negotiations," said Arens Lawrence. "Would it have ended any sooner if some Viet Cong killed Westmoreland? No, it wouldn't have. How about killing that asshole Johnson or that retarded crook Nixon? Wouldn't have changed a thing."

"So where does that put your rifles?"

"At this point putting them in the hands of natives won't work. Canadian Mounties would be swarming all over every tribe up there. The best strategy is that of Mao Zedong. The enemy advances, we retreat; the enemy camps, we harass; the enemy tires, we attack; the enemy retreats, we pursue. Never be seen, ever attack."

Llewellyn Lawrence opened one of the rifle boxes, "Steyr Mannlichers? Aluminum folding stock, adjustable cheek piece and butt plate with height marking, and an ergonomically exchangeable pistol grip, how much did this cost me?"

"They're 30/06's at a thousand a piece."

"You've got to have stolen these at that price Charlie. Straight out of the catalog, what're they about two grand?"

"Yea, a certain white man arms dealer in Germany needs to learn about us Indian givers."

Peter Lawrence looked at one of the two boxes. There were at least six rifles covered with excelsior. "So Charlie, my father and a bunch of Crees are going to gun down people, just common folk doing their job?"

"You don't get it do you, Kemo Sabe? It's a paradox like the insane idea that you can get rid of an ant colony by killing the queen. Not true. Queen's only one ant. Another will replace her over and over again. Kill off the soldiers? Soldier ants only control the drones. Drones are the ones that keep the colony alive, feed the new queen and generate new generations."

"Peter! You came here because of a man who didn't assassinate kings or presidents. He slew one hundred and sixty drones in a colony, a colony of vermin. We're leaving tomorrow for Trout Lake. You don't want to go? Stay here. Charlie and I will only be a day or two. Then Charlie can fly you back to Thunder Bay."

"Why don't you just smoke that damn cigarette outside?" Peter was on edge.

"You got some big chip on your shoulder, don't you? Don't like my smoke? Take one of those sleeping bags and go outside."

Peter Lawrence knew he was at the point where the alcohol would make him lose control of his emotions. With the last bit of clear thinking left, he did just that. Took a sleeping bag and left the cabin.

***

The cold night air had been good for Peter. Sleep came with inebriation and no dreams infiltrated his unconsciousness. He woke up to the noise of his father and Charlie carrying the Mannlichers down to the Cessna. Ignoring both men, he went past them into the cabin and was elated to find a coffee pot on the iron plate above a wood-fed stove. As he sat down, the caffeine slowly rousting his brain cells, Arens returned, having finished loading the seaplane. He sat down opposite his son at the kitchen table.

"Going or not going son?"

"It was good sleeping outside. My grandfather ... Your father tried very hard to replace you. Poppa George got me out of the city and its non-living creatures sometimes wrongly called humans. We lived straight off nature. Something happens inside of me when I sleep in the open air surrounded by trees, birds, forest creatures, basically the living of life. I woke a few times, thought maybe I ought to take my Ruger and shoot you while I had an edge."

"Why didn't you? You're right getting pissed at me. Could have remedied all those years having no father. Here I was, close enough to ..."

"No, Arens, you might have abandoned me physically but you left me with a woman that raised me to be just like you. Poppa George picked up his share of the task and gave me what he had given you. He told me the stories, especially about you growing up. He is very proud of what you became even if you are a murderer."

"You don't really have an anathema to judging and killing, do you Arens?"

"You're overdoing it, Peter. Do I feel remorse killing? No, I have no problem. In Vietnam when I saw babies tossed into the air and blown apart by kids fresh out of high school or college, any moral antipathy I had for thou shall not kill evaporated. I have never killed without first judging the person an evil being. Evil deserves death, period."

"But how can you be sure?"

"You've already seen that. Poppa George, me, and you can sense it. I know when somebody's lying. It's not some paranormal attribute. Everybody has a bit of that sense only it's not as evolved as our other senses."

"I have trouble accepting that. Yes, I sense other people's lies. It's almost a satanic, but that's just too much exposure to books and movies and TV."

"No Peter, it's not. Do you believe that great musicians have an ear for music? Is their ability a special sense others don't have? Is that just some bullshit from the entertainment industry?"

"No, it's not. Mon mere hears music and can draw music out of the air as soon as she sits in front of a piano but ..."

"You can't, right? You hum songs Peter? Have one that gets your adrenaline flowing when you're in a confrontation?"

Peter Lawrence had needed Llewellyn Lawrence when he was growing and developing, "James Bond theme, every time."

"Not everybody has just the magic of music to excite them. Some, like Evelyn, can create from her sense what to expect from people. Everybody has doubts when faced with people who might be scamming them. Most let it ride and then wind up thinking they should have known better when that investment planner sold them bummer stocks. You know that old saying, *if it sounds too good to be true, it probably is?* Intuition, it's called intuition and maybe it's the seventh sense?"

Charlie returned from loading the Cessna. "You two white men gonna sit around drinking coffee and talking?"

The three of them wound their way over the cliff edges, through the throng of pine trees, and down to the canoe. Charlie sat astern and held the canoe firm against a boulder as Peter went aft to paddle. Arens squeezed between the Mannlichers wrapped in oil cloth and the ammo boxes. With the additional weight of Arens, it took them a little longer to paddle to the Cessna. After loading the rifles and ammo on the plane, Peter took one of the two rear seats while Arens sat shotgun. The engines ignited quickly. Charlie went through his checklist and taxied to the middle of the lake. Using the wind direction, Charlie lifted them up above the forest and headed east northeast.

The flight only took fifty minutes, the weather superb despite a little wind and some rain. As they approached Big Trout Lake, Arens pointed out the area where Plate Extract Inc. was only supposed to be exploring. Below the plane was more forest. The ground was green and alive until they neared Nemeigusabinsabins Lake, ten miles south, southeast of Big Trout Lake. The change in terrain was devastating. Hundreds of miles of an arboreal biome had become orange, naked rock hills. Only a few trees rose out of the soil that was visibly drained of any organic material.

Grayrock pointed out their destination, "see to your right? About two miles northwest? That's Big Trout Lake. Beautiful, isn't it?"

Peter could see the barren rock fields just south of the lake. "Does Plate Extract Inc. have leases on any of this area?"

Arens replied, "two hundred and twenty-one mining claims in all those areas below us right now. There are claims on all the areas that have no visible vegetation. Look to the right. They have leases on almost all of the forest areas from the rock scree area up to the lake. You know what that means?"

Peter responded, "it means that probably this desecrated rock land below us was once an arboreal forest just like the land we flew over. The whole stretch is theirs, maybe what a thousand square miles of forest becoming a rock wasteland? That's got to be ..."

Arens broke in, "six hundred and forty thousand acres. Where are we landing Chief?"

"Plate Extract Inc. workers' complex and the mining facilities are on that isthmus below us. See them? Between that rounded lake to its north and Nemeigusabins Lake. The company flies in on a Seair Seaplanes Beaver float plane to Nemeigusabins Lake and it has docks at the north of the isthmus. Other side of the isthmus is a big rock shelf like your cabin's built into. Not a good place to put down a plane. Once down it's nearly impossible to scale the walls and cross the rocks to their camp."

"We're gonna to drop down just above Big Island and moor at Kitchenuhmaykoosib Island, Arens. Danny LaCatt, the Cree chief, will meet us there. Get those belts fastened cause here we go."

***

Danny LaCatt was a solid man who wore narrow glasses for reading and had a braided hair tail with strips of leather twined off the end that hung down his back. His face had pock marks from age and frustration. He was the Chief of the Crees who lived around Big Trout Lake. LaCatt had contacted Llewellyn Lawrence to help them get rid of Plate Extract Inc.. LaCatt's had told Arens that raiders who used Charlie's Cessna in an attack on the mining camp could be caught. LaCatt pointed out the mandatory license numbers on the side of Charlie's Cessna. The plane would surely be observed and recorded.

Arens came up with a different attack plan that was workable and simple as the best plans should be. The Plate Extract Inc. Camp was mostly inhabited by mine laborers and drillers, basic workers. They were supervised by drilling managers, explosive technicians, camp guards, scientists, and company management. These were the operations people. Once every few months, executives from the home office flew up from Toronto to check on production and shipments. Every Saturday afternoon, when morning mining operations were finished, the workers were given time off to head for Kitchenuhmaykoosib Island. The company guards patrolled the island to prevent confrontations between Plate Extract Inc. workers and the natives. After Saturday recreation time on the island was ended, the workers returned to camp and spent Saturday night resting and playing games and sports within the barbed wire topped chain link fence. The operations people were flown into Thunder Bay that night to be with family or to party. On Sunday operations staff and Plate Extract Inc. executives met all morning and afternoon to go over the next week's business operations. The management staff, top level operations supervisors, and accountants spent their time changing or altering production plans. The operations cadre would share an afternoon brunch with them and then fly back to Big Trout Lake. Once their guarded time-off on the island was over and they returned to the mining camp, workers were not allowed to leave the camp. This was the protocol ever since a major confrontation between the mine workers and the Crees at Kitchenuhmaykoosib Island occurred. Plate Extract Inc. decided to protect their staff by keeping them under lock and key until work began on Monday morning.

The Crees marched and demonstrated on the island against the government's leasing of the land to Plate Extract Inc.. This did nothing except lead to a brawl with Plate Extract Inc. employees. The Crees filed lawsuits against the government and Plate Extract Inc., fighting the exploitation of their tribal land. Deforestation was rampant, as Charlie had shown to Peter and Llewellyn during their flight to Big Trout Lake. Massive amounts of trees and vegetation had been cleared and burned, destroying food sources for many of the Cree. The mines were pumping cyanide and mercury from platinum extractions into rivers, streams, and some of the lakes. Without knowing it, Cree families were being exposed to toxic waste. As more and more mining and ore extraction took place, Cree people began developing skin diseases, denigrating rashes, headaches, vomiting, and diarrhea, plus the lethal signs of mercury poisoning. The natives had no money. Not only could they not afford to go to a doctor, most lived in villages that were inaccessible to medical services. Like their ancestors before them, they lived off the land and streams.

Plate Extract Inc. workers were spending down time and limited vacations on Kitchenuhmaykoosib Island. The natives carried signs and yelled at the workers, ironically people who had absolutely no control over the mining. The tension reached an explosive point when one Saturday night the workers got totally intoxicated. Danny LaCatt and some Cree natives ordered them to get off the Cree land. LaCatt told them, "that this land was given to us by the Creator and it is our past, present and future, not the white man's." A massive melee broke out, sending the Crees to jail and Plate Extract Inc. workers back to camp. It was the only confrontation between the two groups. It was at this point that the Cree's chief contracted with Llewellyn.

Arens was sitting across a table from Danny LaCatt, Peter on his left and Charlie on his right. He stood up, pushing his chair backward and motioned for Peter to get up and take his seat. The four of them were at the same bar where the fight between the Crees and Plate Extract Inc. workers had happened. Tonight, nobody was in the bar except these four men. Peter looked to Charlie for guidance but Charlie shrugged and held up his left hand, fingers extended and palm facing Peter. Arens turned his new seat so he was facing LaCatt directly. Scooting the chair across the floor on its four legs, he moved within inches of LaCatt's face. Arens titled his head left then right and spoke.

"You know you're going to kill people?"

Danny LaCatt was scared. "I thought that. It's why we bought those rifles."

"Are those men at the bar, the six you've asked to join us?"

"Yes, they are. I'll call them ..."

"Tell me each one's reason for joining with us."

One by one Danny LaCatt listed off each young tribe member; four Crees and two Ojibwas. Two of them had worked for the mining operations of Plate Extract Inc.. They knew first-hand the dangerous working conditions. They had been beaten by the guards and eventually fired. The man named Cowessess had a wife who died during child birth from mercury poisoning. She had used a stream flowing from a mining extraction to prepare food for her family. Ironically the name Cowessess means little child which was dead. Another watched his father turn into an alcoholic. Instead of a full pay, the company gave him a gallon of ethyl alcohol once a week. He died a horrible death and from that point on, the company ceased hiring natives.

One very small, very muscular Ojibwa was called to the mining camp to pick up his grandmother's body. She had died from a fall into a mine. She had been hired as a cook and according to the mining supervisor on site, was taking meals to workers when she slipped off the rim of a seventy-five foot air shaft. However an autopsy on Kitchenuhmaykoosib Island found that her vagina had been extensively damaged most likely caused by being savagely raped.Llewellyn Lawrence was convinced that LaCatt had done a thorough job of recruiting natives for an attack. Each one had a reason to seek revenge against Plate Extract Inc..

"Call all six of them over, Danny."

The six natives were now facing Arens.

"You each are ready to kill Plate Extract Inc. workers?"

All six gestured with nods.

"You, Quidel. You're name means burning fire. Does your name tell me your courage?"

"Yes, but why are we waiting until the operations people ..."

- 204 -

Arens held up both hands. "Are all of you wondering why we're going to wait until the honchos are gone?"

LaCatt raised his head, making eye contact with Arens. "Yes, it makes no sense. We can hold off until they're back Sunday night."

"Charlie, tell them about being an Aborigine."

"How much do you young warriors know about your heritage?"

There was no response.

"You own this country. You own this whole continent. There were no humans here until people from Asia migrated across the Bering Sea and settled on this continent. For thousands of years these people, your forefathers lived in tribes that slowly filled this land from the Pacific to the Atlantic Coast. Many different peoples shared similar lives and became the tribes you know today. Tribal life is every member's responsibility. Leadership is won or lost man-to-man. No chief gained his leadership by wampum, money spent to gain votes or bribe electors. Our tribes do not have politics, elections. The tribe is you and the tribe is one. The chiefs are not superior, they are the tribe. The tribe can discard them if they are wrong, even kill them. Tribes created their habitat according to their lives. Tribes that survived on fish, lived an estuary life. Tribes that lived by the buffalo, like the Apache and Comanche, claimed the plains. Many tribes crossed over the Rio Grande and formed civilizations like the Aztecs and Mayans."

"We are the best warriors life has seen. Our entire life was war. Your place in the tribe was decided by your prowess in battle. Before the white man came with his weapons, the Comanche bands drove Apaches back to Mexico, attacked Pawnees in Kansas, Utes in Colorado, Osages in Oklahoma, and Blackfeet in Wyoming. Comanches owned the Plains Indian territories. For the Comanche, Sioux, Apache, and every other warrior tribe, there was only life or death. We killed our enemy and left none alive."

"The white men came for many years and we stopped him. When he opposed us, we destroyed him. Killed his people, fired his villages, burned his crops, and cleared the earth to prevent his retaliation. No tribe was more deadly than the Comanche. We went after what was most fundamental to them, their villages with families and homes. We killed and we burned."

"Had not the white man made weapons greater than our power, we would rule all of America right now. A Comanche attacks the whole being by using the Comanche whole being. Each tribe member has his place. A Comanche knows you must destroy the whole nest, not just the king snake. Warriors die but a tribe lives when it is not in the battle. To defeat Comanche, Apache, Arapaho, Cree or Ojibwas you must conquer the tribe, not the leaders."

Arens spoke, "Danny, I know what you're thinking. We should take out the leaders; destroy the mines and the equipment. Have you listened to what the Chief just said? Killing off the Plate Extract Inc. leaders won't shut down Plate Extract Inc. mining and extractions. Gray suits do not run drills into your land. Executives do not run the poison off into the streams. Can't stop it that way. But, no workers means no mining. The land is useless to Plate Extract Inc.. It's useless to the gray suits, executive officers, and every do-nothing honcho getting paid hundreds of thousands of dollars. To kill the tribe, you eliminate its drones. If nobody lives to be a worker, how will their garden grow? How many workers do you think will be there Saturday night?"

"I'm not sure but Makya worked there up until a month or two ago. He probably has a good handle on it. Makya, come up here."

Makya was not a big man. He could still be a teenager. He was sinewy, his thin arms and legs worried Arens.

"Makya, this is ..."

Arens held his left hand in front of LaCatt's mouth, "we all must know as little as possible about our compatriots. Do you understand?"

"Yes. Makya, he is our leader. He would like to speak with you."

"Do you want the others with us?"

Arens spoke, "No. You worked at the mining operation? What did you do?"

"Yes, from start up to last month. I was first hired to cleaned out empty shafts because of my size. I didn't mind because I used to pick up rocks without being caught. No one else was small enough to go through some of the shafts. I used to get gold nuggets, not very big, but I could sell them and feed my family."

"You got caught, didn't you?"

"No, never. It was the big lay-off, when they got rid of the Crees and Ojibwas and ..."

"How many workers are in the camp? Not drillers or smelters or any supervisors, just plain old, hand-by-hand workers?"

"About maybe a hundred or so."

"Makya, I have no idea what we're getting into. You need to tell us what is at the mine and how it operates."

"They are after platinum. It is very, very rare and very difficult to extract. The whole process of getting the platinum takes five to six months, the time spent being a half a mile underground."

"I had no idea it went that deep. How much tunneling is involved?"

"I'm not sure but I think they had a big party when they had finished fifty miles of tunneling."

"Fifty miles of tunnels under ground? How did you find your way, Makya?" asked Antiman.

"It is very difficult since the lighting is not very good until you get to the working area. Their biggest and most difficult problem is how to find a seam. That's why they sent me down there. The tunnels are less than ten feet wide, maybe smaller until the drillers are finished. When the tunnel gets a certain distance, they drill into the wall for the platinum and sometimes they also get palladium. This takes much time and many times they are not hitting a seam. Once they have a seam the machines drill into it. Even when they dig out over seven hundred pounds of rock, they end up with less than one ounce of platinum that is taken to the surface."

"It's got to be ugly down there, Makya."

"You breathe in all the dust. They, the company men, have a full face mask with air tanks feeding into the mask. But only for their people. I got a mask like you get at a hospital, a white cloth. It is useless. They, the workers like to fuck around with you. They all have hard hats, helmets with lights on top. They'll have me squirreling through a small shaft and then cut the tunnel lights off, yelling cave in, everybody out. Scared the shit out of me the first time but you get used to it. I caught on to their fucking around with me. I used to hide the loose rocks that might be gold in crevices I could feel in the dark. Next trip down, I'd pick them up."

"So they have all these tons of rock being excavated, but to where?"

"The surface. There's a big machine that crushes all the rock brought up. It's really bad in the crusher building. Tons and tons of rock are going through the crusher and I've seen men, their own men even, get their hands ripped off trying to dislodge rocks caught in the belts."

"Where does all this crushed rock go?" asked Peter Lawrence.

"A conveyor belts takes the crushed rock powder over a specialized magnetized conveyor belt. The iron is extracted. All of the powder is dissolved into water and air is pumped through it. The platinum bubbles to the top, sort of like the top of a milk shake. Big silver bubbles, erupting into a froth they call concentrate."

"And now they have their platinum?"

"Yeah, but very little, only less than a tenth of a percent is pure platinum."

"How pure must it be?"

"Ninety-eight percent. They take the powder and form it into cakes. It's a bad place to breathe without an oxygen mask. The bags of the powder cakes are thrown into a furnace to burn off nearly all of the other elements. Now they're at ninety-eight percent Platinum. As the molten slurry leaves the furnace, they wash it with cold water."

"Wow, must crack the hell out of it."

"That is why they wash it with cold water. Now the rocks are very fine powder, look like ready mix cement you buy at a building supply store. They funnel the powder into plastic sacks, maybe a gallon size. Drop the sealed platinum bags into cans, silver ones that look like paint cans, and ship the platinum salt, which is what it is now called. It is sent hundreds of miles away."

Charlie stared at Danny LaCatt. "Exploratory operation? What were you Kitchenuhmaykoosib Inninuwugs doing when you inspected the land Plate Extract Inc. was exploring, land that belongs to the Kitchenuhmaykoosib Inninuwugs tribe? What did you say to them? Mr. White Man from Toronto, that's a nice destruction of my land. Please dig hundreds of miles of tunnels, send polluted air over my forests and make yourselves rich?"

Arens ran the situation at Plate Extract Inc. through his mind. He had to take down a hundred men who may or may not be armed. The Steyr Mannlichers had a 10-round HC-magazine so there was room for misses with only six Crees and Ojibwas, Peter, Charlie, and himself. He could not help himself but to worry whether Peter would kill.

"You men are tribal so says Chief LaCatt. He says you all have personal reasons to take down Plate Extract Inc. workers. Tell me what they are."

Llewellyn Lawrence already knew their stories from Danny LaCatt. Each man told of his denigration, ranging from personal sickness from the poisons being dumped into their water supply to having a relative die from a mining accident while working for the company. Arens could feel the anger in each man. One man's wife gave birth to a deformed baby, having no arms, and later the mother died because he could not get her to a doctor.

Arens had to lay it out in no uncertain terms. "You must kill. We must take down every man in that camp. No survivor means a total defeat for Plate Extract Inc. and a warrior's victory for the tribe. Is there a problem?"

Arens saw the rage and knew that none of these men would back out now. If anyone had a problem and wanted out,

Arens would kill him. There would be no choice. Once the attack ended, the only security for each of them was knowing that should they be found out, all six would buy a noose. No one spoke.

"The plane to Thunder Bay leaves late tomorrow night as usual. From what I know about the camp on Saturday night, the workers more or less have a night of drinking and playing games. Movies are shown and women are brought in. Sunday night, on the other hand, is basically a lock down. Is that right, Makya?"

"Yeah, been that way since the big fight on the island."

Arens continued, "The company plane returns Sunday at about five in the afternoon. It will not land. When they try to bring in the Seair Beaver float plane, Chief LaCatt will block them from setting down in the water. He's taking a skiff out onto the lake to block the landing and keep the plane air borne."

"So when do we go in?"

"Sunday night at dusk. The company will radio the authorities about the skiff blocking their landing. It might bring out the local police and probably the Mounties."

Antiman spoke, "we kill them all?"

"Condor of the sun, isn't that what your name means Antiman? Do you see a better way? When tribes battle, they know they must take down the whole tribe. Charlie Graystone made that clear. You know how many survivors Sitting Bull left at Little Big Horn?"

"Not one white mother fucker!" said Wayra whose name meant the wind.

"We're gonna get some practice with the rifles?" asked Quidel, the burning torch.

While his father went through the attack preparations and continued emphasizing taking out every worker and employee at the Plate Extract Inc. Camp, Peter Lawrence watched the natives and listened intently to what each one, including Chief LaCatt had to say. Llewellyn did not have to tell Peter or Charlie that if one of them posed a danger to this mission, he would have to be eliminated. Everyone had to escape from the attack knowing that no one would dare rat them out. Peter was certain his father would kill anyone that did. If he thought tonight one might expose any or all of them, Arens would kill him. Peter was having some worries about Shikoba who had said little and seemed to not care much for what was being discussed.

"That's why you're here now. Chief LaCatt and my friends and I are going to teach you how to handle the Steyr Mannlichers. Let's go." Llewellyn Lawrence led them out of the bar to Danny's aged Ford pick-up truck.

After running each man through rifle training, Llewellyn, Peter, and Charlie returned to the Cessna to do a fly over the mining camp. The more they recognized now, the less they would miss on Sunday.

***

It was late afternoon when LaCatt took them across Big Trout Lake and down a narrow river into Nemeigusabins Lake. They were about two miles north of the camp. Since the base was on the north side of the barren orange rock isthmus, they were not worried about being heard. When they spotted the loading docks on the south side of the isthmus, LaCatt turned off the engine and let it glide them to shore about a half mile above the docks. This was no tactical Army unit. No one had greased their face or wore black outfits with helmets and Kevlar jackets. Each Cree had a Mannlicher shoulder strapped to their back and a belt carrying 30/06 cartridges in magazines. The weather was clear with a slow, cool breeze. Arens kept them on the narrow shoreline of sand at the edge of the forest. They reached the rocks and boulders of the Isthmus quickly. The camp was about a thousand feet northwest of them.

The rocks were not huge. They were nearly flat having eroded, with spaces between them where the tundra forest grew through, nearly covering the rocks. Peter reached the camp entrance first and signaled for the others to stop. Arens came up from the rear and told Peter to stay still for a few minutes. As they silently waited, Arens scanned the front of the camp. There were two large chain fence gates with barbed wire across the top. A chain was linked between the two, secured by a padlock. Makya had given them a very good overview of the compound. There was an entrance guard hut perpendicular to and to the left of the fence. No guards were patrolling any visible section of the camp. Arens told the men that he was going to rattle the gate and see if he could get a guard to come out of the hut. They fell back into the tree line, hidden by the foliage.

Arens did not carry a rifle. Instead he had a Sig Sauer P22 elite pistol holstered at his back. He carried four loaded magazines in his front pockets. It did not take long for a guard to exit the hut once Arens started hollering and rattling the gate. The guard was a very dark skinned black man of about six feet six. He was wearing military khakis shorts and a short-sleeved matching shirt. His black hair was very kinky, the side hair forming a white ring around his head. He wore aviator styled sunglasses dark enough to hide his eyes. The guard brought with him a leashed Doberman pinscher that was so strong he nearly pulled the guard off balance. The guard had an attack pistol holstered on this left side, the holster flap fastened. Arens could outdraw him easily.

"What the fuck you doin' here? You on private property. I can shoot your ass right now and let Baby eat you for dinner."

The man had shortened the choke chain so the Doberman was tight against his right leg. Both man and beast were now directly in front of Arens with only the fastened chain link gates separating them, "Baby? That killer mongrel's name is Baby?"

"You better stop with that fucking laughter, now! Get out of here!"

Arens got as close as he could to the gate. "Look, I got a skiff back up the shore and the motor's conked out."

"What the fuck you doing out on the lake anyhow?"

"I'm on vacation and I was fishing. Can I use your phone to call the boat rental people so they can come get me?"

"Ain't gonna to happen, Bro'. Better start walking."

Arens saw what he needed. The guard had a key ring with an extendable cord attached to his belt. "How about you watch me and get one of your cohorts ..."

"Whores? Ain't no whores here, asshole."

"No, no cohorts. Cohorts are people you work with. You can keep watch over me while another guard calls the boat rental people to come get me. Is that too much to ask?"

"Ain't no cowhores here. No work here on Sundays. Only need one guard to ..."

That was the information Arens needed to know. The key to the gate was right in front of him, within a foot or two. There were only two barriers preventing him from getting into the camp - - the dog and the guard. In one fluid motion, learned from many practice draws, Arens had the Sig Sauer out and had put a bullet through the nose ridge that held the dark sunglasses of the guard.

"Sorry, Baby!" The dog's jaws remained open, still salivating despite the .45 bullet that blew away the dog's right rib cage and heart.

The guard was dead and no other guard would come to the gate. The dead body was within an arm's reach of Arens once he lifted the anchor pole that kept the chained gates from swaying back and forth. He reached over the dog's body, grabbed the key ring and yanked the extension cord as far as it would go. Flipping out his jack knife, he severed the cord and took possession of the mining camp's locked doors. He dragged the guard's body to the side of the guard house, and then did the same to the Doberman's. There was a firewood trough against the building a tarpaulin covering the logs. Arens yanked the tarpaulin off and placed it to over the bodies.

Pulling the gates together and wrapping the chain around them without the padlock, Arens ran back to the forest.

"We're good. Lock and load and let's go."

As they started toward the camp entrance, Peter shouted at them. "No, stop! Get back in the woods, quickly."

Llewellyn injected a bullet into his Sig Sauer. What he feared the most was his son being a coward. "No, fucking way, Peter. There are no guards, the gate's unlocked, we're not backing out ..."

Peter came face to face with his father, "shut up and listen."

All nine raiders turned back facing Nemeigusabins Lake, just south of them. The sound of a single engine plane was getting louder as it came in from the east. Within a few minutes they saw the Plate Extract Inc. company plane emerge from the trees, dropping in altitude for a water landing. Peter raised his hand to keep them still and silent. Within seconds, the roar of Danny LaCatt's skiff topped the airplane noise as it headed over from the other end of Nemeigusabins Lake into the landing path of the Plate Extract Inc. Seaplane.

"The plane's going to try a couple of approaches. If they circle into the lake by going over the mining camp, there's a chance they'll spot us. The Mounties will be called in and we'll be busted. Just wait."

The seaplane took three more approaches, each from different directions but LaCatt's skiff was light enough to infringe on their landing zone each time. After the last try, they could see the seaplane raise its nose and head for a higher altitude. More than likely, it would return to Thunder Bay and contact the authorities from there.

"Charlie, what do you think, two hours probably back to Thunder Bay?" said Peter.

"Easy, they're fully loaded. Time to go, Arens?"

"Ready, Dad?" There was a hint of sarcasm in Peter's voice.

Arens waved them out of the darkening forest, bringing them up to the gates about fifty yards away. He grabbed Peter's arm as he past, "I would have killed us all if you hadn't caught that plane's engines. I was ready to take you down, Peter. Would have and I usually do kill warriors that endanger the unit."

Peter shrugged off his father's arm, "we've got a lot of pain and lost years to conquer between us. Might not be able to, but I need to give it a try. Now's not the time."

The workers' housing was a large one-level military barracks with double doors facing south and directly in front of their approach. The doors were at the top of a flight of steps leading up to a porch that encircled the building. The doors were closed. The rear of the building had lavatories, showers, and a recreation room with no an access out of the building. Single, heavy-duty doors were at the north end of the building, one facing east, the other west.

Arens assigned two natives to guard each side of the front doors. He told them to lock and load. Charlie would lead them, making sure no weapons were fired into the building. The rest of them would be entering at the opposite end of the building. If any worker came out, they were to gun them down until all were dead. He teamed one Quidel with Peter and took Makya for himself. The two squads had to duck down as they went past the barrack's side windows. It was nearly dark and the dormitory lights were on. From the outside, they could see workers on their bunks reading newspapers and books. Some sat at tables in the aisle between the double level bunk beds playing cards.

"Makya, we're busting through the side door at the other end of the building. There are two rooms at the rear. One's a bathroom with showers, the other a small dining and kitchen area. I'll shoot the workers on my right. Peter and Quidel will take out the left. You've got to take down anybody to our rear, both the bathroom and kitchen. If you fail to kill them, the three of us will have men at our backs. You understand?"

"Easy, Arens. You'll be covered."

The killing of ninety-seven men did not take long. The Natives had learned well how to use the Mannlichers. They were expert at firing and loading ammo cartridges. Peter used his Ruger, taking careful shots so as not to waste bullets with scatter shooting. Charlie had brought a shot gun. Arens did his share of killing with his Sig Sauer. It took ten minutes.

No worker escaped, no attacker was fired on. The company did not allow the drones to have weapons. Arens walked around kicking each body, making sure no one was alive. The Natives started to chant, slowly and quietly at first, then becoming louder. They walked among the dead white men chanting. The dead on the front porch were covered. Charlie joined them inside and began chanting along with them.

"How are you doing, Peter?" asked Llewellyn Lawrence.

"There's a certain energy that went through me. I was afraid I'd have a problem killing so many people. With each body I killed, I thought I would see or feel the evil I did. It wasn't what I felt. I know tribe life makes you loyal to your tribe. The Cree and Ojibwa know these men as their enemy, even though they are only the drones of the enemy. The chants, the music of Makya and Shikoba, made sense of the deaths. If these deaths did not happen, the killing of the tribes of Makya, Shikoba, and all the others would continue. The war on these workers will be a sign to the leaders that their tribe will be dead. They have no workers."

"You're point is good, Peter. But will Plate Extract Inc. know which tribe is at war with them? All they will find is dead bodies."

"Yes, Arens I see that. Accuse, they will accuse but not recognize the tribe which is at war with them. There is one way to stop them from attacking any tribe. We set a war of fire on them."

Peter Lawrence pulled his jackknife from his pocket, flipped open the pumice stone, sharpened the blade, reached down to a dead worker, and scalped him. His father's eyes widened in shock, when he saw his son holding up the scalp of a dead man.

"Charlie, Comanche Charlie, this is not the Adobe Wall Battle, but it is a battle won. Chant us a song of violence as all of us leave each body with the same message I just sent."

In less than a half an hour every dead body's head was bone and blood.

Danny LaCatt met them at the shore of Nemeigusabins Lake, having successfully forced the Plate Extract Inc. sea plane back to Thunder Bay. He had heard the chant but preferred not to find out what happened at the mining camp. He and his skiff were the only means of escape for the attackers and now they were returning to the skiff, each chanting nearly forgotten wars songs of his tribe. When he saw that each attacker carried a scalp in his hand, he was horrified. He started yelling at them; afraid they had gone too far and would bring disaster upon every Canadian Native in the country. Llewellyn Lawrence stopped him cold. He walked LaCatt down the shoreline. When they were out of hearing range, he turned and took LaCatt to the mining camp.

"What happened here, Arens? My god, they've scalped all of these people?"

"Danny, you are too old now and too much a white man. You brought me here because your tribe was slowly being eaten away, destroyed by the mining company. It was for certain that future mining companies would piggy back on Plate Extract Inc.. You brought me in to fight your monster. You wanted to stop the horror of cyanide and mercury flowing through your rivers, streams and into your lakes and bays. You wanted to see no more dead bodies, natives killed from the toxic waste and going to their graves after suffering months of vomiting, diarrhea, and brain eroding headaches. You know that pain and that pain is their weapon, Danny. How many of your people died like that? How many tribal men found no way to care for their family and wound up stealing, going to jail, or drinking alcohol until their minds were incapable of coherent thought? How many Natives were using drugs and getting the money to buy more by selling drugs to Native children. Your women were raped and sexually abused by these workers. Their men could not protect them because they were laying in their own vomit, unconscious from booze and coke."

"I know, Arens! I know! But ninety some scalps lying next to bared heads of dead people?"

Llewellyn Lawrence and Danny LaCatt just looked at each other. Arens knew what he had to do. LaCatt was starting to break, putting the six Native men, Charlie, his son Peter and himself in great peril. The Sig Sauer was raised and fired before Danny realized that Arens was going to blow his brains out.

Back at the skiff, everybody saw Llewellyn Lawrence and looked for Danny to be behind him. Peter had heard the shot. He knew what his father had done what his father had to do.

Llewellyn Lawrence needed to keep the faith of the avengers so he told them "one of us let a worker get away with pretending he was dead. The man was under two other bodies. He had a little .32 special. LaCatt is dead. We've got to leave him there. Nobody but the nine of us know what actually happened at the massacre of Nemeigusabins Lake."

"We leave Danny there?"

"He will go down as a legend, the Kitchenuhmaykoosib Inninuwugs warrior who killed ninety-seven enemies. Now, let's get to the skiff."

Peter Lawrence hung back with his father. "He broke, didn't he?"

"Yep, there was no choice. We'd a wound up at the end of a noose. I guess they hang people in Canada?"

"What about the six Natives?"

"They know I killed him. They also know that either I or Charlie or you, will hunt them down if they talk. More importantly, they know they'll be just as guilty as we are. Should you worry? Yes, but when don't we worry? Besides they have no idea who we are or where to find us. Especially me and Charlie."

After navigating the rivers north then west back to Big Trout Lake, Llewellyn, Peter, and Charlie did not wait around to find out what happened when Plate Extract Inc. finally landed the next day. More than likely Plate Extract Inc. would be followed by the Mounties. The six aborigines shook Lawrence's hands and hugged Charlie. Arens did not let them leave without a final warning.

"You know what will happen if you tell our tale?"

Makya spoke, "I am a Cree warrior. We are also Ojibwa warriors. Arens is a warrior, a warrior chief. I will kill before you have a chance to hunt us down."

Llewellyn took Makya to mean that he would kill the informer, hopefully not him.

***

Charlie fought back his fear of taking off in the Cessna at night. As the plane leveled off, Arens called him a coward, a disgrace to the Comanche tribes who used night as a weapon. Peter edged up from the back seat and got between them, worried a fight would start until he saw them smile.

"What now, Arens?"

"Charlie flies us out of here. My bet is that Plate Extract Inc. will let this wash over and pull up stakes. Make it look like a manufacturing accident happened last night at the mines. Probably blame those damn grinders and that explosive dust in the air. Could also be they'll find one of those deep mine shafts and dump the bodies down into the run-off of hydrochloric acid. "

"You live the life of the aborigine, don't you?"

"The Natives where I live don't have problem's like Plate Extract Inc., yet. Population around me is very small and all the people are tribal. They live the life their ancestors lived. I am thankful I can be friends with them."

Llewellyn Lawrence paused and looked into his son's eyes.

"Peter, you have learned from Big Trout what life is."

Peter smiled a bit gratuitously and spoke, "and Arens, just what have I learned about life? That there are bad guys and good guys?"

"You have not fucking learned anything, have you? There are three words for what all life is - - production, product, and profit."

"You hear him, Chief? We've got some bullshit going on here, Charlie. All capitalistic life is product, I'll grant you. But your three 'P's' theory is juvenile at best. Come on, where's the production, product, and profit of the Comanche for instance?"

"What is better than looking at the tribe, is looking at each Comanche. What is the driving force of all life, Peter?"

"Continuance, reproduction, leaving your DNA in the future."

"Son, you are one dumb ass and I'm embarrassed to call you a Lawrence. Reproduction, is producing anew. Having sex is a human's greatest physical pleasure. Intercourse with a mate is production and ...?"

Peter smiled as he swigged his second gulp of Gooseberry whiskey from the canteen his father had brought with them. His father had already downed half of the canteen and his inebriated mind was stripping away life's extraneous functions and espousing its goal, "so having a child is the product? I hate to say it, but you are a sage, maybe the best ever. Profit is what your offspring produce to survive and pass along to life."

"Peter, there's more, much more to life, but there is only one path for life. From microscopic euglenas to capitalistic societies, if you don't produce the profit of life, a new life, than life will die without life profiting."

Peter was shaking his head back and forth, the shadow of a smile preceding a laugh, "so somehow tribes and families, clans and societies, become extinct if the profit of life is not met. Ironically your three part scenario of living is played out by societies that have only three parts."

"What three, Peter?"

"Look at every level of life. How does a society use its member species to survive, to profit? They go by many names, but life for each member is at three levels - - drones, soldiers, and kings."

"You are wrong, Kemo Sabe," said Charlie. "Comanche, Arapaho, Apache, Sioux all are the same. Chiefs, warriors, and our women are one with all in the tribe. There is no royalty. There are no drones. Quanah Parker, Crazy Horse, and Sitting Bull all were equal as warriors; all were in the tribe's battles. The white man's leaders are never in war, only at it"

Llewellyn Lawrence spoke, "you're right Charlie. The tribe is not a society. The tribe survives as a group or dies as a group. The White man's wars put soldiers in graves and more drones become soldiers to replace the dead. The kings and queens survive by sending the drones who survive on to new wars."

Peter Lawrence spoke, "isn't that Arens' lake down there? I hope so cause the shit level in this plane is getting very deep."

***

Charlie flew up to Lake Wunnumin at sunrise the next day, leaving Lawrence, father and son, alone until his return later in the afternoon.

"It'll be interesting to hear what the Lake Wunnumin Natives have learned about Plate Extract Inc. overnight when Charlie returns, Arens."

"Did I hear right that Charlie's going to fly you back to Thunder Bay tonight?"

"Yes, I need to get back to my world," said Peter.

Both men were sitting on Llewellyn's roofed front porch as darkness ebbed. Dawn's light eased upward through the forest in front of them, rising over the trees to the east. It was raining, a light drizzle.. Both had hot coffee.

"So this is your dum-dum Lord Greystoke?"

"My what?"

"I've seen the books you left with Mademoiselle Southern. The complete Burroughs set of Tarzan. When Tarzan wanted out of civilization, he headed for the trees and dropped down in the apes ceremonial grounds called the dum-dum."

"Evelyn never got rid of them?"

"Their mine, now. You can't have them Arens. I have my own dum-dum back in Virginia City, actually in the Back Bay of Coastal Virginia. I have some papers I want to show you. You might be able to give me a perspective on what they mean."

Peter Lawrence went back into the cabin, opened up McVeigh's satchel, and pulled out a folder.

"McVeigh had written down a bunch of companies involved in the Iraq War, Desert Storm. It surprised me how many businesses we have at home who were making money off of the war. Companies like General Electric, General Tire, Mobil, TRW and so on. Even Rolls Royce did business with the Defense Department. When I got on the internet and searched out defense contracts, I was in for a big surprise."

Llewellyn Lawrence pulled his chair up to the round picnic table on the porch, "I might be able to help you here, Peter. When I left Vietnam, I got involved with a bunch of radicals in Europe. Mostly they were chicken-shitters who didn't have the balls to go in and blow up some of the war profiteers. But they had a good grasp on what companies they should go after."

"Here's the list for the year 2000. Know any of these?"

"Jesus, look at this. Boeing, Lockheed, General Electric, Rockwell, damn near every one of the big boys. Holy shit, is that dollar figure just for 2000?"

"That's right, Arens. Boeing got over 12 billion dollars in contracts. Lockheed over 15 billion. Hell, General Electric must have sold a lot of refrigerators to the government to get a check of 1.6 billion dollars!"

"In the dead middle of the Vietnam War, 1965, GE had contracts totaling $825,000."

Peter pointed out a table on one of the sheets. "Here's the chart to blow your mind, the Eisenhower years."

Arens was stunned, "Nearly half or more than half of those companies listed during Nam aren't even on the Eisenhower list. Damn, the early 60's the Kennedy years aren't much different."

"But how many top ten contractors in 2000 were on the 1964 list, the middle sixties?"

Llewellyn Lawrence went back and forth putting a check mark next to each company listed in 2000 that also was listed in 1965, "all but three. The first six of 2000 were also under government contract in 1965."

"What do you remember about Eisenhower?" asked Peter.

Llewellyn replied, "Looking at the contracts awarded to war profiteers, Eisenhower warned the country of a tremendous military establishment uniting with a large arms industry. He saw a potential for misplaced power endangering the life and liberty of the citizens. I remember him on TV, looking directly into the camera and calling upon every citizen to be alert and knowledgeable so peace and security would live on in the United States."

"The military-industrial complex, Ike stated we must guard against it. It might be too late?" summed up Peter.

" Look at the parent companies for your 1965 government contractors. What do you see?"

"What I'm trying to show you, for Christ sake! We are a government of war. Our survivability thrives on being at war."

"And?"

"And what?"

"All of those companies are military, arms, and war materials builders, right? Do you realize where they're located?"

"No, I've got no idea."

"I'll give you a clue. Who was the president in 1965?"

"Johnson, wait a second. In the top ten, how many do you know were based in Texas?"

"Lockheed, General Dynamics, General Electric, and Boeing, Peter. Look at your charts and you will notice the first and second highest contracted companies made over 3 billion dollars combined, Peter."

Peter had too much information running through his mind. As the caffeine gradually took hold, his mind opened up more, much more than he would have expected.

"When I was in Europe after leaving Vietnam, there were a lot of protestors that felt Johnson had something to do with Kennedy's assassination."

"You're playing games with me Arens."

He continued, "Johnson had all of these multibillion dollar industries in Texas putting pressure on the government to send the military into Vietnam. I remember reading that Kennedy had blatantly told Johnson he was a war monger out to serve his financial backers. It was rumored that he had told Johnson to look for another job after his four years were up. Kennedy was not going to put the military in Vietnam. In fact, he was threatening to decrease the outrageous defense department spending. "

"Everybody involved in Kennedy's assassination was a Texan. Oswald could have been hired by the military-industrial establishment. Jack Ruby could have been sent in because Oswald was too close to talking."

Peter Lawrence smiled, taking his father's story as just another great myth, "let's go on here, Llewellyn. Look at these charts."

It was a list of the Top Ten Defense Contractors 2000 and 2001.

Llewellyn just shook his head. "What do we got here? Let me count. Last year the top six parent companies being awarded government contracts were identical to 1965. Four of the six were in Texas. In the year 2001 all ten top contractors were also on the '65 list. Jesus, look at the change. All three years had the same highest paid contractor, Lockheed Martin known as Lockheed Aircraft in 1965. Lockheed went from 1.7 billion dollars to 15 billion dollars in 2000 and profited 14.7 billion dollars in 2001. Wow, what a shame. Lockheed lost 300 million dollars from the previous year's contract."

Llewellyn Lawrence continued, "Follow the times. In terms of reality the great depression ended with World War II and its profits. Kind of scary, isn't it? Fifteen years later, the country was suffering a recession. Boom, here comes the Vietnam War and the economy perks up. The GNP yields profits. Think about post Nam, where oil embargoes and stock market crashes threatened the economy. In the late 80's, we have the Gulf War, courtesy of George Bush senior, also a Texan. We profited. War is recognized for its value. Fight a war and some of your sons may die but the military-industrial-financial complex profits from the taxes we pay. Billions of dollars go to companies during war. What we are seeing are the faces of dead soldiers on television and in our newspapers. Oh my, the Smith's son was killed in Iraq. What a shame. We were going to invite him and his wife and four children up to our Maine sea cottage to celebrate his homecoming. So sad, isn't it? We should be proud. He's a hero now."

Peter was stunned. His father's hatred had exploded. Making war produces wealth. Life or death is a product. Money is the profit. He watched his father's red face. But

Arens had a serious problem. Names, companies on McVeigh's list, also appeared on another list which he could not reveal to his son. Names such as Marsh & McLennan, Cantor Fitzgerald, the American Bureau of Shipping, Deutsche Bank, and a prime target, AT&T.

Llewellyn had no more to say. He got up and walked down to the boulders on the edge of the lake. Stripping down to his underwear, he dove into the cold water. Peter saw him surface about fifty yards out in the lake and understood why his father was the man he should be. Sculling on his back, he slowly edged himself back toward shore, feet first. He picked up his discarded clothes and walked to the porch.

"Where are my grandchildren, Peter?"

Llewellyn Lawrence could not know the pain that shot through his son. Peter was angry, but he did not want to leave his father's lair with any malice toward him. No one knew about Lawrence's aborted child.

"How many Vietnamese children have you in their genes?"

"As shamed as I am, I am a man. Many. But I am not a man who could raise a child. I am a fugitive, a killer, and a demon. Hopefully, they will never know. You're red in the face Peter. If I hurt you, it is not for reason, only ignorance."

"There's a woman in Virginia. She has a child, fully grown. She is old, at least too old to have gotten pregnant. She felt being a mother again would be wrong. It was my child."

"Did you agree to the abortion?"

"No, I didn't even know she was pregnant. She wasn't going to tell me. Her daughter, who works with me, told me by accident. I have yet to confront her since the abortion, I will when I go back."

"Peter, can you really trust this woman?"

"I thought I could. We did well together. I was very involved with ..."

Peter Lawrence paused when he remembered what he had fought back at Oceania. Military, the military-industrial-financial world, like he and his father had just finished discussing. Life had changed. Industry had teamed up with the military, investment brokerage and city councils. They had beaten Lawrence.

"She and I work well together. We shared a battle against a different military complex. This military was involved with the financial investment industry. We had it beaten but it fell apart. I don't know why."

"How did this woman feel about your losing to the investment business?"

"She tried to walk me around it, help me lose my anger, put myself up to another challenge. Her name is Susan Yoder. She's a bit moody at times. She's an extremely good fuck."

Both heard Charlie's Cessna pass over. They watched him drop the left wing and circle back . He kept the nose prop slightly up, dropped flaps, and cut speed. The plane made a smooth and even landing, stopping about a quarter mile east of them. The plane turned a hundred and eighty degrees and slowly eased itself on its pontoons to within a hundred yards of the boulders where the two Lawrences were standing.

They grasped each other, father patting his child's back, child tearing up, "I left my Ruger on your table. I'd never get it through security at Thunder Bay."

"Save up some money and get yourself a Glock-17C. Goes for about $550, but it's synthetic, carbide constructed. Carries nine millimeter rounds and is just a tad lighter than most niners. Carbide goes through most scanners without being detected. I carry mine everywhere I go, airline or just crossing the border. I've never been stopped. Ask Charlie to get you one. Less likelihood of the law catching you and Charlie's sales are legit."

CHAPTER TWENTY NINE

To Kill Beasts

"They are all alike. Cheating, murdering, lying, fighting, and all for things that the beasts of the jungle would not deign to possess - - money!
. . . Edgar Rice Burroughs, <u>The Return of Tarzan</u> 1915

"Colonel Togo? I need to talk with you," Llewellyn Lawrence held his cell phone to his ear.

"Lawrence, Llewellyn Lawrence, you know you're a wanted man in my country. You also know I'm no longer a Colonel."

"Why don't you call me Arens anymore?"

"Because I am not a military leader. I am now the official translator for the Ambassador of the Socialist Republic of Vietnam."

"They really fucked you over, didn't they?" Lawrence looked at the digital clock next to his queen-sized bed in the motel room. He knew the drive would take almost 6 hours and it was nearly midnight.

"Arens, in my position in the government of Socialist Republic of Vietnam, I commend you for what you did in Vietnam. It was earned by the number of enemies you killed."

"Togo, you still have that venom ..."

"The hatred of America? Yes, the United States continues to denigrate the people of Vietnam, Arens."

Lawrence spoke. "Hiroshima and Nagasaki can never be avenged. Would you like to see America get some of what is deserved?"

"Arens, we … You and I have a thirst for revenge that will never be quenched. What can I see that will change that?"

"You still live in Brooklyn, right?"

"Yes, on Gold Street near Sands."

"Good, best way is to show you. Is there a park or something near the East River, maybe near the Brooklyn Bridge where we can get together for a few hours?"

"Yes Arens. Brooklyn Bridge Park would be good. Why don't you just come to my home? It'd be easier."

"No, park works best. You'll see why. How do I get to the park?"

Lawrence had to trust Togo completely now.

"Where you flying in? LaGuardia?"

"No, I'm driving down from Maine. Takes about six hours."

"You'll be coming down 90, merge onto 95. Stay on 95 until it turns into 278. Go past exit 28B, that's for the bridge. Next exit is 28A. Take it and follow the signs. There's a long row of benches facing the East River and the skyline. "

"See you tomorrow." Lawrence and clicked END on his cell phone."

* **

When the United States evacuated Saigon on April 30, 1975, Llewellyn Lawrence was no longer a warrior fighting with the North Vietnam Army and Viet Cong. He was a deserter of the United States Army and had to avoid any combat zone or be killed. Months later on television he was able to see the U.S. Military running with their tails between their legs trying to crowd people into a small Huey helicopter that would eventually be dumped into the ocean. Lawrence lived with the Quyens, the people he had saved from the United States military onslaught. After the North Vietnamese, led by General Nguyen Van Toan, bombarded Saigon, chased out the Americans, and invaded the city, ending South Vietnam's reign, Saigon became Ho Chi Minh City. There was now just one country called Vietnam, a Communist Vietnam.

Lawrence and the Quyens avoided the violence from the government take-over. They grew rice over many acres of paddies. It was their life and livelihood. Less than 5 miles from Da Nang, their village, Hoa Xuan, was just east of Phan Hung Trail. There was peace. Villages and villagers were left alone, even though the single United Army of Vietnam continued its war economy by invading Cambodia in an effort to destroy the Khmer Rouge who had been attacking and murdering villagers on the border. Fearing worsening relations with China, the new Vietnam established relationships with Soviet Russia to increase economic and military assistance.

Llewellyn formed a family unit with the youngest of the Quyen daughters; he would never reunite with Evelyn Southern. With permission from the father Quyen, he made a home with Quyen, two daughters, and a son, but Arens would not seek marriage.

As years went by, Lawrence found himself missing a high protein diet. He ate the rice, fish, and chicken, but not enjoy it. The economic strife of the life gave the villagers no meat protein, and Arens physically needed this. He could feel it in his body, especially his arm and leg muscles. To this end he sojourned east to the forests. The hunt proved successful when he returned with a small deer-like animal Muntjac of species *Muntiacus* but known as a Barking Deer by the natives of the area. The Quyen's initially declined the gutted and butchered meat. They ate fish with Arens while he dined on the aromatic and juicy roast. But when Arens' mate tried a rib, she asked for more, leading the rest of the family to not just take a bite but inquire when Lawrence would go hunting again.

He hated leaving his family to hunt. His son was still too young to join him. Arens looked forward to the future hunting trips he would have with his son, just as he had many times with his father. He remembered the trips to the forested hills of Pennsylvania with George Lawrence looking for deer.

The Muntjacs were small both in providing meat and in being difficult to track. The first kill produced a warning, a barking to the others in the area. Lawrence doubted he could ever bag more than one at a time. Too much delay in returning with the first kill would cause the meat to rot. What he really sought was the Sambar deer, a much larger creature than the Barking Deer. A Sambar weighs over 500 pounds and could provide treated meat for many meals.

On his next trip, Arens traveled into the Sambar habitat. It was a tidal area with a dense cover of deciduous shrubs and grasses. The problem for the hunter was sighting on the deer before the deer sighted the hunter. In a dense forest, a tree stand makes being detected less difficult. Over a large marsh, hiding is close to impossible. One has to burrow himself into sedge with rising tidal waters; forcing the hunter out before he drowns or is tuck in the black mire being unable to pull his boots out of the quagmire.

Lawrence arrived at the shore of a marsh just before dusk. While most deer are nocturnal, hunting deer in the dark is considered unsportsmanlike by all hunters, and especially true concerning deer who stop in their tracks when facing a light in the dark. Lawrence's purpose was to prepare for the hunt at sunrise. The marsh was brackish. The water was sucked from the China Sea and flowed back to the China Sea. He stalked through bunches of weeds taller than himself and within reasonable wading distance from shore. He silently bemoaned the lack of waders like the ones he had back home. At least the tides were with him. At sunrise he would only have a few inches of ebbing tide water to wade through to make it to a dense group of sedges. With a little bit of luck, the same hoof prints he was reading now in the mud bank going down to the rising water would return in the morning with their marker, the Sambar deer.

It was pitch black in the tidal forest and since Lawrence saw only deer prints, thankfully no tiger or panther prints, he braced his body against his backpack at a tree and fell asleep quickly.

The bugs covered him but did not bite. The Quyens father worked rice paddies in mosquito dense marshes and swamps and years ago he had given Lawrence an ointment that insects loved but died after tasting. He refused to tell Arens what it contained. From the smell, Lawrence guessed it to be excrement but from what creature, he could not guess.

Rising, Lawrence chambered a round in his AK-47, given him to courtesy of the Viet Cong, and slipped an extra cartridge into his vest pocket. He waded out to the thatch of weeds. The tide was rising, but early morning was a usual feeding time for most prey. He waited cautiously and in between the weed stalks and keeping his rifle at shoulder height, silently. It did not take long before a huge Sambar deer trotted out of the forest where Lawrence had been sleeping. It sniffed the air, smelling the fecal content of bug repellant, not a human scent. Arens raised his sights and tried to move to his left for a better angle. His feet were stuck in the deep, black muck underneath the water, and he could not move. If he forced his way out, the Sambar would surely sense his movement and flee. Lawrence was in a no win situation.

It did not make any difference. He heard the shot from behind his left shoulder and saw the deer rise on his hind legs, only to get hit by another bullet at center mass. The Sambar fell dead.

A humming sound approached him from behind. Lawrence turned his head and saw the flat-bottom skiff powered by a battery driven propeller. The man guiding the skiff was dark- skinned and taller than Lawrence, quite unusual for a Vietnamese male. He shut down the motor and poled up next to Lawrence.

"Damn thing is awful quiet. You bagged my kill."

"No, I bagged the Sambar, not you. You American? What you doing here, Yankee?"

Lawrence got his left foot out of the muck and turned to face the man in the skiff, "used to be an American. If anything, I'm a Vietnamese adoptee now. Been that for going on ten ... no, eleven years now."

"What's your name, Mister ..?"

"Lawrence, but most people call me Arens. Please feel free to."

"You ought to get out of water, Arens. Tide's going up. Are you stuck?"

Lawrence could just barely twist his feet in a half circle, "might need a little pull from you if you don't mind? Who are you anyway?"

"Trinh Pham. My father is cashew farmer just north of this marsh," responded the boater as he edged up to Lawrence and pulled him, black muck and all into the boat.

"Thanks, got to look out for leeches, you know?"

"Yes, I have burned off many of them wading through marsh. Why I use this boat."

Lawrence pulled off his low cut boots and soaking wet socks to find three leeches. He reached into his top pocket and pulled out a pack of cigarettes and a lighter. He would go through a pack of Asian cigarettes every month. He almost quit but placed the blame on leeches. He lit the cigarette, drew in a deep and satisfying cloud of smoke, exhaled it out of his lungs, and put the glowing red tip of the cigarette on each leech. They fell off.

"Cashew farmer? Cashew, like in nuts?"

"Yes, we have good sized orchard just north of the swamp. Where you from?"

Lawrence told him of the village where he lived with the Quyens.

"Oh, rice farmers. Not much money with rice. Many farmers have rice fields. Not get good price at market."

"They grow it to live by. The family's not interested in making profits."

"Not good. Vietnam growing agriculture country. Rice not much profit."

"And nuts are?"

"Yes, Arens. Major cashew growing areas in Brazil, West and East Africa, India and Vietnam control cashew agriculture for whole world. I show you our orchards."

After tying down the dead Sambar, Trinh Pham guided the skiff throughout the dank smelling marsh, "you've eaten Sambar before Arens?"

"No, I heard about it but the Quyens are only eaters of goats and chicken. Thought I'd give it a try."

"You got to know how to prepare it or else it's tasteless. My baì ngoaòi [grandmother] has old, ancient recipe. Very flavorful, maybe too much for first timer."

The skiff edged out of the swamp into a small river.

"Don't' just eat it as meat?"

"No, not good favor, very tough. Cook in water, when half cooked add pieces of drumstick and vegetables. Cook till is very soft. In another pan heat oil and add mustard seeds. When they stop splattering add chopped garlic, menthe seeds, dried red chili pieces, asafetida and curry leaves. Fry for two minutes and then add to vegetable mixture and boil it for 1 minute. Add chopped coriander leaves."

Not far down the stream from the swamp, Trinh pointed out his family's orchards, "and yes, also add cashew, cashew chopped."

The trees were short and bushy. The Pham orchard covered what must have been a hundred acres, with the trees tight together much like an apple orchard. They reached a small wooden pier off of a stone and dirt road passing through the cashew trees. Once Trinh secured the skiff and disengaged the battery, he led Lawrence along the road, carrying the removed battery with him. Lawrence asked him to stop and went to one of the cashew trees.

"The cashews are growing out of the bottom of a fruit? Looks like a pear fruit."

Trinh laughed as Lawrence lifted up a branch with pods of hanging red fruit-like structures, "the nut isn't inside the pod?"

"No, Arens. It grows outside. Nut grows outside of apple fruit which can also be eaten. Commercial product of the cashew tree is the nut. Rarely is apple fruit eaten, as taste is not popular. I've been told by Da Nang buyers that in South America and West Africa, local inhabitants think the apple, not the nut kernel, is a delicacy. I am told in Brazil, the apple is used to make jellies and alcoholic drinks. In India, it is used to distil cashew liquor called "feni"."

"You want me to carry up the Sambar?"

"No, I'll send worker down."

It was not an estate nor an agriculture mansion. The huts were not much different from where Lawrence and the Quyens lived. The orchard dominated their lands. As usual Lawrence was treated with cautious respect. In his years living in Vietnam, he always found meeting Asians for the first time awkward, almost as if they feared him.

A bulky man stood on the front porch of the hut. His face was slightly swollen with scars from what must have been a battle with acne. Typical of many Asians, his eyes were narrow slits and were focused directly at Lawrence as Trinh walked up the steps and on to the porch with Lawrence following.

"Father let me introduce you to Mister Lawrence."

"Llewellyn, but most call me Arens," said Lawrence extending his hand.

"Arens, my father, Pham Thao."

"I know who you are Arens," said the father grasping Arens fingers tightly with his right hand and clutching Arens elbow with his left. "At least I think I know who. You American that turned on his country to fight for mine. You are a legend."

Lawrence wanted to forget the war and rarely discussed his alliance with the Viet Cong. "Those times are past. I don't need to relive them."

The father smiled, "to forget is to risk, Arens. I lost a son and many friends. We need to remember their lives. Don't you agree?"

""Those who cannot remember the past are condemned to repeat it. Only the dead have seen the end of war."

"Yes, Arens, those are the words of George Santayana. Trinh did you bring back our dinner?"

"Yes, father. A good sized Sambar. It's in the boat.I'll get it."

Trinh returned to the skiff. Thao escorted Arens into his home. A small woman was sitting in a rocking chair darning a shirt.

"This is my wife and Trinh's mother Arens, Pham Anh."

Again, as uncomfortable as he was meeting Asian men, Llewellyn was more so with Asian women. Unlike American women, they evidenced uneasiness in males, especially males that were not Vietnamese. Lawrence bowed at the waist to her and smiled. "Your son has my mouth watering for your Sambar recipe."

"My son ass like father. The sambar has to be butchered and prepared before I get out cooking pot and clean it. Take many days."

Lawrence felt awkward and speechless at the mother's mild rebuke of males. He was relieved when the son returned.

"Sambar being butchered right now. Me Pham, you going to make Sambar?"

"You even dumber than father. You know it take many hours how I cook it."

Trinh's face turned a rosy pink but smiled, as a child. She returned the smile in what Lawrence guessed was an ongoing ritual of the female badgering the males in the Pham home. "I fix meal already. Wait for you to return. Arens can come for meal tomorrow for Sambar. We eat what is done."

Lawrence felt at home. The atmosphere was much like living with the Quyens. They sat at the table and went through a meal that was spicy and tart. He had no idea what the food was and had learned years ago not to ask but just eat. Vietnamese women knew how to prepare a meal using many assorted plants and meats.

"Ba, Arens not know cashew trees great crop to grow. Make good produce."

"Arens, cashew tree great asset. Seedlings grow two maybe three years. Take long time but need little care. Can be grafted in less time. Maybe two years or less."

Lawrence spoke, "who buys the cashews?"

"Go to Da Nang after harvest. Take many barrels. Produce agency buy all we can grow. Cashew grow fast as weeds. Many barrels. Much voucher."

Lawrence described the Quyens village and the rice fields.

"Cashew do good there. You say soil sandy, yes?"

"Not drained of earth but sandy enough you can rub it in your hands and feel the sand particles."

"That good. You try?"

"I'll think about it. It's not my decision. My family, the Quyens, will make the call. Might need to bring it up with the other villagers. We're very tribal."

Lawrence rolled quickly out of his chair, turned around and scanned the room behind him, looking for the source of the guttural moan coming from the far corner of the hut.

"Sorry Arens," said Trinh. "I forget to tell you about hôÌn ngýõÌi chêìt [ghost] who moans."

Lawrence was startled that he had not even detected the man's presence in the hut. The man sat in a dark corner, bundled cocoon-like in a wool blanket wrapped around all but his head.

"We call him ghost because only sound is the moaning you heard."

"Damn, he looks like a corpse. He's face is all gray and his eyes are glazed. Is he a relative of yours?"

"No Arens," spoke Pham Thao. The father walked over to the grey man. "He's an omen we took in. We fear losing him. Our crops have been good since we brought him here."

"You brought him to your orchard and home and he's not related to you?"

Trinh spoke up, "let me explain, Arens. I make deliveries with truck to Da Nang and I used to make them to Saigon. Truck empty when I left Saigon. Not empty when I got back."

"What happened? Did this man climb into your truck without you knowing?"

"No, Cheit ... Cheit is name we call him. He could not climb into truck."

"Why couldn't he?"

The father walked over to the man in the corner. He spoke gently to the man who maintained his low rhythmic groans. As the man calmed, Pham Thao unraveled the blanket exposing the man's anemic, almost skeletal body. Lawrence did not see the man's disability at first. With the blanket removed, the grey man started his chant again, raising his arms as if begging to the people in the hut. Lawrence shuddered, taking in a deep breath, his eyes wide. The man had no hands.

"Damn! He's got no hands. How the devil did he get into your truck?"

The son spoke, "only way had to been somebody or maybe with help from others threw him into the truck bed."

"But he doesn't speak? Why did you keep him? Why didn't you turn him over to the police?"

The mother came up beside Lawrence and took his right hand between hers, "he is our pariah, only he's good pariah. You have lived how many years as Vietnamese?"

"Almost twenty counting my time as an American soldier. Why?"

"We cherish the poor and maimed. We believe it's our test from our god. We took Cheit in and he has survived, giving us prosperity. He is family now."

"Yet he never talks? He just groans? You are amazing people."

It'll be dark soon so I better get hiking back to my village."

The father spoke, "my son will drive you back. Don't argue."

Outside, after bidding farewell and thanking them for the meal, Lawrence followed Pham Trinh to a hut where their harvesting equipment was stored.

"How did you ever get a United States Army M35 2½ Ton, 6×6 cargo truck?"

"Very easy, Arens. Your army took off like bats in the sun after Saigon and Da Nang fell. All they needed was paint for the yellow stripe on their backs! What was yours is now mine."

Lawrence laughed, "I'm impressed with your cashew crops. It's getting dark now but I'd like it if you could look over the Quyens' fields. Can you stop by and take a look?"

"I had planned to. My guess is my mother will be sending me to your village as soon as Sambar recipe is done. Oh, in back of truck is head of the Sambar. Sorry, but Pham Anh never gives up meat."

The next morning Lawrence was returning from his morning two kilometer run through the rice fields and along the road to Da Nang, when he saw the Pham's truck outside the Quyens hut.

The mother, Thi, was talking with Trinh.

"So did you bring us some of the Sambar stew?"

"Yes I did, Arens. I think you may be in trouble with Thi Quyens."

Mother Quyens started in on Lawrence immediately, chastising him for needing another woman to cook for him.

"Ma Quyens, leave poor man alone. It is gift to us for me hunting the Sambar for their meal."

She looked both men in the eye, knew Lawrence was lying, and went back into the hut. She took the Sambar stew with her.

"Arens, I have come to help you start your own cashew nut orchard. Pham Thao wants me to make sure you're able to grown and cultivate an orchard. We make you a split-off from Pham orchard."

"Okay, I'll walk you around."

The Quyens village was no different than other rice paddies farm seen throughout most of the rural areas in Asia. To grow cashew trees sandy soils with good drainage were needed. Cashews cannot thrive in marshy areas. They flower during the winter when it is usually dry. The mature trees will grow up to forty feet. Because they branch out, it is best to keep them at least thirty feet apart. Trinh walked around the perimeter of the rice fields. As he got more to the east, he stopped and rubbed handfuls of soil between his fingers.

"The river is very close and the ground falls gradually to it. Means good drainage. Also good base to drain or pump water. Soil is sandy, maybe too sandy. You will need fertilizer with nitrogen and phosphorus. Maybe zinc too. We'll work on it. This fair to good area Arens."

"So when do I start?"

"Got seedlings in truck. We start now Arens."

"Not now. Thi Quyen is waving to us. Either she warmed up the Sambar or she's going to dump it on the ground and give you the bowl back."

She had no bowl with her so they would be eating. Sitting at the table with Lawrence and Trinh were the rest of the Quyens. In front of each person was a steaming bowl of Sambar stew. Everybody looked at Lawrence to see his reaction.

"This is excellent! What's in it?"

Trinh listed the ingredients and sauces that he knew his mother added.

"It is not Sambar," said Thi Quyen. It has meat in it."

"Sambar," said Trinh.

"Yes, I know it's sambar. Sambar does not have meat."

"My mother adds Sambar to it. You see ..."

"How can you add Sambar to Sambar?"

Lawrence started to laugh but held it in check. "Ma Quyen, let me explain. There is an animal much like a deer called a sambar. Trinh's mother diced some meat he hunted yesterday and added it to the stew sambar. Wait a second."

Lawrence left the table, went outside and returned very quickly holding the head of the sambar Trinh had given him. "This is the animal sambar that you are eating in the stew sambar."

"Makes no difference. Meat is tough," said Ma Quyen, who despite her rebuke at having sambar in sambar managed to wolf down three bowls of sambar.

Before Trinh left he and Lawrence went back over the proposed orchard.

"This is good area, Arens. Here six seedlings for you to plant. As they grow, they will produce seeds which you can use to extend orchard. If you have fruit bats, they'll actually plant seeds for you. They eat cashew apple, the part that looks like pear. They don't digest all the seeds but excrete them as they fly over orchard."

"How long before I have fruit?"

"This good, very good area. The forest along river has strong, very tall trees. Cashew trees not strong in wind.

You've got good protection. May take three years Arens. Could have fruit in year and a half though. Take good care and fertilize with good irrigation. Before long, we will be trading cashews in Da Nang."

Lawrence turned and looked Trinh in the eye. Trinh could tell that Lawrence had a problem but he knew he had to wait for Lawrence to bring it out in the open. Lawrence walked down to the river, Trinh following him. Lawrence sat down on the river bank. Like most rivers flowing from the rice fields and farms, it was brown from the sediment.

"You know who I am?"

"Yes, you are Arens. You are American that saved many Vietnamese lives."

"I saved them by killing Americans."

"They were killing us, Lawrence."

"No Trinh, they were murdering you. There's a big difference. The United States had no reason to kill Vietnamese people. When you kill for profit, you are a murderer. America could have cared less about Vietnam being a communist country. They were everything that war was meant to be in a capitalistic world. A country at war is a country with profit-making for its industries. Your dead people made thousands of businesses in the United States rich. That was the reason. No matter how much the government clouded the war issue, your people died to make people rich.

"How this affect cashew trees and selling product?" said Trinh.

"As your father told you, I am well known. Maybe famous to the people I fought with to save their country. I am definitely notorious to those I fought against, especially the United States. I can't risk any exposure in a place like Da Dang. You'll have to take my crop and market it for me. Can you do that?"

"You are hero to my people. I don't see danger but I not you. I will market your product with pleasure and thanks Lawrence."

***

It took almost four and a half years before the seedling cashew trees with their large leaves and very beautiful pink flowers, reached six feet. One of the original seedlings shriveled up and died. Trinh caught Arens chasing away wild birds and fruit bats at the first bloom and scolded him since the bats especially were excellent seed planters and would increase the orchard growth.

When the first flowers on the starter cashew trees ripened into fruit, instead of asking Trinh to aid him, Lawrence picked unripe cashew apples. Their red sections were very alluring. He knew from Trinh that the red fruit was not a fruit but part of the stem that had swollen. At the bottom of the apple fruit is a kidney-shaped, light-colored shell. The cashew nut is inside of the shell. Because Lawrence was careful in removing the false red fruit from the shell, he took a small bite finding the apple to be tart but quite juicy and refreshing. The refreshment from the fruit enticed Lawrence to break open the cashew shell without thinking.

He didn't notice the noxious smell fast enough and the liquid surrounding the nut flowed onto his fingers. Burns causing severe pain lasted for many hours and would leave life-long scars on his hands.

When Trinh arrived with his truck, he knew what Lawrence had done and chastised his stupity in front of the Quyens. Lawrence just shook his head and smiled. Trinh laughed, but not at Lawrence's scolded hands. He was laughing at Lawrence's crop.

"You have two problems here Arens," said Trinh. "First you stupid not waiting for me to show you how prepare cashews for market. You think commissary buy cashew apple fruit? Fruit no good as product. Buyer wants nut ..."

"I know that Trinh. That's why I burned my hands."

"You know nothing Arens. But you learn. Burn fingers many times. You need bucket of water and rubber gloves. Shell nut under water and change water many times."

"Yeah, seems smart to me. Then package them for trip to Da Nang?"

"No, must process them. Nuts no good until processed. Processing very easy but must be careful of nut acid. Two ways Arens. We do roasting in oil. Give better flavor, better market value. Drop in boiling oil two, three minutes, no longer. Shells get brittle and useless, no sell. Cool off in bucket of water. Shell come off very easy. Be careful when boiling. Acid from shell hisses and cashews squirt it out."

"The other way take long time, not taste as good. Heat nuts in open frying pan that has holes in bottom to drain acid liquid. Heat over open fire but keep from fumes, very caustic, make you sick. Dump in water, then put into sawdust to absorb any acid left."

Lawrence spoke, "Okay, thanks for the lesson. Sounds like oil roasting is the best way. What do I need?"

"Brought materials with me. We can process your cashews very quickly. Did you see back of truck?"

"Yeah, go ahead and brag. We'll compete with you in due time. What have you got back there? Couple of 50 gallon barrels of cashews?"

"Got thirty Arens. But got room for your cashews in glove compartment!"

Both of them laughed and punched each other's shoulders in camaraderie. They had known each other for almost five years. As hunters they built up a close friendship that found them disappearing for weeks at a time on hunting excursions. Always they returned with a kill or two that provided meat for both the Phams and the Quyens. On their last hunt Lawrence had brought his son, the son he had with Hoa Quyen. The Quyens, especially Hoa's mother Thi, did not like the non-marriage arrangement until Lawrence made two things clear to them. First, he was a renegade, one with a reward on his head. Should he be captured and it was discovered that he had a wife, she would be in danger, as would the entire Quyen family. Second, Lawrence might one night disappear forever. Precarious at the start, the family accepted Lawrence more as a son than an in-law. They also accepted the son and two daughters through the union with Hoa Quyen.

Trinh took charge of Lawrence's cashew processing and finished just before dark. He would spend the night with Lawrence and the Quyens and in the morning leave for Da Nang.

"Poppa L, can I go to Da Nang with Trinh Pham tomorrow?"

Lawrence knew his son would rush adulthood like a true Lawrence just as he did, "since you have now bagged your own wild animal, a tapir, I see no reason to treat you like a child."

"Poppa L, will you ever stop teasing me about the tapir?"

Lawrence smiled. His son had bagged a medium sized tapir on a trip with Trinh Pham. Nobody would eat it, including Lawrence. His son was upset that he had killed a living creature for no more than the sport of it. Lawrence repeatedly tried to qualm his son's frustration but it did not go away. Lawrence knew his son had learned well the value of being alive."

"I'll try. Can you handle all of those cashews Trinh is processing for us?"

"No problem Poppa L. I'll just put them in my pockets."

His son ducked quickly enough to avoid Lawrence's swat to the side of his head. Both laughed.

At dawn, Trinh and Lawrence's son had washed and eaten breakfast. They were ready for the trip to Da Nang.

"Be back by dusk, Trinh?"

"Probably. Not much to do but wait in line and unload. Then barter back and forth with vendor."

"Think you can get a couple thousand Vietnamese Dong?"

Trinh laughed since two thousand Dongs equaled to about two American dollars.

"Trinh, your vagrant Cheit? I've been going over and over trying to understand not just who he is but why he is?"

"It bothers you Arens. Doesn't bother Thao or Anh Pham. Doesn't bother me, either. We feel honored we can help him even though there's little we can do for him."

"I know your family. You're good people. He's a challenge, but don't you want to know more about him?"

"Our God has sent him to us. It is blessing for the Phams."

"It bothers my sense of understanding. He cannot speak, right?"

"No words Arens. Sounds, he make sounds. There are times when his sounds make us afraid. But afraid of what? The man is old and cannot move much."

"His hands, Trinh, it's in his hands."

"Arens, he has no hands," said Trinh shaking his head as if talking to a lunatic.

"There lies the secret Trinh. What is he doing when he shakes his arms? It's as if he's trying to use his hands."

"That good point, Arens. My father notice this early with him, but nothing came to mind to describe the man's gestures. We're off now," said Trinh, as he pulled himself up and into the cab of the old U.S. Army truck.

Lawrence absently waved to his son and Trinh as they left for Da Nang but his mind was with Cheit. He could not rid himself of the image of that old man moaning and waving his arms, around with stubs where his hands should be. He needed to visit Cheit, rile him a bit, listen to the moans and watch each movement of his arms, looking for a hint of what the man's situation might be. He had to do this now. He told Hoa he was visiting the Pham's and might not return until tomorrow. It was a long hike but it would give him time for his thoughts.

Pham Anh met Lawrence at the door to her hut. "Arens? Arens is something wrong? Has Trinh ..."

"No, there's no trouble. Trinh and my son left hours ago for Da Nang. I came to see Cheit. Is it okay with you?"

"Yes, very all right with me. No men here to help me. Cheit must make water and he too much for me. You can help?"

"I'll take care of him. Out back?"

"Yes, he go there. You not need help?"

Lawrence could sense her relief and was glad he could help. It meant he could get very close to Cheit. The old man was very light, easy to carry to the shed behind the hut. Lawrence unwrapped the man and could see that Anh was too late in assisting him. The front of his burlap sewn shorts was slightly wet. The old man was probably aware of this and was trying to hold back, hoping to be helped. Lawrence quickly got him seated on the shed's wooden seat situated over top the hole for excrement. Making sure the man would not fall over, Lawrence slowly pulled the shorts down his thighs and over his knees.

"Lawrence saw the circumcision, definitely not a doctor's cut and stitch. More than likely the man is a Jew."

The man's weak body tried its best to empty the bladder but only a few drops hung at the end of his penis. Grabbing the rag hanging on the side of the shed, Lawrence wiped the man clean. The man stared at Lawrence. His eyes were grey and glazed over. There was little doubt that Cheit could see not much farther than a few feet. Lawrence spoke to him on the off chance the man might have a better shot at hearing him since they were so close. There was no reaction. Lawrence pulled the man's shorts back up, covering his genitals. He lifted Cheit up and carried him back to the hut.

"Did he make it okay, Arens?"

"Yes, he's fine now Anh Pham. Did you know he's Jewish?"

"No! How we know that?"

"He's been ritually circumcised."

"I not know what that means Arens."

Lawrence did not want to embarrass the poor woman so he just told her that Thao Pham could explain.

"Does Trinh still do business in Saigon?"

"No, we give up on Saigon after night Trinh found Cheit in truck. Viet Cong causing riots and he afraid for his life. They kill many French people, especially ..."

"Especially what?"

Anh Pham put her hands up to her face, covering her mouth and nose. Her eyes widened and her narrow eyebrows arched, "the Jews, they chase out French Jews. It was last of French peoples."

"Can you get me a towel or a clean rag, wet please."

Anh returned and handed Lawrence a clean, dripping wet cloth.

Cheit was on the Phams rattan sofa. Lawrence had wrapped him back up like a cocoon before placing him there. He pulled over a little step stool from the Pham's kitchen and placed it directly in front of Cheit. He took the damp towel and gently washed the old man's face, mopping up the tiny streams of water running down his cheeks.

"Do you hear me? Blink if you hear me."

Lawrence realized how stupid the request was since the odds of the man understanding English were slim. He continued gently wiping the damp cloth over the man's face. He handed it back to Anh and asked her to wet it again. The second time he began washing the man's face, Cheit smiled. Lawrence was getting somewhere.

"You can hear me, can't you?"

Lawrence pushed his stool back from the old man, giving him some room. He didn't want to make the man feel like he was being interrogated. The man lifted his handless arms up and made various movements with his phantom hands. Lawrence could see Cheit was trying to convey a message through his gestures.

"He's making signs! He's fucking making signs! He wants to talk to me but he has no hands to make signs."

"Arens? He talk to you with no hands?"

"Yes, Anh, I'm almost positive that's why he waves his arms around. It's bad enough that he can't speak with his hands but he can't hear either. He's a deaf mute. The people who cut off his hands knew this! It's horrendous! I've never seen such malicious horror."

"He see though. He see somebody make signs to him?"

"Yes, I'll bet he can. And the odds are he's one of the French Jews that were attacked. It may be a long shot but I think I've got it."

Lawrence looked deep into the man's glazed eyes, eyes that mimicked those of the dead. They scared Lawrence. They mimicked eyes of dead people. He lifted his hands, palms up in front of the man's face. The eyes followed Lawrence's fingers. Lawrence gestured his right hand to the left side of the man's head, gently brushing his cheeks. He retracted his right hand putting the tips of his fingers on his own lips, signing speech. Holding up his left hand's fingers, Lawrence gestured from his lips to the tips of his left hand's fingers. He hoped he was signing that he knew the man could only speak through the stumps of his arms.

The old man gave Lawrence his answer with tears and a grateful smile.

All three were smiling and crying.

"Now I've got to learn how to sign in French. There's only one person I know who can help, the mother of my son in America."

* **

For two years the U.S. Army had designated Llewellyn Lawrence as MIA but eventually changed the designation to KIA, not because they believed Lawrence was a loyal soldier who died for his country, because the government was satisfied that he had been killed during one of the many incursions he led against American troops. What they failed to recognize was that Arens, as the Vietnamese soldiers called him, had more heart in defending the people of Vietnam than any American had in fighting Vietnamese soldiers. With the fall of Saigon and thus America's ignominious fall, Llewellyn Lawrence became a dead man that the United States wanted to keep in a grave. Not all agencies, particularly the CIA, agreed to this. They chose to keep Lawrence's listed as a traitor, wanted dead or alive but only within the bureau itself. In the first five years, they offered generous incentives for allies in the Orient, generous in the amount of five million dollars. No foreign agency responded.

Lawrence was not aware of any of this. But the odds were, he was still being hunted and would probably remain a fugitive top the United States until he was caught or died. Yet he was still able to maintain communication with the mother of his child, Evelyn Southern. While the communication was not ideal, it was pretty much untouchable by any United States agency. Evelyn had two sisters. The three sisters came from a close knit family and would go to their death before any of them would imperial another sister's safety or her family's. One sister remained in the birth place of the Southern's, Paris, France. Evelyn moved to the United States in the early 1960's and the third sister immigrated to Canada.

Fortunately when Llewellyn took French in high school, he was in the class of the very dynamic teacher, Mademoiselle Southern, who arranged for her classes to write letters to real French people. As Llewellyn and Evelyn's relationship grew close, she assigned him to write to her sister living in Paris. He wrote so many letters that he never forgot the elaborate mailing address. Once he was no longer a United States Army barbarian, he took a chance. He sent Evelyn's sister a letter. The odds were in his favor that nobody would be spying on her or checking her mail. It was nearly a year before the Quyens received a letter addressed to Tuant Quyen.

Mother Quyen had told the mail deliver that no one by that name even lived here. Tuant, translated meant "magic." The man shrugged and left it with her anyway. She left it lying in the hut and by chance Llewellyn found it. The sister wrote that she cried for hours, knowing her sister would be ecstatic knowing the father of her child was still alive. She did exactly as Llewellyn asked her to in contacting her sister. It would be a very long time before Evelyn would know. She sent a letter, along with a copy to her sister in Canada. Her first thought had been to call Evelyn but in reading Llewellyn's letter for the fourth time, realized he would be in grave danger should the U. S. government be tracing or tapping Evelyn's phone. Two letters left Paris that day: one was sent to Tuant Quyen, the other to the sister in Canada, along with a copy of Llewellyn's letter. Six months later Tuant Quyen received an envelope containing two letters, one from Canada and one from Evelyn Southern.

It had been a long, brutal wait before the United States left Vietnam. As Vietnam regained its own existence, there was the tremendous growth in the country. Lawrence was still a wanted man but his ties to the Quyen family grew and so did his visibility. Yet, there were places he had to avoid. Da Nang especially worried him. Companies from other countries were establishing economic resources in Vietnam and it did not take long before American businesses set up distributers in some of the major cities of Vietnam. The risk of exposure might have seemed low but the consequence of being captured was not worth it.

Llewellyn Lawrence avoided Da Nang. He looked south at the growing city of Quang Ngai and found what he needed. There was a Western Union store which also served as a mail box rental agency. Telegrams would be perfect. Instead of waiting months upon months for a letter which might be traced, he could telegram Paris within hours. It was not without risk; his telegrams could be tracked down. But years had gone by and his fears about being sought were lessening. Sio he used telegrams and it worked.

The answer to Cheit would depend on Evelyn's ability to find a means for him to communicate with the old man through sign language. It had to be in French. Being vigilant, he telegraphed Paris asking for a book or lessons that would let him sign in French. Once the telegram arrived in Paris, another would go out to Toronto, to be followed by one to Pennsylvania. A confirmation would be relayed back so he would know the request was with Evelyn. How she could get this information to him, he had no idea. It was a long shot, but the only one he had.

The Western Union account and mail box were private; Western Union was paid monthly in cash, with no address needed for Thuat Quyen. Lawrence would only know he had a response to his telegram by visiting the store in Quang Ngai. Figuring he would have a response within two weeks, he returned to Western Union at that time to discover not only a telegram but a package as well, one that did not fit into Lawrence's small mail box.

The telegram was from Paris stating his request had been forwarded. The agent brought Lawrence a FEDEX corrugated box addressed to Thuat Quyen from an unnamed person in Toronto, Canada. Thanking the agent, Lawrence paid his bill. He hesitated before walking out the door. Was he being tracked? Did the CIA break through his communication chain? Would he be gunned down in the street? Damn, he didn't even think about carrying a gun.

He shook his head, twisted his backbone to the left and to the right, making sure his paranoia was just that. He walked to an open bar and ordered a beer even though he hated Vietnamese beer.

He pulled out his jack knife and cut the glued edge of the FEDEX box so he could ease out whatever was inside. There were two books and a letter inside the larger book. He looked at the larger book first. It was French Sign Language: Reading Comprehensive Activities by D. L. Ellis, M.R. Pearce. The other was a French/English dictionary. He read the note after taking a good swig of beer.

It was from Evelyn telling him that he should forget the war and forget the U.S. Army. It was over. He did not need to hide any longer. He might not be able to come back to the United States but he should feel safe. In typical Evelyn Southern style she ended by saying, "Mon ami, you are reading my letter. You have seen the books. Are you under arrest? Non, you are safe, is it not so?"

Evelyn was right. Nobody cared about Llewellyn Lawrence.

He worked diligently with Cheit trying to find a way to communicate through the moans and grunts. At first he signed simple things, like asking Cheit if he was indeed a Jew. A nod from Cheit confirmed he was. This followed with a confirmation that he was French but it was ot possible to verify if the old man was from Saigon. When Lawrence signed asking Cheit how he lost his hands, Cheit began moaning and crying. Because Cheit was so aggravated and would not respond to Llewellyn using his own hands to image those of Cheit's missing ones, the session ended.

There was no logical reason for Llewellyn's determination to breach the insanity that surrounded Cheit, one that the Pham family had endured for many years. Trinh tried to get Llewellyn to give up, to let Cheit be, but Arens was too driven. His determination to communicate with the old deaf man, at least meant that Lawrence visited the Pham home and orchard on a regular basis. By now, the Quyen cashew tree orchard was no longer miniscule. It was a source of humor for the families farming rice in the village. During the first years the Quyens teased and taunted Lawrence and his son, their grandson but eventually the trees matured and blossoms gave birth to the cashew apple and harvested a crop. The humor was replaced with admiration and support since the Quyens' cashew crop was bringing in commerce debenture notes from Da Nang. The only Quyen who continued to tease Llewellyn was the mother of his son, Hoa Quyen, who described the kidney shaped shell at the bottom of the cashew apple as a copy of his penis.

So prosperous was the Quyen cashew orchard that the Pham's merged with the Quyens making them a subsidiary of the Pham Plantation. Since the Quyens marketed their crops by hitching a ride with the Phams, this made for a mutually satisfying relationship between the families. Llewellyn monitored both orchard productions. This gave him many confrontations with Cheit. Since Llewellyn was reluctant to travel with Trinh Pham to the market in Da Nang, this gave him an excuse to work with Cheit. Despite the limited communication with Cheit, his drive to learn was yet another good excuse to not visit Da Nang. His son Cao rode with Trinh to help unload the cashew bins in Da Nang.

Lawrence had been working in the fields before facing another useless session with Cheit when Trinh and Cao returned from Da Nang. His son was all smiles as he ran quickly to his father.

"Arens! Arens, guess what I discovered in Da Nang? A tourist company that'll take you to all the battle sites during the United States invasion."

"Why do you want to visit the war sites?"

"Because you, my father, were probably at some of them. Grandfather Ba told me you were a hero and fought against the American's. I'd like to see where you fought for us."

"This tourist company? Is it run by Vietnamese people?"

"Yes, mostly. The tour guides are all Vietnamese but the boss man is an American."

Lawrence shrugged, leery of an American who would sell that showed Americans getting their asses whipped, but money, no matter how you made it, was the obvious reason. It piqued his interest as to what would actually be shown to the tourists and he couldn't help but wonder just how well known was he?

"Cao, listen to me carefully. Your grandfather Ba should have not told you those stories."

"Ba was not telling the truth?"

"No, Ba would never lie. Since he has passed away, you and I are the only people who know what war stories were told. I owe it to you as my son to tell you how I became a soldier for Vietnam, fighting against my country. When we finish our work here, I will tell you what I remember."

"I know you will. Maybe after you tell me, we could visit those places?"

"Let me think on it Cao."

The crops were harvested and processed during the next two weeks. Lawrence knew he promised Cao the history of his war with the United States. He planned on waiting until Cao and Trinh returned from the last delivery of cashews from this growing season. His plan would have to change, maybe for the better.

The last of this year's crop had been loaded on the U.S. Army truck when the flu hit the Pham family. It was by no means a deadly flu but dangerous if they did not rest and take care. They could not do this and deliver the crop. Thao Pham pleaded with Lawrence to deliver the crop to Da Nang. Considering what the Pham family had done for the Quyens and Lawrence, he had no choice but to make the delivery. The Quyens' crop had to get to market so like it not, he was obligated to help.

It worked out well. Cao had not been with the Phams during harvesting so he was not likely to get sick. Lawrence almost never got the flu or any illness.

The trip was long. He had been working with Cheit at the Phams for the last three days, making just a little progress. He had Cao buy a map of South East Asia the last time he went to Da Nang. He showed some places on the map. Cheit could nod yeses and noes, but there was a problem naming the countries and towns. Of all places, Cheit recognized Afghanistan. His head nodded a yes for Kabul. So now Lawrence knew at one time Cheit had been in Kabul, Afghanistan. Now to find out why he left? Maybe he could find some history books in Da Nang that would help.

The huge truck bounced up and down on the hard dirt roads to Da Nang never allowing the chance to nod off. Lawrence told his son the whole story, from being drafted, turning against the U.S. Army, saving the Quyens, becoming a prisoner of war, and finally joining the Viet Cong. Cao mentioned his Grandfather's versions when he heard Lawrence tell the stories differently. Ba had been quite accurate.

"You know why I had you pack clothes?"

"In case there's an accident?"

"No, we're staying overnight, maybe two nights depending on what I see when we find this tourist company. Seems good, we'll do their tour. But you've got to keep your mouth shut about me. Understand why?"

"Yes, and I know better."

***

Llewellyn Lawrence had only been in Da Nang twice. The first was when he was sent by the U.S.Army to Vietnam in 1966, the second time when he fought with North Vietnamese forces as they chased the Republic of Vietnam's army, ARVN, out of the central highlands of Vietnam and followed them to an attack on Da Nang. On March 28 1975, Easter weekend, Da Nang was chaos as artillery and rockets bombarded the airbase. It had been evacuated by U. S. Army's 1st Air Division in response to low morale and conflicting orders issued by America's military stationed in Saigon.

Crazed mobs of Da Nang citizens turned coat and attacked any and all United States military personnel left. Of the over 200 aircraft that could have evacuated the trapped Americans and their new Vietnamese families, only 20 planes made it out and only 130 people were saved. The other 180 planes were abandoned and sat on runways fueled up and loaded with ordnance. Lawrence had watched as a crazed mob of American soldiers tried to use anything that could float to escape Da Nang by sea. All were gunned down.

It was a day Lawrence chose to forget.

The Han market at Tran Phu and Bach Dang Streets is impressive but as not as impressive as the ever motor scooters racing up and down every street in Da Nang. The commissary where Lawrence had to deliver the cashew barrels was just south of the Han Market bordering the Han River. There were four loading docks and a long line of trucks waited bumper to bumper to back into the docks. Cao had directed his father to the docks very well.

"Does Trinh let you drive the truck?"

"Poppa L, he sleeps on the drive here and once in line, leaves me to dock and unload while he visits …"

Arens smiled at his son since he knew very well why Trinh always made the trips instead of sending one of the workers. "I figured he had a friend or two waiting for him. He's a handsome man and there are not many ladies he would match up with at home."

Cao smiled back at his father.

"You do it. I'm going to take a walk around and find a place where we can stay for a couple of days. Park the truck …"

"I know!"

It did not take him long to find a place. Just a few blocks to the east of Han Market was the Sunriver Hotel overlooking the Han River. Its entrance was a tall glass tube going seven stories high. He asked the man at the counter if he could take a look around and was told to go ahead. The man gave him a key to one of the rooms so Lawrence could see what they were like. After taking the elevator up to the room which overlooked the beautiful view of China Sea, Lawrence went back to the ground floor, checked out the restaurant, and seeing the bar was open 24 hours a day, went back to the desk counter and took the room.

"How's the tourist guide situation?"

The desk man spoke, "depends on what you want to visit."

"I've heard a lot about the war sites around Da Nang. Is there a tour of some of the places where the battles were fought?"

The desk man's smile disappeared, "you an American soldier that fought here?"

Lawrence knew the war had left deep scars. "No. I went to Canada so the draft wouldn't get me. Heard a lot, saw a lot, and was embarrassed about what the U. S. did to your country. I'd like to know how the U.S. got its ass kissed."

"Here's a card," the desk man had turned to a rack behind him and pulled out an advertising placard with photos of wrecked tanks and destroyed bunkers and villages. "His name's Lionel Hanover and he runs tours called Battle Tours. Just three blocks west and one south. Can't miss it."

Lawrence back-tracked to the commissary, found Cao still waiting to unload the cashews, and told him about the Sunriver Hotel, giving him a room key, "I'm going to check out a place called Battle Tours. Shouldn't be that long. You get unloaded, go on to the hotel. Here's some cash in case you get hungry."

The hotel concierge was right. You couldn't miss it. The façade looked like a fallen pagoda, colored red and a yellow that made it look like a bus from Birmingham Alabama. The door was locked and no one answered Lawrence's knocks.

"Hey, over here!" The voice came from under the bus and when Lawrence turned he could see two feet sticking out. "Heard you knocking. You interested in a tour?"

"Got a problem under there?"

"Yeah, fucking oil leak. Lost enough oil to cost me a whole tourist fare. Think I stripped the threads the last time I changed the oil filter. Almost finished putting in a new one. Don't look like the motor threads are fucked, just the filter."

The man wiggled out from under the engine. He was an old man, between sixty or seventy. His face was covered with grime. Sweat created little rivulets giving him the appearance of having stripes. At least he was smart enough to be wearing coveralls.

"You do tours, right?"

"That's what the sign says. You a vet? Here during Nam?"

Lawrence smiled. "Yeah, went home with bad eyes. Lucked out I guess."

"Looking for a battle site tour, huh? Well that's what I do. When you want to go? Got close to a bus load for tomorrow. In fact, got three Nam vets goin' out. Rest are just plain Vietnamese tourists. You wanna go?"

"My son's with me."

"Want him to see where kick ass went down?"

"Guess so. Good for him to learn. You get many vets? I mean we did lose this war, right?"

"Don't give a fuck. Tour makes U.S. look like war heroes. Only reason I make any money here is that I'm subsidized by a company back in the States. They got a bunch of small little set ups like this one all over Nam. Good tourist market."

"What time tomorrow?"

"Get moving about 8:30. Be here around a quarter after. Ain't cheap. Cost you a C note, maybe two. How old's your son?"

"He's an adult. Two hundred's fine. Do we need to bring anything like food or drinks?"

"No, got some stops. Hope your stomach can handle Vietnamese food, beer too."

Lawrence just laughed. He knew Vietnamese food very well indeed. "See you tomorrow. Your name's Lionel? Lionel Hanover. Unusual name for a down home American boy."

"My daddy loved electric trains."

"Good thing he liked the big trains. Could have named you after those small gauge ones. You know HO."

"Yeah, then I'd been a Ho. Fuck, there's enough Hos around here as is. See you tomorrow."

***

The old school bus was filled by the time Lawrence and Cao made it to Battle Tours. Lionel Hanover was waiting patiently at the bus door with his arms folded over each other like a parent prepared to discipline a child.

"Lionel, it's my fault. I should have had the desk clerk at the hotel ring me. You got room for us?"

Lionel was not bothered. "No sweat, Mr. Lawrence. Most of my customers are Vietnamese. They're here when the sun comes up out of China Sea. Hop on up the steps, there's seats behind my driver's seat. You need some coffee before we leave?"

"No thanks. Probably would make me have to go too much. How long a ride?"

"Thirty-five maybe forty minutes if Route 607 ain't bottled up with farmers and their carts."

"Your battle site is in Ho An, right?"

"Yep, that's the one we're doing today."

"How many you got?"

"Ho An was our first and we're up to eight now."

"Eight battle sites?"

"Well I don't want to pull the wool over your eyes. They ain't really battle sites. They're more or less simulations the company built around areas where there had been some major skirmishes. It's how these slopes fought. Reason they kicked ass in fact."

Lawrence put his hand on Cao's shoulder when he saw his son's reaction to the word slope.

"You might want to cool it using that name for Asians if you don't mind." Arens sat behind Hanover, who had started the bus and had both hands on the driving wheel.

Three rows behind Lawrence and on the right side of the bus sat three non-Asian that Lawrence had noticed as he was getting on the bus. He wasn't sure they were American's until the bald-headed, gangly white man yelled at Hanover. "Yeah Lionel! Just call them Chinks."

Llewellyn felt the hairs at the back of his neck stiffen. He knew the three men were Vietnam veterans just by hearing the voice of the bald man. He could not chance a confrontation, so he would let the remark go. Lionel closed the folding doors of the bus and headed south to Ho An.

They reached the Battle Site in just over 30 minutes. The three white men never let up on their derogatory and demeaning comments about Asians, especially about the people they passed as the bus drove through the village.

Lionel announced first in Vietnamese, followed in English that they had arrived at the site and should leave the bus. There was a large, open air building with a long banner welcoming tourists to Battle Tours Vietnam. Hanover told the passengers that they had fifteen minutes to use the facilities before the tour would began. He directed them to an enclosed building with rest rooms and a souvenir shop. Arens and Cao walked around the site trying to get a handle on just what Battle Tours Vietnam had to offer. When they returned to the lecture building, the three white men were just leaving the lavatory and were lighting up cigarettes. Lawrence got a better view of them now. The mouthy one on the bus was quite tall with a bald scalp of grey hair from one ear to the other. He squinted, even though there was no sunlight. When he walked, he a loping pace, similar to a circus clown wearing large shoes. He also tended to sway back and forth. He came across as a bully.

The shortest of the men could have been an albino. Even with a tint of color to his skin, he still looked anemic. He had curly blond hair cut close, making his head look like a cartoon character. His eyes were very blue flickering continuously, as if there was dust in the air. Unlike his bald compatriot, he kept his voice low. His comrades constantly asked him what he said.

The third man was a rat, a large rat. He had a snout like a rodent and eyes that were in constant motion, moving from side as if searching for something to kill something or attack. His upper body was thin, with long skinny arms easily grasped and encircled the opposite arm, fingers touching thumb. What really stood out was his oversized rear end, a bubble butt. He spoke little and when he did speak it was not much more than a whisper, his mouth next to the listener's ear.

"Okay, folks!" Lionel called first in Vietnamese and then English. "Come on into the Battle Tour Instruction hut and take a seat."

The instruction hut had a large map of Ho An with color marked areas of battle sites, a display of the area of the camp showing a pathway of tunnels, and a large screen monitor connected to a desk top computer. A young Asian man wearing black slacks and a white, short sleeved shirt was waiting for the tourists to be seated. Pointing to the ground map, he labeled a system of tunnels that the Viet Cong used to fall into to avoid being caught by American and ARVN forces after an attack. The tunnel system was a tremendous weapon against their enemy. After a quick strike at enemy forces, then turn and go no more than a few yards, and drop into a tunnel, a perfect hiding spot.

The bald man spoke, "that makes no fucking sense! Just follow them down the hole and into the tunnel. Or better yet, follow those fuckers to their hole and drop grenades down the hole. Or gas 'em!"

"Sir, if you would please," said the instructor, "could you watch your language when speaking?"

"Fuck no!"

The rat grabbed his friend's arm, as he slowly looked at everybody in the room, and whispered to the bald man, "keep it down. Don't get riled up. Just stay calm."

After viewing a short video, the instructor escorted them out of the hut and through the woods going northwest.

"Sir, you a brave man, no?" The instructor spoke to the bald man, "you see enemy fire from here?"

"Sure, right here. He disappears right here. Where's the tunnel?"

"You standing on it."

The bald man looked at his feet. All he saw was dirt and leaves.

"You brush away dirt leaves, please."

When he kicked the soil below him, a block of concrete with a square in the center appeared. Two ropes formed handles on each side of the square. The bald man grabbed the ropes and lifted out the square revealing a deep, narrow tunnel passage going straight down.

"It's just a hole."

"You go down hole and at bottom another hole is tunnel running from here to other drop holes. Viet Cong are very good at dropping and running tunnel to new hole to kill enemy soldiers. You try?"

The bald man hung his feet over the hole and eased down in to the hole. When he touched bottom, his upper body was still sticking out of the hole.

"How do I crawl into the tunnel? When I try to bend, I only get my head under."

He pulled himself out of the hole and turned to the albino. "Hey, fat ass! You give it a try."

The bald man was right. When his compatriot tried to drop into the hole, he got stuck and the instructor and his bald friend had to pull him up out of the hole.

Lawrence could not resist the challenge, "Cao, come here. You try, okay?"

"Yes, Poppa L! Let me try!"

The instructor called the boy over and whispered something in his ear. Cao went back to the hole and dropped like a rock. He disappeared.

"You now see Asian advantage. Asian warriors, Viet Cong Army, all small, short and ..."

Lawrence finished, "don't have fat butts!"

The albino leered as Lawrence laughed.

Lawrence walked over to the hole to help Cao out. He was gone.

"Where's my son?"

The instructor smiled, "him not in hole? Oh, good thing. Him escape ARVN. Come follow me."

They walked down a path and there was Cao sitting on the edge of another hole. Lawrence pulled his son up and out of the hole, giving him a big hug. The tourists followed the instructor as he pointed out escape holes one after the other. They passed a Viet Cong armored tank and a display of models dressed in army fatigues holding weapons. After passing a flower garden, they came to a large concrete firing range. Targets of American soldiers with concentric scoring circles embossed on the surface were placed a hundred yards away. There were AK47's welded to rotating pivots which could only be aimed down range.

"AK47s? Just what your friends the Russians sold you. They live or just models?" asked bald man.

"Yes, look at the ground below the wall," said the instructor.

Hundreds of spent shells were below the four rifles. The instructor started to demonstrate how to load the AK47s but the rat man went by him, cleared the breech of a weapon, inserted a cartridge, chambered the first round, and sent a spasm of bullets at the target in front of him. The albino and bald man took up the remaining positions and went through their cartridges, asking for more.

"For the money you pay us, only one cartridge load." Lionel had been sleeping in the bus but now joined the group. "You see how the Viet Cong set you up? Small, easy built gun turrets over top of the tunnels. Not more than four shooters wasting GIs coming out of the woods. Boom, boom, boom, and boom they're dead. The four Viet Cong go down the pipe, with their weapons and head to another turret."

Lionel took over the tour, escorting the tourists from one wooded area into another. In the middle of the woods they came upon a hut that looked like a subway entrance. The shape and size benefited the Asian tourists but was difficult for the Americans to maneuver. This tunnel went deeper than the other and was completely dark. The albino started screaming, turned, pushing people out of his way, and ran back up the stairs. The rat man stayed at the front, seemingly right at home crawling through his nest.

Lawrence asked Lionel, "how many kilometers of tunnels are here?"

"Want to walk all of them? Over 250 kilometers."

"That's what? 150 or so miles?"

"Sounds about right. They housed over tens of thousands of people. Ah, here we are. The kitchen," said Lionel swinging his flashlight around as he looked for an oil lamp.

The rat man was looking around and said, "cook ware? That's stupid around Airplanes see smoke, they'll know where you are. B-52s probably killed a lot of people down in holes like this one."

The instructor had returned. "You are making a very bad error in thinking my people were not smart enough to divert the smoke. There are ducts running very far from here. Never a bomb took out our barracks."

Rat man continued, "I remember my company trying to go into these tunnels. It was a big mistake. Viet Cong set booby traps all around possible entrances. I got caught in one that when I put my foot down into the hole a spring was tripped and rusted steel rods swung on a pivot, gouging my leg. Still got scars."

"Viet Cong set similar traps at all entrances. Urinated on spikes to make enemy get infected," said the instructor. "Need get to top. Got surprise before you go."

They returned to the entrance hut where a Vietnamese woman was sitting before a large wok pan placed on burning coals. She had a large pot filled with a white paste next to her. She scooped a ladle full of the paste and spread it evenly on the wok, placing a lid over it. The tourists were tired and took seats, watching the woman. After a few minutes she removed the top, took a tube about the width of a large drinking glass, and rolled it over the now hardened thin cake. The cake wrapped around the tube and the woman turned behind her to a bamboo mat. She unrolled the cake onto the mat and turned back to make another cake in the wok.

The instructor spoke, "you see how little smoke she make? This is how we lived. Try some of her food. See what we lived on."

When everybody had tried the food, visited the rest room, and visited the sparse gift shop, they were escorted back to the Battle Tours bus.

The albino spoke, "what are you doing? This isn't how we came from the bus."

Lionel turned a smile on his face. "Want you to see the kinds of souvenirs the Vietnam people got from the war. Just follow me."

As they neared the end of the woods, they came to a small clearing and could see the bus just off to the right, maybe fifty yards away. At the exit from the battle site of Ho An was a memorial of huge bomb shells stacked upright.

"B52s, all of them," said Lawrence.

"Yes, that's what the people of Vietnam got from the war," said the instructor who had followed the tourists out to the battle site.

Instead of heading north on Route 607, Lionel took the sightseers west on Route 608 through Thanh Ha, an old village of waterways where each morning fishermen sailed into the rising sun via the Thu Bon River to the South China Sea.

The village was well known for its carpentry, the technique of its carpenters exceptional. Their work produced on the heads of building columns, rafters, pillars, altars, tables, chairs and beds were masterpieces. The carpenters still keep their traditions alive, many of them making fishing boats for the fishermen in Central Vietnam.

Further along the road Route 608 split, Lionel went north for a half a mile and then made a left turn onto a rural road that followed a wide, deep stream. Within a few minutes they approached another village, this one with a sign welcoming all to visit the death of the village, Qua Thoi Loi, which according to Cao, translated to passing pig piles.

Lawrence asked "What's here Lionel?"

"New village. We are adding to Battle Tour Sites a village where American's attacked, killing for no reason. There are some Vietnamese survivors of the massacre who rebuilt the village. They welcome people to see what happened."

"That's sort of morbid."

"Yes, I'm sure you've heard of other massacres. These villagers have tried to bring back life by encouraging visitors to experience the pain and horror. You'd be surprised at how many American Vietnam veterans leave with tears in their eyes. The people of Qua Thoi Loi hope to bring closure to their shame. At the end of the walk is a monument to those whom wish to cry for the villagers of Qua Thoi Loi who died in the massacre."

How ironic that a survivor of the massacre acted as the tour guide. A thin, frail woman, probably a grandmother exhibited a radiance of youth and wellbeing. She first led tourists to a well in the middle of the village. Here the helicopters came into the village in the early morning without any resistance by the villagers; the only people in the village that morning were women, children, and the elderly. She motioned the tourists around the well and explained that children and small women were picked up and dropped into the well. The American soldiers watched, laughing and ridiculing their victims, eventually gunning down those that did not drown. The well symbolizes entrance to the afterlife for those who died in it. Villagers drop flowers into the well for those living in the hereafter.

The albino spoke up. "Hey, I like that. Instead of flowers we can have tourists drop money down the well."

The bald man laughed and punched his friend on the soldier.

Lawrence was startled, "Lionel, what are they talking about?"

"I'll tell you later."

The tour guide led them to the rice fields, "most of us men were in the fields when the helicopters came. We knew there was a war going on but we were not part of it. We were just living our everyday lives. But the planes started shooting down people in the rice fields. Those who escaped the rice fields by way of the road in back to the village got stopped at both ends by soldiers that dropped out of the helicopters."

She motioned the tourists to the ditches on each side of the rice fields, "the ditches are drainage when we have storms.

They help save our fields from flooding. They are quite deep. The leader of the Americans, I believe he was a Captain, yelled at his men to fire, kill everybody. Shove them into the ditch. Some village women went up to the Captain bowing to him and begging him to let them return to their huts. His men beat them with their rifle butts. See that sign down there?"

Everybody turned to see the metal sign staked at the edge of the ditch. The tour guide read the sign in Vietnamese and English. It honored a village boy whose arms had been shot off as he walked. Before he fell dead he asked "what did I do?"

"The captain ordered us to stand in the ditches so his troops could pass. As soon as we did, the gunfire started. Bodies fell as the Americans gunned down the women and children. I grabbed my infant daughter, and lay down between the dead bodies in the ditch, pulling the dead over my body as best I could. Fortunately, they did not shoot where I was."

The tourists followed the woman down the road leading to the village, as she told the worst of all horrors. "Babies were a rarity, much desired by the Americans. As they went to the village, they could hear babies crying, covered by their dead mother's body. A soldier reached under a dead woman and yanked the crying baby out ..." The tour guide stopped, turning to face the tourists. With tears in her eyes, she spoke softly, "what I show here puts me close to the dead. Forgive my crying. It will never stop on this road of death."

"The soldier reached under the woman and held up the baby with his two hands over his head yelling 'who wants a shot?'"

Painfully she continued. "Four American soldiers hold up guns and took sight. The man with the child tossed it into the air above the rice field..."

She sat down on the edge of a ditch, looking out across where this happened, "they shot the baby so many times nothing left but bits of bone, skin, muscle, and tissue."

The rat man nudged the bald man, "here's good one for the site. You know how the other site had the AK47's stationed in the gun tower? How's about we match that with baby dolls tossed up over the field?"

The bald man slapped the rat man's hand in a high five, "yeah, that'd be a money grabber."

Lawrence had overheard most of the conversation and was beginning to understand some of what was happening. He needed to know the whole picture.

The tour guide led them into the village with their rebuilt huts. "If you look over there to the right, there's a big hill with a door in front, a strong wooden door."

They walked over to the hill. "This is a bunker. These people were villagers, not soldiers. They did not have a tunnel system like the one you saw today. Yet, they could hear the bombs. This was their bunker for when the bombers were overhead. The villagers who were still alive had squeezed into this bunker thinking they would be safe from the invading American soldiers. With the door shut, it would be difficult to get them out of the bunker. One of the soldiers was smart enough to realize they needed air inside the bunker. He found the vents and the soldiers dropped hand grenades into them. My daughter and I were lucky to have escaped into the woods."

The guide led them back to the village and to a large L shaped, grass-roofed hut with raised window shutters to help keep the humidity outside. The hut was set up like a family with chairs, tables, bunks and a kitchen. The inside walls were covered with photographs.

"These pictures were taken by American soldiers," said the woman. "Many we found in old magazines from United States. We cut them out and posted them. Many came from United States war veterans who have visited our village. They were ashamed but knowing we would use their pictures to show the tragedy of our home helped them feel better."

Lawrence and his son gazed at the pictures of war.

"Poppa L, what is that soldier doing?"

"He's poking out the man's eyeballs, one at a time, trying to get the man to talk."

Next to that photo was a one of the body of the boy who had his arms shot off. Llewellyn put his arm around Cao seeing the tears in his son's eyes. The next photo showed a village woman being held back from trying to stop five GIs from raping her twelve year old daughter. The photo after that showed the woman face down in the dirt with the back of her head blown off.

"Cao, let's and get out of here."

"No Arens. I need to see this. Always I questioned your desertion. Now I know you did the right thing. Please, let's keep looking."

The horror was captured in each photo. There was a man dead on his back with his brains oozing out of the top of his head. Another photo showed villagers in front of huts, their bodies shattered by bullets, the blood seeping into the dirt. There was a very young woman on her side, her arms bound behind her, naked from the waist down with blood smeared over her anus showed a photo of rape. Next to her was a stick covered with blood. Lawrence was glad that Cao did not speak.

On the next wall was a series of photos showing the rice fields, the ditches draining the fields, and the roads between the fields. Each picture showed bodies strewn atop each other. All the bodies had been ripped apart by gun fire.

The guide came up behind Arens and Cao. "Those bodies saved my life and that of my child's. We were under the bodies until the Americans left. We will never forget the smell or the bugs and snakes as we laid under our dead friends."

She motioned for the two of them to follow her to the back room which ran perpendicular to the hut. Inside were more walls filled with photos and one large engraved plaque. At the top of the plaque was the name of the village, the words "list of victims killed by the GIs" and the date of the massacre.

Llewellyn did not need to guess how many since she said, "one hundred and two. Look behind you. See those pieces of paper taped to the bare wall? This is the shame wall. These are note cards we post whenever an American visits this memorial. I will ask you, as I did these Americans. Would you like to post your name admitting shame for what your country did?"

He could not do that and she did not push him, "we understand, sir. But I will put a note there so we remember the tears in your eyes. No name on it."

Trying to control himself from embarrassment, Lawrence spoke, "these photos here are not of your village. They are battle pictures."

"The inside walls behind us recognize our village. These are photos of your war against the people of Vietnam. These are our victories."

The guide excused herself and returned to the other tourists still in the first room. Lawrence and Cao took their time looking at the different actions the VC took against ARVN and the United States. They were harsh and even though amateurs, they did not fail to get the message across. Vietnam ran America out of the country.

All of a sudden Llewellyn Lawrence felt dizzy and nauseous. He was looking at a photograph of the 1972 Easter Offensive and there among all of the Asian faces was his face. He staggered out of the hut. Cao followed him, fearing his father was very ill. Deep into the woods, he vomited up nothing but bile, the bile burning his throat. His dry heaves lasted for five minutes before he got back control.

"Cao, relax! I'm okay. Don't worry about it. Go on back to the village now!"

Cao held his head down, embarrassed for his father, and returned to the village as asked. Lawrence recognized the photograph that had been taken at Nguyen Hue. It showed him with the Viet Cong climbing over an ARVN tank they had destroyed, killing its crew in the process. Even though fifteen years had passed, Lawrence was still a traitor. It took him a few minutes for his stomach to settle and to regain his equilibrium.

When he got back to the room of the North Vietnamese photographs the rat man was standing in front of the tank photograph staring at it. Stunned Arens moved off to the side so he could watch the rat man unobserved. The rat man was strangely built. He could put both his arms behind his back and grasp both his arms akimbo. Lawrence could not even get his arms anywhere close to that position. The man was examining something in one of the photographs.

The man turned but not before Lawrence had eased his way outside. He heard the rat man call to his associates. Both were talking to him. Lawrence heard the bald man say he saw nothing familiar in the photo the rat man was standing before but the albino snickered.

"Yeah, that's the asshole with the chink kid. Sure of it."

Lawrence felt trapped. He had his .38 holstered at his back with six bullets. He knew he could take the three of them down, but at what cost? He would have to flee and in doing so bring shame and humiliation to the Quyens. Even worse would be the effect on his son. Shooting the bastards was not the answer. He would have to be patient and bide his time. He had to let them make the first move. Even if they tried to take him down or called the police, he could still kill them. He would just wait and see. He knew from years of battle that you did not react to what your enemy might do, only to what they can do.

As he returned to the village, the three men eyeballed him but that was all. The tourists were slowly wandering back to the tour bus. Cao caught up to his father, saw that Arens seemed okay, and both climbed back on the bus. Lionel took role as the tourists took their seats, started the engine, and headed back to route 607 toward Da Nang.

Lawrence could see the back of the bus through the rear view mirror in front of Lionel. Every so often, one of the three men would take a quick gander in Lawrence's direction. He knew better than to let it bother him, but it did none the less In a little over twenty five minutes, they were disembarking in front of Battle Site Tours.

Lawrence and Cao headed to their truck but not before the bald man yelled to them. Lawrence stopped, telling Cao to wait while he talked to the three men.

The rat man did not make eye contact, "you destroy that tank?"

"That's right. What's it to you?"

Rat man's eyes darted left and right, from Lawrence, to the street and then back to Lawrence, "you're a legend. Do you know that?"

Once again Lawrence reminded himself of the code of war. Find what your enemy can do, maybe.

"We're here as part of a franchise investment. You know Battle Sites of Vietnam."

"Yep, just went on the tour."

"They're going to be big time Lawrence. It is Lawrence, right?"

"It'll do."

"My associates and me could use a man like you. Set up our Battle Site franchise, you leading the tours. You know a lot more than Lionel."

The albino butted in "Lionel is an asshole. We need someone that's been in the fight, can get the tourists excited."

The bald man had left the conversation to the other two. Lawrence could sense from the sneer on his face, the man was not so sure of using Lawrence as a tour guide.

"Is baldy with you on this?"

The bald man straightened his body and gritted his teeth, "yeah, but I don't like it. You're a real shit. You killed off men who might have served with me in Nam. I oughta ..."

Rat man told him to shut up, "Lawrence, he's in it. Doesn't matter anyway. It's the money is what counts."

The albino snickered. "Hell, he'd fuck a dog if he could make a buck."

Rat man turned back to Lawrence, "can we get together and discuss my plan?"

"Sure. When?"

"How about now?"

"Tonight. Where are you staying?'

"Okay by us." The rat man gave him the name of their hotel and room number. "How 'bout 8:00 PM?"

Lawrence had control. They were not interested in blackmailing him but rather wanted to use him. The tour had been a piece of work. Using a war that should never have been fought to make money, that is America's way. Before Vietnam, America was headed for a financial depression. Start a war and end a depression with money spent to fight, arm soldiers, build weapons, and recruit workers for a pittance they paid to the drafted soldiers.

Now the war was over and America was still finding a way to make money off the war that ended with 58,156 dead Americans, 17,725 of which been forced to serve creating a franchise to relive history where you can come and visit Vietnam and its famous, or infamous, twenty-year war. Where you can see the actual battle sites, crawl through tunnels, shoot AK47's, and toss up baby dolls that you can gun down like the U.S. Army soldiers did.

The United States was a farce. From George Washington to Richard Nixon, it has been a country of money merchants. Human life is not important. The USA is money.

Lawrence was lit, smiling as he found Cao. "Cao, I'm staying here for a few more days. I want you to drive the truck back and make sure you tell Trinh about the bidding on the cashews. Give him our commissions. Do not explain anything else. If they ask you about me, just tell them I'm working on a deal."

This would have to be quick and buried deep. There was little risk of being caught without a bunch of police work, but by then he would have disappeared. First stop was Lionel at Battle Sites Tours.

"Lawrence, what're you doing back here?"

"Gotta talk with you about your franchise people. Can we do it in private?"

"Sure, come on in the back. As you know, I am Battle Tours. There's no one else, just me."

"That's why I'm here."

There was not much in the back room except a kitchen table with two chairs, a refrigerator, and sink plus a used Honda moped.

"How much did the Honda cost you?"

"US dollars? About $325, not much sense owning a car in Da Nang."

"Lionel, those three men on the tour, what do you know about them?"

"Not much. They were recruited by the franchise leasing company back in the States. The company sent them here so that they would see that their investment would make a profit, a big one. It also gives them a feel with how the Battle Site is run. The company oversees the site but the site can only make money if they can handle it properly."

"So you won't be communicating with the home company until you've gone through the investment with those three men?"

"No reason to contact them. I've got to go through the steps with them tomorrow. What's on your mind? Have they talked with you about the investment?"

It was obvious that Lionel knew nothing about Llewellyn's past and therefore had not communicated anything to the outside world.

"Lionel, do you realize that Battle Sites Tour makes money by selling war and the dead people who died because of it?"

Before Lionel could respond, Llewellyn put a .38 mm bullet through his left eye. He searched through Lionel's pockets and came up with a set of keys, one of which belonged to the Honda. Lawrence found a tarp, covered the body, and turned off the lights before leaving. Only three people could identify Llewellyn Lawrence as a suspect in Lionel's murder. Those three would be dead before the night was over.

The Vinpearl Penthouse Condo was located on the edge of the South China Sea and stood five stories high. The three Americans occupied one of the penthouses on the upper floor. The resort desk clerk phoned their room, and after hanging up, directed Lawrence to the elevator. As he entered the penthouse, Lawrence was taken aback at the magnificence of the Vinpearl. An oak hardwood floor with two large windows offering a clear view of the sea and beach comprised the entrance. There were two bedrooms, one on each side. The right one had its door closed. Lawrence had been met at the door by the bald man who showed him into the main room. To the right was a luxurious dining room with glass fronted cabinets containing very expensive china and glassware.

"My two associates will join us in a few minutes. Care for a drink?"

Lawrence rarely turned down a drink but he had to be in total control. "You got a diet soda?"

"Diet soda? You're fucking kidding me? This ain't a MacDonald's. Can't get ya a beer?"

"No, thanks anyway."

The rat man came out of the bedroom in his underwear. He finished rolling a marijuana joint and lit it. After slowly taking in a drag he spoke, "Lawrence, how do you like this place. We're giving it a try, might buy it if we get our Battle Site Tour franchise near here. There's three villages with tunnels only an hour or so away."

The albino had come out of the bedroom also clad only in a white night gown. His baby blue eyes sparkled as he snarled.

"Mr. Lawrence, you look shocked? Got a problem with fags, boy?"

"What you do is your business."

The albino opened his mouth, moving his tongue back and forth over the lower lip. The rat man offered him a drag on his joint. The albino inhaled deeply as his eyes rolled up into his head.

The bald man spoke, "don't drink, don't fuck fags."

Lawrence was on edge. He had one advantage over the three men. The bald man had let him into the penthouse without frisking him. He had reloaded after taking down Lionel, and it took all he had to hold himself back from killing the three of them right now.

"Let's get down to business. What do you people see in me?"

Rat man passed the joint back to the albino to finish off. The albino's eyes were clouding over and he was swaying a bit. He would be the last one Lawrence took down.

Rat man assumed the same pose that had amazed Lawrence earlier. Akimbo, that is what it was called.

"Mr. Lawrence, Vietnam Battle Site Tours is an LLC. You know what an LLC is?"

"Yes I do. It's a limited liability company where the investors are not liable for any malpractice by the GP, the general partner."

"That's correct. We invest in an LLC for a battle site or two and gain not only profits but big tax advantages. Our GP fronts his investors with a no expense trip to Vietnam to get a feel for the investment. It is our funds that will build the battle site. That's why we're here. The GP wanted us to see the potential of Vietnam Battle Site Tours. He wants to know if we see any changes that need to be made to make more profit. Being Nam vets, we could get a better perspective on it."

The bald man spoke. "We saw you at the site today. Saw that photo of you with the Viet Cong ."

The albino spoke, "yes, dear boy, we know who you are. Got a reward hanging over your head, don't you?"

"Still a hundred grand?"

Rat man grabbed the albino's left arm. "Cool it. No need for that. He's safe here in Nam and you know it. Now go get dressed."

Lawrence couldn't help but laugh since the rat man was still in his briefs. "Quit fucking around with me. What do you want?"

The bald man's neck hairs were erected, "hey, don't throw the shit around. We got an offer for you. Keep up that attitude and you could put your head on the block."

Rat man spoke. "You know Lionel right?"

Lawrence smiled, thinking about the dead man lying on the store room floor, "man who directs the tours. What's he got to do with this?"

"He keeps the tours too civilized. Take the AK47's. It's his biggest attraction but he won't expand on it. You know, more shooting and killing. Do a My Lai on the site. Bring in a bunch of vets from the States."

"That throwing the baby doll up and shooting it would be a killer attraction," added the bald man.

It was getting to be too much for Llewellyn. He folded his arms over his chest and looked each of the three veterans in the eyes. "Money maker, right? Sort of like a mini Disney World devoted to war and killing. Doesn't that bother you? You really think people will spend thousands of dollars to come here for that reason?"

"Are you fucking blind, little man," asked the albino. "Didn't you see the full bus? Not only will we attract Americans to see our side of the Vietnam War, but busses will be filled with Asians wanting to see what the Viet Cong did to the United States soldiers."

"Calm down, you three. If we open up the battle site with an American deserter, that would be you, Lawrence, leading VC into battle to kill off the American's, the Vietnamese, Chinese, and nearly every other Asian population we've screwed over will flock to the site."

Lawrence smiled. These men were insane. It was time.

Lawrence pulled the .38 out and shot rat man center mass less than three feet away. He fell backward, his arms still grasped behind his back and died. The bald man ran toward his bedroom but a bullet exploded the back of his head before reach the door. That left the albino. He was lying on his lover's body, the rat man as he died.

Lawrence put the nozzle of the gun on the albino's neck and killed him.

It was over. The only people who knew he was still alive and living in Vietnam were now dead. Since he had touched nothing, there would be no fingerprints when the bodies were found. With Lionel's case, the moped would be the only clue. Even then the police would probably believe he had been killed by somebody stealing his Honda. He saw a 'DO NOT DISTURB' sign hanging on the inside door knob. He went to the door, grabbed the sign, and was ready to leave the penthouse when he stopped.

"It might be a good idea to do a search of the penthouse," he thought. Following his instincts, he searched the bald man's room first but found nothing worthwhile. The other room was disgusting but he went through it all anyway, looking through the closets, bathroom drawers, and dressers. Before leaving he stopped at the night light table next to the bed.

"I'm dead." There laid a copy of a telegram the rat man had sent the LLC's general partner just hours ago. All of their recommendations for their franchise including Llewellyn Lawrence's proposed role in the Vietnam Battle Site Tour were there. Eventually the bodies would be discovered and the LLC general partner would learn that his investors had been killed. Surely he would bring forth the rat man's telegram and then Lawrence would become a fugitive. His life in Vietnam, his relationship to the Quyens was over. At most he would have two or three days before the hunt for him would begin. Maybe no connection to the Quyens would be made and he would be safe. After all, very few people knew Lawrence by name.

"No, no, no. It won't work." The franchise GP would have knowledge that Llewellyn Lawrence was a U. S. Army deserter and he more than likely would report it to the United States Army. There would be a large dossier on him including photographs. These would be sent to the Vietnam police in Da Nang. A wanted campaign, complete with a posted photo would be released to the public. He would get caught. He was at a loss. Where to go now?

He spoke out loud, "where is not important but right now go is."

He returned to the Vietnam Battle Sites Tour office, took the Honda, and headed back to the Quyens village. It was not a long ride but was made dangerous by Lawrence's lack of concentration on the drive. He almost crashed.

"Think, Lawrence. You've got to think and still drive."

He had money, ironic since he had not paid much attention to finances living in the village. He also had the American dollars and Vietnamese currency that he had taken from the four men he killed. It was a great deal of money, but spending the money was not as important as where to spend it. He went through the countries surrounding Vietnam but his limited knowledge of these countries made them improbable as escape routes. The Quyens would be of little help. They had lived their whole lives within a few miles of the village. He would need to turn to the Pham family for help. Would he have to lie to them, give them some cock and bull story? No, he knew them pretty well and the truth would be the best way to go. There would be no questions asked, just advice to help him flee the country safely.

He drove the moped through the night, stopping two miles northeast of the Pham home. The jungle was too thick to ride a moped through but there was enough room on the trails to walk it to the swamp. Lawrence and Trinh had hunted through this swamp a few times. It was foul smelling, the fauna covering quicksand pits. Trinh had once thrown a javelin like limb directly into the middle of the pit and they watched as the seven-foot branch got sucked down and disappeared into the quick sand. Lawrence parked the Honda on a small hill edging the sand pit using some stones to prop up the rear wheel. He knew the deeper into the pit the moped went, the less likely it would be discovered. It would be tricky but he started the Honda, hand throttling the speed of the rear wheel. Keeping the wheel slowly spinning, Lawrence used the edges of the seat to lift the rear end of the Honda off the rock supports. Aiming for the middle of the pit, he eased the rear wheel down until it was an inch from the ground. Giving the throttle a little more gas, he let the wheel go and the moped flew out toward the middle of the quick sand. An hour later the pit had swallowed the entire Honda.

He walked the rest of the way to the Phams. The sun had started to rise before he was risen half-way there. He knew that Trinh's father Thao and his mother Anh would already be up beginning their work day. Stepping up on their porch, he called out asking if anybody was awake. Mother Anh Pham came to the door and yelled at Lawrence.

"You wake everybody Arens! Be quiet! You hungry?"

"Sure am. Since it's not noon yet, I'm betting Trinh is still asleep?"

"Boy drive Thao crazy. Thao said could get in whole crop of cashews by time the boy out of bed."

"Did Cao get your truck back okay?"

"Yes, with no help from father."

Thao Pham came into the hut right behind Lawrence, "Arens? What happened that you not come back with son?"

"I need to tell you the story once and only once. Can we get Trinh awake?"

"Only, if you got dead fish to lay over his face! I'll get him. You eat breakfast with him and me."

Lawrence looked over to the corner of the family area, "I hear Cheit still snores. Maybe we could train him to do some kind of signaling with different snore sounds? What do you think Mama Pham?"

Anh beamed at him, "you be surprised Arens?"

"How's that?"

"We wait til Trinh here. Yes, him here now."

"Arens, what happened to you? Cao was scared to death having all that responsibility. You not do right Arens."

"What I'm about to tell you may change our relationship."

As the four friends ate their breakfast, Llewellyn Lawrence related the events of the last two days. Mama Pham moaned when Lawrence told them about killing Lionel and the three Americans. She moaned not for the men killed but because Arens had to kill them. They should have been killed and Lawrence did it.

"If I had known about the telegram, I might have changed my plan. But it really makes no difference, I still would have killed them."

Father Pham spoke, "you think they not track you down?"

"I think that's not likely. It'll be in the papers that three Americans were shot to death in their penthouse in Da Nang. The Da Nang police will probably tie it in with Lionel's death at the Vietnam Battle Site Tour office. I'm sure they'll contact the owners and get a list of clients Lionel over the last few days."

"You gave them your name?"

"I didn't even think about it. U.S. government thinks I'm dead, so who cares?"

"They don't know about your family here?"

"No, the Quyens are safe. I never used their names. I didn't even use Cao's last name on Battle Site Tour."

"What are you going to do?"

" I need your help. I'll ask you. Where can I go?"

Trinh started to speak but his father broke in, "not many places, Arens. Cambodia bad place for Americans. Laos not much better. Have to go cross border with no passport. That no problem. Many places to cross. But where you settle? Thailand little better, but not much. America might send out wanted notices to the governments. You get caught."

"I'm a dead man!"

The four people sitting at the dining table turned as Cheit let out a loud moan.

"Big surprise for you, Arens. Cheit learn to talk."

"He can talk?"

"Not talk, talk. He sign talk."

"But he has no hands?"

Anh smiled. "You go, I take over using your signs in French. I better at it than you. I learn much French from when they were in country. I work better with it. Go slow but get response. Noises not do any good. Only use sign of hands."

Trinh spoke, "you'll never guess what Mama Pham did."

"Make facial signs?"

"You let me tell, son or I hit you on head," said Anh. "Feet!"

"Feet? I can't believe that?"

"Course not. You dumb American," said Mam Pham making everybody including Cheit, laugh.

"It not easy but he understand. We change some finger signals which feet could not make. But most hand signs could be close with feet.'

Cheit started a long chain of moans which got Anh to turn to him. She went over and took off the socks he wore when he slept. She propped up his feet so all of them could see.She spoke out loud as she gave Cheit hands signals for, what is your name?

Lawrence watched in awe as Cheit slowly signed letter by letter.

"His name Zohar, means light," said Anh. "What did you do before you were hurt?"

This took longer and he had to stop many times, getting frustrated until Anh spoke, "he was rabbi and teacher. He teach children like him, deaf and dumb."

"Did he tell you how he wound up here?" asked Lawrence.

"Yes, but let me sign him same question," which Anh did.

It was a long story much it not decipherable.

"Arens, watch feet. He trying to tell you something."

Anh translated Zohar's signs as best she could. She had to sign him to go back over what he signed many times.

"Arens, think a minute about Zohar. He been many places in this part of world. He grew up in France, deaf and dumb but after becoming rabbi went to Afghanistan in 1979 to teach others like him. Arabs forced him out and he went to Saigon. He lived and taught at synagogue in Saigon for six years, one of only twelve French Jews. The Khmer Rouge raided his synagogue and killed everybody but him. His terror was worse a deaf mute could have. They cut off his hands and threw him back of Trinh's truck."

"He's been all over the Arab world, Mama Pham. Ask him where I could go. You can tell him as much as he needs to know. Tell him why I need to leave Vietnam."

Anh Pham spent over an hour signing and reading the feet signs, going back over the places which he did not elucidate well.

"He say Afghanistan."

"You're kidding?"

"Watch when I ask him again."

Signing, she asked why Afghanistan. His response was that Lawrence was a warrior and the Afghanistan army needs help fighting off the Russians.

"Who? Who can I fight for?"

"He signs the Taliban, whoever they are?"

CHAPTER THIRTY

Tabernacle of the Beast

Exiting Route 278 in Brooklyn, Lawrence parked on the street next to Hillside Park. It was a little after 6:00 AM and still dark. He popped the trunk of the Alamo rental car and took out the license plates he stole from a car in a rest area outside of Hartford, Connecticut. After changing the stolen plates to the rental car, Lawrence took the old plates to the Brooklyn Bridge Park on East River. Tora Togo was right. The park provided a great view of the world's greatest columns of lucre. As he walked to the river's edge, he could barely see the flowing river. The sun was just beginning to break through as Lawrence looked around for any witnesses. There being none, he threw the rental plates into the river. His next rental would be with Hertz. He took a seat on one of the park benches facing Brooklyn. Togo wanted to meet early since he had a full day ahead of him at the United Nations. Lawrence took advantage of his inherent ability to sleep under any circumstances. This posed no danger to him since he was a light sleeper who awoke easily.

At twenty minutes before seven, the rising sun nudged him awake. On Cranberry Street a grocery store was opening and Lawrence found his needed caffeine. Returning to the river's edge, he could now see downtown Manhattan. The noise had picked up on the expressway behind him but he still heard the clumping sound of a man walking on a bad leg using a cane.

He turned and yelled to Togo, "Colonel, over here."

Tora Togo was now an old man. His crew-cut hair was grey, gradually turning white. They embraced as Lawrence spoke, "what's with the limp?"

"Shot my foot off at Saigon. Took down GI trying to catch copter ride out of Saigon. Disarmed him but lock was off. Gun blew away front of foot."

Since Togo was smiling, Lawrence did not feel bad laughing. "What's there now?"

"Prosthesis foot. Good foot. Never itch. Maybe shoot off other so I don't get dry rot."

Both men laughed.

"Arens, why you not go back to Vietnam with family? Your son big man with Phams. Market many cashews."

"Because I have no desire to go to jail."

"What for Arens? Men you kill? Bah, no crime. Never solved. Men had hotel room for two weeks. Left do not disturb sign at door every day. Hotel never see them. Smell got bad, Da Nang police find dead men. No suspects. Police found Battle Site Tours man who was probably killed by thugs wanting motor bike. Bike never found."

Lawrence smiled. "Of course you had nothing to do with this?"

"I government official. Franchise general partner of dead men was contacted. Somebody called him and warned him that Vietnam not need horrible battle site tour. Vietnam people run site tours, not defeated Americans. Never heard from again."

"Do you know who contacted him?"

"No, me not involved."

"You know I speak Vietnamese? You're battering the English language Colonel."

"Need practice, Arens."

Lawrence looked at his watch. They must have left the hotel and arrived at Logan by now.

"So, why are you here, Arens? Thought you hated America?"

Lawrence walked slowly over to the line of vacant benches along the edge of the East River facing the Manhattan skyline.

"Rather impressive, isn't it?"

"I see it every day, Arens. UN just up the river. Take bus every morning, across Brooklyn Bridge."

"I've never seen such massive buildings before today. Know a lot about them though. Center of attraction is the World Trade Center, right Colonel?"

"Yes, very impressive. Big buildings. Much dollars made there. I'll take you to lunch at WTC 1 if you like?"

Lawrence's smile turned into a sneer. "I don't think we'll be able to do lunch there."

"When you leave Vietnam, where did you go?"

"Did you happen to talk with the Phams at all?"

"Yes, Arens. After the franchise partner brought up your name, I personally went to the Quyens and spoke with them. They told me you left after visiting the Phams. You learn something from a deaf man?"

"Yes, a man we called Cheit. He had been in Afghanistan and knew my anger at Americans. He also knew I needed to escape … no, forget that. He knew I was a fighter. As I was leaving he called me a warrior. He told me that Afghan people needed warriors, especially the Taliban."

"The Taliban? Does that mean you fought with Osama bin Laden and Al-Qaeda?"

"Yes. A big mistake happened though. The Afghanistan leaders let the United States get in the fight against their Russian enemies. Even bin Laden accepted them at first, despite my warnings that they would take over the country. Money, that's how the United States gets into a country's blood stream. After setting the war-torn country up financially, in comes the United States military. Afghanistan could not stop them. The problem with Afghanistan is that it's a tribal country. Leadership is extremely weak. Despite their hatred of the American's, they were forced to let the military in."

Togo replied, "we've seen this at home in Vietnam and I've seen it at the UN. There's no empathy or altruism brought to any country by the United States. American soldiers debase Afghan soldiers and mock the people. Look what they did during Gulf War. Oil, they plundered Arabian Peninsula, stealing its riches by spearheading attacks against Muslim peoples. They clear oil fields with their military. If you don't bow to Americans, they eliminate you. Pakistan will go down. America is shaking in fear at its atomic arsenal."

"America killed over a million people in Iraq. The United States military is hungry to continue their ferocious and horrific massacres. My years in Afghanistan proved the ethics of America; greed, sin, and selfishness."

Lawrence looked at his watch. It was now 8:15 AM. They should be in the air.

"So why are you now an American?"

"I'm not an American." Lawrence trusted Tora Togo with his life. He knew Togo would never turn on him, yet people make mistakes. Lawrence would take no chances, not even with Togo.

"Arens, I am sorry. It was just a ..."

Lawrence smiled, "don't sweat it. Tell me how you got here and why anybody with any intelligence would make you their UN representative."

Togo was the type of man who, once started, would be difficult to silence. Lawrence could not resist looking at his watch but he did so discretely. He was getting concerned. Already they were fourteen minutes late.

It was while Tora Togo was talking about his family that Lawrence once again looked at his watch. It was 8:47 AM when Togo's scream jolted him up from the bench..

"My God Arens, the tower has been blown up!"

Both men looked across the junction of the Hudson and East River, the Statue of Liberty on their left, welcoming the world to America. Lawrence raised his hands in front of his face making the sign of victory.

Smoke was pouring out the south side of the building and drifting with the wind south.

"Arens, somebody got a bomb into the North Tower?"

"No, Mohamed Atta flew a Boeing 767, American Airlines Flight 11, into the tower."

Togo was stunned, "that can't be so? How could he do that?"

"At about eight o'clock this morning, he and four Saudi Arabians hijacked a Boeing 767 at Logan International Airport shortly after take-off. The flight was bound for Los Angeles. A cross country air flight means full tanks of jet fuel. You are not seeing the results of a bomb. You are seeing fuel tanks exploding."

"How do you know this Arens?"

"You were kind of surprised that I was here in the United States. I came here to help make what you just saw happen."

Despite the distance across the waters, they could hear the sirens waking up to the destruction of WTC 1, the North Tower. Smoke was flowing down river, a slight smell wafting even toward the other side of the East River.

"I not believe you Arens. It not possible that an airline let hijackers get through TSA that easily. How they take over such an airplane? Were they pilots?"

"Training. They've been in the United States since last summer. None of them knew how to fly a plane. They took lessons."

Lawrence was standing to the right of Tora Togo when he saw Flight 175 coming up the Hudson River from the south. He pointed to the plane. "It's not over yet. Look to the south just up river from the Statue of Liberty."

Another Boeing 767 was heading straight toward the South Tower. Like its predecessor, it was a scheduled cross country flight to California with full tanks of fuel. Its speed was slow, the flight uneven. The plane was at an angle to the South Tower making the hijacker abruptly turn left turn in order to crash into the building. It slammed hard into the South Tower somewhere between floors 77 and 85. The velocity was so great that flames shot out of the other end of the tower. Parts of the plane scattered, landing as far as six blocks away.

"The pilot was Marwan al-Shehhi from the United Arab Emirates. He was twenty eight years old."

"Is it over Arens?"

"No. Colonel, look at the South Tower. It's collapsing."

"But how? What cause that? Plane isn't enough."

Both men watched WTC 2 collapse story by story in only a few minutes, each level turning into dust, a stack of cards falling in line. A gray-white cloud formed, growing higher and higher as the collapsed layers hit the bottom. Like magic, the wind cleared, revealing a pile of debris where once a building stood.

"No other explosive was needed. We knew the amount of intense heat that would be generated by jet fuel. If the high temperatures of the exploding jet fuel melted the metal supports of one story, it would incinerate the entire building, floor by floor, until it was dust."

"Lawrence, this you knew? How could you know this?"

"Not me, Bin Laden knew it. He was as a construction engineer. It was well planned."

Tora Togo's cell phone rang.

"Arens, they are evacuating the United Nations complex. Is that necessary?"

"No, there were no plans to take it down. Listen, that restaurant up by the bridge seems to be open. I want to see what's on television."

The River Café was open but with few patrons. The café did have the television on. Lawrence and Togo took seats on stools at the bar in front of the television. Videos were coming in from all channels. They watched as people jumped off the roof of the North Tower, choosing to fall to their death rather than die by burning.

Scenes of people fleeing the North Tower filled the screen as firefighters rushed in the North Tower to save those still trapped.

Lawrence spoke. "It's a great feat those men are doing but the North Tower is going to go any ..."

And down it went. It went just like the South Tower, level by level, as layers of concrete collapsed onto other layers of concrete, people trapped with each layer, the rescuers, firefighters, among the dead. A message across the bottom of the television screen, read that New York Mayor Rudy Giuliani had ordered an evacuation of Lower Manhattan.

"Lawrence, come home with me. I need to be with family now."

"You got anybody you know caught in this disaster?"

"No, but I am scared and so will be my wife and children. Please come with me."

"I can't. I'm going into the maelstrom. I'm part of it."

"Why, Lawrence? What part did you have?"

"I told you I went to Afghanistan in 1986. You also know that I fought with bin Laden against the Russians. I was at the battle of Jalalabad. I saw the lack of support by the Americans. That lack of support only tightened the relationship between me and the Taliban. Togo, you are a good friend. We owe each other our lives, surviving against the United States in Vietnam. America is lucre. They rule, those who are rich. It is no different than any country with royalty and peons. The Towers, remember the two columns, erect, reigning over New York City? Put a big "S" over the columns and what do you have?"

Togo tried to see what Lawrence was saying but not until he closed his eyes, could he visualize the Twin Towers with an "S" was a dollar sign.

"Colonel, those hundreds of companies in those Towers rule America. I've read the list. They are mostly money merchants. They control America … no, not just America but the world. The people, they work in order to survive. The owners' sit in tall buildings and drain the workers of their right to live."

A news alert flashed on CNN. Flight 77 out of Reagan National Airport was headed toward the White House. The White House was being evacuated.

Togo stopped to the watch the television.

CNN reported that Flight 77 had turned and was headed back to Reagan National Airport.

Within minutes another news release has Flight 77 headed once again back toward the White House.

"Fucking Hanjour!"

"Who Lawrence?"

"Hani Hanjour is the hijacker pilot on Flight 77. He is one of the reasons bin Laden had me enter the United States. All the other hijackers did what they were told. My job was simple. None of the hijackers knew their mission. I visited each hijacking team and gave them their flight information and target. Only the pilots knew they would die. The others involved thought there would only be a hijacking. I sent each team off, making sure they knew exactly what to do, how to do it, and ways to get weapons on board. I met with Hanjour yesterday morning at a motel in Laurel, Maryland. He was going to bail out. He did not believe he and his compatriots could hijack a plane with only box cutters. They had been trained how to fight with them and how to subdue the flight crew and passengers. He didn't care. If he could not have a real weapon, he would not pilot the DC mission."

"In order to get his ass in the pilot seat, I gave him my Glock-17, which is almost impossible to detect during a TSA since it is made of carbide. And that was it. The irony is that his strongmen, that's bin Laden's name for the hijackers that capture the flight crew and passengers, were more than capable of killing the crew and all of the passengers. Damn, just looking at some of these guys incites fear."

"All of that training and my weapon, too and Hanjour's fucking up. I just can't ..."

CNN was back on. "The Pentagon has just been hit by Flight 77."

"That son of a bitch did it!"

The other people in the cafe turned to look at Llewellyn Lawrence. His eyes made contact with each of them and they moved away.

Togo spoke. "Arens, you better be careful. Maybe we should leave here and go to my home?"

"You're only a few blocks from here, right? Let me walk you home."

"Arens, what I do not understand is how these men fly a huge airplane like a Boeing?"

"They trained for many months but what most people don't understand, flying a jet is not that difficult. Once you breach the security and take over the cockpit, there's only five steps. You turn on the main switch; activate the starter and run up the speed. When you're about 250, 300 yards down the runway, you pull the stick back and you've taken off."

"Surely there is more to the training?"

"That's what they have been doing, training. Five pilots to hijack five planes. As crazy as it may sound, their initial training was with Microsoft's Flight Simulator 98."

"We're here. Would you honor me by entering my home?"

Tora Togo lived in a condo that had to go for nine hundred thousand dollars easily. Togo lived in the neighborhood known as Vinegar Hill. His children attended a city school called Freedom Academy.

"No, but thank you just the same. I need to go."

"Where? To the World Trade Center? People leaving there as fast as they can, Arens. Look down the street. A cloud is covering World Trade Center. Hear all the alarms? They never let you in."

"I'll get in. That will be no problem."

"Arens, I still not understand why they hate America so much? And I cannot believe a man would die like they did."

"It's kind of amazing how America managed to turn an ally, bin Laden and the Taliban, into an enemy. When I was fighting with the Taliban against Russia, I told bin Laden that the United States should not be part of his war. He did not see it. When they came into Afghanistan, it became apparent quite quickly that America had no concern for the people of Afghanistan. They saw oil fields and they saw a war economy. The merchants of war fed the battles with the money of war. A nation at war is a nation of money and debt. Bin Laden finally saw America for what it valued: greed."

"But those people killed in the towers today, how are they merchants of war?"

"Take just one company, Cantor Fitzgerald. Five floors of the North Tower. They are money people. They deal in fixed-interest securities and government bonds. Go around the world and you'll find them financing governments with all types of securities. They have over two thousand employees worldwide with one thousand working out of the North Tower. What is their work? There is no work. They provide money to those who need to build and fight wars."

Togo spoke, "you still do not wish to come into my home?"

"No, I appreciate the offer. You've already put yourself in danger. You have been seen with me."

Togo laughed. "Arens, nobody anymore give one fuck about Llewellyn Lawrence. Go back to Vietnam. Nobody will care. Live where you must. Have family, make children."

"Colonel, we are deeply connected, dear friends. You live in New York City. The essence of New York City is money, making it. Never cover for me. I will not hold it against you. I know the pain you must feel for those thousands of people who died today. I do not have that feeling. They rule the world by money. From custodian to secretary to CEO, they fuel the wars that massacre people. Their profits were made from the blood bleeding out of the victims of war."

"You are very harsh my friend."

"Colonel Togo, why did the United States invade your country? Why were we there? Money. The country was in an economic downfall. War feeds the cash flow. The cost of that economic windfall? Why it only cost the U.S. 58,000 dead soldiers. And the people we were fighting for to give them freedom from North Vietnam and communism? 400,000 South Vietnamese. Then there's you, the North Vietnamese. How many?"

"I have no idea, Arens? Couple hundred thousand?"

"Two million dead. One third of all the people living in both North Vietnam and South Vietnam were left homeless."

Colonel Togo had tears in his eyes, "I know Arens. I've always known but I keep it out of my life. You are warrior, Lawrence. You will always be. It is your life. Thanks to God, you are not warrior for money."

Llewellyn Lawrence hugged him one last time. "Probably won't see you again. But I'm going to try. It won't be today or next week but one day I hope to. Right now I'm going to see this battle won."

Lawrence waved as he headed off to the walkway of the famous Brooklyn Bridge, two streets over. It was filled with thousands of New Yorkers leaving the city and heading into Brooklyn. It would take him longer then he thought, since the mass of survivors was dense and Lawrence needed to be very careful not to shove anyone. They were living a horror none could have imagined. Lawrence needed to find, to witness the horror he had helped to create.

The bridge had a cat walk for pedestrians above the middle lanes for cars. There were no cars today. Instead thousands of New Yorkers were escaping the city by foot. Few were lacing their way through the Brooklyn bound crowd to cross over to the city side. Lawrence crossed to the Manhattan side, over the Franklin D. Roosevelt Expressway and continued to slowly work his way through the escaping crowd. Lawrence stopped at the Fulton Street Transit Center. He would visit the graveyard that was ground zero or at least as much as the hundreds of police and fire fighters would permit.

Like all grave yards it marked by a tombstone, a reminder of the dead. As the dust cloud slowly disappeared, part of the North Tower of the World Trade Center appeared to rise out of this grave, a spire of forty feet, clouds swirling about the steel, and God's light illuminating death. Thousands of New York's congregation stared in awe, weeping for the dead as this last symbol of all that was lost collapsed into the dust.

It was 10:30 AM and police, firemen, physicians and EMC workers fought a losing battle, looking for anyone who could still to be saved from death. Lawrence walked through tons of dust and debris for over an hour finding little pieces of flights 11 and 175. Circling back to Fulton Street Metro station, he heard cheers rise up where WTC North Tower used to be. Firefighters that had been trapped and given up as dead, now walked out of the only stairwell section still standing. Under the rubble that had covered them were also two survivors of the fall of North World Tower.

Lawrence stopped. These people had been buried under ground zero since this morning when WTC North collapsed on ...

He looked closely at these survivors. A towering building of steel and cement collapses on them and they walk out of the debris with very few injuries? He listened to the fireman talking with their compatriots as they shifted through the rubble. The stairway they were descending collapsed, acting as an elevator, finally stopping in the underground subway tunnel located under WTC North. The Cortlandt Street IRT station had collapsed. Trains could not run through the tunnels but there was enough room for survivors and this is how the firemen had survived.

Llewellyn Lawrence skirted back to the subway entrance he had passed on his way to ground zero. The sign still stood. The sign was a map showing the subway transit lines running over all of Manhattan and up to Central Park. He needed to find whatever might still exist from the flights that took down the World Trade Centers. He did not expect to find much, but for some strange reason, he needed a memento of the attacks. Pieces of the planes had been found on the surface but what about the parts embedded into the levels of office space? Was it all gone, burned to ashes? Probably, but an unexplainable drive kept pushing him on, in search of any small piece of the deadly attack on Mecca of Greed, New York City the mecca of greed. Those survivors he just saw were exiting the subway of the North tower so there might be a chance some pieces from flights 11 and 175 could exist.

His problem was how to get through the blockades of police and firemen and into the subway tunnels. They would stop him but what about the tunnel north of here? The subway below was the Broadway-Nassau-Fulton Street subway. The first stop back of the WTC was Canal Street. The only way he could do this was station by station. It took him twenty minutes to get to the Canal Street Station. It was closed, gates barring access to the station. He looked through the bars, the emergency circuit lighting dim, an after effect from the attacks. Of course this close the electricity would be cut off.

Next stop was Spring Street. It took him twenty five minutes, partly due to a quick stop at a retail store to buy a flashlight and batteries. Spring Street was not gated but no trains were listed to stop here. A neon sign scrolled the message that the only subway line running was IRT Lexington between Midtown and Lower Manhattan.

"Why were the stations not gated?" thought Lawrence. "Of course, there had to be some way a person trapped in the tunnels could escape. The Canal Street station was too severely damaged, its power lost."

As he looked down at the tracks, Lawrence knew there was no power and therefore the subway train hot rail would not be alive. It gave him no peace of mind. He was touching the hot rail and at any time power could return. He had been smart enough to buy a dozen D cells for the flashlight. He estimated the walk from Spring Street station to WTC would take about forty five minutes to an hour. He had to go slow. He was walking through tunnels that could kill him if the trains were running. There was little chance of that happening. This run of the subway would be down for many weeks.

Twenty minutes later an odor began to permeate the tunnel. He had smelled this odor many times. It was the smell of death. Should he flee before he became part of the tunnels' smell of death? He got past Canal Street quickly and was at the Chambers Street station, only a couple of blocks from the World Trade Center North. The smell was getting worse.

When the WTC station came into view, he stopped quickly. The roof at the north end of the station had collapsed. Angling down at 90 degrees was the shattered port side of a Boeing airplane. The smell was attacking his gag reflex but he swallowed and spit out phlegm. He had been around the dead enough to stay in control of himself. The plane was a Boeing 767 meaning it was either flight 1 or 175. The emergency lights dimly lit the station. Lawrence kept his flashlight on the fuselage. There were no burning signs which meant the plane broke apart at collision. As he neared the plane section, he thought he heard someone speak but ignored it as he observed the horror in front of him. He crawled underneath the fuselage and viewed the plane from its starboard side, except there was no starboard side. Instead he was looking at a cross section of four rows of seats midway in the cabin. The smell of death was coming from the bodies, still secured in their seats with the wide black seat belts. Four of the passengers had no upper bodies.

The smell overtook him. Turning his back to the dead torsos, he retched on the train rails below the plane. As he was finishing, he heard the crying.

Somehow, someone was still alive in what was left of the Boeing. Pulling himself up on the aisle of the plane, his knee gave him enough of a hold to allow him to bring the rest of his body up. He saw the little girl underneath the seat in front of two torsos, their bodies having been separated at the waists. He did not want to stand because the fuselage was unbalanced and could turn over.

"Hello? Can you hear me?"

He heard a "yes" between the sobs.

"Come on out from under the seat. Can you move?"

"No, it hurts too much. Help me, please help me!"

In order to get to her, he had to unbuckle the dead torsos and lift them from their seats. He dropped the torsos gently onto vacant seats behind. He reached slowly for the girl.

"We're going to do this slow. Nothing's going to hurt you now. It's over. Let me have your arm so I can help you out," said Lawrence as he lightly gripped her left arm. She screamed out and began crying, the tears washing away the dust of the WTC North off her face.

"I'm so sorry! Is your arm broken?"

"Yes, and my eye is ..."

Lawrence knew from her cries that he had to help her quickly. He grasped her right shoulder lightly and there was no reaction. He edged her out from under the seat slowly avoiding her left shoulder. As she came loose Lawrence saw her dangling left arm.

He had been moving the girl using only the dim emergency lighting. He laid her down in the aisle of the fuselage and turned on his flashlight. What he saw drew him back. The bile began crawling into his throat. The girl's left eye, smashed like an egg, was hanging on her cheeks held in place only by the optic nerve.

He pulled her gently to his chest. Through his tears he told her he would get her to a hospital as quickly as he could.

"My name is Lew. I am going to carry you to the hospital. I have to go slow so ..."

"My mommy and daddy were sitting here."

"They're not here, dear. They're gone."

"I knew that."

Lawrence placed her back down in the aisle and dropped to the train bed below. He was still able to reach the girl.

"What's your name, sweetheart?"

"Angela. Can you get me help soon?"

Lawrence picked her up but stopped. He placed her down on the train tracks and reached for a blanket that was still folded over one of the seats. He wrapped her in the blanket; each time he adjusted her, she jumped from the pain in her broken arm.

"How old are you, Angela?"

"I'm six. We were going to Disneyland."

Llewellyn Lawrence was forced to face the reality of his part in 9-11. He could not stop the tears from running down his face. He had killed her parents. He had ripped the eye out of this beautiful six year olds' face and snapped the bones in her arm. He tried to tell himself that he had not done these horrible acts but that was not true. He was as responsible as bin Laden and the Taliban. He was as responsible as the President of the United States and the greedy money merchants.

He shook it off. His priority right now had to be Angela.

CHAPTER THIRTY ONE

Niche of the Beast

"... he had killed ... not because he had wanted to but because somebody had to." Ian Fleming, <u>Diamonds Are Forever</u> 1956

"Mon Mere, I have something to tell you before I return to Virginia City." Peter Lawrence got into his car that Evelyn Southern had driven to Philadelphia Airport to pick up her son. "But you must promise to me not to tell anybody including, Judi."

"Oui, mon frère but I know what it is. Vous Pere c'est Canada. Do you think I'd tell on him to the FBI? "

Peter was embarrassed. He knew his mother would risk her own life if she had told the authorities where Llewellyn was. They both knew the United States had written him off.

"Pardonez moi," said Lawrence, leaning over and kissing his mother's cheek.

The ride from the airport would take just over two hours but they would be good hours for mother and son.

"Arens, as his Vietnamese family calls him, creates a very strong enigma. He has this deep hatred for Americans that makes him want to kill."

"Do you know much about his life with the Quyens?"

Peter was a bit surprised that his mother knew so much about her ersatz husband, "I know he spoke very little about them with me. How could you know anything about them?"

"Ah, mon fils, you are just as stupid as the U. S. Army, CIA, and FBI. Llewellyn set up a contact link between vous tantes from Paris to Toronto to me. I knew he sired a child in

Vietnam but he did not marry the mother. They lived with each other. She probably had those taunt little breasts and hard protruding nipples an old woman like me have lost!"

Peter had grown used to his mother's embarrassing sexual comments. "At sixty-five, you're still doing alright. At least Judi doesn't complain, does he?"

She smiled and spoke, "what is it that upsets you?"

"He and I along with an Indian named Charlie Grayrock took down ..." and he stopped. He did not want to get his mother involved by giving her the details of Plate Extract Inc.. "Arens believes that the answer to controlling harmful people is to kill them. He has divided the world up into two peoples. He calls them aggies and huggies. I'll explain."

"You need not Petra," said Evelyn. "Your father and I had very quick communications, very random. It was necessary to keep him dead, as far as the United States was concerned. Had they found your father through our communication, they would capture and execute him. I would be cut off of the money I receive as his widow. He was not full of hatred when he first went to Vietnam, not at all like the man you know."

His mother told as much as she knew about the change that over took Llewellyn Lawrence as he experienced the horror America brought to Vietnam. It surprised Peter and made him a little less apprehensive about his father's killer instinct, his lethal thirst for revenge.

"Look about you, Petra," said his mother. "Aren't we all either hunter-gatherers, huggies, who work to survive or are we aggies the ones who own the world and hire us workers to expand their ownership of us? I'm sure he spelled it out to you. Aggies are people who own property as in the concept of agriculture. We are workers, huggies, of the property and create equity in that property."

"I know that. It's economic evolution. Humans started as hunters of animals or as gathers of plants and fruits, both for the reason to feed their families. They roamed looking for food. Aggies were the people who stopped roaming and started to grow food. They captured and breed creatures to eat.

They did not roam. They built farms and ranches and then took on the hunter gatherers as their workers, servants."

"Then you should know what he's talking about. The aggies own us. We live with it. They own men, men they send to kill people, as your father was sent. Owned, Peter, you're owned. I am owned by the state of Pennsylvania. If I don't do as they tell me, I do not survive. That is being owned."

"Come on, it's not really an ownership. But I see where you're coming from. I think that Llewellyn felt on the same level. The work the government forced him to do in Vietnam went too far. Damn, I had the same problem in Upstate New York. They owned me and expected me to do what they said. Fuck, we are huggies, aren't we?"

Evelyn took her right hand off of the driving wheel and softly slapped her son's face.

"So, when do I get a grandchild, Mon Amie?"

Lawrence turned red, not responding.

"I have touched a sore spot, oui?"

"I was in a relationship with an elementary school principal in Virginia City. There's a bad problem, a big one."

"My son, who is this woman?"

"Her name is Susan. She's a bit older than me."

"You are no better than your fucking father!"

Evelyn's face turned red since she had just slapped her son for using the "f" word.

Peter reached over and put his left hand gently on top of her hand on the stirring wheel. "No, I'm not going to slap you but stop. You need to stop breathing so heavily. Your face is bright red and your knuckles are turning white from gripping the wheel so tight."

Peter waited a few minutes, giving Evelyn time to relax. "She's forty-three."

"Mon fils, what is the problem? You are only nine years younger."

"Mon mere, it's not the age difference. It 's that she had an abortion without telling me."

"Oh, mon dieu, what reason did she give you for not telling you?"

"I haven't seen or talked to her yet."

"Then did you know about the abortion?"

"It was pure coincidence. Her daughter works with me on the V City Server. When I called the newspaper, she slipped up and told me her mother was in the hospital having the abortion. She thought I knew about it."

Evelyn Southern was speechless. Her grandchild was dead and her anger was rising. The rest of the drive was done in silence.

"Petra, when are you going back to Virginia? Will you stay a couple days?"

Peter Lawrence encircled his tall, thin mother within his arms, "you stopped talking to me many miles back?"

"It was my grandchild."

"What should I do Mon Mere?"

"I do not know, Petra."

Peter Lawrence had 386 miles, a seven and a half hour drive to put his emotions together, intelligently and with empathy. He knew he loved Susan, that was not the problem. Could he accept his dead child?

"Give me a hug, please Mon Mere. After all, we are both huggies."

Neither knew if the tears were from pain or from love as Peter Lawrence headed home.

***

"Peter, Peter! When did you get back? Why didn't you call me?" exclaimed Susan Yoder as she opened the door of her condo.

The ride should have calmed him. He knew he had to confront Susan. The ride should have given him time to decide how to approach her about the abortion. The ride only made it worse.

"Why did you kill my son?"

Susan lowered eyes. She clasped her arms and turned from him. She was scared.

"How do you know I had an abortion?"

Peter knew one thing for sure from the seven hours and thirty minute ride. That was that he stilled loved her and would never physically harm her. "I found out by accident. I called the paper when I left McVey's execution and spoke to Kat. I asked about you. She thought I knew about the abortion. She told me that you were doing fine after the abortion and would be released soon."

"...and how did you know it was a boy?"

"Called the hospital. I have some contacts there. We get a lot of news stories after people wind up in the hospital. My contact found out you aborted a boy."

Susan knew it was over between them. She owed him the truth. There would be no sexist excuse about it being her body and her decision. He had to know the real reason but telling him would be making him part of the danger she faced.

"I should never have gotten pregnant. I had my tubes tied years ago. The asshole gynecologist didn't do it correctly and my ovaries started popping out eggs. I should never have let a goddamn Asian GP fuck with my body. I thought we were safe. I'm so sorry that I wasn't honest with you."

"Peter, I am too old to take care of a baby." This was not what she wanted to say.

Peter watched her, her arms hugging her body as she gazed out the condo's large windows, looking at the harbor but seeing nothing.

Peter knew she was hiding something. He knew she needed him. He walked up behind her and gently put his arms around her. She could feel his tears falling on the side of her face. Her love for him should not be destroyed by hiding the real reason she aborted their child. She turned from the window, nestled her face in his left shoulder, and wrapped her arms around Peter. They held tight to each other, each knowing they cannot lose the other.

"I would lose my job."

"What?"

"Peter, this is the South. Virginia City Schools and the parents would go after me. I would be no better than a whore, a despicable example to the children under my care."

"That would never happen."

"I know you'd like to believe that but you don't know V City School's administration and school board. Peter, wake up. This is the south!"

Peter backed off.

***

Lawrence awoke to a teal blue sky. He was an early riser. It was a little after 6:00 am. Quietly he rolled off his side of the bed and went to the bathroom. He put on his underwear and walked out of the bedroom, a smile on his face. Susan was a tall, well-built woman who slept face down with her hands under the pillow. She proved the adage of sleeping like a rock. He did not wake her as he ran his hand gently over her taut ass, left the bedroom quietly closing the door behind him. Even though she did not drink coffee, she kept a Keurig brewer in her kitchen for guests and Lawrence. Inside the cabinet he found three different boxes of K-cups. He chose the Sumatran Reserve extra bold. He was itchy but it was too early to go to the newspaper office. He drank the coffee, sneaked back into the bedroom, and picked up the rest of his clothes.

"Leaving me already, Peter?"

Both smiled at each other. She sat on the edge of her bed and patted the other side. Lawrence dropped his clothes, stepped out of his underwear, and laid down on the bed. Once she finished draining him, Lawrence fell back to sleep. It was nearly ten in the morning, when he awoke to the smell of bacon broiling.

***

When Lawrence entered the V City Server's building, he could feel a tension magnified by an unusual quietness and avoidance of his presence. Lawrence walked to his glass walled office surprised that only Kat waved to him while the other staff members avoided eye contact. Kat had a forced smile on her face. Before he could ask her what was going on, Dr. Sauers came out of his private office and called to Lawrence to come over to him. Patting Peter on the back, Judge Sauers asked him how his little vacation went. Inside the office, Sauers closed the door so no one could see or hear what was going on between the two men.

"Peter, have you read your certified letter yet?"

"No, I didn't go straight home last night. What certified letter?"

"The newspaper was been bought out."

"How's that? You own it you?"

"It's a partnership. I had a little more than half of the capital to buy The Server so I took in some investors to complete the sale. The investors sold out their shares. Sold them for less than they paid."

"That doesn't make sense? How could we be losing equity?"

"Peter, you're doing a great job here, too great for these hayseeds down here. Your articles pushed the businesses down here over the edge, especially those last articles about Tim McVey. Ads get yanked nearly every week. And we've been watched. A group of potential investors want the paper. They made me an offer for my share I can't refuse at my age. I really need to retire. I don't need to print a newspaper. I need to sit back in my recliner and read a newspaper."

"What about the other investors?"

Judge Sauers was an honest man. Lawrence could see his eyes blink and avoid contact with Lawrence. Peter knew he would not lie and knew something wrong had gone down.

"They are converting their business shares of the paper into partnerships with the LLC that's buying the paper. I hate to say this but it was a brilliant business maneuver on the part of the GP, general partner. You know about LLCs and GPs?"

Lawrence knew more than Judge Sauers thought since Judi was managing his own off shore investment under an LLC, "yes, he runs the show. Who's the GP?"

In all of the years that Peter Lawrence had been taught by and been a deep friend with Doctor Judge Sauers, he had never heard the man use profanity, "fucking asshole Czeed."

"You're kidding me? After that real estate fraud he put up with the jet plane noise?"

"There's no fraud. Our law suit against Virginia City was dismissed last week by the circuit judge. The city lawyers claimed sovereign immunity."

"What's that?"

"You can't bring a suit against the so called sovereign government without that government's consent. Basically the doctrine of sovereign immunity means that the king can do no wrong"

Lawrence could not push Sauers since it was Lawrence's battle to sue the city for their illegal real estate deals. He knew Judge Sauers had put a lot of his personal money into the legal attack.

"Why didn't the lawyers know this and stop us from the law suit?"

Sauers just shrugged his shoulders, "they were blindsided. They never thought that a judge would consider a municipality as a sovereign realm. In fact it had never been done before. They thought the judge would toss the case. Obviously, he didn't … Whoa, hold a second Peter. I know what you're going to say. The judge got paid off. Our lawyers would not dare attack a judge, even a circuit judge. Neither will I."

"Czeed wanted me fired?"

"Amazingly, no. Czeed stressed very emphatically that he wanted you to stay as V City Server's editor-in-chief. He was honest about it."

"Judge, you make me laugh. All these years I've never heard you make a derogatory comment about anybody or tell a lie. Now, you're trying to tell me Czeed is a good guy?"

Dr. Judge Sauers' faced turned red, "he's an asshole. But he's a very smart asshole. This newspaper would fall apart if you left. He knows that. The LLC partners know how good you are. Peter, you just got to learn to kiss some ass, and then keep them honest."

Lawrence started to laugh, a laugh that was more a chuckle with a slight throbbing of his chest, "how soon does he need to know?"

"He told me no rush. Take some vacation time. Kat can keep the press running for a week or so. When you return, just be the editor and resign anytime you want. He said he's got a great severance check just waiting for you. He also said it's got six figures on it and could be a bonus check instead."

"When are you out of here?"

"Got some boxes in my trunk and very little to load out of my office. Could use some help. Sarah and I are heading for Erie PA. We'll be there in time to watch the fireworks at Presque Isle next Wednesday with our grandchildren."

Lawrence helped Judge load up and he followed him home. The Sauers were already to hit the road which made Peter Lawrence a little ashamed. Had he gotten back to Virginia City sooner, they would have been back where they grew up by now. It only took four hours to finish loading up the U-Haul that Judge would drive and hug goodbye to his wife Sarah whom would be driving their car to Erie Pennsylvania.

Lawrence returned to his apartment above his garage and called Susan. He left a message. He did not want to burden her with the turn of events in his life. He felt very warm with his relationship after their confrontation, confirmation, and connubial intercourse of last night. He had a stack of mail including a certified letter from Dr. Judge Sauers which he had to pick up at the Post Office. He was tense. He could not just sit here to get his life together. It was mid-summer and he knew where to unravel his last three weeks. DumDum. He tried Susan's number again but remembered that she had summer school to supervise. He left a brief message of what had happened at the newspaper and that he needed some think time.

***

The canoe trip was not uncomfortable. Despite being sunny, the highs for mid-week in June were in the low 80's and mild winds of about five miles per hour or less. Coming from north east, even this little bit of wind helped Lawrence reach DumDum via the small stream just to the north. He did not have to evade any marine craft along the coast of Back Bay and into the high weeds of the island. Peter brought very few goods with him, some canned meat, apples and pears, and a cheap half gallon of scotch with two liter bottles of ginger ale.

The rats had invaded his cabin as usual. And as usual they found nothing and were mad enough to leave droppings on the floor, tables, and bed frame. Lawrence got a bucket and followed the path to the south side of the island. Before leaving the tree line, he carefully scanned the small shoreline of the island, the Back Bay horizon for water craft, and the distant west shoreline for possible intruders. It was safe and it took five trips to get rid of the feces and urine. With windows propped open, to keep away mosquitoes, he burned Citronella candles, Cymbopogan nardus, which is a course grass-like plant.

He checked the well he had dug years ago and was able to haul up about a gallon of nearly fresh water. He could only get a gallon or two per day of fresh water which he could not waste on cleaning.

The boom of breaking the sound barrier not only made Lawrence jump up and off of the now cleaned bed. Hundreds of birds were going wild as the Navy's jet planes were flying almost directly over his cabin. Each plane came with two planes following at the same speed and with the same deafening waves. Once the sound lowered and seemed to have disappeared, another came right behind it. This would go on for at least two hours. Another reason he should kill Ken Czeed, not work for him. The thousands of citizens who had signed the lawsuit to get rid the air base, had been bought off, signed a release of the charges in the law suit for anywhere from $625 to $845. The navy air base would stay.

Lawrence was burning with indecision. No, he would not work with Czeed. He would take the severance pay but in his own way. Just the thought of how he would do that made him smile. Of all ironies he asked himself "what would Llewellyn Lawrence do?" Would he assassinate the man and become a hunted renegade? Probably, but Peter could not void his life of Susan Yoder. The hatred for America that he read in Llewellyn Lawrence was trickling into Peter's beliefs. Not everyone is a money merchant making financial slaves out of others. This was his father's scenario. Yes they are. Everybody who works for another person is technically a monetary slave.

"No, that's bull shit communism."

What is wrong about communism? What does he know about communism? We are capitalists. What is right about capitalists?

Lawrence started laughing, "I might as well go back to college and act like some kind of beatnik or protester. I should have lived in the sixties."

His mind played tricks with him until he realized none of this came out of any era. Life in America is the owners and the workers. America was one big ant's nest. The royalty and her soldiers live through the lives of the workers.

"Soldiers! There it is. Every species that lived and all living species have the same ethic."

Lawrence stripped down and headed for the small beach where he had bucketed washing water. The cove was hidden enough from the bay that it would be difficult for anybody sailing or boating to see him swimming. The land side was a dense, mosquito haven marsh with snakes so that a hiker would be driven back to the road two miles west where they entered. As always the bay water was cold and altered his thermo nervous system to react and adjust to a soothing coolness. He liked to scull in the water, floating on his back. He could not shake his last three weeks. What especially tore at his mind was McVeigh. Tim saw life much like Peter was now running it through his mind. He could not become another terrorist. His father lives as a terrorist but is he? The people they killed at Plate Extract Inc. were bad people that took life out of the tribes living where Plate Extract Inc. built dangerous factories. They did this without remorse. They were slaughtered with the same lack of remorse. Their killers did not execute life for a stipend.

On the third day he trapped two rabbits and skinned them. To avoid smoke, he built a pit into the sand outside his door and piece by piece ignited branches into coals. He slow broiled them, turning them frequently inches above the coals. A handmade umbrella of green marsh weeds over the pit kept the smell of the roasting rabbits to a minimum. As the sun dropped over Pungo to the west, he removed the skewered rabbits from the pit and took them into the cabin. Before dining on their meat, Lawrence filled in the coal pit with sand. As he returned to the cabin, he heard mechanical whirring sound of a small out board engine. Walking back outside, the motor noise faded and as it was nearly dark, he assumed the boater was heading quickly back to the main land shore.

Still being careful, he closed the window drops on the cabin so not even the smell of the roasted prey could be detected should somebody be near his beach only twenty-five yards or so away.

"Peter? Peter, can I come in?"

It was Susan. He quickly got up from his meal and swung open the door.

"How did you find me? How did you get here?"

She did not speak but grabbed him tightly with her head buried into his chest. She cried uncontrollably, gagging when she tried to speak. Lawrence surrounded her body with his arms and massaged her neck gently. He let her vent out all of the obvious pain she felt. Peter had no idea from where her pain originated.

"I followed you one day months ago when you told me you were taking some time to yourself. No, don't get mad at me. I had these images of you meeting up with another woman. I nearly lost you on all those winding and turning roads throughout Pongo but caught up at Muddy Creek. I saw you loading the canoe off your car's roof but drove past.

"What did you think I was fucking some mermaid out in Back Bay?"

She laughed a little but could not stop the tears, "no, I really believed you were just doing as you said. Burning off some angst, paddling around the bay and camping somewhere along the shoreline."

"That still doesn't explain how you found me here?"

"I couldn't give it up. You'd be gone for many days but I couldn't believe that you camped out any place on this side of Back Bay. The shore is not very wide and there aren't any places where you could beach and camp. So I snooped around. I did an internet search of property that had been put up for sale or abandoned recently within ten miles of Muddy Creek Boat Launch. On the site for Virginia City government, the department of real estate, you're named popped up. You took the deed and ownership for this island in the swamp."

Lawrence smiled, "how did you get here?"

"When I drove down here, your car was parked at the Muddy Creek Boat Launch. I rented a skiff with a small outboard and rode down the shore to where your property was on the map."

This explained the engine noise Lawrence had heard, "only place to beach is down through the trail and alongside of the small creek. Why? I'm going to go back home tomorrow or the next day."

"I've been put on administrative leave with pay."

"What for?"

"Conduct unbecoming a school administrator. I know you've got some scotch or brandy here."

"No ice. You should have picked some up at the boat launch."

Susan smiled. One of the many virtues she loved was Peter's sense of humor, "well get into your fucking canoe and go get some, asshole!"

As he handed her a plastic glass with warm cheap scotch, she continued, "the aunt of one of my students is a nurse at the hospital where I had the abortion."

Lawrence chugged down the last of his scotch and poured himself another, "she ratted on you."

"Yes, went to the girl's mother. The mother is one of those stuck up snobs that fuck over anybody that doesn't kiss her ass. She's also a devout Catholic. Here fill it back up."

Lawrence took the plastic cup, leaned down and kissed her cheek, and got her another scotch.

"She's a devout member of the V City elite. Went straight to the superintendent, didn't even wait for him to be available. Her husband's got big dough in the beach. Told his secretary to sit down when she tried to stop her, and walked right into a meeting already going on. Called me an unwed, pregnant whore, and demanded I be fired!"

Lawrence put his cup down and went to her. Her face was red and sweaty, "slow down. What happened next?"

"Director of Human Resources walks into the school with a letter from the superintendent putting me on administrative leave pending a hearing with the school board."

"When?"

"It's summer. Most of the school board members aren't available. It's scheduled for second Tuesday in September, a week after the schools open."

"Are you a member of the V City Teacher Union?"

"Yes, I'm meeting with them and their lawyer next week."

"I'll be there too."

"I need a good fuck!"

Lawrence smiled, pulled the stuffed mattress bag off of the fragile cot, laid it on the floor, and covered it with two blankets, "you got it."

Both felt no obstruction from the hard packed dirt of the cabin's floor as the physical spasms of intercourse ripped through their bodies exploding in orgasms not but seconds apart. Without the luxury of air conditioning, their bodies were covered with perspiration, beads sliding into their eyes.

Peter Lawrence gently wiped his fingers over Susan Yoder's eyes, alleviating the acid sting, "you got your cell with you?"

"Yes, what for, Peter?"

"The skiff has the Muddy Creek Boat Launch's phone number on it. Get out your phone while I get the number."

Once back, Susan spoke, "so what am I to do?"

"Stay overnight. Tell them you stopped along the bay line and met some campers. You're going to spend the night with them and bring the boat back tomorrow."

She called and the Muddy Creek Boat Launch proprietor told her there was no problem.

"You really think you'll get fired?"

"Peter, you're a northerner. The union has no power down South, and in fact they really don't give a fuck. I had to call the national offices of the union to get them to force the V City Union to get me a lawyer. There's something else, though. I had a run in with V City Schools superintendent, Dr. Samuel LaMer a few years ago."

"Let me guess? He tried to get into your pants?"

"He was not successful like a certain horny ass I know."

"Yeah, I know who he is. Tall guy about six three or four with a grey haired rim around a bulbous bald head. Has a mustache that looks like a toilet brush. Talks southern and makes you want to shake your head believing anybody that droll and ignorant could get a doctor's degree."

"He's a Georgia man from some boon dock town near Louisiana. He got his PhD from a community college in Louisiana. He was a special ed teacher when he started out. Kissed ass and moved up. He's been looking for a chance to burn me for years but knows I'd rat him out. Here's his chance."

"One thing I don't grasp. How come your hearing goes straight to the school board?"

"The school board overrode any preliminary meetings. The claim is that the charges against me are too severe to go the normal path. I'm sure Sam the man had his say about it."

"Well, you shouldn't sweat it. Their charges violate your personal rights. Your lawyer will nail them and get it over quickly."

Susan Yoder showed a smile with her mouth but her eyes spoke uncertainty, "will you stand by me?"

Lawrence pulled her naked body against his, both on their knees, "you have given me a good reason to not take severance pay. Freedom of the press is nearly impossible to avoid. The school board and Dr. LaMer cannot stop me from attending or speaking. Yes, I will be there."

They stayed united, body to body for many minutes, then Lawrence stood, gently lifting her arms bringing her up to a stance, "the bay water is not extremely cold, but cold enough to refresh us."

"You want me to swim in shark infested waters in the dark?"

"Water in the bay is brackish. I doubt any shark could survive in it."

They spent two hours, naked and as one body up to their necks in cool water watching the stars and moon then returned to DumDum and sleep.

***

Peter Lawrence spent the day before the hearing with Susan Yoder. They went over and over what the union lawyer had told Susan to say. He stressed that she should not freelance any testimony he had not confirmed. He tried to keep Peter Lawrence from attending, sensing that Lawrence would not have any testimony to give and he did not belong at the hearing. Lawrence called the newspaper's lawyer, whom he had already contacted, and handed his cell phone over to the V City Teacher's Union's lawyer. There followed an aggressive conversion between the two lawyers of which only the Union lawyer's conversation could be heard. That was all that was necessary to Peter Lawrence since the frustration on the Union's lawyer told the tale.

Handing Peter's cell phone back to Peter, he spoke, "you and your lawyer are out of your fucking minds. Freedom of the press? This is just a hearing between an employee and her employers. All that's going to happen is a reprimand and a slap on your wrist, Mrs. Yoder"

"That's Ms. Yoder," said Susan as she got up from her chair. "Tuesday in the school board room at 7:30 AM. We'll both see you there."

With Susan Yoder there was a great difference between her time of rising and Peter Lawrence's. Peter was an early riser, usually at about 5:00 AM. He would bicycle ten miles and then go to the gym for a half hour of weight lifting. This he had done and was now showering in her bathroom. Lawrence finished showering, got dressed, and drove to the newspaper office. Just days after Yoder's visit to DumDum and as much as he wanted to take the check and run, he met with Ken Czeed to accept the bonus check, not the severance pay.

"So you pulled off dropping the citizen's law suit of the Navy Airbase and the LLC. All those tenants in the apartment for which you were the general partner of the LLC, agreed to let you off free and the jets would keep on flying."

"Not free, Lawrence. They each got from $600 to $835. They could have moved. But you know what? None of did."

It took only four hours to cash the $150,000 check, obtain a cash voucher in the name of his offshore account, and have it register on his online bank account. Czeed had not demanded Lawrence to keep off of the jet noise fight. Czeed had successfully stopped any possibility of the Navy being evicted from Virginia City. There was nowhere Lawrence could go.

Lawrence spent about an hour and a half going over the stories for the September 12th edition and advertising layouts, and then he left them for Kat. Kat was very upset about her mother's hearing later today, had tears in her eyes, but had grown to trust Peter Lawrence's love for her mother.

It was a little past 8:00 AM September 11, 2001 when Peter Lawrence walked into Susan Yoder's condo.

"Peter, Peter, come over here, right now!"

Lawrence saw that Susan had on CNN and was watching a televised burning of a very tall building, "where's this happening?"

"It's New York city, one of the twin towers of the world trade center."

"Christ, did a bomb go off? How the hell could it have gotten all the way up that high?"

They got the answer as the voice over for the burning building video said he "saw a slow flying plane crash into the middle of the tower. He did not know which tower it was." When asked he added "it was a two engine jet, a large passenger commercial jet."

There was a close-up of the building with dark grey clouds of smoke pouring out its south side.

"Peter, who could have done this? How did they steal a huge jet air plane and crash it into that building?"

"I've got no idea? You remember when a truck tried to blow up that same building in New York? It's one of the twin towers. My guess would be it was the Taliban again. I'm sure bin Laden's involved."

Susan and Peter, like the rest of the United States, sat with their eyes and ears locked onto the television. When the second plane hit the south building, Lawrence called the V City Server Offices knowing they would also be enraptured by the terror in New York City. As he expected all of the writers were surrounding the high definition, wide screen television in the paper's conference room. They were writing tomorrow morning's paper as they watched the United States' history unfold in front of them.

Shortly after noon, Susan got a call from the secretary of the superintendent for V City Schools.

"Fucking assholes! They postponed the hearing. It's not going to be until November. Said there's too much terror going on to put the school board together."

"Yeah, right, maybe bin Laden would send a plane to blow up the board room," said Lawrence.

"Somebody ought to, Peter."

Lawrence had thought the same, only his was not sarcastic. Susan's phone rang and he could tell by the conversation it was the lawyer for the Virginia City Teachers' Union. She slammed the phone down and said, "take me somewhere. I got to get out of here."

***

The V City School board's meeting place was a large conference room attached to the main administrative building. The only entrance or exit to the outside of the building was locked from outside entrance and barred from inside exit as it would sound off an alarm if anybody tried to leave. There was a large mahogany table with five chairs on each broad side and one throne chair at the entrance/exit of the room. A sole chair was placed at the opposite end of the throne chair. Around the outside of the room were hard wood, low back chairs for spectators and individuals on the agenda of the school board meeting. There was a padded chair with an arm rest wide enough on which to place a writing pad directly behind the throne chair. Obviously it was for the superintendent's secretary to record the minutes of a meeting.

Peter, Susan, the teacher union's representative, and the union's lawyer arrived on time, gaining seats together near the entrance and exit. As to be expected, the 7:00 PM meeting did not get started until five minutes after eight. After the school board members entered and took their seats at the table, the secretary arrived, opened her steno pad, and moved her seat closer to the throne seat. She was followed by a short expensively attired man whom the union rep identified as the school board's attorney. Hustling in and looking around the room as if he was making an impression that Susan Yoder's case was wasting his time, Dr. LaMer edged back the throne chair, sat down, and pulled his seat closer to the table.

Peter Lawrence could not believe that this tall, bald headed, toilet brush mustached red neck with a PhD from a boon dock college, ran a school system not a backwoods junk car shop.

"Who's this gentleman with Mrs. Yoder and the union people?"

The union lawyer identified Peter Lawrence as the editor-in-chief of the V City Sever.

"Mr. Lawrence, you have no business attending this meeting. Please leave," was spoken with an arrogance both Lawrence and the Union lawyer expected.

The Union lawyer spoke, "there are two reasons that Mr. Peter Lawrence has every right to attend this meeting. First he is a tax paying citizen of the state of Virginia and the city of Virginia City. Most importantly he has the right to attend this meeting as guaranteed by the constitution of the United States. It is called freedom of the press."

Dr. LeMer's face turned red, "that does not mean anything in this …"

The school district's attorney eased out of his seat, approached the superintendent, and whispered something into his ear. LeMer's face got even redder and redder. He ran his index finger around his collar clearing the sweat that was forming.

"I will tell you this, Mr. Lawrence. One sound from you during this hearing and I will have the policeman arrest you for disorderly conduct."

Everybody in the room looked around trying to find the policeman. The school's attorney had left the room and returned with the administrative building's assigned V City police officer who covered the school administration campus.

"Let's get this started. Mrs. Yoder, I have a few questions to ask you. My secretary will give you a bible to swear on indicating that you pledge to tell the ..."

The union's attorney stood up immediately, "this is not a trial. Mrs. Yoder does not need to swear on a bible. Mrs. Yoder, just answer the questions as best you can. If you are asked any question you don't wish to answer, don't. Go ahead Superintendent LaMer."

Lawrence was watching LaMer's eyes. He had tracked down a wolf with his grandfather who eyed his hunters with a stare like LaMer's. His grandfather had stopped the hunt which upset Peter. The grandfather said the wolf was leading them into an attack. The wolf was distant enough and in an environment he knew better than his hunters. It was too dangerous to keep on his track.

"Mrs. Yoder, you are the principal of an elementary school in the Virginia City Public Schools, am I correct in saying?"

"Yes."

Lawrence smiled. Susan would not let LaMer bully herself. "Simple answers only" was what her attorney told her.

"As a leader of small children between the ages of six and twelve, are you not an example to them of the kind of adult they should become?"

Lawrence sprung alert but was kept in his seat by the strong arm of the union's attorney.

"Yes, you and I and all adults set an example for our children," she replied.

LaMer's head came up quickly but he stopped himself from an attack. He could not overcome his red faced cowardly trait. He looked at the school board's attorney who signed with his arms to cut to the chase.

"Let's get down to it, Mrs. Yoder. Did you recently have an abortion at the Virginia City Memorial Hospital?"

"Yes, I did."

"Who was the father of the baby you aborted?"

Susan had had enough, "That's none of your business."

Lawrence saw the eyes of the board members across the table from him. There was shock on their face that Susan Yoder was being insubordinate to Superintendent LaMer.

"How dare you say that to ..." LaMer was grabbed by the shoulder and turned his head as the attorney spoke into his ear.

"Let's go on, Mrs. Yoder."

"Superintendent, LaMer, it is Ms. Yoder. If you expect respect than give it."

It was all Lawrence could do to control his laughter. He wanted to stand up and clap. When he looked about the school board table, everybody was wide eyed with their hand over their mouth. LaMer had turned scarlet red, "Do you think it is right to let children believe that killing babies is not immoral?"

The union's attorney turned to the union representative and they whispered something between them. There was no doubt there conversation was not good for Susan's case.

"I have no comment."

LaMer knew he had her, "Was Mr. Yoder the father of the aborted baby?"

"I refuse to answer that question. It is none of your business."

LaMer just smiled, "I agree, Ms. Yoder. For you and your husband to make such a decision is your own business. But, wait a second? You are no longer a married woman, right? I take it Mr. Yoder has been gone for quite a while?"

"That's correct."

LaMer eased back into his throne chair and folded his fingers together. His grin raised the hackles on Lawrence's neck.

"Then who is the father of the dead baby?"

Susan refused to answer.

"This is a good Christian community, Ms. Yoder. You are an example to our children. Should these young girls see you as a figure of what they should become? Do they admire a loose woman who sees nothing wrong with having sexual relationships and not being married?"

Again the attorney grabbed Lawrence keeping him in his seat.

Dr. Samuel LaMer had his coup de grace and brought the axe down, "I think we can deal with this right here and now. Dear school board members, my secretary will read off a roll call. I am asking for a vote to terminate Mrs. ... I'm sorry, Ms. Yoder's contact with the Virginia City School District. Please respond aye if you sanction this termination or nay if you oppose."

Lawrence watched the board members eyes as every one of them voted aye. A few of the most arrogant stared at Susan, each showing a sarcastic smile. He could not take it any longer and as he rose he shook off the union representative's grip on Lawrence's shoulder.

Lawrence saw the edge his grandfather missed on the snarling wolf and applied it to LaMer, "I cannot stay here and watch a group of ignorant, ass kissing southern hillbillies run a kangaroo court against Susan Yoder. I'm out of here."

His exit was the door behind the throne seat. Stopping he stood akimbo to Samuel LaMer. He grabbed him by the neck and forced him to stand, "Your wife might like to know the cock hound you are."

The assigned Virginia City policeman tased Lawrence before Lawrence could wring the superintendent's neck. Writhing on the floor, he went unconscious.

***

"Hey, you white boy! Get the fuck off the bunk. Lawyer's here and you out."

Lawrence had a severe head ache, part from being Tased; the rest from the treatment he had gotten when was taken to the ocean front Virginia City Police Station yesterday. The desk clerk abused him and ridiculed him, telling him he was going to put Lawrence in a cell with a black homosexual rapist, and laughing at Lawrence. The other cops had their laughs when they made him strip down totally naked and waddle like a duck so they could be sure he did not have any weapons hidden in his anus. The black magistrate who took down all the information of his arrest and wrote up the charges against him kept up the onslaught of ridicule and debasement by threatening to tell her black boyfriend, who Tased Lawrence, that Lawrence called her a nigger.

The newspaper's attorney was waiting for him.

"Nice outfit, Lawrence" said the attorney referring to Lawrence's orange prison canvas suit. Lawrence did not laugh. "The school district dropped the charges. It seems the superintendent felt merciful."

"That's not the reason. Sam the man didn't want his wife to find out about his lechery."

The lawyer left leaving Lawrence the release form from the circuit court judge. The day cops and magistrate were different people so he could not pledge revenge. Still he would get it. Getting his cell phone back, he called the newspaper and asked Kat to pick him up. The ride back to his car parked in the Virginia City Schools administration lot found two parking tickets stuck under his wind shield wipers. He tore them up and threw into the slight breeze.

Before she left, he asked Kat how her mother was doing.

"Not too good. Besides your arrest and her being terminated, her lawyer told her that ... No, I'll let her tell you. She's at home, now."

"No, got to go home and get a shower. I smell like a convict."

Kat replied, "well, you should. After all you are an ex-con."

Lawrence laughed as she finished by telling him she loved him for trying so hard to help her mother, "it's a shame you didn't ring that bastard's neck. Mom said you were damn close."

"I'll get to it."

There were numerous calls on his phone answering machine but the one he chose to dial first challenged him. It was from an attorney for the Comanche Nations General Counsel in Lawton, Oklahoma. His name was Nacoma Quan.

"Yes, I am Nacoma Quan. What can I do for you?"

"Got me? I'm just returning your phone call. Name's Peter Lawrence."

"Very good, I have been trying to reach you. I represent American natives especially Comanche's that are being falsely arrested. Do you know a man named Charlie Grayrock?"

Lawrence had to stop a second and consider how he knew Charlie. It could get Lawrence in trouble since probably Charlie already was.

"Charlie Grayrock is a great man, a proud Indian. I know him."

"Mr. Lawrence, I know Charlie very well. I know how he does business. Our brothers come before the government of the United States or any other agency that might be ... Let's just say our tribe is first. Charlie counts you as a friend. Charlie is in much trouble. I cannot discuss this over a line phone. Is this a line phone?"

"No, it's safe. I'm on my cell and I have it on an AP that cannot be monitored."

"Charlie needs to talk to you. He's in Leavenworth Prison in Kansas. We got him moved to there. He was imprisoned at Guantanamo Bay Naval Base, Gitmo in Cuba."

"Jesus, what for?"

"Terrorism. He was charged with being ... You're pushing me along too fast and what you are asking is not why he wants to talk with you. Can you come out here and visit Leavenworth with me?"

"When?"

"I'll have tickets waiting for you at Norfolk Airport in less than an hour. If needed, the Comanche Nations General Council will put you up for overnight."

"I hate those teepees. Can't take a shower or a pee in them. Charlie's a good man. I've a person I need to get with for a couple hours. Can I do a late night flight."

"No, problem."

***

"Come on, Susan. The break will be good for you. We fly out tonight to Kansas, stay at a nice hotel, and relax. We'll take a couple days. I shouldn't be long with Charlie."

"Peter, I love you very much. Give me some time. Then we'll be okay. There's something you need to know. The union cannot stop my termination."

She handed Peter a copy of 2006 Virginia Code § 22.1-307.

"Teachers may be dismissed or placed on probation for incompetency, immorality, noncompliance with school laws and regulations, disability as shown by competent medical evidence when in compliance with federal law, conviction of a felony or a crime of moral turpitude or other good and just cause."

Immorality is based on community ethics. Their threat of my sexual activity and having an abortion can be regarded as immorality since it was witnessed by minors.

"You might not get their termination rescinded but you should be able to sue the school board individually for their actions that violent your civil rights."

"Peter, the attorney told me that in any other state but Virginia and a couple others that are commonwealths, I could sue the Virginia City School Board and LaMer but I cannot win in Virginia. They, the school board and superintendent, are protected by sovereign immunity. They cannot commit a legal wrong. They are immune from civil suit. Worse of all they can commit a blatant crime and not face criminal prosecution.

"That's unreal. It's fucking unreal. You read about royalty throughout history being able to send people to the gallows, or taking away people's property, but you'd think this country would never sanction that. Why the fuck did we ever have a revolution?"

Lawrence caught a wisp of the bad air bad covering America. Nothing changes. Wars fought for independence only change the names of the czars and kings. He understood

Susan's need to shake off the past three days without him. He knew she would still love him but he had no idea where she would find her future. Susan helped Lawrence shape both of their futures.

"Peter, you know my thoughts about violence. You also know I love you. My love stays but it sees a necessity to fight. I will be with you."

***

Peter Lawrence nearly went into tears. Expecting to meet with Charlie Grayrock in a visitor's cell like most prisons, Charlie was confined to a special cell equal to twice the size of most cells. It was as close to the infirmary as possible. Locked and barred like most cells, its size allowed the imprisonment of severely ill prisoners. Charlie was severely ill. A man, a Comanche warrior of great height and large physique, was a scarecrow being gnawed at by a dying body. The fleshy face was gone and replaced by sinews of flesh draped from his eyes to his neck.

Nacoma Quan spoke, "Charlie Grayrock, I have brought Mr. Lawrence here as you asked. Do you hear me, Charlie?"

"Peter, Peter come closer. My eyes are very bad."

Lawrence could see the cataracts growing over his pupae. His entire eyes were almost opaque and Lawrence noted that the light from above had no effect on Charlie's sensitivity. A very bright flash of light would probably burn out his optic nerves.

"What did Nacoma tell you?"

"The FBI arrested you and sent you to GITMO. You would still be there if a Marine from Oklahoma who is almost pure Comanche didn't secretly get in touch with the Comanche Nations General Council," said Lawrence. "That's all I know?"

"Nacoma, you did as I asked. Thank you, my brother."

"Charlie, are you safe in this room? It's not wired?"

Nacoma spoke, "yes, we had a tribe member trained in rigging sound recordings for the government visit it before we contacted you."

"The Feds let you do that?"

"For once in our confrontation with the white man, we backed them down. Ask and speak what you will. It will not put you in danger."

"They tortured me in Cuba. Worse was the water boarding that Ass Hole Bush okayed. Ever nearly drowned, Peter?"

"Yeah, I got trapped in a wave back draft when I was only nine at Atlantic City. I couldn't make the surface and got dragged up by my mother. Spewed ocean out of my nose and mouth before I could breathe again."

"I was tied onto an inclined bench, maybe seven feet long. My feet were elevated about a foot above my head. They laid a rag over my face, hair line to chin and saturated it with water. My air flow was restricted to about thirty seconds to get some air. During those 30 seconds, they poured water continuously from a height of twelve to twenty-four inches onto the cloth. The cloth would be lifted and I was allowed to breathe in the open air a few breaths. The procedure kept being repeated. The water boarding would go for twenty minutes or so for one application."

"Shit that's horrible! What did you do to be tortured like this?"

Charlie was having breathing problems and Nacoma pulled an oxygen mask from the cart next to Charlie and affixed the mask over his nose and mouth. He gave Charlie a couple minutes with pure oxygen.

"They tracked me down by the serial number on your father's Glock-17 carbide 9 mm," said Grayrock.

"Where did they find it?"

"Peter, sit down, pull the chair over next to me. I can't talk too loud."

Peter Lawrence felt a chill up his back bone.

"The FBI search team found it in the debris left from the plane that crashed into the Pentagon."

"My father was on one of the terrorist hijackings?"

"Serial number on the Glock matched Llewellyn's Glock. They back tracked it to me. I'm a licensed arms dealer. The manufacturer registers my name when I buy it from them. Arens bought it from me. It was his gun on that plane."

"Did you rat him out?"

"No, I could have since his remains were burned to dust. There was nothing the Feds could do to him once he rode the plane into the west side of the Pentagon. I didn't need to throw shame on your mother or you. Fuck the FBI. Told them I was robbed and it got stolen."

"Which is why you are here. Arens killed for me, my people, and our ancestors. He was a hero."

Nacoma Quan had left the room for about twenty minutes. He returned with a broad smile, "Charlie, we got a release for you. FBI wrote you off. I have the release papers here. I called Lawton and the Comanche Nations General Council has a room waiting for you at Comanche County Memorial Hospital. They don't trust the Feds so you'll have to wait for an ambulance from an ambulance service I contacted. I sure Peter will be glad to stay with you for a couple hours?"

Lawrence told Charlie he would stay with him. He took a later flight back to Virginia. As Charlie was being wheeled out of Leavenworth Prison, he grabbed Peter Lawrence's hand, "I ain't got long to go, Petey. My son's name is on the card I just crumbled into your hand. If I'm not able, he'll get you whatever you want. Don't ask for a Glock-17 carbide. It's a bad omen. See ya later, big guy."

***

"Susan, I know Charlie Grayrock from my time in Canada. He's one hundred percent Comanche. If you ever imagined a brave Indian warrior, Charlie would foot the bill, but not anymore. He's a dead man. His body has shriveled and his eyes are glazed over. Yet he's still fighting. Can he make it? If anybody can, Charlie would be the man. The fucking government tortured the life out of him. All Charlie knew was that he had sold the Glock-17 to my father. But through all of the torture, he never squealed. He held to the story that when he was in Canada, his Cessna had been robbed at the airport."

"They didn't believe him?"

"No, and everything they did to him was useless. He never ratted out my father."

"Peter, where are you now? I know you're standing in front of me but where's your head?"

"Don't you see it's time?"

She knew what he meant but could not accept what he needed to do, "as much as the world has collapsed for me, I can't bring myself to kill somebody, Peter."

"Yes, I know it's very difficult for you. This is not what you expected from life. Neither you nor I have made it a world of rulers, enforcers, and slaves. That's what life is in the United States now. I can't live with it anymore. This country is feared by people all over the planet. In this piss-ant piece of insignificant life called Virginia City, tyrants like Czeed and LaMer rule sycophants like the city council, police force, and the school board. They obey these Tsars because these men gave them the sweet taste of power. You saw the self-righteous smiles when you were voted to be terminated. How many citizens accepted a pittance to waiver off the law suit against the Navy? Every one! How can the state government allow school boards and city councils to violate the human rights of its citizens? Eminent domain and sovereign immunity or more atrocious crown immunity, are the laws made to protect the kings.

"Peter, Peter, I know all of that! But I can't see myself killing people. Isn't that just as heinous as what is happening here?"

"Susan, we've got to fight back. I don't expect you to accept that. Just don't give in is all I ask. I'm not going to let the rulers and their soldiers take me down. My father died trying to rid the world of obedient soldiers attacking foreign countries so the United States can control the flow of oil to the United States. The Unites States military is taking over countries so that American petroleum companies can keep making profits at the pumps."

"What can I do?"

"First I have to avenge myself of the police force of Virginia City. I have seen bullies and I have dealt with them."

Through Lawrence's mind ran his fight with Frick. Frick and his gang ruling the school yards with violence and fear.

Violence and fear had added ridicule and shame when Lawrence had been arrested. He would not let it pass by.

"I am going to leave in a few minutes. I cannot tell you what I am going to do. Probably you will be contacted by the Virginia City Police. They might even take you into jail. What is it you can tell them?"

"Why, nothing. You have told me nothing. How could they arrest me since I know nothing?"

"Remember, these soldiers, this police force of the city council and the city manager, let alone the mayor, will push you, attack you, but you must force them to let you contact your lawyer. You have his number, right?"

"Yes, should I call him ahead of time?"

Lawrence came chest to chest with her, placed his two hands behind her head, and spoke, "no, because that would mean you knew I was planning some action. Just don't say anything until the lawyer's with you."

Susan began to cry, "am I going to lose you?'

Lawrence knew the odds were against him surviving his sortie.

"When I call your cell phone, you'll know. Make sure it's fully charged and hide it somewhere as soon as I leave. Make sure it's turned off."

They held each other tightly not wanting to leave the other. Tears formed in both of their eyes, "you will be getting a large and heavy package from Comanche Hardware and Lawn Furniture and a smaller, but heavy one also from them. You must sign for it. It will not be delivered until the following week after next week. Here's a key to a small space in Jack Rabbit storage on Birdneck Road. You're listed as the renter. Put them as soon as possible in the shed and do not return to it. A have another key in case you lose it."

They held for a few more minutes and Lawrence left. It was snowing outside of Susan Yoder's condo unit at Ruby Inlet. Lawrence left his car back at his house over a garage after he had taken his Grumman canoe to Ruby Inlet and secured it under the piers. He did this after dark and the blinding snow storm assured his not being observed. At the canoe he discarded his jacket and rigged his The Miami Classic II holster over his shoulders and around his back. He checked the two Colt 45 M1911A1's for a chambered round in each, dried the pistols off from the snow with his shirt tail, and holstered them. Surrounding his body with his grey rain coat, Lawrence headed for the Ocean Front Virginia City Police station which was only sixteen blocks north.

Peter Lawrence was more primed than ever in his life.

CHAPTER THIRTY-TWO

Three Preys of the Beast

"Vengeance, sir, is the hollowest of all the mockeries that go to make up life."
… The Sea Hawk 1915, Rafael Sabatini

When did they come after you?"

"Peter, where are you," said Susan.

"I need to know what happened."

"Like you said, the city police were here in the middle of the night. They had a warrant and took me in. They did not take me to the Ocean Front jail, obviously. I wound up down at the court house."

"You could have waved to good old Sam. Virginia City Public Schools is only a block away."

Susan responded, "You haven't answered me?"

"You know what happened at the ocean front jail?"

"Of course, am I alright discussing it on this line?"

"No, the cell phone can't be traced but my bet is your condo is bugged. Delete my cell phone number off yours as soon as I hang up."

"I need you, Peter. I'm scared, very sacred. The lawyer had me out within five hours. Police couldn't prove I had anything to do with …"

"No, remember what I just said. I have had a challenging journey and when I'm there I won't be so dumb. I've got three more to go. I love you."

Susan knew where he was headed and knew only she could translate his message. Now it was the long wait of time to pass.

It took Lawrence four days to cross Shipps Bay to Bridge Cove which was nearly five miles from his start. The initial journey was the simplest and safest since it was the dead of winter and no one was allowed on the refuge. He paddled north up the east side of Back Bay Refuge which even in fair seasons was virtually without life, let alone during the winter. Just north of the main body of the island was a wash breech linking the inlet on the east to Shipps Bay on the west. Once through the gap to the west side put him less than three miles to the south of Bridge Cove and DumDum. This was the riskiest part since he would be in open water. There should be little or no water traffic but his silver, light reflecting canoe could still be sighted during daylight. He found a muddy organic slime pool at the isthmus and used the muck and mire to coat the canoe. On the journey were several patches of reeds as tall as six or seven feet. The camouflaged canoe would spend the daylight hours in those patches giving Lawrence a chance to sleep.

During the night on the fourth day, Lawrence headed the canoe out of the last batch of reeds and to the small cove below DumDum. It was a tiring and physically painful stroking but it got him to the shore just as the sun rose behind his back. He struggled to go as fast as possible and cursing the weather which could have been cloudy. There were no lights at the cove or at the site of DumDum. This did not mean he was safe but he was so exhausted that he said "fuck it." He removed one of the .45s from the holster wrapped in oil skin. If they are waiting, they will have to kill him.

His best approach was to land east of the creek running up to his cabin and wait an hour or so. No, he changed his mind. Darkness gave him and edge. Any noise was intensified in darkness. A reflection off on somebody's glasses or an accidental flashlight turned on, would give Lawrence notice he was being trapped. He could just see the edge of his cabin. He squatted in the reeds, resting on his haunches when the alert came.

With his .45 held barrel down and alongside of his right leg, Peter Lawrence walked slowly the edge of the creek to the cabin and knocked on the door.

"Susan, open the door. You've got to wear something besides that Versace perfume."

She opened the door and rushed him. He did not fear that she would be part of a trap.

"Explain, right now!" she said shutting the door behind him pointing to the ice chest at the sink. It had three bags of melting ice in it. There was a bottle of Johnnie Walker Red Scotch on the kitchen table. She pulled curtains over the windows and lit a small but well-rounded candle.

Lawrence did not go for the scotch. Instead he poured the melted ice from the ice chest into a glass and oohed at the ice cold water. After two glasses of ice water, he had a scotch on rocks. Susan had brought food, two large subs from *SUBWAY* that she kept in another ice chest.

"No, you explain. How did you pull this off?"

"They didn't care about me. They tore apart your apartment and office at the newspaper and found nothing. I asked them to search my condo. This was really dumb even though we're close to each other. Of course they found nothing because they were blind. The day after you killed those police officers, those packages you said to watch out for came and were lying on my dining room table. One of the policemen asked why I bought stuff from a hardware store in Oklahoma. I told him because I support the Native Americans of this country. He shrugged and let it go. What's in those packages, Peter?"

"A black widow AK47 is in the big box and the smaller contains 7.62X39 mm armor penetrated bullets."

"What do you need them for?"

"Susan, you seem to have changed a bit. You're not backing off about killing people. You know I killed those police people at the Ocean Front Police Station?"

"Of course I knew that."

"You risked my freedom coming here. They could have followed you. In fact they might just be out there in the marsh ready to take me down!"

"That won't happen. Here, read this."

Susan Yoder handed him a V City Server paper still in its recyclable plastic bag.

"You're dead!"

The headline made that clear, "COP KILLER'S BODY FOUND."

"What the hell's this about?"

"Read the newspaper."

Peter Lawrence was dead. His body was found strewn in pieces over the rock jetties on the south side of the inlet into Rudy Inlet. The body size and structure exactly matched the size and shape of Lawrence. The estimated time of deterioration coincided with the elapsed time of his fleeing the Ocean Front Police Department. The blood samples earlier found on the jetty rocks were identified as Lawrence's and were only two feet above the water level where the decomposed body was found. The body had been torn to pieces by marine animals. A positive identification was not possible.

"Peter, you're old news now. You've lived in Virginia City long enough to know these self-absorbed, egoists couldn't care less. You're dead. Forget about it."

"Are you sure?"

"Go to the editorial. Czeed let go on you."

Lawrence slowly read Czeed's editorial on Peter Lawrence. A first grader could have written more intelligently and Lawrence smiled knowing that Kat did not advise Czeed how poorly he wrote. The real clincher was that Czeed graduated from William and Mary with a degree in business.

Lawrence chuckled as he read through Czeed's attack on Lawrence. He said that the only reason he kept Lawrence on staff was that it was part of the deal with the previous owner. He stated that Lawrence was not only disliked by the newspaper staff but spent many days intoxicated at the paper.

"You want me to ignore Czeed? How about Sam LaMer and the school board?"

Susan Yoder turned away from Lawrence. He gently put his hands on her shoulders.

"I should let Louisa Santiago never see the man who killed her baby pay for his drunken stupidity?"

Susan turned to him and buried her tear stained face into his shoulder, "I know, I know, I know."

"Is the bribery of Czeed and the city council to be forgotten since it was washed away by the pittance given to people who live every day with jets scaring their families and threatening their lives?"

"No, Peter. I have changed. With you being safe now, I thought we could take the easy way out. It wouldn't be hard for you to take on a new identity. I know you have contacts all over the country, and probably most of North America. I ask myself why?"

Lawrence gently held Susan Yoder's face between the palms of his hands, "we will. I must take down the four preys or I will not be able to face any life myself in a mirror. You must understand that, Susan. I know you don't like violence or believe in retribution but they will happen only three more times."

"You said four?"

"I have killed the first and I died in the rocks washed by the Atlantic Ocean. The other three must go. Can you bear through it?"

She shrugged with deep breaths, "can you? Will I still have you, Peter?"

"Yes."

***

Susan Yoder sat on the satin covered sofa of Evelyn Southern's home in upstate Pennsylvania watching the AM America's morning news program. The entire school board, the superintendent, and a police guard were murdered by an assailant last night in Virginia City, Virginia. The murderer had shot out and destroyed the outside video camera, the hallway video camera, and the school board conference room's video camera. This lead the Virginia City police to believe the assailant was a former employee with a grudge to settle. They were inclined to think it was a maintenance man at one of the schools that had been fired because he came to his school intoxicated.

"That's two" said Susan Yoder.

"Mon Cher, two?" said Evelyn Southern.

Susan had been living with Peter's mother for two months. The day after Peter's return to DumDum, she had packed, had a moving van pack up all of her belongings, said goodbye to her daughter Kat, and drove to Pennsylvania. Peter's mother had been waiting for her. There need be no explanation to which Evelyn made no query. Evelyn's lover and first husband had been a rebel warrior. Like father like son, now her son was a rebel warrior. Both were paladins like the warriors of Charlemagne's court, who appeared in the songs of heroes such as The Song of Roland. They fought with Christian martial valor against the Saracen hordes.

Susan fell immediately in love with Evelyn Southern. Feared she could not trust her, Evelyn spent five hours the first night telling the life of Peter's father. That this woman could shed off any action by the United States government made Susan fear naught. Peter had told his mother very little when he called telling her Susan was on her way. Susan filled in the blanks.

"He's going to do the city council and city manager. The city manager happens to also be his former boss, the one whom tore him apart in the newspaper."

"Peter has chosen the best woman a warrior can have. You respect his valor and do not challenge his battles. But as all women in waiting for their love, you fear his death, Mon Cher," said Evelyn Southern.

Susan Yoder smiled, absorbed by this woman's cavalier view of her son, "Peter has set the battle ground. To the people of Virginia City, he is a dead man. They see the slaughter of the school board as revenge by a dismissed employee. Peter will have little problem with the school board and he will be in heaven when he takes down Czeed."

Evelyn smiled and spoke, "let's hope that is the only heaven, Mon Cher."

***

Peter Lawrence had lived long enough in Virginia City that he had canoed every waterway covering most of the city including the air base and the city hall/city school administrations buildings. The myriad streams washing eastward into Back Bay were not navigable by any water craft larger than his canoe. Best of all was the lack of any horticulture of the environments abutting the streams. Basically you had to cut your way through a ravaging growth of trees and weeds and briars to get to most streams. Lawrence came through them via the stream just north of DumDum. It drained like nearly every stream to the west and into the North Landing River. He had used the stream putting him only a hundred yards from the Virginia City Public School's administrative building.

He waited two weeks for the city council meeting. Ironically, it was on the same day of the week and at the same time as the school board meetings. They met on different weeks. Tonight the meeting would be *In camera*, a closed board meeting covering information not recorded in the minutes or divulged to the public. The city manager and city council members would discuss personnel, financial, and other sensitive decisions. All must be kept secret. Peter Lawrence years ago completely loss respect for the people of the south and especially Virginia. That elected officials should hide behind chamber doors negotiating the lives of its citizens was abhorred by Lawrence. Yet, the people allowed it to happen.

Waiting in a stream only ten or twenty yards from the city council building, he unwrapped his .45's from the oil skin, dried them off, and chambered rounds into both. He wore his notorious grey rain coat that was two sizes too large for him and held two more cartridges. Lawrence was armed enough to take out a seal team.

He knew the board room configuration from previous visits as a newspaper man. He also knew the police officer that stood by the double doors. Lawrence shifted his weight from the canoe port gunwale and sat on the large roots of a tree. Grabbing the rope at the front of the canoe, he stood, shaking the kinks out of each leg one at a time, and secured the canoe to the tree. The foliage here was excellent for keeping the canoe hidden and he was glad he wore the grey coat since the briers were sharp.

It was too dark and the street lights of such low wattage, that he was sure the police guard on the inside would not see him. As he expected, the double doors were now locked, meaning that all of the board members were present and so was Czeed. He knocked gently on the right door. It took a few seconds and just before he was about to knock again, the police guard opened the door.

"Building's closed. Move on."

"Got to piss real bad. Come on, you gots a men's room in there, don't you?"

"You can't come in."

Lawrence pulled his knees together and formed a grimace on his face, "I'm gonna have to whiz back that bush, sir. Might have to take a dump."

The policeman spoke, "come here. Come on, you bum. Follow me."

He lead Lawrence to the meeting room doors and gestured to the right, "make it quick."

"Thank you, sir."

The cop turned showing his back to Lawrence. Lawrence cold cocked him at the base of his head. When the cop fell, Lawrence put his fingers on the man's throat making sure he was out cold. He was dead which was better. Lawrence also knew that there was another police officer inside the meeting room. With both .45s drawn, Lawrence kicked five times on the bottom of the right door.

The inside policeman swung open the door and said, "what are you doing ..."

Lawrence put a bullet through the man's left eye that came out of the back of his head, blowing hair, scalp, and bone fragments into the air. The city council members rose and Lawrence took out two them yelling to the remainder to sit back down. They did but Czeed tried to escape through a door on Lawrence's left. He shot him in Czeed's left leg just below his knee.

"Get back to your seat my friend the editor or I'll shoot the other knee."

Czeed dragged his spent knee and leg to the head of the council table and sat.

Lawrence now had out both .45's, "in my family there is a trait rare to others. We sense when people are lying. If you lie to me, I will kill you. There is no second chance."

A fat man wearing khaki pants too small to accommodate his rear end thus displaying his crack as he stood up spoke, "you're full of shit."

Lawrence put a bullet in him at center mass, "anybody else wants to stand up?"

Lawrence shot a woman with her back to him, blowing half her skull away, and spoke "person next to her body. You! Pick up the cell phone she was hiding under the table. Do it! Now!"

"Listen completely to what I have to say. You voted down the city's law suit against renewing the Navy's lease of the air base. Yet, your constituents filed a petition to evict the Navy from Virginia City. They had enough numbers to do just that."

Lawrence walked around the council members, completing the circle one and a half times by stopping above Czeed who was applying a tourniquet to his leg. He was using his neck tie and a broken wooden pointer used during visual presentations.

"You can just keep lying on the floor."

"I want a show of hands now. Who voted to null the petition?"

Nobody raised their hand and Lawrence shot an old black woman at center mass.

"Now, what did I tell you? If you lie, I'll kill you. Do you need me to offer a better explanation?"

Lawrence was playing with a stacked deck. Even though their voting down the petition and forcing a recount was held in camera, Lawrence had found out it was a unanimous vote. Anybody who did not raise their hand when he asked for a show of hands of those who did vote it down was lying.

"Let's try this again. Who voted against ..."

Before he finished asking his question, every hand went up.

"Now that's more like it. One more question. How many of you knew that Mr. Czeed had an economic interest in keeping the Naval Base here?"

All hands went up and Lawrence was surprised, astounded. It meant that Czeed had revealed his LLC for the apartments to the city council. He had them in tow, scared to lie to him so he pushed them into their own criminal act.

"Last question. Answer correctly and you'll be going home soon. How many of you got a financial bribe from Mr. Czeed's LLC?"

He did not have to shoot anybody which he was not going to do anyway. All the hands went up.

"You people are America. You are the slaves of the money merchants. Yet, it is voluntary slavery. I feel sorry not for you, but for people like Louisa Santiago. Your lust from gilt comes from lack of guilt."

Lawrence walked up to Czeed who was now sitting upright on the floor, his damaged leg stretched out and the tourniquet stopping the flow of blood to his foot.

"You're going to lose that leg. At least it won't kill you. But I will," said Lawrence putting two bullets into his head, one through each eye. He ejected one of the cartridges and inserted a full one.

"All of you killed the baby. All of will die," said Lawrence.

***

Peter Lawrence had been doing surveillance on the Oceana Naval Air Base for three weeks. He had circled the base in his canoe using the stream system that connected to North Landing River. At dusk every week night he would watch and note when the F-14 Tomcat's took off. He waited for their return. Ironically their return did not change much. Still the weather and darkness of winter, the noise of the jets would be heard well before seeing wing lights and the cockpit halo soaring in from the Atlantic Ocean, north east of the air base. There was no target at the height they flew approaching the base. The Black Widow NNOAK Spud AK- 47 could not hit a plane at that altitude. The jets tilted at the north end of the landing strip and made a sweep to their port. On their turn the wings were nearly perpendicular to the ground. The F-14's leveled at a lower altitude and began their descent until they were parallel to the landing zone. There was no target at that point even though they were low enough for the AK-47.

The descent posed the perfect target. Using binoculars Lawrence saw the descent parabola of the F-14s. At a low level and near the end of the runway, the planes executed an 180^0 turn which put at that few seconds the F-14 at 90^0 to the ground. It left the cockpit fully exposed and well lit. Within seconds the pilot would level off the turn into a drop to the runway with very little target exposure. Peter had to fire at the precise time the plane was perpendicular making the pilot an excellent target. From his position in the stream north of the runway, it was an impossible shot. The AK-47 did not have that range. There was no tributary extending to the south of the runway. He tried three runoffs of the stream but to no avail. His only approach had to be on land. His chances of hunting through the land around the east and west of the air meant suicide. It was all farm land. He would be detected by the base sentry towers and the roving guards with attack dogs. It was time to give up. He had taken down three of his targets and would have to be satisfied.

Lawrence backed up and skewed the canoe a half turn so he was facing east and toward North Landing River. His arms and shoulders were exhausted since the three hour trip from Muddy Creek to the naval air station. Turned and headed south put the canoe running with the current. He ceded paddling and only using the paddle for a rudder. Easing back he rested with the flow. Within minutes he heard a slow flow of water to his starboard. Floating past the noise, he turned the canoe a half circle and headed back to where he heard the water.

He heard it but even with the clear sky and bright moon, he saw nothing. Reaching inside the waterproof bag he toted when canoeing, he pulled out his Husky flask light. Scanning the south side of the stream from which the noise came, he saw a flow of water rushing out of a hill of bushes. Lawrence paddled up to the bushes and slowly into the bushes. As he slashed his way through the bushes, he found himself on a very short stream flowing from a concrete culvert that was also covered by bushes. It was a drainage outlet directly north of the Oceana Naval Air Base. It had steel bars hinged to the opening of the culvert. The lock on the culvert had been busted and was hanging loosely off the latch for the door made by the steel bars.

Lawrence beached the canoe into the bushes and tied the bow to a bush. So over grown was this area that it would be nearly impossible to reach the culvert by land. The briars were so barbed that anybody trying to force through them would get badly scratched. He waded in the stream with water half way up to his knees. Even with the lock broken, the question was, is the iron barred grate so rusted it would not sway open. Removing the busted lock, he grabbed the grate and with a strong heave and a loud creak, it swung wide enough for him to enter.

The smell in the pipeline was rank but at least it was not a sewer line. The flashlight carried well down the pipeline showing a very low level of water, less than two or three inches deep. Lawrence knew his position in relation to the runway. It would be a long march but if the pipes kept aligned south to north, the drainage pipes would go right underneath the landing zone. What choice did he have? None, so he covered the canoe with briars in the off chance someone would come hiking through the bushes, took the two spare "C" size alkaline batteries from his waterproof bag, and started wading.

The flashlight started to worry him as he noticed the time. He had been walking for nearly an hour and had no idea where he was going. There were turn-offs every fifteen minutes or so but the pipe sizes were too small. He sensed he was going due south. Ready to give up, he turned off the flashlight and was about to head back to his canoe, when directly in front of him was a very dim glow. With the light leading him on, he continued another hundred yards or so and found himself directly under a narrow pipe rising up to the surface from which light was descending. On the exit pipe were u-shaped rungs serving as a built-in ladder. Above he could see a grate covering the exit pipe. Slowly he climbed up the iron rungs to the grate. While the light was very minimal, at the top and below the grate, he could see it was brighter to the grate's right. Now there was a problem, two in fact. First, was should he dare pushing the grate up to see where he was? Second, was could he push the grate up? He knew that manhole covers weighed over two hundred pounds.

Putting both his palms on the sides of the grate, he slowly pushed upward. It did not budge. He lit his flashlight keeping the beam directed down. Bringing the light up slowly, he saw that there was hard clay which had sealed the edges of the grate. Pulling out his jack knife, he cut through as much of the clay as possible and returned it to his pocket. It did not give and he was ready to try cutting deeper but he saw a trickle of water oozing through an edge where he had cut. He went to the grate again and slowly but firmly kept up the pressure on the bars. It moved. Lawrence reasoned that a push and drop repeated action might loosen the grate. It did and he slowly pushed the grate out of the pipe hole and to the side.

Knowing there was a chance that peeking his head out of the drainage pipe could get him a bullet into his head, he slowly stepped up another iron step, then another. With his head above ground level, he was looking at the lit runway of Oceania Naval Air Base. Only minimum lighting flooded the air strip. He needed to get his bearings even though every second his head was up meant being closer to being detected. Nobody was anywhere around. He was at the north end. Since there were no flights leaving the air base, no one was policing that end of the runway. He did a full 360^0 of the view from this drainage pipe and knew his night was not over. If this distance found him his first drainage pipe and exit to the runway, going south would find more exit ports. It took him three hours to find every drainage grate for the entire length of the runway. None of the grates were secured to keep threats like Pater Lawrence from exiting them. The next to last was to be his attack bunker.

During his return trip which took an hour and a half, Peter Lawrence mapped out in his mind the assault. Despite the fatigue his body felt, he slowly paddled the canoe back to DumDum and managed to not be spied along the North Landing River except by a couple older black fishermen waving to him from the shore. Lawrence waved back and yelled if they had caught anything. The response was a couple catfish.

***

The wait was excruciating. The repeated trips to the attack pipe took hours of paddling from DumDum to the culvert and another two hours hauling the AK 47 through the tunnel pipes only to be disappointed that Lawrence either missed an early landing, the landing was reversed and came in via the north, or there was no landing. He changed his strategy. He had noticed that there were many side pipes draining into the main drainage system. What he also noticed was that during periodical storms, while the side pipes were gushing, some ran dry. He would camp there. This gave him every night a shot at the Tomcats. Living on very little and bored beyond sanity, it only took one and a half weeks of being a sewer rat before he sat in the up pipe of the attack drain and for the first time heard and then saw the first F-14 Tomcat head over the north end of the runway, ready to enter the landing parabola at the south end.

The Black Widow NOOAK AK 47 had a low profile Dragon Lock bipod attached directly to the barrel. Each magazine held 30 rounds of 7.62x39mm ammo which in this case were high explosive incendiary/armor piercing ammunitions also known as HEIAP. These rounds used high explosives which could blast through two inches of rolled steel armor. When the bullet strikes a target, it blasts a path which ignites a second incendiary explosion that triggers zirconium powder that burns for as long as ten minutes. Lawrence had two cartridges ready for attack.

"Okay, Black Widow, here we go!"

The noise is always irritating and tonight's Tomcats were no exception. A loudness that rattles people's windows, wakes sleepers, and let's crying babies die, filled the air for miles around Virginia City.

The first F-14 dropped speed as it entered the landing parabola less than fifty yards to the right of Lawrence. Since it was night and very dark where the drainage ditch grate was located, Lawrence stood on the fourth iron U-shape step with the AK-47's tripod resting on the concrete runway. The specially designed groove rail top gave him optimal viewing through the front sight. The rubber rail guards provided handling comfort and protection.

None of this mattered on the first shot. Lawrence hesitated a split second when the F-14 reached the U-turn to his landing and all he saw were a few sparks where the first bullet of three nicked the tail of the Tomcat.

Silently to himself, Lawrence said "Peter, you're an asshole! How many kills did you and your grandfather make under worse conditions than this? Lead the prey, lead him!"

That he did. The second Tomcat entered the landing parabola and as soon as Lawrence saw the cockpit, the AK-47 fired out ten HEIAP rounds that hit the Tomcat as it was at the U-turn. The plane did not continue its curve to 180^0 from the approach. The cockpit exploded and the Tomcat spiraled into the ground, first in fire, and then exploded. Before the Air Traffic Control Tower could abort the landings of all the F-14s arriving from the north, the third Tomcat tried to exit the parabola but exposed the cockpit just long enough for Lawrence to put ten HEIAPs into the plane. It went past the runaway to the south and hit a farm.

The third Tomcat tried to pull up before the landing parabola, but seven of ten HEIAP rounds hit the cockpit from the side sending the F-14 into a spiral. It exploded as it hit ground. There were no more planes to shoot. Ground control had gotten the other planes out of a landing approach and back into the air. They were redirected to Joint Base Langley which is a United States military facility located in Hampton,

Virginia under the jurisdiction of the United States Air Force 633d Air Base Wing, Air Combat Command.

The grate down, Lawrence was prepared to be discovered. He would not make it easy for them. He went down the iron rungs of the drainage pipe, he heard the sound. Lightning and thunder waged an up roar and a storm flooded all of Virginia City and the Tidewater area for hours. Lawrence made a run for it and got to the canoe as the rain intensity increased. He had policed every area of the drainage system, leaving nothing behind, not even toilet paper. The storm hid Peter Lawrence from sight during the canoe voyage to DumDum. So violent was the storm that Lawrence met nobody near the waterway, on roads next to the river, or cars passing over him on bridges he went by.

"Mon Mere! You'll tell me it was the voice of God."

***

Only Virginia City could have a blizzard on Ash Wednesday, the first day of Lent and in the middle of March and spring. A storm along the Atlantic Ocean coast had stalled with continuous rain, wind speeds of nearly 60 mph, tidal surges, and best of all large quantities of snow. Peter Lawrence knew his targets would probably not let a little rain and wind stop them from their weekly sojourn to the Oceana Gentlemen's Club. This he learned from Kat Yoder's research during the story line dealing with jet noise and the death of Louisa Santiago's baby dying when her mother could not hear her cries because of the jet noise. The pilot was intoxicated when buzzing the apartments where Santiago lived. That pilot, Commander David Johnstone, and his Tomcat buddies had no flights on Thursdays and they made it their good buddy's night. The problem Peter Lawrence had was whether the cadre of pilots would show up during the storm.

Lawrence had reconnoitered the Oceana Gentlemen's Club when he learned that his shoot down of Tomcats at Oceana Naval Air Base had not taken down Johnstone. He would not stop his quest to destroy the prey he swore to kill. All but one was dead. Knowing Johnstone spent Thursday nights at the Oceana Gentlemen's Club, Lawrence had easily discovered that the nightclub was a whore house at the edge of a military base which meant the powers to be of Virginia City ignored the club using the good old excuse of men need to be men and Virginia City did not want to lose the money the military personnel spent in Virginia City.

The club was an old cinder block building painted light grey with triangles painted dark grey. There were no windows for obvious reasons. If there were to be a raid on the club, the police could not claim seeing the strip shows and drug deals. The procedure was simple. The authorities would knock on the steel double doors, yell it's the police, and wait ten or fifteen minutes for the proprietor to let them in. Except for a few busts for possession of marijuana, very few arrests were made. The police never investigated the four bungalows behind the club since they were told they were storage buildings which seemed logical as there were no windows on any of them. These were where the prostitutes took their clients. There was neither electrical power nor heat in each of them, just an old iron bed with a scrawny mattress.

The storm had covered the doors of the bungalows with snow which made little difference since it was too cold even for the most seeking patron. Lawrence arrived via the same stream he took when he attacked the naval air base. It was not too far from the culvert for water flow. On the east side of the stream was a golf course which obviously was not open since it was dark and had not been open since the onslaught of the storm. The canoe ride had actually been better than usual since the tide was very high and the wind at his back. Empty bungalows meant no threat of discovery from any of the whores or their customers.

He had secured the canoe and hiked the hundred yards or so west and slightly north of the club. He nestled himself in a copse of trees, pulling up branches to cover most of his body. There were no cars in the parking lot and the weather was not improving. He could not put it off another day. As it was Susan Yoder was near panic waiting for Lawrence. Before leaving DumDum he had called her at his mother's in upstate Pennsylvania. He had sent her there a week before his assault on Oceana Naval Air Base. She had packed up all of her belongings and what she could not store at Evelyn Southern's home, she stored at a Jack Rabbit Storage facility. Peter's mother had been more than eager to get Susan and eventually Peter to her home.

A grey colored Toyota Cruiser pulled into the parking lot and three men got out. They were wearing Navy flight fatigues without any coats. Knocking on the front door, a very big black man opened one half of the steel framed door and let them in. Lawrence gave them another ten minutes. The weather did not bother Peter Lawrence at all. He had spent a few winter hunts with his grandfather and learned from his patience. He learned to sit still when a prey or two appears. With snow, usually preys emerge from the forest and are followed by other herd members. In less than a quarter of an hour, a Jeep Wrangler Unlimited rushed into the parking lot and took a space adjacent to the Toyota Cruiser. The man exiting the Jeep was very tall, bald headed, and clad in a black T-shirt and jeans. He knocked and was let in. Lawrence gave it another half hour.

The black man opened the door enough to speak to Lawrence, "I've not seen you before. Are you a member?"

"Nope," said Lawrence.

He was carrying his two Colt M1911A1s. They were recoil operated and locked breach semi-automatic. Lawrence carried both pistols in a "cocked and locked" condition. This meant he had chambered rounds. Lawrence had wrapped adhesive tape around the grip panels since the checkering made the pistols slippery especially with the snow. The Colts held seven .45 ACP caliber rounds in each of their magazines. Lawrence wore a buttoned, grey rain coat that was one size too large for him. Lawrence also wore his Miami Classic II shoulder holster system. Lawrence built his system without ammo carriers. Galco's patented Flexalon swivel back plate made the set-up not only comfortable, despite the 1080 g weight of each pistol, but it was the best possible harness for allowing very fast withdrawal during a cross draw. Lawrence had polished the saddle leather system with saddle wax to keep it supple during the cold weather of this night and to keep it smooth for fast draw.

"Can't let you in. This is a private business."

"I'm sorry for staring but didn't you used to play for Virginia Tech? I thought you had a contract with the Red Skins?"

"Did once. Got kicked off and it ain't none you business why?"

"No reason. How do I become a member?"

"Can't just do it like that."

Lawrence pulled out his cell phone, "you know who Kenneth Czeed is?"

"Put down you phone. Cost twenty five for a one night trial. Hundred buys you a year."

It was a stab in the dark especially considering Lawrence had killed Czeed. Obviously the club manager was not up on current affairs in Virginia City so Lawrence pulled out two twenties and told the man to keep the change. He was given a grey card with Oceana Gentlemen's Club embossed on it. The club was desolate without a bartender, waiters, and having only one exotic dancer. She was a black, very black older woman with an Afro bouffant and breasts with only her nipples covered by stick-on stars. Her ass bulged and wobbled on each side of the G-string.

"Hey, Jack. Ken told me I'd see some action here?"

"There she is."

"That's it?"

"Sent the young ones home. Weather too bad for doing our executive suites. Doors are already blocked. Momma stays with me. Course if you are that hurting, Mama do you in my office for a dime."

Lawrence knew that in the drug world vernacular a dime was a hundred dollars, "I'll pass on that. Fucking bad show here. I'll just do a few drinks and leave."

"Where's your car, white boy?"

Lawrence was ready for that, "want to walk about a mile up Oceana Boulevard and see? Caught the edge of those damn ditches and got stuck. Triple A's so busy tonight that they told me about four hours at a minimum. That means I got almost three hours to down some brew."

Lawrence sat at the bar while the manager asked him what he wanted, "you got St. Remy Martin brandy?"

The manager reached into a cabinet below the mirrors on the wall behind the bar and came out with St. Remy Martin, "on ice?"

"Yes, sir."

Lawrence needed the brandy. It peaked his nervous system but only if he stopped after one or two jolts. He sized up the room, making sure that there were only seven people in the club including himself. He did not need some manager's assistant or cook, appearing out of nowhere. His eyes roamed the room for cameras. There was one above an emergency spotlight in the south east corner of the club where the rest rooms were. This meant that some place in the club was a recording device, probably in the manager's office which was perpendicular to the alcove for the rest rooms. Lawrence finished his brandy.

"Where's your bathrooms?"

"Rest rooms over there," said the manager pointing to the south east alcove.

Lawrence walked to the men's room and had luck follow with him. The manager's office door was open. Behind his desk was an old video tape recording unit with wires running into the ceiling. Once inside the rest room, Lawrence turned on the hot water for the bathroom sink. His hands were still a bit numb from the cold and he needed the blood flow. Opening and closing his fingers on both hands, he got feeling in both hands and turned off the spigot. He flushed the toilet to verify he really used the lavatory. Returning to the bar, he glanced at the four men sitting at a table watching a preseason baseball game on the television mounted to the wall. He intentionally made eye contact with all four of them which had them huddling close together as Lawrence reached the bar. Another brandy was waiting. He would take only one more but not until he finished what he came to do.

"Hey, you! Old man at the bar. You," said the bald headed man. "Come here a second."

Lawrence just smiled. Old man? Guess that's his genes speaking and nurturing his grey hair. He picked up his brandy glass and walked over to their table. The show was starting.

"What you need, skin head?"

Well into their Thursday night drunk, the other three oohed, aahed, and laughed at their compatriot.

The bald man stood up abruptly. This was not Lawrence's choice for action but just in case, he unbuttoned the front of his grey coat giving him access to the pistols which were still covered. The bald men's friends told him to sit down and leave the man alone which he did. Lawrence came to their table.

"Don't like being called an old man. Gotta blame my mom. She grayed early in life. You guys pilots or something?"

"Not baldy, he's a seal. We, us three are though."

Lawrence smiled, a friendly smile, and reached out to shake the bald man's hand, "can you balance a ball on your nose?"

The other four went into an alcoholic deep and unnecessary laugh which infected their friend to smile and shake hands with Lawrence.

Lawrence turned to the manager, "give these men whatever they want all night long. It's on me!"

The bald guy spoke, "you better watch out! Johnstone's been wanting a taste of that old rat ass woman dancer!"

Lawrence verified that Commander David Johnstone was indeed the same man he sought.

Lawrence spoke, "you guys flying when those planes went down couple weeks ago?"

A silence gripped the four men and Johnstone spoke, "not baldy, but the three of us where tail end. Ground control pulled us off a landing approach and sent us to Langley."

Lawrence nursed them along, "wow, had to been god awful watching your buddies crash like that?"

"Yeah, it was bad" said another pilot.

Lawrence abruptly stood up, put both hands on his hips, and rotated slowly his upper torso, "it's my back. Get's a pain at the hips. Gotta rotate them a bit. Gotta piss to. Be right back. Boss man, these men need some refreshment!"

In the men's room, Lawrence checked both .45's making sure a round was chambered in each. He practiced pulling his grey trench coat behind him and held fast by the holster leather. Four times were enough and he kept his grey trench coat unbuttoned.

Sitting down as the four men were starting on their just delivered drinks, Lawrence asked, "what I don't understand is what happened? All the press tells you is the planes' cockpits had an issue?"

The third pilot spoke, "wish we knew. I'm not just saying that. You probably think we were ordered to not disgust what happened. Actually we weren't. If Navy security can't put a handle on it, makes no difference what would say. All we know is just what you said. The cockpits exploded."

Johnstone punched his friend very hard in the shoulder, "you dumb fuck! Press doesn't know that, asshole."

Lawrence smiled and leaned back in his chair. He pulled the lower part of his trench coat so it was under his legs and held firm. With his elbows he felt the grips of the .45's, "want me to tell you?"

Not only did the four Navy officers stare into Peter Lawrence's eyes with their mouth agape, but the club manager came from behind the bar and took a seat at the table on their right. Lawrence had all prey ready to kill. The old black woman dancer was sound asleep in the manager's office on a couch. He had seen her on his return from the men's room.

"Okay, I need your word. Let me spill my story before you challenge it. Does that work?"

They all looked at each other and nodded except the bald man. Johnstone nudged him and got a yes.

"Your Tomcats take off north east on the Naval Air Station runways. They land from the south west. The landing is a parabola."

Johnstone spoke, "how the fuck you know that?"

The two men on either side of him punched his shoulder and told him to shut up.

"Maybe I should just forget about it," said Lawrence as he got up from his seat. "I'll just meander back to my car. AAA might already be there."

"No, no, no," said the man to the left Johnstone. "He's gone to keep shut."

"There's a time frame when the Tomcat is turning the parabolic curve so that if you are on the top side of the plane, you have a target that a good rifleman could hit."

"Yeah, we know that. But go ahead. You'd need a damn good weapon but you never be able to blow the cockpit."

"Black Widow NOOAK Spud AK-47 loaded with HEIAP bullets."

The bald man spoke, "I know AK-47's but what's HEIAP?"

"High Explosive Incendiary Armor Piercing ammunition. It will not only detonate the HE charge but the incendiary material can burn throw two inches of steel. Plexiglas windshields are no barrier to these bullets."

"That's all well and good old man," said the pilot to Johnstone's left. "An AK-47 does not have the range to make that possible. There is no where somebody could get that close. Gunman would have to be standing in the middle of the landing zone."

"So?"

"What do you mean so?" said the bald man.

"I was. Well actually I was standing on the top step of a water drainage pipe in the middle of the landing zone."

Before anybody could jump from their seats, Lawrence stood; cross drew the .45 pistols, and shot the bald man through his temple, blowing out the back of his head.

"Sit down."

They did.

"Johnstone, Johnstone, Johnstone. You don't remember me? Peter Lawrence, editor-in-chief of the V City Server?"

"The police killed you when you tried to escape back many months ago from the ocean front police station."

Lawrence watched the black club manager's eyes. He was going to take a run for it so Lawrence shot him center mass. The power of the 45's slammed him across a table and crashing to the floor. Lawrence nearly made a mistake. He forgot about the old black woman dancer and video recorder. Keeping the gun in his right hand aimed at the three remaining pilots, Lawrence backed up to the office and found the woman still asleep. The reason she had not been awaken was the needle on the floor besides her sleeping body. He shot her center mass and turned quick enough to shoot one of the pilots easing his way to the door.

"Let me tell you something. This country is based on a three tier life to live. The government is royalty and you are its warriors. Rests of us are workers. I'm not a worker any longer."

He shot another pilot leaving him alone with Commander David Johnstone, "Santiago, Louisa Santiago. Beautiful woman. Her mother was a whore and her father a dago who worked on an oil tanker. You killed her baby."

"Her fault. Should have moved. I just follow the flight plan."

"I didn't know being intoxicated was part of the flight plan. Warrior, that's you. Just like any warrior, the royalty defended you."

Lawrence wished he had the time to make Johnstone suffer. He did not, so he shot him dead aim at the bridge of his nose. Brains blew out of the back of his head.

He returned to the office to check the recording machine. He ejected the VHS blank and took it with him. He would burn it when he had a chance.

***

Lawrence knew the Amtrak bus from the Ocean front stopped to pick up fares at the Circle D store and gas station on 17th street at 6:00 am to transport passengers headed for the Newport News Amtrak railroad station. He used the Oceana Gentleman's Club phone line to call Amtrak's computer operator. All Peter Lawrence needed to know was whether the trains would be running tomorrow. The computer answering voice said that all train routes would be on schedule tomorrow. This did not surprise Lawrence since the storm had not hit the Hampton Roads peninsula with very much force. Only the south east Tidewater area was snowed in. The Amtrak bus route took the Monitor Merrimac Memorial bridge tunnel via Route 264 and around Norfolk via Route 64, both of which were passable but slow. Amtrak would reschedule the train departure if necessary.

He did not need many hours of sleep which he could take once debarked on the train but he did need a couple or three to keep his eyes open on his trek from the club to 17th street bus pick up. His Grumman canoe and he were to be parted this coming morning. He pulled it out of the stream and took off the tree branches we used to cover the hull. Turning it so its port side was down, Lawrence crawled into the cavity on the leeward side of the snowy winds. Wrapped in a canvas tarpaulin, Lawrence nestled his head atop of his back pack. He slept well considering he had just killed six people. Fatigued had saved him at this point in time from sleeplessness fighting what dangers he faced.

He awoke well before sun rise which was a trait he mastered many years ago on hunting trips. The prey moved at sun rise. Even though the preys were all dead, he still awoke to face them. He saw no sun light coming from the east, yet. He had at least an hour to reach the bus stop. Covering the Grumman with branches, he swung his backpack straps from left to right, shook the backpack back and forth a few times to make it more comfortable and headed east. He was walking over a small golf course as the sun was rising. Still a bit cloudy, there was no snow. Walking north from the 16th hole of the golf course, he went uphill to the 6th tee and into the woods. Following a well-worn path, he skirted a camp site of homeless who also were just arising and starting small fires in front of the various shelters they created. Lawrence waved to them but continued his hike without stopping.

At the Circle D he found himself a good half hour ahead of the bus. He bought a large coffee and a sealed in cellophane pastry, covered with sugar glaze. There were five or six other people waiting for the Amtrak bus. It was not a long wait. It arrived exactly on time, running through the slush and muddy water left over from the storm.

Trying to regain some of the sleep he lost did not work, as the bus caught 264 at Birdneck Road and headed west. By the time they reached the Hampton Roads Beltway at the Route 64 bypass, there was very little snow. The storm seemed to have launched its attack on Virginia City Beach and only spit on Norfolk and Chesapeake. At the end of the bypass the bus caught Route 664 straight to the Monitor Merrimac tunnel. Sitting on the right side and against a window, Peter Lawrence caught his last view of Virginia City in the distance. He had met many people in his life. Some he liked, a few he loved, and nearly all he tolerated. The people of Virginia City were beyond respect. For the most they were self-righteous and egocentric. It was a good place to leave and a bad place to have visited. Money was their god and "me" was their Jesus.

Once out from under the James River, the bus turned off of Route 664 and on to Warwick Boulevard. The train station was only about three miles north. Lawrence knew this would be his first challenge but probably not a viable one. There was little doubt that anybody had discovered the bodies back in the Oceana Gentleman's Club. A little was enough to worry him. He started to search through his backpack for one of the .45's, then stopped. He was being paranoid.

The train station was a stone-faced building just to the east of Warwick Boulevard with a good-sized parking lot separating it from the road. Dawn had arisen and a few cars had pulled in. Departing the bus, he swung his back pack up and on him. If there was going to be a search of baggage, he was in trouble. There was not. There was also no police at the station, just a woman verifying and selling tickets, a janitor cleaning up the rest rooms, and a conductor looking at his watch. Lawrence had to smile at the conductor since he was attired exactly like ones he had seen when he was a little kid going to Philadelphia with his grandfather.

Once he had his ticket verified and issued, Lawrence sat down for a wait. He walked out to the boarding area and watched a set of passenger cars being pulled north along tracks four tracks east of the station's main track. Since Newport News was a dead stop, he guessed correctly the cars moving north would be the cars leaving the station for all points north. Looking a long ways down the main tracks, he could just barely see the last car now switched to the main track and reversed and heading back to the station. The conductor got on the loud speaker system and warned people to stay behind the yellow line until the train fully stopped and boarding was announced. It took a few minutes for Lawrence to see the engine. It was a diesel.

Unlike most of the passengers, Lawrence did not sleep on the journey up the peninsula. There would be four stops before the train was out of Virginia. He doubted the first one, Colonial Williamsburg, would have police searching the train. By the time the train reached Richmond, it would be a very long shot the Richmond police might be notified to do a search. The last dangerous stop would be at Staples Mill Road which would lift the anxiety off his shoulders. After that was a quick stop at Ashland Virginia and Randolph Macon College with little to worry about. It was the last stop in Virginia.

Lawrence finally relaxed. He enjoyed the ride. In Washington DC; the train changed to another engine run by pantographs. It brought back memories of the famous Pennsylvania railroads G-G-1's which Lawrence had seen running the rails when he was a kid. He guessed that below DC the railway could not put in overhead lines. The stopover was for almost an hour and Lawrence left the passenger car and roamed Union Station, stopping at televisions in a few of the eating places to see if there was any news to warn him. There was none.

The train made it to 30th Street Station in Philadelphia a little after 3:00 pm. Carefully, doing one step at a time, he lugged himself and the back pack down the steep steps to the platform. As the 30th street station's escalator peaked and leveled off, Lawrence could not restrain his smile. There on the other side of the turn stiles stood Susan and his mother. They had to be involved. They could not let him catch a bus to his mother's house. He tried to stop them but got nowhere. He was glad.

***

Of the two hours and eleven minutes it took Evelyn Southern to drive from Philadelphia to her home in northern Pennsylvania, Peter was awake for only seven minutes. He sat in the back seat with Susan Yoder, started to tell Susan and Evelyn about the Oceana Air Base attack, but put his head down on Susan's lap and stretched his legs out on the rear seat. Inhaling the slowly secreting fluids seeping from out of her vagina, he fell asleep.

He awoke long enough to exit the car; walk up Evelyn's front steps, then walked up the steps to the second floor. He went to the bathroom and then fell onto the bed in his childhood bedroom.

Susan would not let him go to sleep. She undressed her semi-comatose lover, leaving him naked, but covered by a wool blanket. He would not awaken until a little after none o'clock the next day. Susan was sitting in the rocking chair in which his mother lulled him to sleep when he was a baby.

"Damn, what time is it?"

She told him it was the next morning, the time, and added, "you owe me a good fuck, baby boy."

Lawrence saw the tears in her eyes, pulled the covers off of him, and knelt before her, causing her to stop rocking.

"The bedroom door's not locked, Peter."

"Ma Mere is French. She knows better," said Peter Lawrence as he spread Susan Yoder's legs, lifted her skirt front up to her hips, lifted gently her hips so as to remove her panties, and had a delicious breakfast while listening to the erection producing music of a female orgasm not once nor twice, but five times."

Once her breathing slowed down and her senses recovered from ecstasy, she stood, lifted his arms to get him up from his knees, and sat him in the same rocking chair. Her moans and grimaced faces had exceeded his but not by much.

Evelyn Southern had breakfast ready as Susan and Lawrence trotted down the steps to the breakfast nook. Placing omelets with bacon and toast before them, she spoke, "it is good to have a house filled with the aromas of sex."

Lawrence had become immune to his mother's bawdy speeches but Susan Yoder turned red.

"Are you having another one, Mon Cherie?"

"Ma Mere, ease up. Are you not getting enough from Judi?"

All three began laughing.

Susan spoke, "you need to tell us. Not because we have to know. You need to release it from inside of you."

Lawrence saw Evelyn's eyes lift and head tilt. She loved direct and abrupt people. Hiding oneself hurts both lovers.

They knew some but not all. Lawrence gave every detail including a repeat of much that Susan Yoder already knew.

"I know there are bad and deadly people in everybody's life. Killing is not the way. That's the mistake we make in life. If you have a tumor, you exorcise it from your life."

Lawrence took a sip of coffee and continued, "the trip back home got to me. Actually it started after the killing at the Oceana Gentleman's club. I began feeling guilt in my gut. I was a bit dizzy on the train just after it left Newport News. I killed so many people I couldn't even put a number to it. A sweat covered my body, not a severe sweat but enough to make me uneasy. So I rethought why I killed, who were these people?"

"More coffee, Mon Fils?"

Lawrence handed Evelyn Southern his cup. She kept it black as she knew he liked and asked Susan if she wanted a cup. Susan did not like coffee.

"They thought nothing of anybody but themselves. If they could absorb profit from you, they would drain you like a leech. Look at who they were. School board members and the superintendent. As long as you graced them by letting them rule, you were admired. It made no difference if you knew better then how to teach them and promote education. You could not give them kickbacks like the vendors who sell school supplies that were useless. The worse group is the city council. Keeping the air base open was physically detrimental to the citizens they were supposed to represent. But keeping the military base meant money and the city rulers sucked in the profits.

"Then there's the law, the police, the warriors. What more need I say about them? You have no rights if you cross paths with them. They serve the rulers, the royalty."

Susan spoke, "Peter, you're close to going over the edge. We've discussed this over and over. You and I cannot save the masses. History shows they always lose. You have killed those who would kill us. You have that moral right. You did no wrong."

"Mon Fils, Susan is right. No one can win a battle better than you. You are your father's warrior reborn."

Lawrence was all of a sudden put into a dilemma. Did his mother know that Llewellyn Lawrence was dead? Did she know that he was a 9-11 terrorist?

Lawrence stood up and walked behind Susan Yoder. He whispered in her ear and she had tears forming in her eyes. Despite the effect it would have, Susan knew that she would want to know. It was not anybody's, including her son's, privilege to keep the death of her first husband from her.

Evelyn Southern spoke, "why the tears, Mon Ami?"

Lawrence knelt next to her chair, "ma mere, you have a right to know. Llewellyn Lawrence was killed in the terrorist attack of 9-11."

"No! It is not possible. I know he lives in Vietnam with a family called the Quyens. They raise cashew ..."

"No, Mon Mere. He left Nam to fight in the Mid-East wars on the side of the Taliban. He was in the plane that crashed the Pentagon. It's true, Mon Mere."

Her arms began to tremble and then the three of them heard the front door open. It was Judi Dougherty coming home from a job in which he had been involved overnight.

"My Cherie, why are you crying?"

Lawrence told him as his mother left for the bathroom to get some tissues.

"I never told her about my time with him in Canada, Judi. Maybe I should have."

"No, Petey. You did right. She'll blow it off. She's a strong woman."

The day went slow and grim. As night approached, the four of them sat in front of a fire and ate take-out for dinner. The silence was threatening. Each feared an outrage from Evelyn Southern claiming infamy. She changed.

"We must go on. Mon Frere, where do you go from here?"

Susan spoke, "Peter is almost absolutely safe. He was legally pronounced deceased when he attacked the Ocean Front Police Office and disappeared. They found a body, obviously not his. He was ruled a dead man."

Lawrence spoke, "see what I mean about these people? If there's an easy way out, even though it is totally in error, they'll take that path. That's why the powers to be control the people to be."

Susan spoke, "Peter has a very close friend who was nearly killed by the FBI. He's a Native American named Charlie Grayrock. He was brutally treated and near dead when he served in the United States Army in Vietnam. After 9-11 he was tracked down because of a gun he sold."

Lawrence spoke, "he had absolutely nothing to do with the attacks."

"But your bastard father did?"

Lawrence backed off, "the attorneys for the Native American Rights found out about the tortures Charlie was being put through and stopped them. They got him released. I thought for sure he would die. Charlie's too strong to let asshole white men kill him."

"Evelyn, your son had a hand in helping Charlie Grayrock escape the FBI's torture. If he hadn't, Charlie Grayrock would be dead."

"So why are we talking about this Indian?"

"Because he's going to visit us in two days, my mother." Lawrence smiled at referring to Evelyn Southern in American terms.

***

Charlie Grayrock was a dead man only he would not accept it. His son brought him to Upstate Pennsylvania at the request of Peter Lawrence. The taxicab pulled up in front of Evelyn Southern's house early in the morning. Charlie's son had flown them here in a Cessna. They landed in a small aviation station only a few miles to the west. Lawrence had received a cell phone call from the son when they landed and waited on the front porch. The Charlie Grayrock being lifted out of the cab and carefully settled into the wheel chair had not long to live. Lawrence had been told this by Charlie's son but Charlie refused to not take the journey.

"Hey, white man, get on down here and help this poor excuse for a warrior get me up these porch stairs."

Peter smiled and inside his mind hoped he would have a strength like Charlie's when facing death.

"A taxicab? Where's you pinto, Tonto?"

"You still fucking Silver, Kemo Sabe," said Charlie as he and Lawrence embraced. Peter expected a weak man but got a strong one.

The son and Peter got Charlie's wheelchair onto the porch and through the doorway. Inside Evelyn Southern had just come downstairs.

"Kemo Sabe, is this fine piece of woman your sister?"

"Ma Mere, this is Charlie Grayrock, last of the great Indian warriors."

Lawrence heard an uh hum behind his back, "oops, I mean the next to the last. This is his son."

Evelyn knelt and put both her hands to Charlie's face, finishing by kissing him on the fore head.

"Used to be I got kissed on the lips. Sometimes with a little tongue added."

Everybody laughed except Judi. Lawrence took Charlie's luggage to the downstairs bedroom where he would stay and followed the rest into the dining room. Susan was in the kitchen doing breakfast. His son lifted Charlie onto a dining room chair, easing him under the table. Evelyn went into the kitchen and returned with a coffee carafe and ceramic mugs.

Only Charlie's son asked if she had some juice. Hearing the conversation, Susan walked into the dining room and placed a medium-sized glass of orange juice in front of Charlie's son.

"I've got some tomato juice, if you like."

"No, ma'am, OJ's okay."

"My God look at that lovely woman," said Charlie Grayrock. "This ain't the female wants to marry you, is it, Peter?"

"Same one, Charlie."

Susan blushed and returned to the kitchen. Peter could see his mother was a little taken aback with Susan doing breakfast in her kitchen but reacted warmly to her son putting his arm around her shoulder with a hug.

"So you are going to marry my son to this beautiful woman, Charles?"

"Charlie, ma'am. Ain't nobody'd stay alive calling me Charles. Sure am. Somebody's got to take this ungrateful white boy from your apron strings."

All of this was both exciting Evelyn Southern and irritating her. She had spent too many years without a grandchild or husband but she also was used to being the executor of the event.

"Mon Fils, when is this wedding supposed to take place?"

Susan walked back into the dining room with a stack of pancakes in one hand and a dish of sausage links on a plate in the other. She placed them in the middle of the table where Peter had already had placed silverware settings, butter, syrup, and jelly.

"Peter, it's nice outside and the temperature's just a bit cool. Do we do it around noon."

"Mon Dieu!" Evelyn Southern nearly fell backward out of her chair, saved by the quick reaction of Charlie's son. She stood up and walked about the room, fanning her face with her right hand.

"Mother," said Peter using his American English, not French. "Votre Dieu heard you and he'll be there, too."

"And how am I to get a priest for you by noon?"

"That's why Charlie's here. He's a tribal chief with the power to unite people in holy matrimony."

She sat down but kept her hand wafting air across her face, "you really do love her, mais oui?"

"Oui, mon mere."

Susan wore a silk flowered dress with wide and long sleeves. Her hair was pulled back into a bun with small yellow roses pinned to her hair knot. Peter had only one suit, a light grey jacket and pants with a matching vest. Threats from both Evelyn and Susan forced him to wear a striped flowered tie. The ceremony took place in Evelyn's back yard with Charlie Grayrock sitting in his wheel chair between the couple. It was a simple and beautiful wedding nearly ruined by Evelyn Southern. Near the end of the ceremony, a priest from Evelyn's church showed up to bless the married couple. Peter felt his hair rise at the back of his neck but gave in when he saw the brilliant smile on Susan Yoder's face as she became Susan Lawrence.

Charlie shared religious thoughts with the priest along with many drinks. The priest had to be driven back to the church parsonage by Judi.

The wedding cake came from a fast trip by Judi to a bakery down town. The birthday candles had to be removed and a husband-wife figure put in their place. Judi had paid ten dollars extra for it since he saw it on another cake and made the baker an offer he could not refuse. It helped that the baker was also Italian.

As they finished a wedding meal straight from the local delicatessen, Charlie broached the second reason he was in upstate Pennsylvania, "Can we talk about ... You know ... What we discussed on the phone?"

Lawrence saw his mother's eyes open and staring. She hated surprises if she was not the person making them.

"Mother, you've got to take it in, what we're going to decide. There's more than one reason Charlie Grayrock's here. Charlie is a very high chief in the Canadian First Nations peoples."

"Why is that important?"

"We can't live in the United States. Eventually I'll be recognized and it will be the end for me. I cannot be touched in Canada."

Evelyn was holding back tears, "Your father should have taken that path."

"Charlie has set us up to meet with many tribes. The Cree look very good. They live in and around Lake Superior, places like Ontario, Manitoba, Saskatchewan, Alberta and the Northwest Territories. Nearly 15,000 live in eastern Quebec."

Evelyn began to absorb and see the necessity his son and daughter-in-law faced. Quebec would not put them too far from her and her sister.

Peter continued, "Susan and I have also discussed the Métis which are one of the Aboriginal peoples in Canada who can trace their descent to mixed European and First Nations parentage. There used to be an important distinction between French Métis born of francophone voyageur fathers, and the Anglo Métis descended from Scottish fathers. Today the two cultures are essentially one Métis tribe.

Susan spoke up, "I am older than Peter. I am not as strong as in my youth. I could have competed with him. He and I are running through this emigration in great detail. We are not going to become American Natives. We are not American Natives. We know the American Natives thanks to Charlie Grayrock. He will help us find a compatible relationship with a tribe. Mrs. Southern, we both want to settle as close to Peter's family as possible. You are our family."

Evelyn Southern had to face the truth. Their future depended on living with a society they admired and could share life. She walked up to Susan now Lawrence, her daughter-in-law and wrapped her arms about Susan, "you have my love and I will never give it up, Mon Amour. I am not so old I cannot travel. Judi is a great man and will be with me as he has been all these years.

Judi grasped his wife's hand. Tears were flowing down his eyes. Evelyn turned and lifting a handkerchief held in her sleeve, wiped away the tears.

Susan faced Peter Lawrence with a smile and tears, "I have two presents for you. I am your sole and only lover you will ever need. We are one. I've never felt that with anyone."

Peter Lawrence wrapped his arms around his wife, "I'm sorry but the only present I have for you is me."

Susan eased back a few inches not releasing her hold on her husband, tears still flowing, "you gave me your present. I will give birth to your second present in three months."

~*~*~

Also by John Kinsler

Thirst for Revenge Trilogy

Book 1

Llewellyn Lawrence, the Father

Llewellyn Lawrence watches as his friend Charlie is humiliated and physically assaulted by members of the school's football team. Knowing he cannot stop the assault, he turns to the teacher for help, only to be told the boys are only having some fun. Lawrence knows the teacher is afraid of the thugs and will not help stop the assault.

The thirst for revenge runs deep in Llewellyn Lawrence's soul. It is not just the rage he feels over his friend's assault. He is still bitter over the confrontation he had with his father over his mother's death. The father and the son have become distant. They once hunted and camped in the Upstate Pennsylvania game lands. Both know how to survive and kill within the forests. But what will happen when the hunters leave the forest?

Llewellyn Lawrence is one of 1,728,344 high school graduates drafted and sent to Vietnam. 17,725 of those graduates were killed. Assigned to the Corps of Engineers, he works with Vietnamese civilians helping improve the villages and solving health problems. Then Mai Lai explodes in front of him and his life changes forever.

The horror of the war reaches unthinkable levels. The rage Llewellyn feels toward his country can no longer be held inside him. He becomes a turncoat, fighting with the Viet Cong. He becomes part of the Quyen family, telling his new family, "it is better to die in heaven's fields, then ignore the abortion called America!"

He is thousands of miles away living a new life when he learns that his wife, his former French teacher, is now pregnant.

Thirst for Revenge Trilogy

Book 2

Lawrence the Son

Lawrence the Son, book 2 of Kinsler's Thirst for Revenge Trilogy, a new dynamic action adventure thriller series, finds the son, Peter Lawrence, facing a vicious gang leader and drug dealer. Peter almost gets killed. The gang has already killed the ice cream man, so Peter has to kill the dealer.

Peter meets Eileen Ledger while teaching in Upstate New York. Nearly killed by her ex-husband, Peter rids her of her ex. While home teaching, he finds his student dead. The boy's death was written off as a suicide, but Peter proves the boy was murdered in a cover-up by the school superintendent and the chief of police. Peter, seething with anger, confronts the school superintendent and the chief of police. Their responses leave Peter filled with rage. He needs a father-figure, but his father is MIA. He learns the truth about his father. It wasn't pleasant. Like father, like son; the thirst for revenge must - and will - be quenched. In blood.

Available in print from www.a-argusbooks.com
available in ebook from W & B Publishers

www.ingramcontent.com/pod-product-compliance
Lightning Source LLC
Chambersburg PA
CBHW071509260626
47170CB00002B/311